CRUSHING STEEL

Cover and Book Design by Nick Zelinger, NZGraphics.com

Nehamen, Dennis A Author

Crushing Steel
Dennis A Nehamen

Printed in the United States of America

First Edition

This story was originally produced as a screenplay entitled, *The Last Patient*. Then when I finally overcame my hesitation over writing a novel, I picked up this piece and began what turned out to be a long journey in the study of creating fiction. As it happened, several other works were to be told before I came back to what is now, *Crushing Steel*, the fourth of The Zach Miller Adventures. To my amazement, it was to be two books in one—I'm grateful for the detour and from the perch upon which I now rest I can take pleasure knowing that it ended for the better.

PROLOGUE

SOW THY FIELDS WITH seeds of love and thou shall reap kindness, compassion, forgiveness and joyfulness.

But some seeds are rotten.

My best friend, Preston, claims to recall it perfectly. It was a Friday afternoon. He parked at a Kwik Stop Convenience Store on White Sands Boulevard in Alamogordo, New Mexico. After filling up with gas, he went inside to buy a few provisions for the rest of his drive. He was standing in line holding a quart bottle of Dr. Pepper soda, a bag of Lay's Smokey Bacon Potato Chips and a package of Bubblicious Cotton Candy gum—he was a devout enthusiast for damning the imaginary health movement in America.

There was a man standing behind him. As Preston reached the cashier and set his three items down to pay, the other man started laughing. My friend turned to determine why the fellow was bellowing. Then the stranger proceeded to methodically put his three identical purchases on the countertop, carefully matching each to make pairs.

Preston described him as a man with dark burgundy-hued skin. His face was flat and the tautness of his features left one with the impression that he was a stern guy, not seeming to be practiced in levity but overmastered by what he obviously perceived as a hilarious coincidence. He was wearing a worn chocolate-colored sleeveless leather vest with what at some time had to have been a bright red and yellow feather embossed on the breast; the dye faded after at least a decade of use. His muscles were remarkable in that they were comparable in size to those sported by body builders, yet were a natural endowment of this powerful specimen.

The giant stood motionless, as if he were calculating the remarkable improbability of the circumstance. Then he put his massive hand on Preston's shoulder as gently as he could—which was still described as sufficient in grip strength to cause discomfort—and smiled as if they were brothers.

"Wait for me outside," the man who would soon identify himself as an Apache Mescalero Indian petitioned Preston.

Thus, after both had paid an equal price for the mirror image purchases, they became acquainted in the parking area.

"Come. I'll take you to dinner," offered the Indian man.

It was that encounter that preceded a series of unimaginably unlikely events impacting up to the time of the writing of this chronicle, mainly...my life. More times than I'd like to admit since that fortuitous encounter between Preston and the man named Walter, I've been trying to quash my hapless dwelling on one huge question: "What would have happened had Preston picked up a Pepsi instead of Dr. Pepper?"

Preston's meeting with Walter had resulted in me being drawn into a terrorist plot against Israel and America, being introduced for the first time to love and then family, and finally becoming an investigator into the disappearance of a musical icon as well as corruption on an Indian reservation.

Preston was once more serving as my conduit, unintentionally instigating experiences of high adventure and life transition. In fact, some months before he had innocently mentioned to me that one of his relatives was working near our nation's capital and had a very close friend who had the distinction of being the youngest senior criminal investigator to ever hold that title for the Washington, D.C. Metropolitan Police Department.

This friend-of-a-cousin had a story to tell. It was promoted to me as something extraordinary, although I quickly discovered that Preston didn't have a clue about what made the tale outstanding. What he did know was that the owner of the experience had knocked herself silly at the computer trying to scribe the adventure, but "failed miserably." (I asked if there was any other way to fail, but the question couldn't stop my friend's enthusiasm for selling me on the project.)

Knowing my passion for writing, Preston thought that helping out the lady would be right up my alley. Therefore, he let me know that he'd taken the liberty to suggest she contact me. Normally, I'd have thought nothing of it because on the surface it seemed a perfectly benign request for me to advise the woman. But coming from Preston, I knew I wouldn't be getting off easy.

She did get in touch with me. It was about three months after he first mentioned her. The timing coincided with a premier musical presentation that I attended at The Center for the Performing Arts at Kuruk. This small theatre was located next to my restaurant, which was an establishment with the same name, Kuruk. She approached me and introduced herself as Nadine Street. She then told me that she thought she was ready to talk about her "harrowing adventure"—and then inexplicably, she disappeared. I could only assume that the reason she came in the first place, was to test if she was prepared to meet the ghosts that had been chasing her.

I didn't hear from her for another six months. It was a rainy November afternoon. I was at Kuruk, finishing a bowl of lentil soup. I leaned back in my chair and gazed at the thinning lunch crowd. Then, I noticed a young lady entering. She took a table across from where I sat—I recognized her immediately as the same woman who came to talk to me after the musical performance.

Nadine Street never looked up, also avoiding eye contact with the waitress when ordering. Her brunette hair was combed in the same meticulous style as when I had first met her. Swooning toward her shoulders with a flip at the bottom, it looked like the perfect slide for a child on a hot afternoon to take flight and joyfully drop into the coolness of a swimming pool. She was wearing a tan long-sleeve blouse. Around her neck was a feathered choker in soft shades of blue, orange and yellow that fanned out across her clavicle.

Her features were small and delicate. The eyes were round and pretty. Upon closer inspection, I noticed they were filled with sadness and they made no apology for the surrounding dark tint. Only prolonged suffering could have hardened her cheeks, mouth and chin. Still, beneath the mask of tension, tenderness was evident.

After several minutes of staring at her, she finally glanced my way. However, she withheld any gesture to signal that she recognized me. She seemed hopelessly locked in a trance-like state. I walked to her table. By the time I stood next to her, she had dropped her head.

"You made it, Ms. Street," I greeted her.

She looked up without inclining her head, her face still lacking expression.

"Would you care to join me, Mr. Miller?" was all she was able to say.

"I assume you're ready," I said softly.

"You make it sound like I'm headed for open heart surgery...and by the way, please call me Nadine."

"My tools, Nadine, are limited to a digital recorder, pad of paper and pen, and keyboard—no sharp instruments," I jested.

"Well, I think you're right," she contemplated. "Words cut to the heart. That's what this is about, isn't it, telling the truth?"

As she spoke, I noticed a rogue blemish on her face. It was a thin wrinkle running downward from the inside corner of her left eye, paralleling the nose and then branching like three prongs of a pitchfork unceremoniously before disappearing on an aborted mission to reach her lip. I later learned that fault line was the sign that she was preparing for battle.

"We can meet at my office. How's about nine o'clock tomorrow morning?"

"I'll be there…if you're ready to meet 'The Killer.'"

She painted a smile on her face. It spoke to the sense of defeat she unabashedly admitted, a disclosure that was light years from the truth. She had been submerged long and deep beneath the sea's surface, but she was cousin to the Humpback whale, having the characteristic of lurching far out of the water and splash-landing on her backside just when the pressure would cause most mortal beings to self-destruct in a massive explosion.

I'd soon learn that this off-duty, temporarily disabled detective, Nadine Street, had been subjected to a force equal to that needed to crush steel. It was her hope that by coming to Mescalero to recount her story, she might heal her ailing soul. Instead, she was to receive an urgent come-to-the-rescue call. Unimaginable…inconceivable… was that she would be the subject of the emergency—she remained in the eye of evil, the apparition was on the chase, thirsting for a single kill, zeroing in on Nadine.

She came to see me certain that the final chapter of the story terminated in Washington, D.C. Yet as it turned out, while she was narrating the history to me, several more acts were added to the play, convincing her that madness can be a not-so-cool cat with nine lives; there was to be a new setting for the finale.

What this unexpected continuation of terror meant to me, in addition to drawing out the writing of this tale—one I'll admit is well suited to my taste, a who-done-it human drama where who done it didn't do it—was to place me in the not unfamiliar position of playing a role in an unfolding drama that was frankly, none of my business.

1

AND THANKS FOR STOPPING BY

I'M TOLD THAT THE weather in Washington, D.C. in early spring is whimsical. If it's a crystal clear day and the sun invites the residents and visitors to take off their sweater, global warming is the explanation. If conditions are freezing, it's a local joke for the late night talk shows. Either way, it's safe to say that most people welcome a day rivaling what most Southern Californians enjoy routinely. But Nadine posits that there is one group that has discovered distinct advantages of bad weather: professional killers.

For one thing, people unfortunate enough to be out in a blizzard, hail storm or snow, pay little attention to anything or person around them. They fail to notice the subtle clues that detectives seek after a murder. Everybody moves quickly. Unusual action or behavior does not stand out. And we're not to forget, lots of heavy clothes permit weapons and tools of the trade to be easily concealed, as well as appearances to be masked.

I learned that the man initially deemed the star of this drama—a man of many talents, killing just being one of them—is savvy enough to function under any condition. Still, he wouldn't handicap himself if a job could be carried out in the most inclement weather.

Glance at that gentleman over there on Vermont Avenue hailing a cab. That's right, the one who just stepped off the icy curb with a large metal briefcase—almost the size of a small suitcase—held in his left hand. He's the one wearing a long black wool coat and matching fedora.

Doesn't he appear to be a normal fellow? He does, but the truth is he's a cold, calculating killing machine on his way to a very important strike. Dress warm, come along, but hurry. If we jump into the cab just behind him, we can catch a glimpse of a true pro in action.

Up Vermont Avenue NW, left on "R" Street, NW—a bit out of the way, but the cabbies in Washington are no different than anywhere—and up to Johnson Avenue. Turning right...slowing...he's getting out.

"Cabbie, pull over if you would. Here, keep the change."

Ready everyone? Don't get out quite yet. Wait a moment until he scans the area: it's a habit they all have, looking around just in case they're being followed. Let's go. Notice how he strolls casually, not a care in the world. This murderer is an expert. He's trained himself in many disciplines, transcending fear just one.

As we get to know him better, and we will quite intimately, descending deep inside his head, we'll learn some tricks that most anyone can apply. I hear we all have a killer in us—fortunately, I've never found mine.

Now we'll stay a short distance behind him. He's going down the block to the entrance of Hotel La Gare. After he ascends the steps, we can watch him entering the hotel lobby. Curiously, he doesn't even pause but instead goes directly to the men's room. He's obviously been there before because he moves confidently to its somewhat remote location down a short but obscure hallway. See him entering? Security cameras aren't permitted in public bathrooms. I'll describe the scene because what is taking place out of view is very important.

He walks directly to the last stall and enters. He locks the door, taking off his coat. Precisely, he turns it inside out, revealing a waterproofed dark brown interior. He hangs it on the hook on the stall door. Next, he takes the toilet seat top and closes it, resting his metal briefcase across the flat surface. He stands facing the rear of the bowl and opens the case.

A mirror is extracted. As he lets the top of the case fall closed, he reaches behind to hang the reflective device temporarily from the same stall door hook. He now picks up the case and rotates so that it sits on the toilet cover with the case resting on his legs. Opening it, he stares at the contents: make-up kit, hairpieces for crown, brows, mustache and goatee, large scissors and other incidental objects.

First he takes off his hat and carefully stuffs it into his case—only the finest, soft wool that can be scrunched into a closed space and later reshaped to its original form. Now, he takes a hairpiece, reddish-brown in color with medium length straight strands and positions it carefully on his head.

Without looking up, he reaches for a matching colored medium length well-trimmed goatee that he carefully puts in place. With a brush taken from the make-up kit, he colors his eyebrows and then slightly broadens them so that they appear heavier and sharply outlined—his application is perfect, in fact, some women might express jealousy at his dexterity. He then takes a pair of thick brown-rimmed glasses with a Gucci insignia and slips them into place, pausing momentarily to inspect his work.

He reverses himself so that the case, opened, is again on the seat. He substitutes one-by-one a pair of dark brown loafers for his black ones, storing the latter in the case. He reaches behind for the jacket and puts it on. He turns to inspect himself by crouching down to the level of the mirror. He then places it back in the case. Finally, he extracts objects of rubberized material. While holding them in his hand he places the scissors so that they're wrapped within yet sticking out of the middle—he puts the precious assorted items in his jacket pocket.

He closes the case and grabs it with his left hand. He's now ready to exit the stall. On his way out, he smiles at a man entering and... there he is, coming down the stairs. The show is about to begin.

We notice him heading back down Johnson Avenue from where he approached. At the very corner where he was let off by the cab, he directs himself back along "R" Street a couple of short blocks. He comes to a small building and goes up a few steps to a landing. He presses a buzzer. The noise from cars passing on the slushy street makes his few words inaudible, but he proceeds directly to the front door—electronically released for him—and he enters.

There is a doorman, but the infrequency of visitors due to the whipping cold temperature this evening, discourages him from his assigned position at attention outside the door. Instead, the uniformed clerk is lounging indolently at a small desk reading a copy of *Mad Magazine*. He never glances as the man we're interested in, walks past him and up to the elevators.

During the ride up, he extracts the package from his coat pocket. It's a pair of latex gloves and another pair of rubbers to cover his shoes. He puts both on while in the elevator and holds the scissors with his gloved left hand in the pocket of his coat.

He exits on the fourth floor and walks down the hall. He's looking for 4D, the third unit on the right. He knocks.

"Wesley, it's me."

The voice lacks volume or enthusiasm, suggesting he might be almost as concerned about disguising his vocal identity as his physical appearance.

The response is eager, joyous, as Mr. Wesley Arnold begins to open the door.

"Hey, amigo, great costume. But..."

In Arnold's world, "buts" are flung around like beer bottles in a bar. There are "buts" tagged "wish I could," "buts" tagged "almost," "buts" tagged "I did everything I could," "buts tagged, "things changed," but every "but" is disingenuous because Arnold hasn't expressed a real, heartfelt thought or feeling since he caught his member in his pant zipper while on a high school date with Mindy Klinger, whom he had every intent of balling until he saw blood oozing out from his wound and lost his appetite. Well, no real emotion until now, as he confronts the disguised figure he has just opened the door to.

Now the "but" is a prick of confusion, quickly followed by a composition of flash-frozen shock and terror. Not a lousy instant is granted the poor man to appeal, pray or repent, and while he hasn't even a thimble full of experience with any of them, he has volumes of material worthy of a gesture of regret. Arnold, in other words, is a ruthless, callous and vengeful figure in every venture of his life, the prime one being CEO and President of Con-Tech Entertainment, the largest media conglomerate in the world.

So powerful is Arnold, that phone calls to members of select Senate committees or Federal Communications Commission members set the ball rolling in his direction for legislative or bureaucratic directives needed to accomplish the spread of his empire.

Nobody likes him but, as is often the case with men of such influence, he could fill a small city phone book with names of those professing to be his "great buddy." In truth, the bastard doesn't have a friend in the world and could not care less. Still, when he comes to Washington for business, he expects at least a meeting with the President and sometimes a private dinner.

What he doesn't expect is a stone-hard killer palming a pair of sharpened, pointy shears in a gloved hand moving at light speed and delivering the instrument with on-the-button accuracy through the right side of his neck, just below the ear and upward into the most primitive structures of his brain.

The power of the arm is sufficient to not only impale the cutters into his head, driving deep into the limbic system, but also to send Arnold to the ground like a wood log. There he lay, the shears sticking out like a meat hook. Blood is slowly draining on to the tan carpet.

"Did you think you'd get away with it?"

The killer speaks in a monotone, raspy voice—harshly and cruelly.

It's as if he's not conscious of Arnold's reduced state. He stares down momentarily at his victim, walks over to a nearby table and picks up a small steel lamp, yanking out the electrical plug. He turns it upside down as he ambles back to where Arnold lays. Then with the solid base he delivers three more powerful blows to the top of the head and forehead, applying just enough force to crack the skull but not splatter blood on his clothing or shoes. He hesitates an instant to consider further cranial damage, but instead he listlessly lets the tissue and blood dripping lamp fall to the ground.

After a few moments, during which he seems to be proudly and delightfully deliberating on the overall scene, he walks to the door and exits. He appears as calm as when he entered. He reverses the order of his action. First, he gets into the elevator—during the ride down he takes off the gloves and shoe coverings and stashes them in his pocket. The door opens and he exits, meandering past the still disinterested clerk who glances perfunctorily as he passes. An instant later, he's out the door.

We see him now proceeding back to Hotel La Gare, where in the men's room he establishes the appearance he presented with when we first witnessed him hailing a cab. Nonchalantly, he leaves the hotel and walks along the street, pausing just long enough while passing a trash container to deposit the no longer needed gloves and shoe coverings.

We hear that serial killers typically select a class of victims for their ugly acts, quite often prostitutes or defenseless women. This killer that Nadine Street has been summoned to snuff out specializes exclusively in the upper crust. His only kills are politicians, financiers, business moguls, bureaucrats and generals. It's hard to tell at this point, if his targets are random or orderly. What's certain is that he's put well-earned fear into some brave hearts.

Well, murder must be more exhausting than most would think. This fellow is stopping for a drink. We'll say "goodbye" and leave him to enjoy his great accomplishment.

*****

After I finished the first draft of the opening chapter, I was on a high. I had set out with a mission, to let me, Zacchaeus Miller (known as Zach to his friends and loved ones), narrate as if sitting on a perch looking down on a stage. That way I could jump off if it were necessary to get closer to the action—as I did with Arnold's murder—but escape at will so as to permit Nadine and the other characters to enact the story like a live play; I thought I had nailed it.

I called Nadine and asked if she could come meet me. It was about eight in the morning and she had just finished her yoga. She informed me she'd be over in half an hour. I recall she abruptly put down the phone.

When she arrived, I could tell she was in a pissy mood; her attitude did discharge my enthusiasm. Still, with hesitancy, I gave what I had written for her to look over—when she finished, she went ballistic.

"How do you know this is what happened?" she demanded more than questioned.

"Because you told me," I calmly answered.

"I never told you any of *that*," she argued, tapping her finger randomly and with unrestrained consternation on one of the pages.

I chuckled, which charged her affect. If she was peeved when she arrived, she was now frightfully inflamed.

"Nadine, if I'm going to write this I have to make interpretations along the way," I explained. I took a guess at what was riling her. "It's not possible to know for sure what every character was thinking, feeling or doing during every exchange. We have to fill in holes with the most logical explanation. If we do that we'll be true to the story."

"That's likely the reason I couldn't write it on my own." In an instant, she had slammed the brakes on her agitation; it was astonishing how quickly her feeling tone could change.

Then I noticed as she spoke, weariness in her demeanor. She had to be reliving the repeated attempts to imagine what her real life adversaries and allies were going through proximate to her during the experience—it must have been excruciatingly frustrating as she tried and failed many times to get it "perfect."

"I'll bet anything that is real close to what did happen," she acceded after a short meditation.

"I think so too, Nadine. Really, how else could it have been accomplished?"

Nadine held up her left index finger, pointing at me. "That's one for you."

"If we're keeping score then I think you're going to lose big," I teased playfully. "You're on my turf; it's what I do for a living."

"Oh, is that the case?" she bantered back. "Preston gave me the impression you hardly made a buck-fifty writing. But if it will comfort you, you're lack of success is not why I asked you to help me."

"You're heartless," I smiled. "Am I supposed to ask what it was then that brought you to me?"

"Yes!"

I motioned for her to continue.

"You know what it is to suffer. You know how to let a person feel." Her eyes glistened from a thin film of moisture. "I lost a lot because of the events I'm sharing with you. I'm still not healed. I don't want this book to end up feeling like a mechanic wrote it."

"Guts on the freeway. That's my gospel," I promised her.

"I know. Neither of us would have it any other way."

She wasn't joking. The vultures were hovering above us.

"By the way, Preeti is having dinner Tuesday night and would like you to come." (The invitation was from my wife.) "We'd all like it, if you joined us," I encouraged her.

She nodded her head up and down to suggest affirmation, but the look on her face delivered a different message: *I'm not sure I'm ready.*

"You can decide up to the last minute," I offered. "Do you want to see how I ended the chapter?" I said, handing the last page to her.

She read out loud: *I have more introductions to make. In fact, we're just on time. Nadine is about to find out what a crackup her new partner Dustin is.*

She laughed herself silly. "It sure started out that way with Dustin—you got that right."

I have to admit it was always a relief when she lightened up. The problem was she was not a light person and she was recounting what had not been a light phase of her life, one that would become increasingly heavier as we proceeded with our joint exercise.

2

BOYS WILL BE BOYS

YOUNG DUSTIN DRAKE WAS in the early stage of instruction under Nadine's tutorship. There's a big story behind this fellow coming to study with such a prominent investigator as Nadine Street, but that's going to have to wait because…right now the boy is in deep muck.

It was a dark night, cloud covered and drizzling. A compact Ford sedan moved slowly along a deserted country road. Looking through the front windshield of the car, one would observe the backside of a late model Porsche. Leaning on the vehicle was a male in his twenties, a tall, stunning man reeking of sexual appeal. That's the toddling assistant assigned to Nadine, Dustin Drake.

The Ford moved to the side of the road and parked, leaving Dustin between the two vehicles. Nadine exited her car and refrained from even glancing at Dustin. Instead she proceeded to the front end of the Porsche, which was embracing the trunk of a stubborn elm tree that had refused to get out of the way of the speeding vehicle.

Fortunate for Dustin was that the tree must have had the presence of whatever mind a tree can have and tried to sidestep a collision: it was the passenger side of his roadster that was badly damaged, allowing Dustin to escape without apparent injury. Indeed, he looked his usual cool and unburdened self, only a little tentative as he watched his boss inspect the crash site.

Forced to role-play the chastising parent, Nadine sauntered up to the fancy racing car to casually inspect every crease of its new body design, loitering to breathe in the fumes belching from the weeping engine. Then she circled the tree and the car, nodding to send a clear signal of approbation for a hell of a job. When finished with her performance, she strode up to Dustin.

"How did it happen?"

Dustin responded sheepishly. "I had a couple…maybe I shouldn't have had even one but…"

"That's for your priest."

The rain picked up, followed by a sudden bolt of lightning that brightened the sky sufficient for Dustin to observe the glare on Nadine's face. A trailing blast of thunder failed to shake her impassivity.

"Wait, Nadine, you know my dad?"

It was more a statement than a question, but it caught her attention. She'd noticed in the past that no matter how irresponsible he'd been, Dustin had never mentioned the man who walked him into the job. She appreciated the fact that he didn't cower behind big daddy's coat every time he was about to take a tongue-lashing.

"Well, a short time ago…I never told you…I was drinking and, uh, he helped me out of a jam."

"What else is new?" She aimed her scorn like a spitball.

"What's new is I promised him I'd never get behind the wheel of a car again, even if all I'd had was a lousy beer."

"So you want me to smooth it over with your father." That thought, considering it was actually what he was suggesting, burned her toast. "Forget the priest, Dustin, you need a mommy."

"All you'd have to do is say you were driving to try out my new car."

At this moment one of those events that we can never quite determine to be either chance or design happened to fall in Dustin's favor. If the last words out of Dustin's mouth hadn't been drowned out by the distinct sound of crunching leaves in the nearby woods, Nadine would have been on her way. Instead, thinking human footsteps to be the cause of the sound, Nadine went on alert. She whisked a flashlight from her purse.

She aimed the light toward a dark, heavily forested area. Then she heard several quick steps, running, as if somebody was disappearing into the dense foliage. Following into the darkness, she scanned the area ahead and the ground around her for signs. Then off in the distance, she couldn't tell for certain, but perhaps two hundred feet away, she caught sight of a pair of eyes she was sure were human… staring directly toward her.

They instantaneously disappeared. Nadine started to move towards the place where she saw them but recognizing the futility, she elected to walk back to Dustin.

"Probably a vagrant."

She dismissed lightly an event she would bank just in case…in case of what she didn't know but she'd learned never to be careless with a circumstance that could signal danger, especially now when she was in the middle of the most exhaustive and potentially perilous investigation of her career.

"Sounded like a mountain lion to me," Dustin assessed.

The interruption by the vagrant, mountain lion, or whatever it might have been apparently stimulated an amusing idea in Nadine's mind. Mirthfully, she addressed Dustin.

"I'm going to fix this up with your father. But in return—"

"Nadine, anything," the young understudy pled.

"You fail me one more time and I'll ask you to resign on your own accord. You won't argue, and you'll face whatever consequences it means between you and your family. Deal?"

"Absolutely. Nadine, thanks, I really—"

"Dustin, I'm not joking. I think I'm going to need you like a real partner. I can't be losing sleep over someone who can't locate his butthole with both hands."

Dustin reached out only his right one to consummate the deal.

Nadine emphasized the urgency of the matter by eyeballing him long and hard. Finally, she offered to seal the deal but as they were about to touch, her phone rang. She latched on to his right hand with hers. With her left, she took the phone out of her pocket, listening attentively.

"Don't let anyone touch anything," she sharply ordered. "I'll be right there."

3

A GENERAL KILL

MURDER INVESTIGATION SCENES ARE usually chaotic. It's safe to say
that the pandemonium witnessed at this one was a multiple of ten of
the standard angry-wife-shoots-husband type. After the little tête-
à-tête just described between Nadine and Dustin, the partnership
was about to be confronted with a real mess. The call Nadine took
was from a junior investigator informing her of another murder presumed to be the work of our star.

The weather had worsened and a dazzling display of lightning
had recently zeroed in on an electrical transformer, reducing the illumination of all the streetlights to less than a candle. To compensate
for the loss of light, the police vehicles—over a hundred, and that's
without exaggeration—were scattered facing every which direction,
generating enough power to service the entire city.

The area had been cordoned off with that stylish yellow designer
tape branded exclusively for murder scenes. There were also numerous officers standing around the perimeter of the area to prevent any
pain-in-the-ass citizen from breaking the line. Comically, the car
around which the entire stage was set escaped any rays of light; it was
as if everything in a theatre production were brightly presented, but
the action on center stage blacked out.

While at first thought, we might assume the circumstance to be
the result of folly or stupidity on the part of the officers already on the
scene, there might be another explanation: even police officers and

detectives sometimes don't have the stomach to look at a murder victim. They'd rather close their eyes and leave the dirty work to those who don't nauseate as easily.

So none too soon arrives Nadine, cast iron stomach and all. Her car glided into an available spot on the outside of the randomly parked clutch of vehicles. She calmly opened her door. If we could hear da-da, da-da background music as she lowered her foot onto the wet concrete, we'd swear The Sheriff had arrived. Bad guys better get out of town, pronto. Standing on the street, she stopped to survey the scene. Then, unconsciously, still with an extra dividend of force, she slammed the car door closed behind her.

What Nadine dreaded most about her job was being called in the middle of the night, which happened with surprising infrequency. She hated having her sleep interrupted; nightmares had troubled her since childhood. If she had one, fortunately, she now knew how to get herself back to sleep so that she didn't feel hung over in the morning. But having to dress and go out at all hours after she'd begun her sleep time, that meant the whole night's rest was lost.

If Dustin's so-called emergency ring requesting her to the scene of his little caper put her in a foul mood, its only redeeming consequence was that it prepared her for this. Still, as she approached the scene, she couldn't hide a sharp edge that not one of her subordinates would have wanted to rub.

Gazing at the mess in front of her, inattentive to her hair taking a soaking from the now heavy rainfall, she readied herself for a brief orientation of the scene. She didn't have long to wait; a novice investigator, Todd Padgett, short on breath, raced up to her.

"Street, sorry to call you so…"

"I was already up." She glanced slightly right to punish Dustin with a reminder she wasn't expecting a repeat performance from him. "What do we have, Todd?"

"Hope you haven't eaten recently. General Crow had a bad night."

Nadine was led to the driver's side of the car, with Dustin a step behind her. The absurdity of no light on that one significant location in the entire setting nettled her. She raised her arms so that her hands were chest high, palms up and looked skyward for an appeal to an unknown source.

"Is it possible to get some light over here?" she irksomely asked.

Padgett ran to one of the other vehicles and reset it so that the headlights were properly directed at the late model Jaguar that would have belonged to General Crow, were he still alive. Now, with the assistance of her lighting director, Nadine was awarded a close up of the general's head.

If it weren't so repulsive a sight it might have been uncommonly humorous. The head was lying sloppily across the left side of the steering wheel with the bottom of the chin serving as a faucet for a slow-dripping chain of blood still splattering into a puddle on the floor mat.

Nadine took her flashlight and shined it on the figure. She leaned into the car, calling to Dustin who was in the process of sheltering himself under a long rain jacket and waterproof shovel hat.

"Dustin. Looks like the first strike was to the right side again, the brain…" Her voice elevated. "Take this down."

Dustin fumbled to get a note pad and pen out, then tried to write under the protection of the coat.

"He used an object…looks like some sort of sharp-edged hammer."

She stopped talking for a moment, leaning through the window and downward.

"What do we have here?"

Nadine pulled herself out the window. In her purse, she found a rubber glove and plastic pouch, putting on the glove and then reaching far up in the area of the foot pedals, commenting on her way out.

"The killer's a meanie; he didn't even let The General finish his cigar."

She faced directly toward Dustin, dropping the smoke in the evidence bag. Her hair, naturally wavy and intentionally worn down was glued to her scalp and face. Her blouse was drenched. Padgett came running back, holding a coat that he draped over her.

"For Christ's sake, Street, you're gonna get sick."

Oblivious to the gesture, the warning, or the elements prompting both, she went on with her investigation. "I think we may have ourselves, what is it, number eleven? He's picking up the pace for some reason."

"Dustin, get his home and office phone records," she instructed, as she pulled off her gloves. "Somebody must've called to arrange a meeting with him."

Nadine paused her reporting of the murder and looked at me with the saddest expression, as if the global tonnage of the world rested on her tiny bony shoulders.

"My boss, Chief Lambert...we'll be talking about him a lot Zach. He hated me," she sighed. "Facebook friends we'd never be...I knew he was always lurking in my shadow, waiting to destroy me."

Nadine left that afternoon with the understanding that we'd meet again the following morning. By then, I had completed the next section. As I did with every bit of writing and every re-write of an entire chapter, I asked her to look it over. She had more time on her hands than she was accustomed to and was always eager to keep abreast of my progress. However, I could tell from the onset that her role as editor-in-chief-number-two was not a pleasant task—she was used to being number one.

As hopeful as she was that this exercise in story telling was going to exorcise the evil spirits the case had placed upon her soul, she was exhausted by the daily ordeal of meeting with me. Still, she'd tear into the material I wrote and dissect each and every word such that at points, I felt like she was a pestilent I'd prefer treating with a Xanax pill.

"Nadine, I have another topic to bring up to you this afternoon," I gingerly approached her after she hounded me about minor issues. I was being sneaky and knew it. The real issue I wanted to address was her vigilance of my work, but I used a secondary, and irrelevant matter, to bring it up.

I had a silly habit when writing. I'd envision the story like a stage production or film. During one of our earliest meetings, I had proposed her as the star of the show. Immediately she protested, insisting I was mistaken to put her in the leading role. I let it pass. Now I was ready to assert my authority, leading to a major blowout with her. It started as a powwow, but ended as a "pow" followed by a "wow."

"I realize I made a mistake when I accepted that the star would be the killer. Really, Nadine, it has to be you."

"What's so important about it?" she rightfully asked.

"To me, it's a technical issue. There's a different emphasis placed on the key character as I write."

"Okay, you happy now? I'll be your star." She stood up and began prancing about my office like an actress, concluding the scene by crouching down with her chin on the desk and with her eyes looking up at me. "Anything else?"

"Actually, yes," I prudently answered. "You have to back off me on the writing. Story elements, sequence and dialogue you witnessed or partook in, character depiction—I'll take all you have to offer. But style and structure, descriptive writing, pace; I'm going to have to make those decisions."

She stood up from her squatted pose.

I was laying down the law and she knew it—I delivered the "pow." Looking up at her, with her lower lip unconsciously tremulous, I didn't know if Nadine's response was about to be a "whoa" or a "wow." I loved the story and was hooked, so it was a big risk, especially considering that while Nadine may have been compromised by her suffering, she was as hard of a cookie as ever baked. I surmised she wasn't beyond walking away from the project.

Waiting for her next move, a fantasy set in. I imagined her magically moving her right eye to the left side of her face like a chess piece, bulking up the strength on one side of the board in a show of force. She was now glaring at me, but with both orbs grotesquely next to one another.

I held my ground (I was in my chair so standing it was not feasible) and waited, what seemed to me an eternity. Then the right eye slid back into its normal position and the slits of her eyes narrowed and widened. She was smiling.

"Let me know when you need me," she declared as she sat back in a rare gesture of submission.

Wow. Wow! I presumed I'd have to pay up someplace, sometime, somehow. For now, however, I came away with exactly what I wanted. I was to be granted greater literary freedom—I felt like I had just won a bluff.

"Nadine, I think it's time to introduce a couple of other performers."

"As you wish, darling," she said with the indifference of a lion closing in for a kill.

Anyone care to meet Dr. Monroe? The esteemed analyst is in session. A little birdie is breaching the cardinal law of client confidentiality, kindly doing so to allow us all to eavesdrop as the doctor "tries" to treat a most unruly patient.

4

ANALYTIC TROUBLE

DR. LAWRENCE MONROE IS not only a professor of psychiatry at George Washington University School of Medicine and a world-renowned expert on deviant and criminal behavior, but he's also a highly successful private practitioner. He is avid about his work, has gem-quality ethics and principles regarding treatment; and…has a collection of friends that would qualify for the label "unique."

His treatment office is large. The patients enter—like most psych doctor offices—into a small waiting room with a button to press that lights up to let the doctor know his next person is waiting. Given the profile of his typical client, it's a wonder they'd tolerate the possibility of being seen by a friend or relative of the person receiving treatment while they themselves are arriving to see Dr. Monroe.

If any of the patients had reservations about being recognized, however, it was apparent they were willing to trade their vanity for the privilege of having their heads shrunk by such an esteemed and competent master of the mind. Still, it should be noted that there was one "special" individual who was granted a private method of anonymity when visiting Dr. Monroe.

If we had the vantage point of a pigeon that often enjoyed resting on the sill outside the doctor's treatment room—the wretched creature with the gall to violate the sanctity of this holy space—we would notice that on the day when Monroe was to see one particular patient, he was oddly out of sorts. Typically presenting to the world a self-assured and relaxed exterior, when he saw the light come on signaling the arrival of his next patient, grim lines blemished his smooth, youthful face.

Sitting in his favorite dark brown leather chair with wood frame, staring at a lithograph by Andy Warhol of Chairman Mao, he appeared unenthusiastic, actually a tad apprehensive. Still, like a good soldier, he elevated himself. He opened the door for his waiting patient. His voice slipped a quiver as he greeted the man.

"Please come in."

The patient said nothing. He seemed bold and gritty. He stared coldly at the doctor.

"I believe last time we finished up discussing some issues about your childhood," Dr. Monroe offered to refresh the patient's memory. "Should we continue there?"

Lots of patients come for help because of anger control issues that have destroyed marriages, relations with children, or even careers. Learning to deal with their stronger emotions is an essential element in their recovery process. At least that's what Dr. Monroe has devoted an entire chapter to in his latest book, *Doctor's on The Couch*. I trust the publisher won't begrudge me briefly quoting him:

"Learning to overcome this negative behavior helps one to gain confidence and enhance his or her self-esteem. Therefore, if the therapy is successful and achieves those critical breakthroughs we as clinicians treasure in treatment, finally, at long last, the patient will be able to appropriate some of his or her anger constructively."

As he continues later in the same chapter, the title of the book begins to make sense.

"An early step in treatment is testing out these healthier expressions of hostility with the therapist. In this way, the doctor can take pleasure in the signs of great progress being made. Still, for individuals who are potentially dangerous, the doctor must be cautious of first-hand experiences with rage only a tissue below the surface of execution. For the

inexperienced, naïve or overly zealous clinician, failing to appraise the upper level of toxicity of a patient's anger may place the doctor in jeopardy of his or her own safety."

This short treatise composing Chapter 11 and entitled *"The Art of Dealing with Anger in the Therapeutic Setting"* is not presented to criticize or judge Dr. Monroe. It is solely to highlight the fact that for some reason this accomplished and talented man is having trouble taking his own advice.

I mention above that he seemed "reluctant" to see the patient? We can't be sure yet as to the exact nature of Monroe's trepidation, for he himself is not on top of it at this time; his closest proximity of insight is merely at the embryonic level.

Before the patient spoke, that visiting pigeon I just mentioned flapped from his perch on one landing outside a window to the one immediately adjacent to it. He now pecked two times on the glass. The patient addressed the intrusion with a grunt, turning next to Monroe. His first words were spoken in a voice that shared, though vaguely, characteristics of the vocal sounds uttered by the killer of Wesley Arnold.

"Let's get this over with, sonny boy," he grumbled, treating Dr. Monroe with equal indignity as the bird still intruding into the session. "What do you need me to do?"

"I don't need you to do anything," Monroe retorted with an odd chuckle.

"Play your games," the patient snarled. "I'll wait until you're ready to cut the crap."

"We have to find a way to bring down your level of anger."

The man's impulses were on a short leash. He pounded suddenly on a table in front of him, the shock startling even to the bird. The man then bellowed. "Thanks to you I deal with my..." He paused to mimic his therapist. "'Stronger feelings' better now." He paused a second time, now to reflect on the point. "I really do."

He then smirked, after which he leaned toward the doctor to whisper at him. "I haven't done anything…" His voice softened eerily. "Bad…for…" Finally, his words trailed off completely. At the same time, his face assumed a proud calm. Then he spoke in a playfully scoffing manner. "So what's new in your life, doc?"

In the corner of the room sits a round table. It serves as a resting place for a metal piece of pop art. It's designed as a track for a small metal ball to travel. The sphere utilizes kinetic energy to propel itself in a state of perpetual motion. Monroe finds it restful to watch the ball's predictable but pleasant journey, especially during those times that he's deathly bored by a patient's redundant chatter, or more aptly, when he reaches the point where he's in need of an I-wish-I-could-strangle-this-idiot pill.

The fact that he's stationed the moving object directly behind where the patients sit, where he can gaze at it while seeming to be focused on what his client is saying, speaks not only to the fact it commands more attention from him during the course of an average day than any other person or thing, but also to a clinical fact: therapeutic growth takes place in tiny, compressed plots separated by vast, ill-defined stretches of wasteland.

Under the best of conditions, this profession chosen by Dr. Monroe has occupational hazards that can be deadly. That ball may be saving his life. If not, at a minimum, it succeeds in cleansing his mind momentarily as he's deliberating on a query or plain response to a patient, precisely as he's doing with this belligerent man.

"Just talk about yourself," the doctor gently instructed.

The man didn't miss a beat, seemed on his game as he impudently retorted. "Well, when I was growing up I went to a school where they taught us that if you masturbate you'll go blind. What do you think about that?"

Monroe for a brief second aired a deep breath. As he exhaled, he seemed to be calming himself. He recognized he'd been fumbling through a mental minefield and might now be able to put things on his own terms.

"It's what you thought that matters," Monroe said, paddling the comment back across the imaginary net.

"I thought it was time to stop going to school," the man stated brazenly.

"You believe you made a good decision?"

"I was fucking by the time I was fourteen." The patient wouldn't let up. "How about you?"

"This isn't about me."

"Don't you think it's about both of us?" The man for the first time altered his tone. Monroe sensed the change.

"No, it is not," the doctor strongly stated, trying to cease what he sensed was an opportunity to reinstate clinical order. "And we've covered this ground several times, haven't we?"

"You mean about you and I, keeping us separate?" the patient queried, curiously shifting his tone to the extent that he sounded timid.

"Exactly. You have your own ego boundaries. So when you come here all you have to do is stay with yourself, learn to thicken the walls between you and everyone else in the world. That's when you'll start to find your true self," Monroe lectured.

"That's what I hate worst. Sometimes I feel like the 'me' inside is bad. I do terrible things. I can't help myself. Look how I've treated you," his voice now assumed the sound of deep remorse, the man taking the role of flagellator of his own evil unrestrained impulses.

"Tell me what happened," Monroe quickly asked so as to capitalize on the easing of his patient's mood.

"I don't know what you mean. Nothing happened."

"Your attitude changed," Monroe pointed out. "Why?"

"I can't tell," the man said almost apologetically. "It was just something here."

The patient pointed to his abdomen, while his face exhibited a sign of pain.

"It's a feeling," Dr. Monroe explained. "That's good. You're feeling regret, and that's appropriate."

"That's a feeling?" the patient wondered. "That's what I'm talking about, a feeling. It happens all the time and I can't tolerate it. It makes me want to…it hurts so much, it makes me want to harm someone."

"But you don't have to," Monroe said in a soothing intonation. "You can learn to tolerate it."

"Never have." A sense of resignation could be discerned through the briskness of his words. "I really doubt it."

"That's where this intervention is going to help. And what you need to remember is that it all begins with how you treat yourself," Monroe confidently conveyed to his patient. "Once you learn to make friends with those painful feelings, you'll see, it will be easier to share kindness with others."

"I think it's too late," the man lamented. "Look how I act toward you. Do you want to know why? It's because you're trying to help. Pisses me off, doc. I don't like people helping me."

"It's part of life. We all have to rely on other people sometimes."

"It would make it easier for me if you let me help you with something," the patient grinned.

"But I don't need you for anything," Monroe chuckled. "Besides, that's not what your therapy is about."

"It is for me," the man insisted.

"We can talk about this more next time. But one of the reasons we try to go back into your youth is to find leads pertaining to what your likes are, what you can do to gratify *you*. You can't wait for me or anyone else to offer you the opportunity to be satisfied."

"Okay, I got it, sonny boy," the momentarily gleeful patient answered. "You'll see how good I can be."

The pigeon winged off his perch, having learned from experience that what he was witnessing between Monroe and the patient was as thrilling as the treatment process gets. Simultaneously, the door gently closed.

Monroe was sitting alone. The whipsaw pattern of his patient was familiar to the doctor but it still left him curiously distraught.

What could account for the patient's dramatic change of attitude partway through the encounter? Guilt? Shame? Would Dr. Monroe, a great analyst, deduce regret or nascent signs of a conscience?

Whatever it is, here's hoping the treatment process helps this man achieve a stronger grip on his emotions. For if he might be the killer, Monroe's skills as a therapist may be the only chance that the lives of many innocent people will be spared.

Is this master of the mind, Dr. Lawrence Monroe, the man for the job? It's a question Nadine is going to get the answer to.

5

THE LOVE COTTAGE

IT WAS A MONDAY evening. Kuruk was closed. Preeti's invitation for dinner to Nadine was for a meal at our restaurant. Reuben, our chef, had volunteered to cook one of his feasts in honor of Nadine. It was near six, the time that Preeti asked everyone to come. Reuben's wife, our good friend, Josea, Preeti and I had arrived, but the other two invited guests had not.

Reuben poked his head out from the kitchen. "What do you smell?" he posed with the jubilance of a quiz show host.

"Oscar Meyer wieners," Josea joked.

"You wait little lady," he quipped back at his wife at the same moment as my father-in-law, Len Cloud, arrived.

The greetings for Len were interrupted when our family pet, Henry Higgins, jumped up and gave a single sharp bark. His short tail was wagging at ninety degrees—which is near record setting for the stump left on the boy. He had developed a fondness for Nadine and his outburst anticipated her approaching the door. By the time she opened it, he took the liberty to be the first to welcome her, landing his two front paws on the thighs of her black jeans. She picked him up and hoisted him with her outstretched arms so she was face-to-face with her buddy. His tongue was reaching zestfully. I believe he was trying to gauge how he might get to her rouge lip balm.

To my knowledge, Nadine had met everyone present, except Len Cloud. I proceeded on that premise and made the proper introduction. Then Preeti had us all sit at a table and brought over a bottle of champagne. Kindly, she welcomed Nadine by toasting her.

"How do you like the little love cottage, Nadine," Josea asked, referring to the living quarters attached to the restaurant that I had invited Nadine to use during her stay.

"There's a charm to the place. I feel safe here." Nadine offered what looked like a strained smile. "I do get lots of love when Henry Higgins comes to snuggle."

"It does have that feel to it," Reuben agreed. "When I was living there alone, I would sit sometimes for hours—it would rejuvenate me when I felt sad."

"So much sadness, so much joy, so much life born in that space," Josea reflected. "I'm glad you came to occupy it, Nadine. I hated to think of it empty. It's a special home and I hope you'll stay in it a long time".

"But why do you call it the love cottage?"

"Everyone who has lived there is either in love or falls in love while occupying it."

"I'm sure I'll be the first to break the string of successes," Nadine snickered.

"We'll see," Josea teased. "You're not the first to think that."

"I have to go back to my life. I can't run away from responsibilities," Nadine sternly reminded herself.

Josea surveyed the other faces in the room. "So be it, Nadine." She couldn't hold back a portentous smirk. "But time will tell. I don't think anyone who lived there went back to the life they had before."

"I never thought about that." Preeti stopped to deliberate. "Your right." She then intentionally altered the course of the discussion. She was sensitive to the awareness that Nadine had enough on her mind and could do without fortune telling by a group of amateur soothsayers. "Zach tells me you're moving along well with the writing."

"Zach is moving along well," Nadine sighed. "I've been ordered to stay out of the creative process, but I've been assigned the lead actress role." Cunningly she added: "Anyone looking for a star?"

"Actually, Nadine, Reuben and I just completed a new musical called, *Brothel*," Josea responded. "Care to audition?" Then she contemplated more earnestly. "It's the story of a little girl whose mother was a prostitute."

"There's an unusual twist in the end," Reuben embellished, "but you'll have to stick around to see it for yourself. I think I see what Josea is getting at. We have a perfect role for you...ever acted?"

"An essential ingredient to being a good murder investigator is acting."

"Then it's decided. You'll audition," Josea declared.

"I think you could do better," Nadine insisted. "I loved your musical, *How Could Wright Be So Wrong*, by the way." She was complimenting the seminal work of Josea and Reuben. "Who wrote what parts?"

"I wrote the book and sections of the music," Josea explained. "Then Reuben did the rest."

"I still think about what Benny did. His devotion to his family was unimaginable," Nadine mused. "It's a simple love story in the end; that's what makes it so beautiful."

"Benny was stuck in a dream and couldn't materialize it in real life," Josea explained.

"Aren't we all stuck in something? On the global level, we call it life, but individually we're dealing with a particular dominating characteristic," Nadine surmised. "Shyness, gullibility, greed, devastation, vengeance, loneliness, ignorance; poverty, worry, fear, hate, denial, lust—this list is vast, but if we look at ourselves, we'll see what is most damning that we can't escape."

"What if we do escape it?" Reuben challenged.

"If you believe you dodged it by running away from it, I promise it'll be there when you look in the mirror."

"It's true. I'll admit that what I've hidden from in my life ends up being there just the same." Reuben stopped to contemplate. "I may be stuck in it, yet I handle it better than when I was younger," he finally concluded

"I think that's the best we can do, Reuben. Since we'll never get unstuck, we have to learn to take it gracefully," Nadine opined.

"Should we do one round, each of us telling what we see as our life-damning theme?" I flippantly suggested.

"No, please," Nadine earnestly pled. "We're off track. What about *How Could Wright Be So Wrong*? I'm sure it'll be on Broadway soon."

"That we will never allow, Nadine," Josea quickly assured her. "Reuben avoids fame like snake bites…at least he tries," she said, giving a subtle clue to Nadine about Reuben's dominating theme. Then she added regarding herself: "And I've had enough of a taste of it to know it causes indigestion."

"So it's just for fun," Nadine assumed.

"And self-satisfaction," added Reuben as he stood to go into the kitchen. "People are entertained. They truly enjoy our work. What more can we ask for?"

At that moment, the door opened and, Preston, the last invited guest walked in.

"I was just about to worry over you," Preeti called out.

"Plane was late. What else would you expect?" Preston humorously disparaged the airline industry's notorious habit of inconveniencing customers.

Preston was a man about my height and weight, six-two and one hundred eighty pounds. He had light sandy brown curly hair that he permitted to dangle loosely but at a controlled short length. He had an easy-going spirit and other than an unconquerable and inexplicable mistrust of Reuben, he liked his fellow man and reciprocally was adored by most everyone who knew him—even Reuben.

He loved woman. With equal reverence Minnesota Fats would

show to a pool stick, he handled his ladies. The main difference between the two men was that the famous billiard player finished the match, whereas Preston was content to lay down the cue and walk away any time it suited him.

The two of us had delighted in that shared state of bachelorhood, but after my marriage to Preeti, I noticed Preston tiring of superficial interludes. Yet rather than vigorously pursuing a more enduring bond, he seemed to withdraw from dating altogether. Occasionally he'd report to me how he'd bore himself with the endlessly stocked river of band devotees who were never selfish with their lust, in exchange for the chance to meet the members of the famous rock group employing him as their sound engineer.

Preston worked for a world-renowned musical band that had lost its iconic leader. Still, the remaining members played to huge crowds of followers who beyond attending out of nostalgia, prayed that someday their idol would return to stage and they would have been able to say they were there when it happened. Regardless of the motive of the female fans, I could tell that Preston had graduated to a state of indifference toward their carnal offerings. As only a best friend dating back to childhood might be able to attest, my mate recently had been culturing loneliness and sadness like warts.

Then I noticed as he saw Nadine from across the room, his eyes popped forward. She had stood up from the table where she had been seated. *Holy shit,* howled rankly in my muted mind as Nadine locked in on him in return. *Kuruk! It's a place where people fall in love,* I laughed inwardly.

It might have been pure imagination on my part, that I had witnessed *the look* by each of them. Yet my first thought was that romance between these two appeared as plausible as a turtle tap dancing. Nadine seemed emotionally fragile and romantically crippled. Preston, historically, was as dogged pursuing love as a bellman refusing a tip.

Yet there they were. Preston looked gaga and Nadine took on the look of a confused little girl. I broke the spell.

"Nadine, come over for a second." I waved instructively to her. She followed my direction like a child. "I assume you both know each other," I said innocently.

"Actually we never met one another," Preston addressed me while apportioning his glance heavily in Nadine's direction. "I'm Preston, Zach's best friend," he introduced himself to Nadine.

She stood looking at him and said nothing, only a silly grin speaking to a fact I couldn't begin to interpret.

"Stacy told me you had this horrible experience in your work. I'm sorry," Preston told Nadine, who still hadn't said a word. "I knew Zach would be the person to help."

"We are making some progress, are we not?" I rhetorically asked Nadine.

"Slow but steady. It's a lot better than I did on my own," she admitted. "Besides, I like it here. I'm really not in a hurry to finish it up and that's not how I typically work."

"Can I ask what it is you're writing about?" Preston queried her.

"Of course, you can," Nadine responded playfully.

"Well, what happened?"

"I can't tell you," Nadine teased.

"But you invited me to ask," Preston insisted.

"You asked if you *could* ask, not if I would answer."

"That's cheating," Preston objected.

"No. You weren't paying attention to the words. Every point we speak is critical. Is that not correct, my author friend?" she posed the question to me like a chess move.

"It is," I agreed. "But you knew what Preston was asking."

"Zach, I'm surprised. I'll bet your friend can defend himself." There was no offense in her voice. She actually seemed more relaxed than I had seen her up to that moment. "I'm toying with Preston on purpose. It's my way of keeping up his interest."

I noticed her punctuate the last statement by staring straight at him. There was no doubt she had accomplished her purpose—his engrossment stood out like an erection.

"Fact remains," Preston insisted, "that I would be pleased if you would share it with me."

"Okay," Nadine consented. "Zach, what if you give copies of each chapter to Preston after they're finished? It'll be like a serial."

The last word set off a neural reaction. Her tone turned somber and the light playfulness she displayed an instant before, scattered like dust particles in the wind. "It's about serial murder, Preston. It's about love, betrayal; it's about dirty, filthy politics, sick people, hateful people, greedy and desperate people…and it's about me being tossed around like a shag mop in the hands of monsters." Nadine's eyes turned watery, but she battled proudly to maintain composure. "It's about every damn thing evil in life…and I collapsed, okay?"

Public displays of emotion were not this lady's style, yet there she was, unwittingly making herself vulnerable. "This is why I can't be with people." Her mascara dissolved in a teardrop that aimed an inky rivulet down the right cheek. "I'm broken, can't you see," her voice hushed to avoid embarrassment in front of the others. "You've all been wonderful to me, Zach. I'm not ready for this," she wept. "Another time, okay? Please let everyone know that I don't feel well."

Nadine retreated back to her room. Henry Higgins managed to slip in just before she closed the door—Preston might have hated the dog just for that second. Preeti had been watching while at the same time talking with Josea. She came over to see what happened. Ever since she arrived, my wife sensed that Nadine was a lady in distress and had instinctively zeroed in on building a bond with the new guest.

"Zach, honey, what happened?" she inquired.

"It was my fault," Preston piped in. "I wanted to know more about what happened to her." He spoke to both of us with a maturity that I'd never heard come out of his mouth. "I think I might be able to love this woman."

"Then go knock on her door," my wife dared him.

6

THE SETUP

WHAT A COINCIDENCE IT was that the goo-gooing initial attraction between Nadine and Preston coincided with the next chapter of Nadine's tale, an episode beginning with all the elements of a love story. This one was between Nadine and the esteemed Dr. Monroe.

The psychiatrist's lectures are always packed. He's respected as a great expert in his field and has the reputation of padding his lessons with the most schmaltzy professional case experiences—cases he's directly handled, involving some of the most notorious psychopaths and sociopaths ever put under an analytic scope. This particular evening is no exception. That explains the densely crowded hall Dr. Monroe speaks to, with seats available in the last row only.

In fact, if we glance to the rear of the lecture hall, we notice a lone spectator with a seat empty on both sides of him. He's a man senior to Monroe by a good couple of decades. His hair is still black, with only the hints of the gray most men sprout in their early forties, and it's thick as well as full. We could say that clinically he looks years younger than his stated age. His dress is simple: polo-type maroon top—forget the labels—a worn pair of blue jeans and white tennies.

He leans comfortably to his right with his left leg draped over the other, hunching slightly. His eyes are half closed, challenging drowsiness he'd have awarded with a short nap long ago had he been home. The purpose in his attending Monroe's class is not edification in psychopathology, a subject he's proficient on in his own right. This gentleman has romance on his mind.

Dr. Monroe in front of the audience is in his element. He moves back and forth across the stage, engages his troops by pausing for rhetorical questions. Occasionally, he humors his flock with quotes he's either picked up on his travels or made up along the way.

At the moment, he's showing his students a video from an institute for the criminally insane. His attention rests on one particular patient, a man displaying multiple characters in each of several sequences. Monroe explains that the patient under study is a convicted serial killer—and more. Have a listen.

"Initially, this man was diagnosed as a sociopathic personality. As his evaluation progressed, it was recognized that the diagnostic process was far more complex than previously believed. The man had developed innumerable personalities, some of which he'd abandoned and others he'd retained.

"It was concluded based on the criminal investigation that the reason his case had become nearly impossible to solve was that each of the murders he'd committed was the making of a distinct personality, each sprouted successively and seemingly with the ease of a kid blowing bubbles in class.

Monroe reached under the stand and drew out a cup of water, taking a sip and then replacing it.

"About a year into the case, I was invited to help the FBI's Violent Criminal Apprehension Program to sort out the killings. You may be interested to know that the man who requested my involvement in the case is seated behind you—Chauncy Meyer."

He gestured with his hand in the direction of our spectator in the last row, who in turn makes a half bow and sits back down.

"Chauncy briefed me on a batch of murder cases under investigation. The files were suspiciously and preliminarily assumed to be the product of one killer. The geography, sex and temporal separation of each act supported it. Generally, serial killers like to operate within a special field—a comfort zone—where they have great familiarity; often, in other words, close to home. They'll typically select a category of victim and stick with it—prostitutes, college girls or teenage boys. Also, there's a feeding pattern; we know that once the act of murder is consummated for the first time, it gets easier. Makes sense, doesn't it?

"But there were uncharacteristic patterns for serial killers in these cases that Mr. Meyer presented to me. Serial killers are into slashing, strangling, mutilating, torturing or sodomizing, but generally not all or in combination. Thus I argued, incorrectly, that these were examples of murders carried out by several people. As it turned out, fortunately for all of us, the case solved itself.

"After the last murder, a man showed up at the crime scene claiming that he could help identify the killer. When he was invited to the office for questioning, he asked if he could go in 'a real police car.' Then on the way to the station, he confessed to the agents that he'd committed the latest murder."

Eager hands were flopping in the audience. Monroe pointed to a male in the front row.

"You indicated that he confessed to the last murder. What about the others?"

"That's a point. His examination spanned over a year from the time of his initial confession, during which time we discovered that I wasn't so dumb after all. He, the man sitting during the interrogations, wasn't capable of solving the rest of the murders for us; he hadn't committed them. Instead, responsible for the atrocities were disparate elements of the same psyche, characters as unique as separate persons. These monsters had acted out the rage, insecurity and hate they all shared in common; they were in fact all operating out of one single physical body.

"As evidence was presented to him of what he had done, there were moments of awareness when dormant personalities were awakened. It was during these interrogations that he was able to recount the acts carried out by individuals, but he perceived them to be separate from himself. Some of the unsolved murders that he couldn't help with we deduced were his, based on many clues we gathered about one or another of his personalities. He was never able, even for an instant, to reacquaint with some of the murderers he had invented and then disowned.

"Modern psychiatry classifies cases like these under the diagnostic category of Dissociative Identity Disorder, whereas previously it was referred to both professionally and colloquially as Multiple Personality Disorder.

"There has probably never been a more intriguing area of human psychology. Yet this case, in my opinion, is at the top of the chart. Just consider the following. This man accomplished what I have until now not observed in another human mind. Many of his personalities have and had relationships with each other; they carried out complex patterns of relatedness but never with awareness of their shared physical space or the reality that they were a product created by one mind."

Monroe's inspiration and scrupulous attention to his material diverted his attention from a late arriving individual. It was a female who had entered from the rear and then moved in the direction of the man just introduced as Chauncy Meyer.

That lady, as you may have figured, was Nadine. Looking sharp. Though it's not her intent to come off as sexy, that pale yellow tight fitting sweater with tan pants hugging her frame would classify her as "tight". The ineluctable sensual air that follows her is a natural endowment she's not foolish enough to hide. She knows that by doing so she could possibly miss that fortuitous romantic encounter sadly missing from her life.

Nadine met Chauncy when she was a junior investigator for the D. C. Metropolitan Police. As their relationship developed, he became mostly her mentor, but also a father figure. Seating herself next to him, close enough to nudge his arm, she gained a snap victory over his dopey state. He smiled kindly, reaching for her hand, which he gave a welcoming squeeze. Turning his head back toward where Monroe continued his discourse, so as to be as unobtrusive as possible, he whispered to Nadine.

"Need I tell you that's Dr. Monroe?"

Nadine nodded. Monroe, precisely at that moment, was interrupted. A man entered the stage area from the side and spoke inaudibly in the doctor's ear. They conversed a few moments. Chauncy and Nadine filled the void, quietly talking business.

"How bad is this sex slave thing you told me about…you know, the mess with La Mont?" Chauncy asked.

"Very bad. There's a lot more bigwigs than La Mont involved. I've put everything together and I'll be meeting with Lambert. I'm handing it over to him."

"What do you mean handing it over?"

"The murder investigation is all I can deal with now."

"Good. This sex ring is filthy. Nadine, the people participating are more dangerous than any of the killers you've sought. You don't need the risk."

Nadine's imperceptible tightening of the muscles of her mouth served to acknowledge she understood the gravity of that situation. While she was still thinking about the danger of the matter she was ready to jettison, Chauncy carried on about Monroe.

"Well, what do you think?"

"I understand. These political power people are the types who deal with opposition by eliminating it."

"Yes, but that's not what I'm talking about." Chauncy laughed, humoring himself over her denseness. "I'm asking about Monroe. What do you think?"

Her blush answered his question, though she tried to temper her reaction with words. "Good looking man…for sure."

Monroe was an attractive man. His salt and pepper-toned hair had a barely discernable part on the left that confidently hugged the head.

The frontal hair cut an even line along the forehead. His face was oval and perfectly balanced; even two vertical creases running from the bridge of the nose laterally downward defined identical twin cheeks that were so flat to the face they accentuated the woman-killer eyes.

The orbits for his eyes gently rose to tuck into the brows, offering that deep-set look of wisdom that makes the ladies' hearts throb at the thought that this is a man who can have any of her competitors. The most insightful women understand that such handsomeness can place a man at an inherent disadvantage with the opposite sex since many fine women give up without trying, and those that make a pitch are often the most cunning and avaricious.

Nadine was processing the vision. There was interest, but it was tempered with prudence. She knew this type of male could be arrogant and self-indulgent, but she was no more intimidated than she'd be testifying against the worst of human kind. She'd always had confidence that she was not deficient in allurement. Plus, she knew as well that attraction alone was good for at most one date, and experience had taught her that most of the hot lookers were also classic bores.

"He's a lot different than he seems on the surface," Chauncy said. "He's deep. I think you'll like that."

Nadine chuckled uncomfortably. "Did you already set up a date for us?"

"No, you'll have to handle that on your own. But I'll tell you, you could do worse."

"I'm sure I've done worse a lot of times."

"You read my mind."

"Chauncy, I can't be great at everything."

Their playful daddy-daughter bantering sputtered to a halt as Monroe returned to address his flock. "I was just asked if I would mind wrapping up a few minutes early. Since we're about finished anyway, I'll see all of you Thursday."

Monroe grabbed his notes off the lectern. A few eager students approached him. Chauncy stood and faced Nadine.

"Let's go to Monroe's office. He'll meet us when he's done."

"I'll be there in a minute. Need to freshen up first."

While Nadine was making herself more beautiful and Monroe was chatting with students, Chauncy, satisfied he'd succeeded with step-one in facilitating a romance, made his way to Monroe's office.

Detective Street and Dr. Monroe? This should be interesting.

7

THAT'S MY GIRL

WHEN HE STANDS UPRIGHT, we may notice that Chauncy's posture is slightly hunched. All those years dealing with gruesome murders and facing the horror of families broken with grief weigh heavily on him. But since retiring, he's noticed himself feeling lighter and more youthful.

He was sporting a perpetual peaceful grin as he entered Monroe's office ahead of both the doctor and Nadine. He passed the time examining a rock collection of the doctor's that he'd mounted on a table. Only a moment later, Monroe entered.

Chauncy possessed a great fondness for the psychiatrist and always had. Empathy is what we'd call it. But could it also be the vigilance of Monroe's eyes, a sign betraying inner turmoil that made Chauncy care for the man so deeply? Chauncy was uncertain. Other than his premonitions about Monroe, and his perception of a stressed soul, he found the man otherwise, well, neat. He dressed and presented himself as neat. His affairs were orderly and neat. His ambiance was neat and calm—neat, neat, neat, an interesting offset to the tight, tight, tight imprint we'd fix on Nadine.

Occasionally Chauncy lingered on another idea to account for his goodwill toward Monroe. Perhaps he saw the man as lonely. The famous doctor never talked about his love life…was there one? Was Monroe, like he, punished by a past sorrow he couldn't talk about, the loss of love? The thought had come to him more than once. A companion thought also visited him from time to time: Nadine. What about introducing them?

Unfortunately, the circumstances never seemed right—until a few days ago when Monroe called Chauncy and asked if he could set up a meeting between him and "the female detective handling the D.C. murders." An emergency at the hospital left Monroe short of time to explain to Chauncy the reason for the request, but ever since the thought of playing matchmaker had kept Nadine's mentor in the frolicking mood we find him in this evening.

"I've thought of getting you two together for years." As he waltzed over to Monroe, now seated on a couch, he continued as in a soliloquy. "Like sprouts from the same seed. Devoted to work; play long forgotten. What about love and romance, family?" He added, almost comically, "I hope I'm not out of line by saying I think you both need somebody."

"Chauncy," Monroe began, "the reason I wanted to meet—"

Approaching footsteps alerted Chauncy that Nadine had arrived. He loped to the door and embraced Nadine while calling out to Monroe who was still seated.

"This is my girl."

As she entered, Monroe was privileged with his first close up inspection of Nadine. The impression caused him to sit straight up, as if unwittingly succumbing to a supreme inner force. He enveloped Nadine in his gaze. She, always even keeled, struggled to keep outside his visual grasp. Neither was much for words; magic filled the silent void until their broker, who gained more from their first encounter than he could have dreamed, came to the rescue.

"Larry, this is the lady you asked to meet, Nadine Street."

Awkwardly, not confident what role to play, Chauncy lifted his arms and hands as if directing an orchestra. "She loves the most challenging cases."

Unable to dismiss, in fact relieved to acknowledge the truism of her personality, Nadine laughed. "I bore easily."

"I'll keep that in mind."

Monroe's coyness pricked Nadine, who responded by trying to regain control of the encounter. She moved forward to friskily shake his hand.

"What's nice about my work is that it's logical; every case can be solved. It's purely a matter of patience and perseverance."

"Sound familiar, Larry? Don't you argue that any patient can be cured, even the monsters who kill for sex and sport?"

"Are you saying we're both ridiculously deluded?"

Chauncy chortled. "No, just a matching set."

Staring at one another, stunned by what might be a frightful truth, neither the detective nor the doctor smiled or blinked. For a few seconds, the dancing rhythm in the room was still. Then Nadine unlocked the stalemate.

"Chauncy tells me you're quite the expert on serial cases."

Straightforward provocative is not her style. Truthfully, when it comes to any area of emotion, she's not uncomplicated. Fear is laced with aggression. Disappointment is tinged with hostility. Sorrow is fused with comedy. How human can you get?

Sometimes it takes an experiment to know exactly what sort of feeling you're dealing with on Nadine's part. It's not surprising, therefore, that on the day of her meeting Monroe, sarcasm would have had to be lab tested to confirm the trace elements of seduction. But it was there. She knew it. More shocking was that Monroe didn't need a test tube and Bunsen burner to distill the brew.

"I'm sure you're about to find out," Monroe bantered.

"Fine. Then if you have a few minutes my friend here suggests I tell you a couple stories."

"Shall I get my blankie and pillow?"

"This is a little gruesome for nighty-night tales. But if you'd like, this may help."

She extracted from her pocket a See's Candy caramel sucker and handed it to Monroe.

"My favorite flavor."

"Then we'll assume this is your lucky day," Nadine teased.

"It seems to be," Monroe cleverly acknowledged his good fortune meeting Detective Street. "I hope I'm not taking your last one."

"Don't worry. I always carry a supply."

"That I will be sure to remember. Now you have my nearly," he pulled out the sucker to highlight his point, "undivided attention."

"Nearly is not going to do it for me," she asserted as an admonition.

No time was allotted to Monroe to get in a final retort. Nadine proceeded, embracing the role of narrator. The great and famous professor was reduced to suckling peacefully while Nadine was in discourse.

"The victim is a tall, lanky man. His hair is jet black, slicked down with a sharp part to the right and trimmed to fit the role of a man of importance. He's sitting at the desk in his office, reviewing the final draft of a proposed tax exemption for designated offshore oil investments that he is presenting to the Senate Banking Committee in the morning.

"We infer this from the material gathered at the scene and confirm it with members of the committee. Anyway, he's wearing wire-rimmed glasses for reading and evidently takes them off and places them on the desk when he hears a knock on the outside door.

"You should be apprised of the fact that his building is secured. There is a night guard in the lobby at all hours. All interior doors of his offices were checked and reported locked at nine-thirty that evening. It was not unusual for Wayne Horton—I presume you recognize his name, ex-director of the World Bank, consultant to the Federal Reserve, and a leading world banker—to work late, and when doing so he was known to lock the outer door to his suite of offices."

She paused, catching Monroe vigorously working the lollipop like an enthralled child.

"I'll refrain from the obvious inferences, if that's okay with you."

"I think I can pick them up."

"If not, I'll have my answer to how good you are right away, won't I?

"Please continue," Monroe cheered her.

"Without any sign of hesitation, Mr. Horton goes to the door and opens it. It's doubtful he ever had the opportunity to welcome his caller. It appears, instead, he was greeted…with a steel blade housed in the left hand of the visitor. We know left because the upward force as the weapon made its way from the lower abdomen to the sternum exerted left to right, though it continued straight up from there through a couple ribs.   "Horton's lips tightened, looking like he was trying to ask a question but never had a chance. We know instead that his last breath was used for a deadly, unheard, shriek. He was wearing a white dress shirt, but it reddened from oozing blood even before gravity assisted his body to disengage from the knife, dead before reaching the ground.

"Later, we talked with the night watchman. His log showed a man signed in at nine forty-five. He registered with the initial 'D' and then 'Mann. The guard recalled it was crisp out. Therefore, he was not surprised to see the man wearing gloves. He did find it odd that the man refused to use the pen at the desk, instead opting to produce one of his own—incidentally, a cheap ballpoint.

"I questioned why there was no security tape of the foyer and the officer on duty said somebody by mistake must have either turned it off or forgot to reset it; typically nobody comes by late so he thought little of it…I still found it odd. Also, there was nothing distinguishable about the man as best the guard could recall. He described him as average in height and weight, estimating six feet tall and a hundred eighty pounds. His attire was unremarkable. He left at nine fifty-five;

no time for chit-chat."

Monroe was expressionless. Pausing again, Nadine looked across toward him just long enough to process his lack of enthusiasm; the man still seemed more pensive on the candy. Seeming impatient, she addressed herself to Chauncy.

"What are we doing here?"

Recognizing the reference was truly directed to him, Monroe calmly responded.

"I'm enjoying your flare for theatrics."

"I don't find any of this entertaining," she jeered at him.

"Must we be so serious at such an early stage of an investigation?"

"Then I'll have to assume you don't read the papers, doctor," Nadine continued, still assuming her mocking tone. "This is not the beginning. The boy has been quite busy. So far, he shows no signs of letting up. The evidence he leaves me amounts to nothing." Her last words made no attempt to hide the consternation starting to brew.

"Shame. If you matched the profile he was looking for, he might come introduce himself."

"What if he already has and I didn't recognize him?" Nadine proposed.

"Then I would say you have a brave killer, Nadine."

"I haven't met one with an ounce of courage yet," Nadine flippantly retorted.

"There now, do I sense some comic relief?" Monroe playfully countered.

Nadine did enjoy the banter. It definitely had a feeling of goodness behind it. It had been too long since she'd had even a tiny dose of interest in a man, let alone a measure qualifying for a tease. The thought rushed through her mind that maybe Chauncy was on to something: even if he wasn't helpful to her with the case, Dr. Monroe might be more worthy of a date. But she was hesitant to allow herself to lean on the fantasy.

"I hope I'm not wasting my time here. But if you want, I'll go on."

"I'd like that," Monroe offered in a more earnest voice.

"Reynolds Oil is owned and operated by Lacey Reynolds. It's the largest independent oil company in the world...hell, you know who he is. A simple reading of the file tells you he took a call from an unknown person and then ordered beer and nuts just before he was killed. A rock singer 'thinks' he saw someone leaving Reynolds' room but the star was likely using drugs. All he can remember, regardless, is that he might have seen surgical gloves. Reynolds was found with deadly puncture wounds in the occipital and parietal regions of the brain."

She threw her hands up haphazardly. "Now, isn't that wonderful?"

Chauncy, who'd been surveying the scene from a seated position on a chair, interjected a comment in Nadine's behalf. "Lambert's like a hornet buzzing in a jar. His personal aspirations are on the line and to say the least, he's not particularly fond of Nadine, who thus far is making minimal progress. She will solve the case, but it will never be speedy enough for him."

"It certainly doesn't help having a boss like him," Nadine conceded. "Plus, I agree that things are moving slowly. It's typically that way until you get a first break."

She paused, seeming irritated with herself for her temporary lack of success. Her impulse was to redirect the discussion.

"Let me go on. I'm sure you know about Wesley Arnold, the most recent case. He also welcomed the killer. That's the most extraordinary fact to me. This is not a bunch of average Joes who unsuspectingly open the door to their house or office and let in a foul draft. These are prominent people who are careful with their time and company. Yet each one of the victims thus far has been as receptive to the killer as...you'd expect to a good friend. Not one of them puts up a fight or tries to defend their own life." The comment returns her to a state of indignation.

"This killer…he really does nothing that extraordinary. As far as murdering goes, it's run-of-the-mill stuff. Really, what's unusual or remarkable about how he carries out his kills? The only outstanding thing to me is that he can get to people who are usually difficult to approach," she ranted.

"I've looked for associations between the victims, people they might all know, any patterns linking them but there's nothing, yet. Sometimes, I wonder if this is the work of several people, like tag-team killing, but I don't believe that. I think this is the kind of killer that could be in the room with us and we'd think he's a good friend. That's what distinguishes him: we would never suspect him, and he knows it."

Monroe nodded for a moment before he sung out off-handedly. "The killer sounds irresistible."

"And I can't wait to meet him," the lady swaggered.

Monroe paused, enjoying this woman's unusual bravado. He knew his next comment was going to stun her…and dumbfound Chauncy.

"The reason I asked to meet you, Ms. Street, was because I'm confident I can help you do that."

That'll earn him a date for sure.

8

DUSTIN'S BIG DADDY

THINKING OF HIS ASSOCIATION with Nadine upset Chief Lambert's gastric reflux. Rather than popping more pills, which he detested taking in the first place, he spent as little time as he could with her. But it was not little enough. In fact, much to his consternation, frequently he needed her. If he didn't, then without a doubt even Chauncy, who had built leverage with Lambert through years of past association, would never have been able to intervene on her behalf and gain for her the compromises he did from Lambert.

The annoying truth was that she was not only a crack investigator, but also his go-to gal—there is no go-to guy—when he needed his royal ass saved. More specifically, the cases that were hand-delivered to him by the mayor or other high-up officials were sensitive, and it was expected they'd be handled and resolved accordingly. Nadine had come through for him more times than his wife had been willing to listen to his sexual fantasies. She loved when her assignments roused her, left her spellbound, and Lambert fed her a diet richly seasoned to her taste.

For Lambert, each and every solved case was window dressing needed to gussy up his resume. It mattered not that everybody at headquarters despised him, they all knew that a sometime-in-the-future moment of great success was going to arrive for him: all he was doing in the meantime was decorating an exterior record to look as sharp as a Saturday night hustler. As unpalatable as his relationship with Nadine was to Lambert, therefore, there were advantages to be reaped.

But there was a circumstance not too long ago when one unexpected rub introduced trouble into the tenuous balance they had established, a situation that necessitated sacrifice on the part of both Lambert and Nadine. A forced compromise was accepted, but one neither was pleased to make...nor foolish enough to refuse. The culprit, though one would sleep better at night not referring derogatorily to him publicly, went by the name of Phillip Drake.

If there could be a human equivalent of a stealth bomber, it would be Drake. For people to whom it mattered, dropping his name under the right condition might earn them a trip to the U. S. Senate or alternatively under the wrong circumstance a one-way ticket from D. C. to Bakersfield, California where, if they were lucky, they might spend the rest of their lives planting onions.

His profession was law, his specialty criminal defense, though, in truth, Drake didn't believe in defenses. To him "defending" a case was like building an Italian tank, five gears in reverse. His theory was that if he was willing to take the client's case, his defendant was as pure as Southern Carolinian soil, and by god the prosecutors better put any idea of culpability out of their cobbled brains.

Drake was never satisfied with an acquittal or even dismissal of claims against his people. He insisted that the outrageous and vilely dishonest charges be vaporized and then a reparation received that would enrich the reputation of the accused. For example, by vindicating his statesman client, exposing the Senator's enemies as the culprits who perpetrated the ugly, unfounded accusations of embezzlement, the politician was able to waltz his way into a second term in the Senate...better yet, set himself up if he so desired for a serious run at the presidency.

So as we might imagine that Drake represented a select group of clients. Aside from being filthy rich or possessing some unique position in society, they shared three distinguishing characteristics: they were innocent, they were innocent, and they were innocent.

Drake knew Lambert; he knew everybody, but he'd known Lambert from way back. So when some time past he asked Lambert to come by his office in the early morning, the police chief gleefully imagined his opportunity to advance his career had arrived—by the time Lambert left Drake's office an hour later, however, he had only one redeeming thought that kept him from utter dismay: at least he could use the situation to punish Nadine.

Drake had a son, Dustin. Yes, the same young assistant to Nadine we've already met. (This meeting between Lambert and Drake, Sr. took place months before the embarrassing Porsche escapade already described.) From early on, Phillip had excused the extravagances of his son as youth-inspired. He comforted himself that someday his son would grow past it. But as the boy reached forward like a fast-change artist from his teens to his mid-twenties, father wondered if he might be wiser to strap him down with a new point of view, some sort of commitment.

Having spent time around his father, and genuinely admiring him, Dustin had experience with various fields of crime and punishment. Overall, he was interested in a possible career pertaining to law enforcement, but not to become a lawyer. Following so closely in his father's footsteps was not the path he envisioned. What he decided to do was study criminology.

Remarkably, he completed his degree. It was then the unimaginable happened: his father raised the awful prospect of a real job. That's how the career of Dustin Drake began, in the office of Phillip Drake, during that meeting with Lambert. Lambert would take him into the department, make sure he was schooled by the best, and then, probably after a few years, the boy would wise up, grow up… and buck up to law school.

Lambert was not foolish enough to cut off his nose to spite his hard-ass puss. In one bite, he swallowed the fact that Dustin was coming on board, like it or not. Always fantasizing subtle forms of revenge to take out on Nadine, by the time Lambert walked out of the meeting with Drake he figured Dustin would be the perfect self-pre-scribed anticonvulsant for all the perturbation Nadine had inflicted on him. "Delicious," he thought to himself as he contemplated telling Nadine that Phillip Drake, not he, was requesting his son have the opportunity to set sail under her tutelage.

He was in a peachy mood when the meeting with Nadine took place the next day. It played out exactly as he rehearsed, with all the sugary deliciousness to please his devilish palate. Even more tasteful was that there was no squirming room for Nadine on this one, and he knew it. She was not so foolish as to believe Lambert had cooked this up all by himself. He was smart and devious, but he never could have engineered this independently. Nadine knew instinctively and rationally the moment the news was imparted on her that Lambert had been backed into a corner; the two of them were each going to have to take a big bite out of a rotten tomato.

Contrary to all expectation, however, the forced merger with Dustin thrived. At first he was predictable; she'd give him immaterial assignments with no time limits and he'd wolf down the liberties she offered like a nine year-old eating birthday cake at a party. Then over time, however, she noticed him coming around more, hanging around. He'd cook up conversations with her; sometimes he would even show interest in cases.

Even more shocking to Nadine, she noticed a fondness for Dustin emerging on her part. Rather than a rich brat bathed in a brand of luxury she'd only peered in on through the investigation of powerful dead clients, he was likable. His sense of humor she found a gentle relaxation for her tightly wired, hard-driven style.

Nadine would never let him know how she felt other than the ir-resistible moments of delightful laughter at his antics, but he was the best balance to her career she could have imagined. He never stepped in her way, periodically he'd show a willingness to learn from her, and he offered her added protection from Lambert.

Dustin would do anything for his boss and Lambert had come to know it—and also came to fear it. Screw with Nadine, screw with Dustin…then face daddy. There was no way Lambert wanted to do that. It was like sprinkling the perfect brown sugar crumble apple pie with cayenne. Lambert never saw it coming. If he had, he'd have assigned young Dustin to one of his less accomplished lackeys.

So had Nadine finally become untouchable? Hardly. There was an upcoming "briefing," followed by a sweet get-together for her and Lambert. We might want to visit.

9

PHEW, PHEW, PHEW

BRIEFINGS. THEY'RE CALLED THAT because they're designed to be brief. If parsimony is an elemental law of speech then those who call such meetings should be legally bound to forbearance. Rarely do they obey.

The boss calls a briefing on a new product and uses it as an opportunity for an interminable discourse on sales and motivation, which in the end proves to be nothing other than intimidation. The director of the hospital wants to brief her staff on new dangerous bacterial strains, ones they already are aware of, and thus bores the lot of them silly as she reads one bulletin after another, word for word, for no reason other than to satisfy state laws. So is that why in work settings most people dread these informal little get-togethers? Probably.

One of the great abusers of such meetings is Assistant Chief, Tom Riley. In fact, his staff was so used to his corny stories and lame jokes they either don't show up or peremptorily beat the man to the punch with a series of comical skits when he called for a *brief* meeting.

A noted prankster in the division was an officer going by the name of Detective Lester Kalman. This fellow rose to high fame amongst his peers. How? He took a local prostitute, dressed her in a uniform, and had her proposition Riley before one of his assignment "briefings."

The propositioning was a diversionary task; the prostitute's real act was to wait until the meeting began, walk up to the front where

Riley stood, strip off the top of her uniform, expose her naked breasts for him, and deliver a simple query.

"Are you ready, big boy?"

Kalman wasn't particularly pleased with his assignments over the coming months, but he professed it was worth it just the same. Eventually Riley let it pass, but he never got the point not to inflict the tiresome meetings on his staff. Other than that, he was considered a lovely man.

Unbeknownst to his subordinates, when Riley called for a "special" briefing one morning and insisted there would be no excuses or exceptions for attendance, the invitations were at the demand of The Chief. Thus, at the stated time of the gathering, we find Riley in the front of the room attempting to quiet the officers by flapping his arms like a bird in flight. His staff is being expectedly discourteous.

Riley averaged being two decades senior in age to most of his people. He was a short man with a soft voice and corpulent figure, the latter reflecting recent neglect of his aging body; he wasn't the physical specimen cop you'd like to imagine fighting the bad guys, but he was capable of rising to the role of calling in his troops. He knew he better do so pronto because the boss man was visiting any minute. He resorted to a loud silencer.

"All right people. Let's quiet down." The last three words are gradually slowed and toned for exclamation. "A few administrative matters before I get to the reason for calling this meet."

Lots of comics are in this group. We hear a few aarf and wuff calls.

"Come on, please. Okay, Pleesy and Nomuro, you're being transferred to the Puller case. Ortega and White, you'll—"

That's about it for Riley, likely the briefest briefing his people will ever recall. Riley's eye catches sight of Lambert entering. The door is introduced to a sample of Lambert's peevishness, as it's slammed closed. Riley stutters to a dead stop. He snaps to attention off to the right of the podium. Lambert's voice, fully operational long before he reaches the front of the room, alarms the remainder of humanity to do the same as Riley: shut up.

"Some time ago Wesley Arnold was killed. We all know who he is, right?"

A foul odor followed Lambert like a shoe smothered in fresh dog excrement. With crew cut hair and broad upper features, he's an imposing figure. If Lambert ever mustered a smile, it hadn't the nerve to crease his grim, militant cheeks. And that's the way he liked it. Why not? He served as a U. S. Marine. Further, he'd tell you those were the best years of his life.

With that in mind, we have to ask ourselves what got into the head of Detective Barry Freeman that morning. He lacked the gift of jest that a man like Kalman possessed. He was probably the most obedient and polite of the group when in public. He'd been under the command of Lambert for several years, so he knew the rules. Then why in heaven's bliss when Lambert asked about Arnold would he extemporaneously holler out, "He's a traitor, I believe?"

More mysterious still, producing another question we can rest assured will never be explained, was the reaction of Lambert. All people who consider themselves champions of the find-the-good-in-a-person polity can take out their warm hugging arms and soft embracing hands, smile adoringly at the poor misunderstood man, even do a feel-good with him, because Lambert smirked…didn't laugh, didn't publicly muss the mean mug, simply put it down and covered it with his hands.

"No, that was another Arnold. The one I'm talking about is one of the most influential people in the country in media and entertainment."

After the unprecedented lapse of prickism, he plowed back to his agenda.

"I'm going to be brief—"

Now as fate would have it, Nadine's fate that is, she caught him in mid-sentence as she quietly entered the room by the same door brutalized by Lambert only seconds ago. She gently moved just left of the door and took a standing post at the rear of the room. She was tardy, a vile interloper, one who instantaneously attracted Lambert's eye.

Her mouth was closed, concealing her small, pearly, paid-for-on-my-own-orthodontia straight white teeth inside lips glossed in a neutral tone. Most outstanding about her face are two cute minutely puffy cheeks, a slight touch of pale pink coloring aiding them to pose half a step forward of her other features; her nose is tiny and unobtrusive.

That day her hair preferred a left sided part. It then cascaded downward in three successive waves, the highly illuminated room bowing the wisps of golden highlights that ended only a few inches below the shoulder line like violin strings. She looked more like a model for L'Oreal shampoo than the prizefighter soon to be called upon to duke it out with Lambert.

She wore a sleeveless plain one-piece moss green dress with black flats. Jewelry was limited to her prized stolen-at-a-sale Cartier Baignoire watch on the left wrist and silver earrings with half-dollar size discs descending like coins from a winning jackpot down her neck. She looked terrific…but she was late.

Lambert's eyes stayed beamed on her with the intensity of a teenage boy sneaking his first peek at a Playboy magazine centerfold. We presume it was only the force that was similar, not the passion, because he immobilized her with his glare and then lashed her one. "If some people placed their attentions as ordered, we might be making more progress on murder cases."

With that he released his visual grip on her and drove home the point with a stern forward nod of the chin. Lambert had more on his mind than murder investigations; we'll get to that next. But the comment baffled her. She was at the time feverishly losing herself in the investigation of her cases.

Lambert had called the gathering as a general motivational for the troops. They were working on many cases of varying degrees of priority, some even overlapping with Nadine's, though she was lead for the overall investigation of the D.C. murders. A lot was resting on ending the spree and him taking credit, yet progress had been nil.

Never anything wrong with a brief inspirational, letting people know that the rewards for victors are plentiful and the punishments for losers are loss of life, liberty and pursuit of career. He wanted Nadine, more than anyone, to be the ears for his speech. Her late appearance must have upset him immensely. It shouldn't be surprising, therefore, that he parted with a taunting climax.

"Frankly, you're all making fools of yourselves. You know what that means!"

He was finished. There was no mistaking when The Chief completed a job. He loved to wrap up with a famous exclamation mark. He stepped toward Riley, still sharp at attention. Then he stopped and refocused on Nadine, who hadn't moved from sentry duty at the door.

"Tom, get her to my office, NOW!"

With that order delivered, Lambert moved toward the rear exit, shooting a killing brow toward Nadine. He then exploded out the door like rectal gas.

Riley moved quickly to execute his assignment of ordering Nadine to the boss' office. He motioned to her to come over to him.

"Chief wants to see you…right now."

She seemed perplexed.

"What's the big deal…that I'm late?"

"Nadine, you have bigger problems than that."

Nadine's jaw flexed as she proceeded toward The Chief's office.

Let's see how this big girl deals with a punishment, or better yet, how the big boy handles trying to give her one.

10

WEARING THE RED TRUNKS IN THIS CORNER...

"THE IRS WANTS TO meet with you."

That's what it sounded like to Nadine when Riley told her to get to Lambert's office. As she headed in that direction, she couldn't imagine what she'd done so terribly wrong. She had a meeting that afternoon that she didn't want to miss, but she knew that if she didn't go see Lambert right then he'd go nuts on her.

I don't want to leave the impression that the boss of the famous Detective Street is bullying her. She had endured private sessions with Lambert in the past, and she wasn't the least bit overmatched. The only mystery was what could be so urgent he had to see her immediately. She is about to be enlightened.

The Chief's office was a large open room, one of several perimeter spaces on the floor. It's the grandest, if you can refer to any law enforcement office so finely. The room spanned both sides of a corner. Thus he was blessed with two separate sets of windows, the interior ones viewing into the central office space and the exterior outward to a drab parking lot: there was never anything cheery about a visit to the Chief.

Typically, he kept his blinds shut so that commotion in "the pen," as the commoners like to refer to it—the area the interior windows look onto, composed of a sea of desks and personnel—didn't disrupt his affairs. Today, the blinds were drawn up; it was show time.

Even with the unwritten invitation noted by Lambert's magnanimous gesture, nobody wanted to be caught looking. But viewing and getting caught viewing are two different things, and not a set of peepers could resist the temptation to watch the matinee.

Nadine entered and closed the door behind her. Lambert was standing. He looked to be twice her size, Nadine surrendering well over a hundred pounds to her opponent. Fortunately, strength of the heart and weight of courage are measured through actions and not on scales. Lambert should have learned he had no upper hand, but he could be dense as a vault door.

From the pen, the gum chewers, coffer sippers, eyeglass cleaners and nose pickers took breaks from their assigned duties to catch a glimpse of Nadine in her supporting role in this silent screen production: they couldn't hear either Lambert or Nadine because years before Lambert had ordered his office soundproofed.

There was no mistaking that he was irate. He was pointing, pointing, pointing, over and over and over, to the boxes piled against the wall. Nadine didn't slump at all as she stared straight at him. A couple of times, the troops saw her attempting to interject a comment, but The Chief silenced her with knifing hand gestures. What was Nadine attempting to get across? Well, have a listen.

"You're the one who told me to look into it in the first place."

"Look into…look into…did I tell you to do anything else? Did I?" he bellowed madly.

"One thing led to another, and—"

"And you were to report back to me before you moved on this, weren't you?" he harshly rebuked her.

"That's not how I remember it."

Lambert roared back. "You had a subpoena issued for records from Todd Henley! You know damn well he's chief counsel for U. S. Senator La Mont. You're implicating a leading senate member in one of the most repulsive messes this town has been shamed by…

and this town is a puss hole! You have no proof. What the hell were you doing?"

"Oh, there's proof. To not see it you'd have to be blind, dumb and—"

"I don't see it. I'm not blind. Do I look blind? Do I seem dumb? Other than my children, I don't believe any of my enemies, and I'm sure I have volumes of them, would make the mistake to think I'm dumb."

He put his hands on his waist, straightened his firm, combat-readied frame an extra notch before turning toward the boxes, pointing and gritting.

"In the sea of dung you generated I could float the entire U. S. Naval fleet. Now I have to clean up this monstrous shipload of disgrace that you've created."

Nadine wasn't getting The Chief's point. She stubbornly pushed her own agenda.

"Sir, I want to make it clear that I created nothing. I'm only reporting the finding of my investigation. I think we have an obligation to pursue this further."

"We…we are not a we. We have never been a we; you are you and I am your boss. You have one assignment now, one only. You are not to follow up in any way on the Henley-La Mont matter, you are not to talk to anyone about it, and you are to devote your full energy and attention to one case only. Don't test me here, Street."

She didn't, but her sarcasm left Lambert mute—that's a grand accomplishment. "Oh, no, I have no intention to. I'm so weighed down with the murder cases, I have no time to worry about twelve-year-old girls being bought and sold by United States Congressmen."

As Nadine would later explain to me, while she detested Lambert and knew he'd go to any length to advance his career, he had entered new territory.

"That was the first time I suspected he actually was corrupted. He was a self-serving dick, of course; I knew that from day one. But for him to express anything other than gratitude for what I had done infuriated me, and also concerned me. Was he going to repress a scandal of this magnitude to protect people just because they would in turn support his career aspirations?"

The manner in which she recounted dismissing Lambert, I found descriptively amusing.

"I snarled my snout. Damn it. I furiously slammed the door, hopefully leaving the lousy bastard with a wretched after burn—his gastritis is as well-known as baby drool."

By the time the door reached the jamb, the pen had become home to innumerable lonesome coffee cups, abandoned noses and clean eyeglasses. Every soul was deep in their study of reports, memos and notes.

Drake was absent from most of the episode. When he did arrive, a few minutes before Nadine ended her meeting with Lambert, Kalman briefed him comically and in detail. After that Dustin, along with the rest of the crew, had been deliberately waiting for the door to open. As Nadine stormed out, Dustin chased after her. Without losing a step, she started venting.

"That asshole. He's got a sex slave operation as profitable as Google in his back yard and his only interest is protecting his cronies."

"This is Washington," Dustin replied. "It's the land of the world's greatest Masters of the Universe. They need slaves. You're about to ruin all their fun."

"Dustin, it's a lot more than that. Today's meeting was supposed to be a pep talk, but that's all a charade. Lambert wants the serial murder investigation to fall on its face."

"What are you talking about? Why?"

"I think he fears it's going to harm him politically, no different than the perversion business. I believe he wants to let me chase my tail until he can justify having to turn it over to the FBI. That's why he's eager for me to work exclusively on the case, so I'll take a tumble. Then he can blame me for having to outsource it."

"Nadine, it doesn't make sense. If he wants you to fail, why wouldn't he pile on more assignments unrelated to the case?"

"I know how he works. If I'm doing nothing else and I still can't get anywhere, I'll look like a fool. So he'll give me only a short time, let me flop, get rid of the case, and then have his revenge on me."

"How long do we have?"

"I don't know, but it's going to have to be enough," she proclaimed defiantly. "And I'm going to disappoint him, just this one more time."

Dustin, lapping it up like a schoolboy reading a Superman comic book couldn't restrain his excitement.

"How? What are you going to do?"

"Solve this case and make sure he doesn't know about it until it's too late."

Fantasizing the upcoming fireworks, Dustin was thrilled.

"Cool. That's really cool!"

11

DON'T EVEN THINK ABOUT IT

COOL? WE ALL KNOW what cool guys are like. They're stuck in a conceit so wondrous they'll own it for the rest of their lifetime. They can bump George Clooney off the set while the star is breezily dodging bullets and luscious ladies are chasing after him. Then they relax by chasing a shot of Johnny Walker Black label with a Bud—that's cool.

Dustin is that cool, but...could he be a young dandy, flying just below Nadine's radar, culpable of the very crime he is assigned to assist in solving? I wondered about it.

As I listened to Nadine recount the tale to me, I also thought about what it would take to burrow beneath her suspicions. As it turned out, she disclosed to me that she had asked herself numerous times if it were conceivable Dustin might be an accomplice. He was deliberately downloaded into her professional life. His powerful father orchestrated his assignment to work under her direction. Coincidence? But what could possibly be his incentive? He had to be set for life financially. He wasn't looking for fame or recognition. He was the son of an esteemed and powerful man. He was a premiere stud who gets all the best-looking chicks in the world.

Go kill? There could only be one possibility: he wanted to protect his father. Nadine stored the thought, just in case.

Poor Nadine didn't possess the word cool, nor would she have known what do to with it if she did. Vengeance, pride; those are words she knew what to do with. After meeting with Lambert, she concocted them in a brew that convinced her, as she proclaimed to Dustin, that she was going to solve the case and serve it up to Lambert at an in-your-face victory party.

Get Lambert!

"I really didn't give a serious thought to Lambert being the killer this early. All I wanted to do was shame him. But if it were the case that he was culpable, I'd be wiping out two monsters with one clean swipe: Lambert, the politically dirty police chief, and Lambert, the deranged murderer. Even for me, Detective Nadine Street, this would be a one-of-a-kind career-crowning case."

Despite Lambert and a murder case giving her grief, all was not dreadful for Nadine. Springtime was popping up like ponies on a carousel. People were skipping and skating, they came outdoors cheering, smiling, dancing in short pants and shirts, eager and hopeful; the birds were chirping, the flowers blooming, the trees birthing billions of servants to shade the earth, children's voices were singing and laughing, breezes were clowning with puffy cloud figures. From the bosom of Chauncy Meyer, amour was being born.

After the meeting at Monroe's office a few days before, the doctor called his intriguing inspector. He suggested they might meet, have a drink one afternoon; perhaps she could bring along some material from her investigation that they could review together. We're going to pick up on the budding romance in its early dawn.

Before we meet the lovebirds launching their affair, however, I might as well embellish upon Chauncy's remark that Monroe is different than he seems. Despite his confidence and obvious attractiveness, Monroe fumbled in the relationship game similar to Nadine. God knows lots of high caliber ladies had dropped their lures in his waters, but he found fault in the end with each. Might it be that Nadine was dealing with a confirmed bachelor á la Henry Higgins of My Fair Lady fame? At forty-five, he might exceed cranky Henry if he doesn't learn that while love is a many-splendored thing, it's also a many-un-splendored one.

The moment he set eyes on Nadine, he felt his pounding heart shooting oxygen to his brain. Reason was clouded alternatively with rainbows, windstorms, rain clouds and stratus formations, yet through this bombardment of his senses his intuition stood at faultless attention. He saw green in her eyes, all signs pointed to go. What he didn't compute was that the signal he perceived meant he was about to encounter a rare variety of female, one he could not expect to drop at his feet.

This potentially disconcerting reality was made evident to him on their first get-together. For on this most auspicious afternoon, Dr. Larry Monroe was about to be delivered a dose of Nadine she swears to me she didn't plan. Sure, she had her explanation, but I had doubts of my own. By that time, I had sprouted my own detective wings.

"I was working at home when I dressed to meet him. I never gave my top a thought because I put a sweater over it. Besides, it was my favorite shirt due to the fabric being so soft that it feels like it's hugging me when I put it on."

She inadvertently shared that it was a designer top in a pastel orange shade.

"It was brisk when I went out. I never thought I'd take off the sweater, but the restaurant was warm. The sun had been out. Beating on the window, it heated it up to where I felt I was about to sweat."

In front of Monroe, she pulled off her sweater and there it was, inscribed from breast to breast like an omen.

"DON'T EVEN THINK ABOUT IT."

"Now that you mention it, there's nothing I'd rather think about," Monroe chuckled while peering directly at her chest.

"I don't get what's so funny," Nadine countered while subconsciously wrapping her arms in front of her such that they covered the words.

"Your shirt," Monroe bellowed, pointing to her breast.

When she looked down she finally realized what all the hilarity was about.

Monroe couldn't stop roaring; he liked it, found it dreamy, refreshing and wonderfully provocative. Add to the sheer tight-fitted top with sleeves so short they hardly traveled past the clavicles, the body fit blue jeans, brown pointed-toe leather boots, chartreuse scarf strewn haphazardly over her shoulder and she was exactly, perfectly, wonderfully…

"Nadine, I love it. Honestly, I won't take it as a threat. Beside, you look…tight."

"And what does that mean?" she asked coyly.

"It's a compliment," he assured her, still delighting over the t-shirt message.

The table Nadine and Larry were seated at was small. It looked outward to the street through a clear window on to tenuous but bright sunlight. Larry was reclining backward. After a few seconds he smiled, stood up, and walked away without uttering a word.

Nadine looked perplexed, but as she glanced up the street she spotted her gentleman. He was offering a bill to a young girl selling roses. In exchange, he walked off with a lovely short-stemmed white bud. He casually made his way back to the table and up to Nadine. He aimed the stem and then wove the gift through her hair, slightly above the right ear where it swirled with the orange top; sweet Monroe had designed a creamsicle.

"It's immaculate on you."

There was no food left on the table. Pity, because nothing would have been more comforting to Nadine than diving head first into a bowl of minestrone. She was in a land of enchantment, like a girl on a real first date. She wasn't sure what to do, what to say, though "thank you" might have sufficed.

Nadine wouldn't have it that simple. Her solution came without conscious deliberation and took the form of an expressionless, metronomic bobbing of her head, finally tailing off into a bewildered smile that would have stretched across, and then brightened, the mouth of the Mississippi.

If we bobbed our own heads to listen we'd have heard a hardly audible, "Wow, really, wow."

Her reaction was fancier than Larry could have bargained for. He was now leaning back in his chair with a poker face hiding the devilish charmer he rarely had occasion to be. But let's not forget, Nadine was no dunce when it came to reading all kinds of faces; she did it for a living, for her survival.

She allowed Larry time to bathe in the goodness of the moment and used the interlude to recompose herself. She'd have to bring the meeting to the alleged purpose of business before she spontaneously drooled out more "wow" exclamations. The question was what diversion she would use to bring about a more serious tone. Chauncy came to mind.

"You must know Chauncy well," she posed to him.

"We worked together for years on cases."

"He's always been there for me; not only for my career but he's shown interest in my personal life too. He sort of tries to look after me."

"Tries, but you won't let him?"

"Well, let's just say being taken care of has not been a big part of my script in life."

Larry smiled. "Maybe someday you'll let me read the whole story."

"I don't think you'd find it anywhere near as intriguing as those patients of yours."

"My tastes are very eclectic; try me."

"We'll see. So you know why Chauncy retired, Larry?"

"Sure. Too much mutilation, savagery and death; it's fairly simple, isn't it? After a while it can make a man sick."

"He's worried it'll do the same to me, but I'm different than him. That's not what would do me in."

"What would?"

"Now, why would I give you a weapon like that? You might just decide to use it on me."

She came to this meeting armed with a full satchel of materials and a well-planned agenda. She was about to take out a few documents but Larry was in no mood for business.

"That flower is so beautiful on you. Really, it thrills me to look at you wearing it."

"Thanks. I like it too," she responded, but with a measure of discomfort. "Let's get down to business, shall we?" She offered Larry no opportunity to interrupt her moving on the agenda she had previously planned for the meeting. "As I mentioned at your office when we first met, I have a killer on the loose who seems not to exist. Try that for a challenge."

"He exists. He just doesn't have the need…yet…to make you his friend."

"Nice choice of word…friend. He'll never be a friend of mine, but I think this one has a need. He won't be happy with anything short of being killed. That's when he'll seek me out, when he's ready to die."

Nadine was eager to tap into Larry's deep well of knowledge, find any clues that might help her in that she surmised her time would be limited to make the case.

"Here's all we know, and it's not much. The killer is very familiar with the territory where he does his work; he seems to know D. C. like he's been here his whole life. He's meticulous. He researches. If there are cameras, he knows how to avoid them. Most important is his command of weapons…he's not just killing. He knows how to do it.

"As we discussed, he has to be somebody of standing because he gains access to these high level victims. But still, as I said, other than his precision with the articles of murder, what is so unusual?"

Larry listened, but his attention was apportioned equally between hearing the details Nadine presented and visually fondling her. Reaching into his pocket to take out his pipe allowed him to maintain a split focus; he torched it with a lighter held in his left hand. From her vantage point, Nadine surreptitiously peeked, then glanced back down at her case. She slowly looked up, peering at Larry's task-busy hand. She carefully dispensed the next fact.

"He's left-handed."

Mirthfully, Larry played with the obvious coincidence, lifting the suspect hand in the air. "I'm your man."

Ignoring his jesting, Nadine plowed ahead. "Now, doctor, you said you could help me."

"I did, didn't I?"

"And I'm holding you to it."

"If I'm correct the violence has picked up as the killings have progressed. Right?"

"Yes, definitely. Why? What are you thinking?"

"These have to be political murders. Would you agree with that?"

"I'm not sure whose politics it might be, but possibly."

"Assume for the moment they are. Now put yourself in the place of the murderer. He…and I assume we're looking for a male?"

"It's not a woman," Nadine stated absolutely.

"Okay, he has an assignment to complete…go kill so-and-so. He's not a hired assassin because you said yourself he has no problem having audience with people who are careful about the company they keep. For the same reason, it's not some screwball psychotic who concocted a list of the twenty most hated big shots he intends to make a game of by knocking them off, one at a time. In other words, it has to be somebody who is not even a killer. I've been mulling it over. Most unusual case I've encountered. How do you have a killer who is not a killer?"

"You needn't seem so perplexed, Dr. Monroe. I promise you he's a killer now. I have almost a dozen dead corpses to confirm it."

Excitement puffed out of Monroe's pipe. "There, you said it... now! He wasn't a killer before; his occupation makes killing as foreign to him as wrestling to a ballet dancer. But he was lured into it, possibly even blackmailed. At first he's hesitant, takes a knife and rams it through Alexander's back, but he can't face the deed, doesn't even stop to say goodnight. He doesn't want to see blood, that's for sure. So he's out before the oozing begins. He's appalled at what he did, sickened.

"He hopes it's over and there won't be a next time. He's wrong. He's forced to act again. This time he's repulsed before the act. But then he's mad. Who is he angry at? Who knows? So he blames the victim; it's his only rational justification for what he's about to do. Now when he meets with Gillis—I believe your second victim—at his office, he takes a long pen and rams it through his neck into the base of the brain. It takes lots of force to accomplish that, but he faces up to the task and leaves.

"I haven't had time to go over the details from all the victim investigations that you had Chauncy send me, but what I would imagine is that somewhere along the way, after a few experiences with his new art, he becomes more curious than fearful, more imaginative than dreadful. You know as well as I do, that once a killer kills just one time it gets easier with each successive event."

Nadine bobbed her head to note her agreement.

"At some point, I believe what evolved was the type of person who started to relish his work. He's done a lot of unnecessary damage to the last few victims. Look what he did to Arnold. He was already dead when he pummeled his head with a lamp.

"Now he likes it, delights in the violence. He starts to question if he was schooled all along in the wrong vocation. Such a middle-of-the-road upbringing, rigid formula for distinguishing right from wrong, educated to think and earn his income by wit rather than force. Now he wonders if possibly all that training in proper values was crap. His mind is moving in new directions. 'How can I plan the attack to avoid the risk of being caught?'

"He has to devote a lot of attention to what he's doing. But he takes pleasure in the anticipation of the act, in every bloody detail. Blood… he likes it. He wants to see the victim dead, not once but several times over. He may even have come to believe they deserve it, whereas at first the sheer anxiety of having to harm someone precluded a more thoughtful assessment of wrongdoing on the part of the target.

"I think this is a guy who lives the good life. He probably plays golf on the weekends, occasionally helps himself to extras with a top-of-the-line hooker when he's out of town but otherwise seems a devoted family man, and generally is as miserable a son of a bitch as are most seemingly happily married men. But now, for the first time since he was a free-spirited teen, he's found true contentment. He's going to live it to the fullest as long as his country is calling on him.

"So when the occasion for killing comes up, he takes full advantage. Merely killing the prey is unsatisfying. A couple of extra slashes with the blade to get a good look at a few body organs, a few thrusts to the skull to witness the inside tomato…he's found himself; he wants to be a professional.

"That's why, in my early assessment, I'm of the opinion that these are politically inspired situations and will continue to be as additional murders are registered. But the wholly unique twist that has never before been encountered, is the personality of the killer; he does not fit any of the profiles we typically find for serials. Here we have two motives at the same time: kill the deserved bastard, the specific subject identified by god knows who or what to be punished, and have a blast of a good time as well."

Nadine sat while Monroe lectured in what seemed like an extemporaneous manner, profiling a one-of-a-kind serial murderer. There was a lot that had been dogging her mind about the case and the commentary by Monroe was slipping some confounding elements into place.

Certainly there was an appealing logic to what he is saying, though

Nadine had never trusted reason alone as substantiation for action. In fact, the successful stratagems she had devised in the past had typically been inspired first by gut instinct and only secondarily tested and refined by deduction. Yet, in this case, her instincts were failing to provide her with sound direction.

Thus, while she listened to Larry, her head was spinning, not because of the puzzlement she brought with her about the case, but due to the fact that a fresh outlook was gleaning hypotheses she hadn't explored. Frankly, the case was exasperating to her and hearing Larry explain it so eloquently and intelligently, aroused a kernel of jealousy.

Knowing how dangerous tolerance of an envious feeling could be, both to her investigation and dawning relationship with Larry, she had to rid herself of it before it crystallized into something destructive. Her solution was to take a mental mallet and pulverize it to an unrecognizable powder that well could have been brewed into a dissuasion drink called "not-a-good-feeling-to-have" tea.

Having quickly snuffed the potentially harmful feelings, she allowed herself to hone in on the background of the killer from a new vantage point. The novel thoughts were elating, but only briefly. For within seconds, her head started whirling oddly, lacking the influence of an ordered gravitational orbit. Then she heard a voice, her senses searching for the sound she couldn't get oriented to, one seeming to be off in the distance, muffled and trailing away as if losing mass.

If she could have asked herself what the hell the disequilibrium was all about, she would. But instead her mind, rather than chasing the voice, turned opposite to it. Then with movement that approached the speed of light—a speed close to that required for transforming from an amorphous shape of matter to pure energy—she raced frantically to escape, only to mysteriously collide with the sound circling back on her from the direction it took off. The impact registered as an atomic explosion, generating loose protons of curiosity, shocking her back to reality. Her mental and physical senses were heaving under pressures and forces she was unprepared to compute.

We, the mass of humanity that has been smacked about a few times by the lightning bolts of love know the frenetic state such powerful feelings can evoke. But we are not Nadine Street, thirty-five, single, very much available, and frightened out of her wits because this time she may have just encountered the perfect fit for her.

The voice that finally circled back to the auditory canals of Nadine was that of Larry, making a simple and benign request.

"Why don't you leave the materials you want me to review?"

Gradually, she collected herself and without a sound from her lips she reached down into her case. Monroe picked up the check. He scanned it and then paused for a long interlude, ample time for Nadine to extract the folders she wanted to give him. She appeared to come back to her full senses and was more at ease. She looked up and addressed him.

"How much is it?"

"It's nothing, really. I'll get it."

"Hold on. You're the one helping me, so I pay."

"I asked you out," he said, teasing like a child.

"It's not a date," she argued.

"Really?"

"Really."

Larry would have no part of her antics. As she began handing him the material, he raised any bet she may have made that he'd back off.

"I'll pick you up at seven on Thursday night. It's a surprise."

His statement launched her back along the cosmic journey from which she had moments earlier returned, now in short time landing her at a point of understanding. He's a man of many complexities. He can be coy, confident and charming, sweet and tender, witty and comical, tricky. And what else?

If only she weren't asking. But she was. That fact revealed to her a terrifying insight, one that did allow her to be aware of what the rest of us couldn't charge more than a nickel to sell: she was hooked.

What luck, to face a glorious opportunity for romance in the middle of the biggest murder investigation of her career, potentially the greatest murder investigation in the history of criminology, with Nadine Street, motherless child from Topeka, Kansas, not seeking but likely to find fame.

"Are you asking me out?" Nadine asked matter-a-fact.

Larry adored her. He laughed delightedly in response to her obvious forced casualness, and rather than a simple affirmation of his interest in seeing her again, he punctuated it with an exclamation point.

"Yes, with urgency!"

It was all so different, so straight, out in the open. It elicited a like response. "How did you know I love surprises?"

What a lovely ending to a chapter. They're both happy, can't wait till Thursday night. Nadine went back to the office to finish up some work. Unfortunately, it was not going to be as pleasant an evening as it was afternoon.

12

FIRST DATES

Since I'm on the subject of dating and romance, it might be a perfect time to digress to what occurred on the evening Nadine had retreated to her room after her first encounter with my friend, Preston. If it had been my wife's intent to embolden him with a dare, to knock on her door, it worked. Tap. Tap. Was it to be the beginning of a new courtship for the lady, proof that the magic of the love cottage was no joke?

"Nadine, I apologize if I upset you," he gently approached her. "I'd like to come in and keep you company."

She cracked open the door a few inches. It was just enough for her to recognize his sincerity, and for him to witness her distress.

"I just can't right now. Call me later," she offered as encouragement.

"I have to be back for work by tomorrow morning," he informed her urgently.

"Then just call me when you get a chance."

She passed a dim smile to him as she closed the door. He stuffed her gesture in his pocket and came back to the table, spending the rest of the evening trying to act his normal self.

Two days later, I was in the kitchen at Kuruk with Reuben. We were measuring to see if we could expand the size of our walk-in freezer. We noticed one of the waitresses carrying a dozen red roses toward the rear where Nadine's quarters were located. When I asked what she was doing and whom the flowers were for, she told me a deliveryman left them for Nadine, but she hadn't looked at the attached card.

I knew for certain they were from Preston, and so did Reuben. Together we shared delight watching as the girl knocked on the door to hand the gift to Nadine.

It was two weeks later when Preston returned. He arrived at the strike of noon, dressed like a dandy. He was wearing a pair of designer jeans and a sheer white v-neck t-top. What alerted me that this was a special occasion were the shoes, tan Lucchese ostrich skin boots. I recall him purchasing them for over a thousand dollars, but I had never seen them on his feet—they looked shiny new, as if they had refused to come out of the box until Preston could persuade them a worthy occasion had arrived.

We talked for a while but I could tell his mind was elsewhere. He walked me to his rental car and opened the back door. There was a box that looked similar in size to what his boots came in. It was wrapped with pretty pink paper and had a beautiful ribbon made of red and white. He pulled it out to draw my attention to it. Then he stood in front of me to model his presentation, as well as the package.

"What do you think?" he said anxiously. "I look okay?"

"You look great. The best I've ever seen you," I complimented. "You'll knock her off her feet."

He held out the package. "Know what it is?"

"How could I, Preston?"

"Took me a week to find them but they are the best of the best. They're super jumbo Medjool dates," he informed me. "These are so grand she's gonna freak. They're the size of small plums and dripping sweet syrup," he said excitedly.

"I didn't know Nadine was a date enthusiast."

"Organic Medjools—her favorites. You just don't find jewels like this anywhere. There's a company in Indio, out by Palm Springs... these are the best of the best," he repeated proudly.

"Nice to see you thrilled," I smiled to my friend. "Just take it slow with her," I advised. "She's raw, but…Preston, did you ever think we'd get to where we are?"

"You grew up. Now it's my turn." He paused for an unnecessary admission. "It was your mom's idea about the dates. I was telling her about Nadine and talking about bringing her something—bingo, the lady knew just what to do."

"She does get it right often, doesn't she?"

I assisted Preston's mission by telling him I had a packed day, thus cutting the conversation short so he could pick up his date. Oddly, I was slightly nervous all day, hopeful that their time together would go well. I knew if it were a flop, Nadine would be a bear to deal with for several days and I suspected I'd be collecting pieces of Preston's broken heart for a longer span—I don't recall him ever experiencing a heart irregularity over a lover, not even being in love for that matter but I could tell this was different.

When we awakened the next morning, I was alarmed that Preston was not at the house. He had told me he planned to sleep the night at our home. I had given him a key. I called Kuruk and asked one of the kitchen staff if he had seen Nadine that morning. He said he hadn't. I knew she always arose early so I asked him to knock on her door. In a moment, he informed me that there was no answer. Preeti was with me when I called. When I told her I was concerned that it appeared they never came home, she laughed.

"Zach, they're grown adults. They probably took a room and stayed overnight in Albuquerque."

"I just didn't think Nadine would be up to that so quickly," I faintly responded.

"Beneath that hurt is a lonely girl. She needs a man in her life," she smiled. "You'll hear soon enough."

I did. Within five minutes Preston called.

"I'm at the airport, Zach. Amazing time. This could be it." His sentences were quick paced, text message abbreviations, suggesting excitement as well as hurriedness. "Got a call last night. The band carried over an extra night in Houston. Gotta go. Catch you up later."

An hour passed before I noticed a cab pull into the parking area of the restaurant. Nadine exited and went around the rear and into her home. It must have been another hour before I saw her come out of her room and prepare to leave. I had an envelope with draft material I wanted her to review, so I went over to her. She took the packet and smiled childishly.

"Separate bedrooms," she chirped. "No need to worry, daddy."

Then she turned and took off to do whatever she planned for the day. Neither of them elaborated to me on their Albuquerque visit. I would have felt badly that they kept it from me had Preeti not assured me that the fact they were private about whatever they experienced together was a good sign.

Nadine was in high spirits for days. Too bad it couldn't last long. Little known, obscure Kuruk was about to get a dose of politics, Washington style. Then I was to be thrust into the odd position of having to write two novels concurrently—and then package them into one.

I'll continue presently with story number one, Nadine in Washington, D. C.

13

WAIT! CAN I OFFER YOU A DRINK?

SOME HABITS ARE GOOD: Nadine asserts that she has learned the importance of brushing her teeth when she arises in the morning and before bed, she eats three wholesome meals a day and makes sure her car is serviced routinely. Some patterns, however, are potentially fatal. For Nadine, adhering to a set, predictable routine must be mindfully avoided. This objection to predictability, to the potentially negative consequences of adhering to strict schedules, pertains to her work: "Don't ever allow anybody to anticipate your actions, to know where you'll be or what you are thinking," she conveys as a cardinal rule.

The reason this is precious to her? There is always the chance that some sicko she put away five years before, is out of jail or has been released from an institution and he wants to make her his first celebration. Or a case she is investigating reaches a critical mass and the killer wants to get to know first-hand the sweet chick he's been talking to on the phone.

So Nadine would rather stop at a friend's house to talk or go out for a drink than come home at the same time every night after work. I guess if one wanted to be picky, they'd call that a habit too, but they'd have to admit it falls into the good habit category.

Nadine lives just outside central Washington, D. C. Her condominium is a sort of architectural oddity. It would strike one who is attentive to matters of style and home design history as a "throw-back" and "push forward" at the same time. Whoever designed it forty years ago was stuck in the Craftsman era, but craning a neck of curiosity into the future.

The building is on a well-established, heavily treed street. The structure is distinct for its high-pitched roof. The exterior is entirely of detailed wood finish, including real wood windows and frames. In other words, it has charm, richness and warmth, hardly fitting with the more modern specimens on her block that are composed of harsh straight lines, prefabricated metal window frames and flat roofs.

At any rate, now that the scene is set, be advised that Nadine after her lunch with Larry, and her visit to the office, stopped at a girl-friend's apartment down the block from her home. It was about nine o'clock on Monday evening when she pulled into her gated under-ground parking area. The night sky was unusually clear. Her street had few lights but the moon was filtering illumination through the moist air. The parking area itself was brightly lit. Nadine was in a good mood, feeling more relaxed than usual as she parked in her designated spot. She exited her car and heedlessly flicked the elec-tronic key lock.

That's when things turned abnormal.

Before taking a single step, Nadine heard a sound she associated with sand rubbing or scraping against an object. It wasn't loud or alarming but it was unexpected and startled her to attention. She looked around, seeing at first only a small ocean of cars. Then she crouched down to view as much as possible of her surroundings through the window glass of her vehicle.

At the furthest point across the garage, was an illuminated area with an exit door leading out from the parking structure to the street. Standing next to it was a man. Nadine observed that he had long, shaggy, dark brown or reddish hair and a protruding, pointed goatee of similar color. He was wearing what appeared to be a lightweight tan full-length coat. His eyes were focused from the distance—no mistake, like binoculars—directly on her.

The figure remained immobile. Even when Nadine's eyes met his, he didn't budge. She went into defense mode, reaching into her purse for her handgun. As a warning to the intruder, ever so slowly, she lifted her arm to reveal the weapon.

The man held his post.

Nadine squatted down further, just long enough to double-check that the safety was off and the gun fully loaded. Then she cocked it. She looked a second time to prepare for the man's next move. But in the instant it took to check her weapon, the man had disappeared.

"Ruin my day," Nadine mumbled irritably to herself.

Rather than racing to her apartment or out the door to catch him, the action she would have taken had she personally witnessed him exit, Nadine employed a strategy she'd rehearsed a thousand times but never had to use. She eased her way around cars, working a path towards the door, carefully checking and rechecking in front and behind them. When at last she was satisfied that he had left the parking area, she opened the door to ease her way out into the street.

Gone. No sign of human life.

She examined the immediate area. The only visible evidence of a human presence was the print of what might have been a shoe sliding through a muddy slick. She went back inside the parking area, closed the door securely behind her, then took a few seconds to see if the man erred and left some identifying evidence where he had been standing.

Nothing.

Probably just a crook about to rip off a car, she thought. *I spoiled his opportunity.*

She figured she'd report it to the building manager in the morning. She waited only a few seconds for the elevator and as a just-in-case precaution took it only to the second floor. She then walked up a flight of stairs to her third-floor condo.

Nadine has always carried an oversized purse; she has to. In addition to what the average women has to lug around—wallets the size of laptop computers, key chains dangling devices to open the houses, cars, safe deposit boxes, mail boxes and gates of parents, siblings, best friends, neighbors and maybe, just maybe, a boyfriend, a full month's supply of Kleenex, makeup kit with enough tools and substances to repair a truck, pill organizers with common vitamins and mineral supplements plus any nutritional capsules prescribed for stress, depression, diet or disease, and mints, breath freshener and gum, not to mention checkbook fully armed with pen and…what am I forgetting…oh, yes, a cell phone—Nadine has to add plastic bags and gloves for evidence, a small pad of paper and pencil, her weapon, her badge, and for occasions like what she's encountered in her hallway, a small flashlight.

Nadine's bags are probably the most thoughtfully purchased items in her possession. She has specific organizational requirements; she has to know where to find what she wants when she wants it. So when a brain cell in the cortex shrieks "flashlight," she wants it in her hand before the nagging little cerebral devil goes into a full neural tantrum.

It's fortunate that everything was at her fingertips that evening because when she exited the door to the stairwell, which was directly across from her front door, she found that the hallway was pitch-black. She reached into her purse, and as expected, her light was where it should be. She shined it down the hall in both directions and saw nothing out of the ordinary. Still, a stray impulse led her to investigate further. She focused her flashlight on the unlit fixture, which looked perfectly normal—except that the glass piece fitting over the bulb was slightly uneven. She touched it and it easily came off; she placed it on the ground. Then she reached for the bulb and twisted it; it went on. This double tweaked an inner alarm.

She put the cover back over the fixture. Then she tried the door to her unit. It was properly locked. She opened the door, turned on the light, closed the door behind her and proceeded to check the rest of the rooms. Nothing unusual. Everything seemed safe. She went back to the front door and double locked it; she tossed her bag on a table in the living room. Then she leaned back on a chair to think about what has just occurred, letting her eyes drift closed.

The phone startled her.

"Hello."

"Hi. It's Larry Monroe. I never got your address."

A smile Nadine would reserve for only her closest of friends, and probably under the circumstances not even them, loosened the tension of the moment.

She'd love to tell him what happened; she'd love to have somebody living with her so that when she comes home after a horrid day, she'd have a shoulder on which to rest her weary head; she'd love to have a man who could protect her, who'd walk her down to her car, look after her; she really would, at least some of it, the part that's not rubbishy fantasy. The truth is she's accustomed to handling these matters on her own. Even if Mr. Right were to come along, it's doubtful he'd be filling some of those roles.

"You know where Allen and Westbrook intersect?"

"Sure."

"I'm on Allen, 1145. Buzz me and I'll let you up. I'm in Unit 32, on the third floor."

"It was nice having lunch today, Nadine."

"It was."

"Well, okay then. Have a nice week. I'll see you Thursday."

"It's an official date," Nadine stated off-handedly.

"Yes, it is. Bye."

He hung up. The grimness in her face returned. Instantly, she was back in the chair, dissecting the two strange events. It would be easy, quite reasonable, to dismiss the man in the parking structure as an insignificant incident. But the light, that's different. Light bulbs don't loosen themselves that much; somebody fiddled with it. Still, was there any sound basis for concluding the two events are connected? Any kid could have played with the fixture. Or a maintenance person might have done a sloppy job cleaning. Happens all the time.

"Well, what do you think, Nay?" she posed to her invisible companion.

Nay is what Nadine tenderly calls out when she's carrying on one of those internal dialogues, mind chatter we all engage in: Nay, Nay and Nay. She likes the sound; it's reassuring and comforting. She's learned that for most problems she has to address there isn't anyone more reliable than Nay, the alter ego meticulously crafted by Nadine to be the ideal best friend you can never insult, injure, exile or abandon.

Nay is composed, always objective, and if necessary, the biggest, baddest and brawniest woman to exist since comic books founded Cat Woman. Nay is capable of sucker-punching the torrents of vitriol, hate, condemnation and rejection vomited up by a superego just bursting to make its day by duking it out with Satan, and then telling Nadine she's next if she thinks she'll ever gain entry to the holy gates of perfection-land.

After Nay is done restraining the beastly conscience in Nadine, she'll usually deliver a voice of moderation. It might be a speech of forgiveness, an encouraging word for a disappointment or failure, or a reassurance that next time it will turn out better. Nay, after many late night sessions, convinced Nadine that if you can't make peace with yourself, if you can't respect, trust and love yourself, you can never accept love from anyone else.

She also taught Nadine that no matter what happens in life, don't—she repeated that word as many times as the tides cycle high and low—don't turn on yourself and don't be an enemy to yourself. And she told her that when she was confident she could follow Nay's instruction she wouldn't need Nay any longer.

That evening she needed her. Old faithful was there on demand, front and center.

Nadine, no need to jump to any conclusions about the events of the evening, Nay surmised. *Look, before you panic, consider that if somebody wanted to harm you they wouldn't have to go to all the trouble of orchestrating scenes like you confronted this evening.*

Still, it's reasonable to satisfy your concern by talking with the building manager, just to see if there have been any similar incidents in the area. Now, also be sure to check your log records for the status of all the criminal cases you've been involved with. Even examine if anything is happening with an investigation that could account for tonight's events. It never hurts to be careful.

Nay and Nadine were in perfect concert on a strategy of both restraint and caution. When a person is aligned precisely with their Nay, they are in a sweet spot. They may even be in a zone to get a short-term gig as a guru.

After the talk with her buddy, Nadine was relaxed. It was lights out for Nadine—say good night, Nadine.

14

REUBEN, ALL SHOOK UP

NOT ONE HUMAN BEING would be speaking the truth if they didn't admit that at some point in their life they dreamed of fame and fortune. Yet the reality is that not all people are cut out for it. The sought after fantasy of acclaim and recognition can take a remarkable toll on the psyche. Many of those who actually do attain it come to feel confined. It's as if the world at their fingertips turns hostile, choking off breath, leaving these franchised souls fearing for their survival.

Our chef Reuben was one of those people who had smelled the sweetness of wealth, felt the electricity of fame, and had seen with his own eyes deep into the magic trick of idolatry. He hated it. Due to those influences, his life became unendurable. He perceived it as draining having to constantly portray to his fans and followers that he was the happiest and most enlightened creature ever to walk the planet. The realization that he could speak on politics or economic policies—topics he knew little about—and people would be eager to follow him he found revolting. Needless to say, being a public figure was not all it was cranked up to be for this man.

So he withdrew and became a chef. Even then, he had the opportunity to rise in status as a noted figure in the culinary field but did all he could to avoid recognition. Why? Because he loved the simple privilege to walk freely among his fellow man and to go unrecognized wherever he traveled. He could visit a movie theatre, attend a concert, shop at a market, stop with Josea for a cup of coffee or get on an airplane and fly as a common passenger. It suited his personality.

So if a stranger happened upon him this brisk fall morning while in the backcountry hiking, and by chance knew who he was, there might be a conversation about food, literature or musical theatre but never would a word be permitted about what he had done in his former life to achieve star status.

Reuben had been walking for a couple hours. He loved the silence and peacefulness of being alone in nature. This morning was particularly alluring. The clouds had pissed themselves void of rainfall throughout the evening and by sunrise they had done a "giddy-up" northward, leaving the sky a crystal blue dome. The air was sharp, cold enough for the tiniest particles of moisture sweeping in the wind to pinprick his uncovered body parts.

Our outdoorsman was wearing a heavy down jacket that afforded his rank frame bragging rights as a full-bodied male. His bottom was clothed in a pair of nylon pants and he wore heavy hiking boots on his feet. The bottom half of him was royal blue in color and his jacket was bright yellow. Reuben had let his hair grow long and his red baseball cap left black tufts dangling to his shoulders.

He was not venturing into unfamiliar territory. He had traveled the area so many times that he had an instinct for where he was and how to get back home. This particular walk paralleled a noisy running creek. After about an hour, he emerged from a long canopied path on to a meadow. As was often the case, the weather did an about face and during the short span Reuben had been out the sky had taken on a dim moodiness. Grey clouds were swirling west to east like a carpet unrolling over a wooden floor. The haze now cast vagueness over the spruce trees that doted the vast expanse in front of him. It caused the tall specimens to take on a bluish-grey shade. They were shaped like perfect Christmas trees.

Most of the ground was covered with a variety of grasses. Clumps of yarrow spread their green leaves to permit pale pink and white puffs. Larkspur showed them up with long deep purple stems reminiscent of gladiolas. Most plentiful was the fleabane. Large clumps of land were home to these waist high specimen, all brownish in shade and bowing uniformly toward a machete slinging sun aggressively slicing sections of clouds for its rays to complete their journey to the earth's surface. Thin branches served as springboards for tiny thinner shoots crookedly jumping into the scene like bolts of black lightning.

Reuben came to the clearing directly in front of him. About a hundred yards away, was the base of a slow rising hilly area that quickly transformed into a more precipitous rock formation of increasingly large boulders. Reuben had visited this spot many times before but never hiked off into the higher elevations.

He took a seat next to one of the spruce, using the trunk as a backrest. He was gazing at the mountain ahead when he noticed a male step out on to a ridge. The man was focused on Reuben and was showing no shyness over the intrusion. To the contrary, he stood his ground and stared the chef to fright.

To the best of Reuben's recall, the man's hair appeared shaggy and not only did the top strands drop as low as Reuben's but the facial covering protruded off his chin in a goatee of sufficient length that it was aiming downward. He was dressed in a lightweight tan pair of shorts with a white shirt—he must have been close to freezing. He looked about six foot as best Reuben could estimate. What was most striking was his stare. He had visually locked on to Reuben and wouldn't relinquish his grip.

Reuben recognized his vulnerability. He also realized the man was content to maintain his post, which alarmed him further. Instinctively, Reuben rose and called out to him, asking what he wanted. The man stood without an inclination to respond. After three tries, the third evoking an intimidating smirk from the interloper, Reuben did the unexpected. He took off after the man, yelling repeatedly: "What is it you want?"

It was not until Reuben cut the distance between them by half, that the man devilishly grinned and then took off, leaping fluidly around, up and over large boulders, deeper into the formation, disappearing from Reuben's sight by the time he was able to reach the base of the incline. Recognizing the futility of catching the spy, with the aim of forcing an explanation for the uninvited trespass on his privacy, he turned and started to head in reverse toward the path leading back toward Mescalero.

As he began his journey, the thought crossed his mind that he had come across a vagrant with a cruel sense of humor. He was ready to dismiss the episode as a chance incident, where it was he who unluckily came upon the man rather than someone else. However, after covering only a couple hundred yards, the man appeared again, this time within close range and with a camera, snapping shots as quick as his finger could move. Reuben stood nonplused, frozen by the temerity this derelict-looking fellow displayed. After several angles had caught Reuben's frame, the man, grinning waggishly, again streaked off, this time into the dense forest.

Reuben made it home without further molestation. Josea was at my house with Preeti and Sousche, my daughter. They had just left to take our dog for a walk. Nadine and I were working on a chapter when the phone rang.

"Is Josea there?" Reuben was out of breath and his voice screeched desperation.

"What's wrong?" I asked.

"Zach, someone's following me," he shouted miserably. "I knew it could happen. Somebody betrayed me."

"Reuben, I have Nadine over," I explained so he'd understand that my communication was about to become cryptic. "We're wrapping up so I'll come over and we can talk."

I hung up. Nadine and I were about to take a break. I packed up the papers she needed and sent her off. I jumped in the car and headed straight to Reuben's. When I arrived, he was beside himself. He had closed all the windows, fearful that the man had to know where he lived and would surely be taunting him by peering into the house.

When I asked what happened, he recounted to me the story of his morning hike. He was absolutely convinced that his true identity had been leaked but couldn't establish a motive for any of us who know him to breach his confidence. We all had adequate money, except my father-in-law, Len Cloud, who could never have been compromised for wealth. Cruelty? We all appreciated and adored Reuben. Jealousy? The man was worth a bundle, but lived a Spartan lifestyle.

Still, it was indisputable in Reuben's mind. Whoever knew about Reuben's former life had found him living near Mescalero and wanted to let Reuben know he was made. The only motive, he then reasoned, was to torment him before extracting a price—extorting millions. It wasn't the money. Reuben would have gladly paid dearly for the privilege of remaining incognito. What troubled him was that he knew blackmail was an offense offering no exit strategy, either for the criminal or the victim.

"Zach, you know what's going to happen, right?" he cried out.

"I think you're jumping to conclusions before you know for sure who the man is or what he was doing," I calmly replied.

"With this sort of crime," he carried on, oblivious to my more rational approach, "in the end, after he's filthy rich he'll go ahead and expose me just the same."

"How do you figure that?" It was futile to do anything other than hear him out.

"Extortion is the most hateful act of vengeance a person can commit, Zach. Viciousness! That's what it's about after the greed is satisfied. He'll seek his joy in the end no matter what I do."

Reuben fell back listlessly into a sofa. I knew what was going through his mind. He had come to hate his prior public life and the thought of having to go back to it was intolerable, even potentially suicidal. In his mind, the rascal had put him in a real life checkmate. In my mind, he was grossly overreacting to a single incident.

While I was trying to logically go through the event step by step he suddenly walked over to the phone and made a call. It was to his closest friend.

"I've been uncovered," he hopelessly began. "Somebody knows."

Only hearing half of the conversation, I had to piece together the friend's reaction. Evidently he was on a similar track as I had been, requesting a detailed account of what transpired. Reuben was beyond that approach.

"There's no other explanation," he asserted in a raised voice. "If you didn't tell someone, and I'm sure nobody here did, then what the hell happened?

The man must have taken offense, assuming there was accusation in Reuben's words.

"I'm not saying you breached the trust," Reuben shouted at him. "It doesn't matter now who did it." There was a long pause before Reuben continued. "Don't come! I'll let you know when he starts asking for money."

We heard a car pull up. Assuming it was Josea, he hung up the phone without another word. He ran outside, looking around to be sure it was safe. Then he dragged Josea into the house to guarantee their privacy before he told her what he knew was inevitable for their future.

Records were about to be set for winter heat in Mescalero. Intense storms were forming on the horizon, but they'd be drenching us in hot rain. For Reuben it would be scalding, but for Nadine the downpour would be acidic. I had trusted my wife's deceased son's assurance that stories would come to me at Kuruk. Now they were raining down torrents.

These yarns would speak to the innocent being ravaged, while the guilty laughed believing God was on their payroll.

15

LOOK MOM, I KILLED MY FIRST STAR

NADINE AWAKENED FRESH AND rested after her tete-a-tete with Nay, but very early. She still hadn't looked at the *Washington Post* from the day before, so she sat down with a cup of tea to do her morning perusal of the daily. She was intrigued with an article in the Arts section by Morgan Astor. It was titled, *"Love Her or Hate Her, Here She Comes."*

Let's take a look over her fleshy shoulder while she sips.

The town is abuzz. I can't wait. Rita Tully, at last, is coming for one night only to do a concert at the John F. Kennedy Performing Arts Center. I don't know about you, but seeing the queen of rock prancing on stage doing 'I'll Take Mine with Sugar,' 'Medium Rare,' and 'Papa, Where Are You?' would be worth a month's salary—and from what I hear tickets are selling for, it may take that.

At least you can think about it, Nadine comically yawned her words as she continued reading.

For her fans that don't know it, what's remarkable about Ms. Tully, besides her unequalled talent, is her indefatigable quest to be better. The fact that she was left fabulously wealthy after her parents were tragically killed in a plane crash when she was a child—and she had the good or bad fortune to be an only child—never squelched her drive to work at a feverish pace.

Ms. Tully is known to impose on herself near-inhuman expectations. She maintains a grueling concert schedule and between performances commits to charity events and humanitarian programs. Of late, she has raised equal applause for her political views. She openly expresses her criticism of governmental authority and she has reserved the highest levels of condemnation for the current administration, that she claims supports dictators around the world while proclaiming a mission statement of overcoming human rights violations. Some may say it's the 'same old, same old,' but Ms. Tulle can't seem to take a joke.

To the contrary, she has been using her recent concerts as bully pulpits to attack the president and his key staff members. Thus, her visit to Washington has been met with mixed reviews; she's exceedingly popular with her fans but reviled by many in positions of leadership. With an upcoming election, the administration has expressed objection to her 'preaching' and is not pleased with the timing of her coming to Washington. No wonder. Her voice might be unequaled in terms of influencing voters.

What Nadine didn't know as she was digesting this article, still before sunrise on what was sure to be a cold, cloudy and dark day in D. C., was that several miles away Ms. Tully had long before left her hotel for a chaperoned walk. Her bodyguard ambled along with her as she strolled up a quiet street. She stopped in front of a store and asked her protector if he might go in and get a fresh coffee for each of them, which, of course, he agreed to do. She insisted on standing in the freezing cold, telling him she found it "stimulating".

When he came out only a minute later, she was gone.

Frantically, the assigned escort started searching. He ran up the block, screaming out her name but there was no response. He immediately called to the suite on his cell to notify the rest of the party of her mysterious disappearance. Within minutes, four private security people working for the star were desperately in pursuit.

About three blocks away from all the commotion, was a small restaurant called the *Avenue Grill*. It was early, but a perfect time for a cup of brew.

Anyone care to join me? It'll be like watching a movie. But beware—I think we're about to see our second kill.

There's Ms. Tully sitting at a table cheerfully talking with a man, both drinking coffee and sharing a sweet roll. She's wearing a fur coat, but it's unknown to anyone but her she's stark naked underneath. Her hair is worn under a brown fur-lined cap and she has no makeup on. Her face is disguised with thick plastic glasses. Nobody would recognize her for the famous celebrity she is—especially at six in the morning.

The man accompanying her is wearing a black cap covering his head, no hair visible. He's also wearing thin cotton gloves and a brown sweatshirt. As they get up, readying to leave, she slowly makes her way to the door. The man takes his drinking cup and furtively pockets it before following her to the exit.

They walk out together and turn to the right. Together, they amble about a block before turning into an alley. They face one another. He looks as if he's about to kiss her. Then he grabs the lapels of her coat and opens them, not seeming the least bit surprised to discover two ripe and panting breasts with dark, hardened nipples.

His mouth moves closer to hers, but before the union, he takes a knife and thrusts it into the abdominal area, pulling upward with great force. His strength is such that he holds her slight frame with the weapon inserted in an upright position for several seconds before letting her fall lifeless to the ground in the alley next to a dumpster. He surveys his surroundings, sees nobody around, turns and walks away.

Confirmed. It's our friendly killer in action, bullying another member of the upper crust.

"Nadine, Lewis here. You up?" The anguishing call by one of her subordinates would erase the thrill of the *Post* article Nadine was enjoying.

"No, I'm talking in my sleep," she ironically responded.

"Better get dressed, Nadine."

"What is it?" Her caustic voice warned she was in no mood for nonsense.

Lewis's words sent a shiver down her spine. She took a final gulp of tea and tossed down the paper. "I'll be right there."

Disconnecting from one call, she immediately placed another. "Dustin, how quick can you get here?"

"Ten minutes. What is it?"

"I dropped off my car for maintenance last night. Just get over here ASAP."

Nadine and Dustin arrived at the murder scene twenty minutes later. By then, the area was secured. Detective Lewis, who took the call, was first on the scene. When he saw Nadine he ran up to her.

"Street, you have to come here, quick."

He led her to the side of the building next to the alley where Tully's body lay. Just a few feet away, stood a heavyset man in a chef's uniform, surrounded by three detectives, all feverishly writing notes.

"As soon as I got here, I went up and down the streets to see if any businesses were open," Lewis explained. "This guy's been on duty since early this morning, right down the block at *Avenue Grill*. You better talk to him."

Nadine walked over. The other detectives backed off to give her the floor. She looked at the man shivering.

"Lewis, how far is his place from here?" she inquired, her annoyance evident.

"Just a few doors down."

She shook her head in disbelief at the insensitivity of permitting the potential witness to be frostbitten while everyone else at the scene was heavily dressed. "We want him as a witness, Lewis. Preferably thawed."

She then addressed the man. "What's your name?"

"Enrique Rocheo."

"Enrique, please. Let's walk to your restaurant."

Lewis dashed over with a coat. "Had an extra one in my vehicle."

"Quick thinking, Lewis. I'm proud of you. Dustin, let's go," she barked out.

She moved swiftly down the block with the witness. Dustin was loping behind. They entered *Avenue Grill*.

"If you want to get warmed up first, go ahead."

"No, I'll be fine, miss."

"So tell me what you saw."

"I didn't think anything of it," Enrique began. "This couple comes in for coffee; the lady said she wanted a Danish. She took a bill out of her coat pocket and paid. Then they sat down. I didn't think anything of it because they were chatting real friendly. Then they left."

"Do you recall anything about the man?"

"Strange. I really couldn't tell you much about either one of them. But we do have a security camera working at all times we're open."

"In here?" Nadine expressed her surprise. "It was on when they were here?"

"Of course. See, where we're located we get a lot of big-shot type people wandering in. The owner said he wants it for his own protection. Every morning when I get in, I set it."

"Where is it?"

He took Nadine to a small office behind the kitchen where the equipment was kept. He showed her how he sets the machine on and tests it every day.

"So we can run the tape from this morning?"

"Sure. I can do it now. It'll show up on the monitor."

He turned it on, but the screen was blank. Perplexed, he examined the settings. Everything seemed to be in order.

"I just put the damn thing on," he said with a measure of irritation.

"How many cameras are there, and where are they?"

"There's four and they rotate continuously."

He led them back to the interior of the restaurant and pointed them out. They were all moving, scanning the room.

"See, they're working perfectly. I don't understand."

"Do you have a ladder?"

"I'll get it."

A minute later he came out with a ten-footer.

"Enrique, can you set it up right next to the camera over there?"

He did as instructed. In a second, Nadine was climbing like a monkey. While on the top rung, she turned her head over her left shoulder, calling out to whoever was present to hear her. "Somebody taped over the lens. Dustin, check the other three, but I'll bet they're all the same," she shouted as she began her dissent. "Enrique, do you have the tape from last night?"

"Sure."

"Can you take a look and see if it was working at closing time?"

"I'll be right back."

Enrique walked out while Dustin was climbing to check the other camera. Nadine sat down at one of the tables and buried her head in her arms.

"Nadine, they're all the same," Dustin confirmed.

Nadine was known for her composure. She rarely showed emotion when dealing with an investigation. This case was an exception in many respects; one being that the killer was acting with impunity. Nadine stood up, softly pressing the palms of both of her hands on the wood top, more an act of deliberation than rage.

"Dustin, I'm going to take this asshole out. Imagine the nerve. He sits here with the victim in public and then kills her—Rita Tully for Christ sakes! How the hell does he even know her?"

Enrique returned.

"I have everything until we closed. The recorder shows that from five this morning the cameras were working. There is not an image from any of them."

"Thanks, Enrique. Here's my card. Please don't talk to anyone about this. If you think of anything else, call me. Now, we're going to have to close shop today while my people take samples and investigate the interior. You might want to call the owner. I'll be right down the block."

She started to walk out, but stopped.

"Enrique, one other thing. Did you do the dishes yet, the dish and glasses they used?"

"Wow, I'm sorry. I forgot. When I went to clean the table I noticed one of the cups was missing. The other was half full of coffee. If you want I have it in the back."

"Please don't touch anything else. I'll need your fingerprints just to eliminate them from the cup."

She moved back toward the front door.

"Dustin, let's get back to the body before any of the morons compromise the scene. He took the damn cup!" she roared.

As they started up the block, Lewis jogged up to Nadine.

"We got her private security people all over the place."

"Get rid of them. We're the police, remember?" she ordered.

Then she turned to edify Dustin. "The fewer people at the scene the better; the more people, the larger chance someone will do something stupid."

By now they were back to where Tully had been killed. The first order of business was to threaten to arrest Tully's private cops if they didn't leave. That accomplished, she was able to attend to the deceased.

"Jesus," Nadine murmured as she observed the body, "this lady sure sang the blues this morning. She's not wearing a damn stitch of clothes." Nadine paused to take in the gruesome scene. "She must have had plans for an early morning screw. Who the hell did she meet?" Nadine called out befuddled.

She noticed the incision beginning just below the navel and rising upward. The weapon must have been at least eight inches long, and whoever used it apparently wanted to attack the heart. He did so craftily, lifting the blade and twisting it once inserted so as to sever the aorta. In fact, the job looked almost surgical.

"Nadine, my dad just called," Dustin interrupted her concentration. "He knows Rita very well. He handled her family's legal affairs, and since her parents died, hers. He said if you need anything or he can help he's available."

Nadine walked over to her fledgling partner. "Dustin, get over to the hotel and let those bozo security boys do something constructive. I want to know anyone she dated or had relations with in the last five years."

"Does it look bad?"

"It's just another corpse."

"No, it's not." Dustin hesitated before tentatively finishing his thought. "She's been over to my house many times."

"Are you trying to tell me you were having sex with her?"

"Nadine, I . . ."

"Damn it, Dustin. If you are, you better confess right now."

"I wish I was."

"Right! Now, I'll ask you again. Were you screwing her?"

"Never, I swear. My dad would kill me."

"Bullshit."

"Okay, you're right; he wouldn't. But the answer is still no."

She gives him her famous you-better-not-be-screwing-with-me-because-if-you-are-I-WILL-find-out-and-make-you-pay-for-it look. Then she goes back to further examine the body.

16

PRESIDENTIAL PRIVILEGE

WHEN MILES DENTON ARRIVES for work, he's wearing his uniform; he carries a lunch box with a peanut butter and jelly sandwich, a baggie usually stuffed with sticks of carrots and celery, a dessert cupcake or small package of cookies, a small box of raisins and a piece of fruit; apples are his favorite if ripe ones are available in the local market.

He's practiced this gastronomic habit for thirty-seven years. His wife packs his food with the same devotion his mother did when he was a schoolboy. If one has the impression that Miles lives a simple and plain vanilla life, his insistence on white bread with his sandwich wouldn't contradict it. What would refute it is a little wrinkle recently introduced into his job description.

Miles Denton was groomed for his career. Those preceding him in the field trained him not unlike a master artisan instrument maker the students under his tutelage. The foundation of his craft was meticulously shaped step by step until the essential elements were ingrained in the deep structure of his mind and body. The lineage for Miles goes back well over two hundred years. Now it's his turn to spawn the next generation of servants to the President of the United States.

The buildup for what Mr. Denton is employed to do is not all puff. Forget the Secret Service, FBI and all the rest of the agents looking after the safety of the President. The staff serving the esteemed Mr. or Ms. President is the people who share with him and his family the most intimate conditions. These esteemed servants are bred to a standard of honor, dignity, devotion, and respect. Miles Denton is the archetypal standard, forged in bronze, eternally at attention, predictable as a sperm.

It should be understood that Miles was asked to take a slightly different assignment during this most recent tenure, in fact, by the president himself. Could the reason for him being selected by The Man be that Miles was nearing retirement age? Or was it possibly his reputation as a servant with undying loyalty, not so much to any particular president as to the title he himself so earnestly respected that resulted in President Howard Haley inviting him deep, very deep, into the president's confidence? That we will never know. I can share a few things we do know for certain.

Fact one: President Haley wanted nothing more in life than to become president, and he succeeded; he wants just as much to serve out a second term.

Fact two: He experiences the tireless monitoring by security of his whereabouts like a leash that gets shorter and shorter.

Fact three: He loves a challenge and will never give up until he finds a way to prevail.

Fact four: He delights in doing things his own way. If a circumstance requires it, he will use whatever means of deception he determines justify the end.

Fact five: He approaches Denton with a proposal that will allow him to accomplish something never done by a modern president.

What Haley wants to do is go out into the world every so often free of Secret Service agents in front of him, on his side, on top of buildings, holding bullet proof plates of glass in front of him, wearing a missile proof vest. He wants to be free to do what any other citizen does, mingle with the ordinary commoners.

It has nothing to do with his Democratic roots—though he fancies himself the spokesman for the less privileged, which makes him a blue-blooded democrat if there is an animal that color. It has much more to do with thirsting for a simple feeling of freedom. He's willing to employ his rebellious spirit to defy those hired to quash his liberty—a license to run free he rates high on his list of things-I-have-to-possess-to-survive.

As time went on after assuming the presidency, he hatched a plan to ease the oppression of his dutiful core of protectors. Shortly after that, he approached Denton with a proposal to move from a position within the White House to working at the guard gate. Denton at first couldn't imagine how it could be accomplished even if he agreed. Still, he didn't dare venture to inquire of the president why he was making the request. As would be expected, whatever the president wanted he would agree to; the president assured him it would be no problem to have his assignment altered. Additionally, Haley let Denton know that he was aware retirement was quickly approaching and hinted that the change would result in a much healthier pension when the departure day arrived.

Little did Denton know at the time he would soon be a partner in a scheme with the President of The United States, a brainstorm of Haley's that Denton would never have to be sworn to secrecy because he was incapable, even under threat of severe punishment, of betraying the trust of the man occupying the White House.

To answer the curious question as to the nature of the activity Denton would be a party to, there's no better way than to catch the two conspirators in the act of subterfuge.

Denton is in the guard booth, having just relieved a retiring colleague. President Haley on this cold Thursday afternoon can be viewed off in the distance, exiting a door leading to a path through a lawn and garden area.

The leader is an attractive president, young and fit. He is in his mid-forties with straight silver hair compensating for a brushstroke of sagacity that his otherwise youthful appearance is lacking. He has an erect gait, one that bobs ever so perceptibly up and down, a hint of pompousness those who actually know him would be quick to con-firm. Yet despite that temperamental chink in his personality, people tend to promote him as a fairly nice sort of man: for the most part, they're correct.

This afternoon he's in a jolly spirit. He just met with the Speaker of the House, Harley Stafford, and he's sure they've worked out a com-promise legislation that he believes will glitter his record on human rights, an area of attack for his enemies in the upcoming reelection campaign. As he walks along the path, notable is a metal case he car-ries nonchalantly. When he arrives at the booth he enters and warm-ly greets Denton with a childish smirk and squeeze on the arm.

The ceremony is enacted in silence. Haley takes the metal case and places it ritualistically on a small counter. As he opens it, the contents elicit a spellbound glint that streaks across his face, as if he's transformed by a hermetic vision. But it is not the items contained therein that awaken his being, rather, it is their symbolic worth, the associations they conjure; inside the container are articles of libera-tion, the essential pieces that will literally transform President Haley into…Joe Average Citizen.

Haley extracts a collapsible cane, lightweight overcoat, a worn pair of tennis shoes and a matching set of gray hairpiece, beard and eyebrows. He squats out of sight within the booth and begins the makeover, his actions not dissimilar to those of the murderer we had the pleasure of meeting earlier, though the president enjoys slightly more comfortable conditions.

While Haley's invisible to anyone other than Denton, the partner in crime speaks for the first time. "Mr. President, it's a dark, nasty afternoon. Are you sure you want to do this?"

Haley is not a man to allow miserable weather to be a deterrent. He was raised in a part of the country known for bitter cold condi-tions. He still seeks out a snowstorm when he can arrange a ski trip. His response to Denton could be put to music.

"I wouldn't miss it. Gives me a marvelous feeling of freedom. Besides," he chuckles to himself as if he were a great comic, "I need to go out and drum up votes."

With that he rises in exaltation, presenting as an inconspicuous, elderly, slightly disheveled man. He grabs hold of the cane like a magician about to perform a new act, assembles it, winks to Denton, opens the outside door of the booth and feasts on the naughty behavior he's about to perform, an endeavor that will bring him those few moments of anonymity as crucial to his mental well-being as a trip to Vegas for a addicted gambler.

Haley, when he went to the university, was an actor. He always professed that to be a politician nothing could provide better preparation than theatrical skills. No longer practicing the arts, he does retain some talents, his favorite pursuit Shakespearean drama. So to complete the makeover he adds in a perfect English accent, "I have a dinner meeting at seven thirty. If I don't returned on time start worrying," he offers as his au revoir to Denton.

In seconds, a sea of people can be seen moving every which direction around an unrecognizable president ambling along with a cane, peaceful as a pup in a bucket of…mud will do.v

17

MERCEDES OR MAZERATI?

WHAT A COINCIDENCE. THE Thursday afternoon President Haley was romping about the city was the same Thursday Larry was having his first official date with Nadine. Our fine head doctor routinely, and I mean routinely, finishes his office at six. Every day he books his last patient at five and the last session ends ten to six. He may make a personal note, possibly a call back to another doctor or patient, but when the clock hands form a perfect one eighty-degree angle, out the door he goes.

The doctor is dedicated to his work, but his interests are broad. Long ago he learned to put limits on the practice lest it become the proverbial tail wagging the dog. Especially tonight, he was not going to linger in the office. He had just enough time to race home, shower and change, and get Nadine sharply at seven as he promised.

On his way home, he deliberated on what to wear and which car to drive. He was tickled with the surprise he had in store for her. He'd been gleeful all day wondering what expression she'd employ when he delivered her a date she was sure never to forget. It wasn't a tactic he'd ever used before on a first date; in fact, it was a tactic he'd never used.

Deliberation over his attire ended with a decision to wear a black Zegna cashmere pullover V-neck sweater with a pale green Armani dress shirt, gray slacks—custom made—and black leather tie shoes by Prado. He wasn't snobbish…he was wealthy, period.

Car? That was a bigger problem. He loved driving his top-of-the-line Granturismo Maserati, but…that might really overwhelm her on top of everything else he had set for the evening. Back and forth the poor man went, until he landed on the boring-to-drive, fat, stodgy Mercedes sedan. He only bought it because his uncle stressed that a respectable man must have a "proper" vehicle for work. Either choice was hardly going to leave her with the idea that he was a struggling teacher, but he opted for the safer bet.

And that's how it happened that we'd see Larry and Nadine motoring along later that evening in the front seat of Larry's big, expensive Mercedes. The doctor could not have known, at that early point in the courtship, that Nadine was less versed on Mercedes' than March Madness—she'd never been to a basketball game.

"Nice car," Nadine said, acknowledging recognition of a fancy machine.

"I leased it for the night to impress you."

"You didn't need to do that. I could have resurrected Smoky Joe."

"Who might that be?"

"My first car. Everyone teased me about him, my old AARP senior. He got his nickname from a perennial cough out the rear exhaust pipe. But I paid cash," she giggled.

"It's the best way to stay out of debt."

"Right. No credit for this girl. I learned early that if I trapped my tiny little ass in a financial hole there was nobody going to help pull it out."

Needless to say Nadine had never walked into a Maserati dealership, unless the owner was running out the back door to escape her interrogating him.

"When I bought Smokey, he was already an ancient specimen. So when I had to bury him, I decided I'd splurge on a new one."

As she was telling the story she was laughing at herself, but fondly. "For most people, buying new is a routine affair. For me it's a study in transactional analysis. What I did first was go to a series of random dealerships that sold the cars I considered to be within my style and price range. I took a brochure from each and studied them until I knew exactly the car that would best suit me. Then I called about five different dealers, telling each of them precisely the car I wanted, exterior and interior color, seat covering, tinted windows, automatic seats—only on the driver's side, sir, so on a cold day you may not appreciate riding shotgun with me."

She paused, realizing she was recounting a story likely of no interest to Larry. "Well—long story short. I get carried away sometimes. All I'm saying is, I buy carefully."

"No. I can tell this is a tale begging to be told. I want to hear all the details."

"You're asking for it," Nadine warned.

"If I didn't want it, I wouldn't be here with you."

"Okay, Nadine the financial wizard in action—take two."

"I'll take a dozen," Larry blurted out as if making a bid at an auction.

"You better hear two first," she quipped before charging ahead with her narration of Nadine Street buying an actual new car. "Well, as I'm calling and getting replies back from each prospective seller, I'm bargaining them one against the other. This went on until I was satisfied not one nickel of my money was going into the sucker pot dealership owners rely on to get rich." Again she chuckled.

"I had a friend who knew the car business. He was nice enough to inform me that the last day of the month was the best day to make a purchase. The dealership would be trying to bring up their numbers because they get better breaks down the line from the manufacturer—in my case it was Ford Motor Company.

"They wouldn't be as inclined, therefore, to let a cash customer go to another store at the end of the month, especially if they were behind their desired sales volume. Then he took it a step further, insisting the ultimate best last day to buy was the last day of the last month of the year, December 31. Oh, and as close to closing time as possible."

She brought the epic event to a fitting finale, fitting to the one and only Nadine. I'll quote her directly so as to rightly credit her for the majesty, mystery and marvel she brings to those who know her: I believe it will enhance intimacy with her for those now making her acquaintance. She's hysterical, hardly able to contain her laughter, describing the rest of the transaction to Larry.

"So it's seven-thirty on Thursday, December 31. I'm the only person in the showroom at Sheehy Ford of Marlow Heights, Maryland. I'm squeezing dimes out of the salesman who want to get out by eight o'clock closing. I know by now I've taken his commission and I'm thinking they might end up chipping in the dealership too. While my friends were having warm up drinks for New Year's Eve, I was writing a check for my new Fusion hybrid with rear splash guards, locking fuel plug, floor mats, keyless entry, security system and, yes, dual heated seats all thrown in. Larry, I think I was the only customer they ever sold a car to—or was it gave a car to—that they didn't tell to send their friends in to buy one too."

Her delight was infectious. By now Larry was sharing the giggles.

"They're probably still talking about you."

"Yeah, hoping I never come back."

"You are amazing," Larry laughed. "Chauncy was right."

"Is he talking about me behind my back?"

"He was enamored with you right in front of both of us."

"I guess I didn't notice. But let me tell you, I'm not always so much fun."

"Then I'll take it as a compliment that I can bring it out in you."

"Okay, but what if it's just the car?"

"I'll take it however I can get it."

Ford Fusion hybrid or Mercedes CL550 coupe: What's a hundred grand between friends? Nadine wasn't balking at sitting in Larry's machine.

She looked stunning in it. Ask Larry.

During this fine exchange, for just one moment, his inattention to driving—measured by his intoxication with Nadine, whose prime derriere was now sunk softly in a glove fine tan leather seat and covered with a pair of designer blue jeans—nearly results in a collision. (It's one of the comical and adorable contradictions of Nadine—we all have them—that she'd fight for an eighth of a point from the bank on her home mortgage but refuse to compromise on clothing and food. She's known to drop a couple hundred every now and then on a swank pair of jeans like the ones putting Larry into a puerile fit.)

Fortunately, Nadine, while truly thrilled to be out with Larry, was more grounded than he. She steered him to alert just in time to avoid a mishap. Despite the near impact, there was a youthful merriment being shared by the two as they glided through the streets of Georgetown.

"We're early. Have you ever been to the Renwick Gallery? It's the Arts and Crafts Museum of the Smithsonian."

He wasn't searching for an answer because the itinerary for this outing was planned, sealed and about to be delivered regardless.

18

UNDER THE SHEET

LARRY HAD BEEN BLESSED with a large dose of culture. His inclination to lecture to Nadine was not contrived arrogance. Rather, what he'd absorbed through his experiences he delighted sharing with her.

Nadine had no objection to his lessons, especially given the radically contrasting upbringing she had. Truth is they both had upbringings deviating from the norm, while still radically different from each other's. But Larry's afforded opportunity to freely browse, explore and discover, whereas Nadine was drudging, plodding and pushing to meet the basic demands of her everyday life.

On one of his leisurely days probing the bowels of D. C., he happened on the Renwick Gallery. That was his destination for the first phase of their first date. He reached a dead end that led to a gated parking area. As matter-of-factly as one would pull a pen from their pocket, he took a card and inserted it into the gate—it swung open. He moved forward and parked.

"By Smithsonian standards it's a sardine can," he informed her as they get out of the car. "But that doesn't preclude it from housing thousands of pieces of our nation's artistic treasures. I think you'll find them amazing. These are not the creative works of Jackson Pollack, Norman Rockwell or Roy Lichtenstein, whom we're all proud of and familiar with. Here you'll see Larry Fuentes' *Game Fish*, Harvey Littleton's *Opalescent Red Crown* or Albert Paley's *Portal Gates.*"

Larry led Nadine to the front steps and then inside the museum.

He continued his discourse, pointing out many objects so unusual that it's understandable they'd find a way into a repository; it would be criminal to not make them available forever for every person to see. As an example, Larry lingered over a piece.

"What do you think? Looks like a common purse, right? Something most women would dispose with no more thought than dropping tissue paper into the toilet?"

"I'd say so."

"The purse has a metal zipper, brass buttons, rope-material strap and roughed leather body, right? But I'll tell you, the only differentiation between the one we're looking at and the billions that get tossed in the trash, besides its residence in a museum, is that it's made entirely of plastic."

"That's plastic? I don't believe it."

"If you could tell with the naked eye that there is no leather, brass or steel you're more a genius than the maker. The marvel of this piece is that you can't tell."

"It's amazing," Nadine exalted.

"That's how I feel. I'm glad you appreciate it. Come, there's more," Larry said, aiming a tad of mysteriousness her way.

One of the pleasures of a smaller facility is that a person can spend a few hours and know they've seen a good part of what it contains. Larry and Nadine were enjoying a slow browse from room to room. As they wandered through a doorway, it opened to a smaller room that faced its exterior to the rear of the building. Entering, they found a few incidental pictures on the walls. But it was the object dead in the center of the room that was the true showpiece.

All one could see was a tall item, haphazardly covered with a sheet—or so it appeared. Its size was on the scale of a living Hulk. The covering hung randomly, dropping close to the floor, creating a hemline that revealed the only visible portion of the piece, a wooden base. Knowing she was on Larry's turf, she posed him an obvious question.

"Where are they taking that?"

"That's the main thing I brought you here to see," Larry answered with delirious pride.

"Really? What's the joke?"

"No joke—look carefully."

And so she did, taking her time to make a thorough examination by circling several times around it. She craned her neck, even leaning over the rope that keeps visitors out of touching range. She approaches as close as possible to the prize, meticulously studying it as she would a crime scene.

Satisfied that nothing was unusual and whatever "the thing" was would soon be disposed of in the museum trash bin, Nadine signaled Larry with a silly agonizing smile.   "Doctor to the emergency room. Calling Dr. Monroe to the emergency room. The patient is dying." She gagged theatrically. "It's the curiosity disease…it's killing me"

He rushed over, quick to follow the dramatic line. He puts his hand on her stomach, just below the breast.

"Is that where it hurts?"

"No, doctor, it's a little higher," she groaned, upping the ante.

But before he could do the proper examination, she playfully whisked herself away.

"Come on, what do we have here that is so amazing?" she asked dubiously.

"When I saw it the first time I reacted just like you. I came into this same room, saw the painting, which hardly impressed me, and turned to walk out. But I did a double take at the center of the room. One of those attendants, you know the type, beady-eyed people hired for no reason other than they have beady eyes and presumed, therefore, to be able to do a job requiring snooping better than anyone who did not possess beady eyes, came smiling at me.

"He was about as delighted as I guess I am to watch you take a proper lesson in beguilement. Well, I turned back at him and with words identical to yours asked why they were getting rid of the piece. I'll never forget the pleasure he took in laughing at me. That's how I took it anyway, that I was being mocked. But he then rather politely explained his attitude to me."

"That *is* the piece!"

"Then he put me through the same exercise I did you. I walked around it, tried to penetrate beneath the cotton shawl that enveloped it, and finally, feeling a tad indignant, surrendered to him the same guess-I'm-dumb look you are just now erasing from your face."

"I can't wait, really! What is it?"

Monroe knew his time was running out. The impatient patient had exhausted her patience.

"Everything you are looking at, including the sheet, is made from one large piece of wood."

Larry leaned her in as close as he could without suffering a severe reprimand by one of the beady-eyed ones.

"Look. See the warp, the fine strands of woven cotton carved into the wood in a crisscross pattern precisely like fabric? The outer surface of the wood is bleached. See it? If you look very close, the darker shade of wood beneath actually penetrates through."

Nadine was starting to get the picture. A look of relief suggested the emergency intervention saved her. The vague characteristics of an old grandfather clock at least seven foot tall began to emerge from beneath the cloth covering.

Her mind wandered, imagining that perhaps the work represented an impression from the artist's recall. Might it have been a treasured monument created to soften sad memories of loved ones? Could it have been inspired by a fond era passed, one whose time was sorrowful to surrender? Or, perhaps the artist wished he could rid himself of a time of horror by hiding time away in darkness under a sheet the way any child would use the covers of their bed to shield themselves from fear.

"Who's the artist?" Nadine inquired.

"His name is Wendell Castle. It's called the Ghost Clock."

"Very human, isn't it?" she posited.

"What do you mean?"

"I was thinking about how this artist went to such length to conceal something. I don't know for sure what, but I'll bet as much as he's dedicated himself to veiling it, he's wishing to have it discovered."

"I see the analyst in you," Monroe complimented. "Funny, I relate to it differently. To me, he's created a perceptual trick."

"That could be. Either way, couldn't we conclude that the key point is that what's inside a person always wants to come out? I weave that awareness into my investigation of every case; the criminal, killer, rapist wants in the end to be discovered."

If Larry wasn't fully mindful of it up to now, he has no excuse in the future if he mistook this lady as a fool when it came to human psychology. They ought to get along just fine, two birds using the same set of principles to peck away at the same puzzles, but with different outcomes as their objective.

"I agree, they do." He took a few seconds before changing direction. "Come on. The night is just beginning—I have a surprise for you."

"Another one, already?"

"You'll see. This one you'll never guess.

19

THERE'S SOMETHING ABOUT REUBEN

THE FIRST WEEK AFTER Reuben was harassed on his hike, he rarely went outdoors except to transport himself between his home and work at Kuruk. Then on the eighth day, Josea was watering plants in the front yard when she noticed a late model car slowing down upon reaching their home. She recalled that the driver was wearing thick-framed glasses and a fedora hat. As he paused the vehicle, he began snapping pictures.

She stared at the man but he was unabashed, taking several seconds to complete his task before driving on. Josea glanced at the front bumper to jot down the license; there was none. Then as she ran after him, she saw that the rear license had been covered over.

The car itself was unremarkable, a common black Chevy of some sort. After going into the house, she sat for a while contemplating what happened. She was gazing out toward the street, when she noticed the same vehicle pull up in front of the house a second time. The car sat for about five minutes before taking off. That was the last she saw of the car or driver.

It had been her opinion up to that moment that Reuben was over-reacting. It was her advice that since a week had passed, he should take a breath of relief that it was a once only peculiar episode he had encountered. Now, however, as she pondered what she had just witnessed, she became increasingly more disturbed. She didn't want to call Reuben and further distress him, so she texted Preeti to ask if she could come to our home.

Preeti's father was visiting. Nadine had arrived and we were preparing to go over a few chapters I had completed. Before doing so, Len Cloud was delivering a short lecture on Apache philosophy and culture to Nadine. It was his favorite activity. Anyone willing to listen could quickly earn a sweet spot in his heart—Nadine had acquired a genuine interest and this was not the first talk that Len, the wise tribal elder, had delivered on her behalf.

He sat in his favorite chair, a padded rocker. His long silver hair hung freely over his back. My father-in-law rarely dipped his chin even when standing, thus his forehead perpetually signaled a communion with a higher power. The agony he had suffered the year before, being involved in settling the first ever murders on the reservation, had nearly killed him. Yet the simultaneous joy of unexpectedly reuniting with a long-lost family member evened out the pain—life had again achieved equilibrium and Len Cloud had resumed his previous state of harmony.

"Don't forget," he cautioned Nadine, "everything precious to my people is built on a foundation of balance. We understand that all forces of nature are associated with directionality. Nadine, the first two days of creation brought the sun, wind, sky, water and earth. Then over the next two days, God created the animals and all the creatures on the surface of earth—all elements, species and objects were created in four days," he proceeded reverently.

"It was not a random process. All living beings and objects of nature had to have their place. The Sun, wisdom and the spring of the year are associated with the East. The Moon, generosity and the women's way are all located in the South. Then the Stars, men's way, the way of the warrior, the place of fallen seasons and death are housed in the West. Finally, rainbows, the height of a warrior's strength and the Eagle make their home in the North."

"But doesn't the Eagle fly south and the sun set in the west?" Nadine questioned." And what's the women's way?" she pondered.

"Why do you ask about the woman's way, but not the men's?" he smirked.

"Good question," she admitted. "Probably, because I'm a woman."

"That's the point. You dwell in the South and your partner is in the West."

"I have no partner," she corrected him.

"You will," he confidently pitched her way. "And the communion you will share will be dependent on both of you understanding you come from different locations—you are not the same," he explained. "Only if you believe you are like creatures, do you set your expectations falsely and doom your love."

"Are you saying I might subconsciously impose on men to act like ladies, and then be disappointed they act otherwise?" Nadine posed humorously.

Len stood and walked around the chair, moving northward and then behind to the west, where he stopped.

"Look at my chair. When I sat I moved it to the north and now I stand behind it, but in the west," Len pointed out. "I never thought about it. There is no other way I could do it. I must be disciplined to be a brave and strong warrior; my place is in the west."

"Am I not brave and strong?" she quizzed him, but without defensiveness.

"You don't have to be," Len chuckled. "More important is that you have other characteristics, ones that if you don't attend to will bring ruination."

"What?"

Len stared at her for a moment before glancing at me. "My son-in-law will explain."

I always felt inadequate when Len asked me to comment on an area of Apache belief. He had tutored me over the last few years to be prepared with answers to these sorts of issues. Still, I assumed that, at times, he was intentionally testing me as much as sending me a compliment. To Preeti, his motive didn't matter; she was proud that her father would honor me with the role of educator.

"Nadine, for the Apache Mescalero, women are vested with most of the power. It's a tremendous responsibility imposed on them. The woman who abuses her force and authority through either coercion or impotence threatens the loved ones who are dependent on her. When the Mescalero talk about 'the world being thrown out of kilter' they are referring to not only the whole of the universe but the tiny subdivisions such as family and marriage. A woman underestimating her power can devastate her sphere of influence worse than one overestimating it."

Much like a counselor, Len would often advise young tribe members about their respective roles, always emphasizing balance and harmony as the core themes for a gratifying union.

"Mr. Cloud, in our society, as you know, it's typically thought that men have all the power."

Len contemplated her statement carefully. "For man, words are dangerous if misunderstood or misapplied. There is a vast difference between power and control," Len explained. "I believe what you are saying is that men have all the control over affairs of state and objects of wealth. But power is the force one hears when they are silent, when they listen. The universe speaks to women through its stillness."

"But not to men?" Nadine asked, perplexed by his explanation.

"Yes, to men also. But men are beings from the West; they are born in association with control—they can have power, but never to compete with that of women. That's why a wise man is comfortable to subordinate to his partner. It is through this awareness on the part of man that the balance of the universe is maintained." Len sat back in his rocker. "What you're talking about in Western culture is an emphasis on control at the expense of power. When that happens the harmony is broken and unless reestablished, it will end with disorder, and potentially disaster."

At this exact moment in the discussion, the text from Josea was received. Preeti had been listening to the talk. When she looked down at her phone she saw the word, "urgent."

"Excuse me, something must have happened," she announced with concern. "Josea said she's coming right over."

Josea usually traveled by car, but if in a hurry, and alone, she'd employ her motorcycle. Within minutes, the bike skidded into our driveway. Josea hadn't taken time to change clothes. She was wearing muddy tennis shoes that she pulled off and then tossed haphazardly as she reached the steps to the front door.

When she saw Nadine, Josea ran up to her. "Nadine, you have to help us," she cried out through heavy puffs of breath. "Reuben was right. Someone is after him!"

After relating what happened with the car and camera, she directed herself once more to Nadine. "What do you think?"

"It sounds bizarre. Unless there's something about Reuben none of you know, something in his background, I wouldn't know what to think," Nadine candidly related. "It could be some sort of misunderstanding. If not, then there has to be a reason and we'll have to find out what it is."

"There's no misunderstanding," Josea shouted frantically. "They covered the damn license."

"For how long have all of you known Reuben?" Nadine, the detective, posed the question as if she were interviewing a witness.

It was the right investigative question. It was the wrong one to ask to the people in the room. We all stared at one another, knowing we were sharing a secret about Reuben—we would prefer cutting our own wrists before betraying it to Nadine.

Nadine had been recovering. The weeks at Kuruk had been rejuvenating to her. She had handed off the writing assignment to me, leaving her in a pure consultative role. She was entertaining a love affair with Preston. She felt safe. She was expanding her activities, including considering teaching a yoga class. She was even smiling occasionally, and the brick she seemed to be hauling on her shoulders was lightening to where her neck was straightening, allowing her head to crane upward.

It was not Nadine's intent to return to her work as a detective in D. C. any time soon. Still, sufficient pressure could wrest the investigative instinct out of dormancy; Josea's plea appeared to accomplish that and she knew it the instant she posed the dilemma to Nadine.

"Look, I'm just upset, Nadine," Josea apologized. "You have your own issues to deal with."

"No, I'm going to help you if I can, Josea. Look what all of you have done for me."

The last thing any of us needed was a crack detective looking into Reuben's history. I wasn't worried she'd ever discover the truth—actually I was comfortable that she wouldn't. The problem was that there was an indomitable force within her she couldn't restrain. She would try.

"I'll be spending some time staking out your house…and I want to talk to Reuben—"

"Nadine! I don't want Reuben to know about this," she pled urgently. "He's already unnerved."

"You have no choice," Nadine shot back at her. "You can't play make believe. What if he is in danger? Until we get to the bottom of this, he's going to have to take precautions. I can advise him what to do."

Josea glanced at me with desperation in her eyes—I passed to Preeti.

"Josea will talk to Reuben," Preeti assured Nadine. "Then it might be best to let the tribal authorities handle it. Nadine, it's not your responsibility—we have a police force responsible for matters like this."

"She's right," Len Cloud, added, aware that danger was brewing. "You just keep doing what you're doing to get stronger."

"I read the transcript on the murders you had here," Nadine commented. "FBI Agent Kershaw made it clear that the tribal police were totally ill-equipped to deal with it, as were the state police. Look, I appreciate the concern for me but these matters can be nasty. At least allow me to informally see what I can do."

There was no way out short of insulting Nadine.

It was at that point, when she announced she was leaving for the afternoon and possibly overnight. Unbeknownst to me, Preston was flying in for the rest of the day and evening: they were meeting in Albuquerque. She left us all in a sweat.

To make matters more despairing, it was Preston, the man who could never shut up about his "absolute certainty" there was something missing about Reuben he couldn't put his finger on, who was about to stoke Nadine's suspicion meter.

What I most feared was precisely what happened. Nadine spent the night with Preston and returned late the following morning. When she saw me arrive at Kuruk, she immediately approached.

"Preston told me everything," she disclosed as if she was in possession of a hidden fact.

"Preston knows nothing," I exclaimed.

As soon as she confronted me, I realized my attempt to eviscerate Preston's ungovernable mistrust of Reuben had only dug me into a deeper hole. By arguing he knew *nothing*, insinuated that there was *something* to know. That was all Nadine needed.

"But you do, don't you?"

I took a long breath of exasperation, signaling that the whole matter was getting out of control. "Nadine, we don't even know there's a problem. He and Josea are upset, but really what proof is there that he's being followed? Let's drop it for now and see what happens."

"You're covering up something," she said bluntly. "But you're right. What business is it of mine?" Her next statement was nonchalant, making me wonder if the investigative animal was retreating from the hunt. "Are we ready to work?"

That afternoon while we were reviewing material for the story, she never mentioned Reuben. In fact, she never revisited the subject... not until it smacked her in the face, bleaching her pale skin a lighter shade of white.

20

NADINE, I'D LIKE YOU TO MEET MY BEST FRIEND

LARRY COULDN'T CONTAIN HIS excitement after getting back into the car following the visit to Renwick. If she were thrilled with Wendell Castle's Ghost Clock, she was soon to be going gaga.

Whether or not one is familiar with the streets of Washington, D. C., they should be aware that the gallery Larry and Nadine had enjoyed is smack in the middle of the city. Larry exited the parking area and turned left on to 17th Street, then did a quick move into the left lane to turn onto Pennsylvania Avenue.

"Larry, you can't go left here," Nadine, who knew the territory, including all off-limit turf, alerted him.

Expecting a speedy validation, followed by redirection of the Mercedes, she was left nonplussed by his dismissal of her warning. The stubborn fool was not only ignoring her, he was smirking with the gall only a husband with a minimum twenty years of service would dare exhibit.

Nadine was misreading him. His perceived silly grin would more accurately be labeled mischievous thrill, the magician's glee as a coin placed under a glass disappears.

Within seconds, the vehicle was halted as it came in front of a security barricade. Larry reached inside his pant pocket and took out an official looking plastic card. One guard approached carefully, another stood in the booth watching. The one at the car took the card to the kiosk and swiped it.

If Nadine possessed three eyes, they'd all be working overtime—Larry, the guards, the building in the background. But the poor maiden only has two, and so busy was she figuring out what Larry and the guard were up to, she lost track of where she was. Only a moment passed before the same guard came back to the car.

"Sir, can I trouble you to release the trunk and for you and the lady to get out?"

Larry responded as compliant as a lamb. "Of course."

He released the trunk as instructed and opened his door. They both exited the car, Larry sneaking Nadine a sly smile. The two stood off to the side of the road. The guard now motioned for them to get back in the car. As he did, the man in the booth approached the car and leaned in.

"Sorry for the inconvenience, Dr. Monroe. Percy there is being trained. I need to let him go through the procedures point by point. Go on ahead."

The guard eyed Nadine and then tipped his hat. "Welcome, Ms. Street."

After revolving her head three-sixty, Nadine mimicked the guard. "Welcome, Ms. Street? How does he know who I am?"

By now she was well aware of the fact Larry was moving forward on a driveway few pass over, the path traversed by the greatest powers in the world, leading to The White House. Another guard motioned Dr. Lawrence Monroe, and his darling lady, forward.

"I told them beforehand I was coming with you. Nadine, since childhood I've had only one true friend. You'll be dining with him tonight."

Riddle solved. President Haley and his best friend, Lawrence Monroe planned a dinner some time before. In the interim, Nadine arrived into his life. Deciding to cast fate to the wind, figuring "why not do something different," he notified Howard that he had met a "special lady" and suggested they make it a foursome.

They were greeted at the door and then taken to an oversized sitting room where they sat in chairs close to one another. Larry touched her hand for the first time, holding his open palm on the backside of hers as it rested on the arm of her chair. The tactile sensation lasted just long enough for him to feel the pulse, the life force surging through a body he hoped to caress more completely. He applied adequate pressure to convey to her that he wanted to embrace her with all of his senses at once.

"I hope you're not upset with me."

"You'll know if I'm upset," Nadine assured him.

The President entered, followed by his wife, Muriel. The introductory stuff was about as mundane as any other first acquaintanceship. In fact, Nadine recounted the evening as no different from any other when she met new people, except...

"There were a few servants...well, quite a few, and the closest most of my friends come to a house helper is occasionally using a Brillo pad. Then Haley popped in. I'd describe him as a calm, on-top-of-the-world sort of guy. His wife is plainly attractive, happy to play a note or two below him as an unassuming and gentle woman.

"Within seconds of Haley and the first lady entering, the room was quietly abuzz with personnel conducting their assigned roles. There was a table between the two chairs Larry and I occupied; Howard and Muriel opted to sit on the couch across from us. It took about five seconds for the coffee table to be covered with treats. My God, there were at least a dozen different types of crackers, with fresh cut vegetables and dips, cheeses and meat slices, hot platters composed of warm cheeses, small squares of beef, and pasta.

"I looked up from the feast in front of me—there was no potential desire overlooked—and I prayed I wasn't being delivered a cruel sidearm curve, my Last Meal. Christ, I would have been happy with a carrot stick and tofu dip from Emil's Deli.

"After a moment, Muriel addressed me: 'If there's anything not out that you prefer I'm sure we can arrange it,' she said, completely unaware of how absurd the suggestion sounded to me."

"I'm fine," is all I could say without breaking into a giggle.

"Well, dear, if there is anything you want, I'll trust you won't be bashful."

"Thanks, I won't be."

"Wow, wow, wow. People who want for nothing, who take it for granted that anything they can conceive is as available as tap water; that's a foreign breed," Nadine shared with awe.

Haley's interest was in Larry. He changed places from sitting on the couch next to his wife to a chair angled just to the right of Larry. He pushed it even closer to his best friend, a position allowing him to communicate with privacy. Nadine was intent to eavesdrop but had her work cut out: Muriel was a gabber. She did manage to apportion one ear to the men.

"Did you hear Solomon speak today at the Fed?" Haley posed in a hushed tone.

"Not too good, was it?"

Haley was a man who would never let an opportunity pass to address a matter of urgency, especially one urgent to him. He had something of great importance to relate to his friend. He had prepared for their meeting, producing a newspaper article from his inner coat pocket. He handed it to Larry, along with a disgusted look. Nadine surreptitiously glanced just long enough to see it.

The headline read: FED CHIEF COMMENTS NEGATIVE ON ECONOMIC OUTLOOK.

Larry was granted all of a micron of a second before Haley directed the conversation. "Solomon likes people to think I'm her best friend, but she's been a thorn in my side all along."

"I know," Larry responded compassionately.

An indignant tone increased as Haley continued. "That's not the worst of it. Hill, that bastard—I put him in the Senate and now he's backing Solomon against me."

Haley proceeded in a calmer, yet subtler manner. One might get the impression that it was all of the sudden Larry's responsibility to address the issues of Solomon and Hill.

"I can't afford a limp economy with my re-election so close."

"I understand what you're saying," Larry commiserated.

Haley shrugged, expressing appreciation for his friend's concern.

Muriel, now seated at a diagonal to Haley, glanced deliberately toward her husband to catch his attention. At that moment, an unexpected intrusion occurred, the ringing of a cell phone.

Nadine fetched her purse. From the precise location it was assigned, she took out the unruly gadget. She looked down on the face of the phone to see who the caller was.

"I'm sorry. I forgot to turn it off."

She hesitated long enough for Muriel to sense the call was important. Muriel led her by the arm to a chair with an adjacent small table. It was out of hearing range, where she could talk unobstructed.

"Don't worry. It'll be quiet here," Muriel kindly expressed.

Then Muriel further demonstrated her warmth by offering a slight squeeze of Nadine's hand, a gesture Nadine returned. Muriel walked away, leaving Nadine to deal with business.

"What is it, Dustin?"

His voice signaled excitement. Receiving the call while off-duty prepped her, for Dustin rarely called other than during daytime working hours unless there was an emergency or critical breakthrough.

"Where are you?" he asked.

"Just getting a bite to eat."

"Well, chew on this. The secretary's phone log in Crow's office shows only three incoming calls the day of his murder: his wife, a niece and the president."

"So? Crow and the…"

Her voice trailed off; she didn't dare say the word, but it was of no difference to Dustin.

"I ran the phone numbers. The one from President Haley was not placed from the White House."

Nadine found herself irked. How could he get all worked up and call her, with an aspersion about the president no less, failing to take into account that the man may make calls from many locations?

"I'm sure he makes a lot of calls, Dustin. I'll bet some of them are placed from places other than where you'd expect them," she chastened him. "Now I'll talk to you tomorrow."

She assumed her tone would wipe him out of existence for the rest of the evening, but with more immediacy than offense he persisted.

"Yeah, but I was able to trace the call. I found out he placed it from a phone booth a few blocks away from the White House. That's a little weird, wouldn't you say? I didn't know we still had phone booths," he chuckled.

"Good work, Dustin," she complimented as she lifted an eye toward Haley, now deep in conversation with Larry. "We'll talk later."

"Howard, did you know Nadine is lead investigator into these horrible murders here in Washington?" Muriel called out to her husband as Nadine returned to join the group.

The president glanced up from his talk with Larry, looking at his wife, shaking his head left to right, right to left and back again. That was all he'd invest in "no," just enough for there to be no mistaking his consummate disregard for Nadine, a dislike that confounded her.

The dining room was more intimate than Nadine expected. Muriel chose to entertain them in the private quarters where she and the president would take a meal by themselves: it was a space made relaxing by its informality.

Haley liked it best because it was where he could get a tamale and rice if he were in the mood, and Muriel wild salmon with broccoli.

Tonight it's beet salad with burrata cheese, non-dairy carrot soup, Chilean sea bass with spinach pasta and grilled yellow peppers. The meal finished off with a dessert, fruit cups with seasonal berries topped with whipped cream. After consultation with Larry, who expressed Nadine's interest in eating "consciously," Muriel's secretary outlined the menu.

Before going forward with the events of the evening, I should mention that I was astonished with the level of recall Nadine was able to provide for some aspects of the story. She would recite word-by-word dialogue as if it were unfolding in real time. When I asked her about it, she smirked as if I'd caught her in a lie. Finally, as if showing me cheat-notes she had hidden in a drawer for all the tests she had taken in school, she disclosed her secret.

"Shortly after I first met Larry I was inspired to start up a diary. Most girls I knew kept one during childhood and into their early teens. I had one very early in life but gave up on the habit by the time I hit nine. I had no free moments for 'trivialities.' Maybe it was intuition, but after I met Larry I started writing."

Nadine would note in the diary that she recognized from the beginning Haley didn't care for her. In her words: "I thought from that first evening he wanted to dress me with lots of cayenne, onions and garlic, then barbeque me on a skewer." But the most fruitful topic she hit on, would be Haley's brotherhood with Larry.

"When did your friendship begin?" Nadine asked Haley as the foursome settled down to dinner.

The answer revealed a different side of Haley. He relished recounting their history.

"We were about nine when we met. We've been proud blood brothers ever since. In my work, friendship is only a theory. That's why I'm blessed to have Muriel and Larry."

It was a sentimental disclosure by Haley, but then abruptly, as if pricked by an invisible needle, he turned peevish toward his "blood brother".

"Larry does have this...quirk," Haley jeered. "I sometimes think he's uncompromising about it solely for the purpose of aggravating me. I know that sounds a bit suspicious, but it's not my imagination." Haley turned to look at Larry. "Well, damn it. Is it or isn't it?"

Larry smeared his face with a boyish grin. He seemed embarrassed that Haley would address an intimate conflict in front of Nadine. He never verbalized a response, instead he let the smug look on his face linger until Haley continued.

"It's that cowardly immutable commandment about patient privacy," he indignantly ranted. "He places it above our *trust*."

Larry bristled at Haley's comment. Muriel took a deep breath and rolled her eyes; she seemed bored, likely having served as a spectator to many prior battles on the same theme.

"What is with this loyalty thing between both of you?" she interceded into what her attitude suggested was a pointless squabble. "Howard, sometimes I think you enjoy rousing him. And Larry...I don't get it. Why are you always letting him get your goose?"

Larry said nothing. He did cross his legs and sealed a mask of stubbornness across his face. Quite some time passed—not an hour, but trying to hold your hand over a burning teakettle for a second might feel like an hour. At last, it was Larry who followed up the taunt.

"Just because you refer a patient to me does not entitle you to know everything about his treatment."

"Depends on the patient, doesn't it?" Haley retorted laconically.

Larry showed no interest in sparring further. In fact, his silence offered the opportunity for both men to commute an agreement to drop the acrimony; it was like frat brothers tossing ping-pong paddles after a match.

"Half men, half boys," Muriel sighed.

Nadine smiled. She wasn't sure that what she witnessed was funny. Within a few moments, the bosom buddies started chatting like nothing had happened.

Anyone ready for a ride home in Larry's fancy Mercedes?

21

SHOP TALK AND CAR TALK

Nadine, as I mentioned, cherishes her sleep. While the evening meeting with Haley had far from bored her, it left her tired from the emotional intensity. In the car, she lifted her left leg first, all the way across the right as she struggled moderately to pull off her boot. Then she reversed her legs to tug off the other boot; she threw them both on the floor in front of her. She eased back in her seat and closed her eyes. Larry peacefully drove, content with the evening silence.

Can't one time it be simple, no complexities, so I can relax and enjoy, at least for a while? She silently posed the question to herself; her lamentation regarding the challenges of romantic relations quickly bowed to confusion. *For Christ's sake, this is only a first date and look what's going on; meeting the President and his wife, sitting in the bleachers and watching a contest between two men as comfortable displaying hostility as tenderness with one another, trying to get a grasp on why Haley dislikes me, and, oh yeah, possibly starting an affair with a man I hardly know.*

She sunk deeper into the lush leather and decided to surrender her queries, waiting to see if Larry would volunteer to answer a few of the questions flitting about in her head—he didn't.

"Definitely an interesting evening," she finally said with the enthusiasm she would display to announce that she was stopping to pick up the cleaning.

More attentive to his driving than earlier, Larry's eyes were riveted to the road ahead.

"Thought you'd find it different."

"Well, you thought right. Larry, why was your friend so offended by your refusal to discuss your patients? You are bound by law, are you not, to keep the privilege?"

"Of course, but his world is different," Larry explained. "Howard can't compute what is sacred about the therapeutic relationship. He wouldn't make much of a clinician, would you think?"

"No, I don't think he's the type to excel in your line of work. But he seemed pretty put out by your refusal. Do you think it's as innocent as he wants to know you trust him? Besides, what would he care to know about your patients?"

"I think you're right. There's nothing extraordinary about the people I see. To him it might be a trust issue but to me it's about the sacredness of the privacy privilege, guaranteed confidentiality for the patient. I know that basic right has been whittled down over the years as laws have encroached, but I strongly disagree."

"You mean if you uncovered real evil in your work, not some common wife beater or drunk, but a rapist or a murderer?" Nadine posed, "you wouldn't want to follow the law and report it, to possibly save an innocent person?"

"So you're saying it's worth violating the rights of millions to *possibly* save one life? Should we throw every foreigner out of our country because we think there might be a few terrorists? What makes our country strong, stronger than our enemies will ever be, is that we have faith in our values; we don't forsake those precious jewels for a few bad seeds. What's happened in my field is shameful."

Nadine stared at him, unable to approve one willingly committing a crime.

"Are you saying that you would break the law, that you wouldn't report what you are required to?"

"If you're worried, I promise I won't get arrested," he answered with a wink.

The attitude of lightness toward what she considered a serious matter perplexed her. But before she had a chance to further ponder it, Larry accelerated into a left turn, the car showing off its handling.

"I could get used to this," she chortled, leaving behind the topic of law and ethics.

"You really like it?"

"Well, yeah. It moves differently than my little Ford."

"Then next time, I will have another surprise for you."

Nadine threw her body back into the seat. She thrust her arms outward in a sign of surrender. "What might that be?"

"You have to wait for surprises."

"Thank you for reminding me. I'm not well schooled in such matters," she shot back playfully.

"You'll learn with me."

"I bet I will."

The completion of her sentence corresponded to the culmination of the trip home; the car pulled in front of Nadine's building.

"I have something I want to give you," Larry announced as he prepared to exit the car. "By the way, I wanted to ask you who you are reporting to on these murder cases."

"Directly to Chief Lambert. You know him?"

"I know *of* him, but I don't know him," Larry answered as he jumped out of the driver's seat and quickly went around to Nadine's side to let her out.

He reached out his arm for her to grasp, pulling her forward. As he did, she landed in his arms. It was a first touch, an exploratory embrace. He noticed the softness of her hair and how it created a smooth, silky film between his and her cheeks. He breathed in the sweet fragrance of her unblemished skin; he yearned for the submission of secrets to be shared between them.

Then gently he pulled back his upper torso; closely inspecting her eyes, reading nothing yet of the pain and hardship to be doled out to him incrementally only as trust would be tested. He was mindful she was beckoning him to come forth, willing to surrender a lifetime of mind and reason to discover the miracle of grace. He kissed her tenderly, but passionately, releasing her from the sensation of a teen-like heart-pounding lust.

It was only a nip he enjoyed; he feared reaching further, feared attempting to untimely satisfy his full thirst. He was struggling desperately, mindful of a mighty libidinal beast yanking at the end of a precarious leash, ready to strike.

"I have my own ideas about this case," he said in a pant.

She stood by as he opened the passenger side door and leaned in. He took out a thin envelope and handed it to her. "You can read it later," he said. Then he put his arm around her and walked her to the front door of her building, stopping two steps from the top as she proceeded up.

"What do you think about spending the day together Saturday?"

What a guy. Perfect timing, perfect control. Still, as he posed the question, he silently petitioned a response by shrugging his shoulders.

Nadine was delighted by his style. "Sure," she fluttered.

"I'll call you tomorrow to make the arrangements. I promise the surprise then."

So we have a date for Saturday. L. M. loves N. S.; write it on a tree trunk.

22

CIGARS AND SCREWDRIVERS

Please don't get the impression it was all fun and games, high class dating, Presidents and First Ladies, and gourmet dining for Nadine. She was working. While she may not have yet been hot on the trail of the madman—frankly she wasn't even cool on his tail—her lack of progress only inspired her to double her efforts; and it appeared she now had Dustin in full service.

Her assistant was proving to not only be more reliable and serious about his career, he was also showing signs of initiative. Most of his assignments he took directly from Nadine, though occasionally he had a whim and nosed his way along without consulting his boss.

This brings us back to the Crow murder scene. When Nadine plucked that cigar from General Crow's fingers and dropped it into an evidence bag, she handed the specimen to Dustin, with specific instructions.

"Enter it as evidence. Also, check the saliva where it was mouthed and be sure General Crow was the only one smoking it."

"Roger that." He loved using clever phrases; they worked well with his chipper personality.

Being bred on luxury, and knowing a few cheroot and Havana aficionados, Dustin recognized fine merchandise when he smelled it. He estimated the single smoke in the plastic baggie might be in the ten-dollar range. He questioned if a general—granted a successful one, with a conservative military background—would be throwing money around like...Dustin or most of the people he knew.

A shot in the dark it was, but he was in the mood to start testing his own detective skills. The thought that one of his endeavors might hit on something that would impress Nadine tempted him deliciously. He owed it to her to at least commit a hundred percent to this case—until it was over—and he intended to be faithful to his word.

Dustin had more than one project he'd been researching independently. When he called Nadine during her White House dinner with what he thought was startling news about the president, her lack of enthusiasm soured the rest of his evening. Nevertheless, just before she hung up on that call, Dustin had made one last effort to impress his boss. He told her he'd see her in the morning, giving her the name and location of a local coffee bar where they could meet at eight.

We catch up with them after having finished breakfast. Nadine had not even mentioned the call placed by the president from a location just outside the White House, nor had she asked why he wanted to see her at this particular place. She knew from experience to expect anything from Dustin.

It might be that Michael Jordan commonly ate at this tiny hole-in-the-wall and Dustin has dreamed up the idea of introducing her to the basketball legion. Dustin had shocked her with oddball experiences exactly like that in the past.

One time he rushed her out of the office, excited over "news" he couldn't wait to share with her. Then he took her to a briefing and introduced her to the whole Washington Redskin football team, receiving a ration of reproof for getting her all worked up over "nothing." How was he to know Red Sox, Redskins, Red Wings and Red Bull meant as much to her as who was the manufacturer of the buttons on her blouse? He pouted, but only for a second. Then he pled his case: "Several of the players thought you were hot."

She was generally sensitive to the fealty he honored her with, earning him credits he might later cash in for the privilege of leading her on little escapades he found of interest. Besides, sometimes she actually enjoyed the moments when he ushered her into a world of celebrity and glitz.

Dustin was carrying a paper coffee cup in hand as they left the restaurant. He took a last sip and threw it in a convenient trash container. Irresolutely, he stared at her.

"Dustin!" Nadine admonished, warning him she was in a no-nonsense mood.

His face brightened. It was lights up on Dustin's stage.

With a magical whisk, Dustin reached to his inner coat pocket and produced a large cigar, fashioning himself a big shot, shoving the end in his mouth. As if he were following a rehearsed script he gave Nadine a huge grin, bringing her impatience to a nearly irrepressible level.

"What are we doing here, Dustin?"

"I'm warming you up for a big morning."

"You're scalding me. Let's get on with it."

He waved for her to follow. They walked only a few paces up the block, two stores exactly. He led her into a shop, Carlos' Tobacco.

"Are you Carlos?" Dustin asked the man behind the counter who was still putting out some of his premier products for display.

"I am, sir. And what can I do for you...or the lady?"

Dustin, now holding the cigar, rested it in a horizontal position across his palm like a small dagger for the man to gaze at. At first the shop owner's glance was cursory, but in a second his eye did a double take, returning to the object he had hastily dismissed. As he came back for a closer inspection, his interest was tweaked. He extended his arm to take hold of the specimen but then halted.

"May I?"

Dustin signaled affirmatively with a nod. Carlos gently took possession of it like a jewel. Then he smelled it, fingered it carefully and finally visually examined. He returned it to Dustin like a sacred amulet.

He had a thick accent and spoke solicitously. "Where did you get it?"

"Actually, I want to buy a dozen."

Dustin was full of the pomp he played so naturally. Carlos' attitude hardened. There would be no sale. He resented the arrogance of a customer he imagined picked up the sample at a fancy shindig for big shots.

"Never in this country; not even in the black market."

Refusing to give up the ostentation, Dustin returned the stogie to his mouth and feigned indignation. He took Nadine—who had silently witnessed the performance—by the arm and directed her to the door and then out to the street. Walking quietly to the car, Nadine's fuse shortened.

"Dustin, I'm not interested in skits," she cautioned him. "If you have something, out with it."

"The laboratory report for General Crow's cigar concluded it was a Cuban blend. I showed it to a few people and called around to importers to see if I could buy some."

"Why was this Carlos so impressed?"

Dustin is about to draw out the story again, but Nadine's edgy eye exhorts him.

"I'm sorry, Nadine. It's worth the wait, I promise. This blend is made exclusively for one client. Do you know what that means? Nobody else can get it. It obviously comes in very small numbers."

"And who is this lucky plutocrat?" Nadine queried.

"I had to pay big for this. Court seats for a Wizard game and guaranteed primo date with a foxy lady to accompany the man. I've got this friend and he knows a guy who…"

"Dustin, you're trying me. See if you can stay on course."

"This brand-spanking-new sample was made exclusively for our President Haley. The guy who helped me works in White House procurement."

"That really doesn't mean anything," Nadine shrugged.

Dustin was undeterred. "No? We'll see. The general, as you know, was retired. But I did some research into how he was spending his gray years; by the way, he was only sixty-two. He consulted. He was considered the most influential person in the nation regarding arms policy. His opinion was undisputed gospel to the Department of Defense and Senate Arms Committee."

Nadine waved her hand, directing Dustin's next movement at prestissimo.

"For some time Crow and Haley had been at odds over military projects. Seems it was coming to a boil and they met privately only three days before the murder. As you know the president put on quite a show of his own after Crow's murder, painting the man as one of the nation's greatest heroes, a lost statesman whose worth could not be calculated. So what do you think?"

"Nothing yet. What do you conclude?"

"The show is just beginning," Dustin bragged, but refused to answer her question.

Nadine knew it was futile to try influencing Dustin's pace. No more battles this morning. She decided to surrender, thinking to herself that the harshness of their work deserves episodes of comic relief. Dustin jumped in the passenger seat of the car and Nadine's Ford puttered off.

This was his coming out party. He directed her to the scene of another gruesome murder: that of Herman Blank, the fourth in what would eventually be a long series of connected killings.

Dustin had been laboring over the findings of all the cases, hoping to beam in on facts overlooked previously or ones that wouldn't have been revealed at the time but would now that more information had been assembled. He was celebrating with the level of delight a poker player might after being dealt a straight flush to the Jack of clubs.

Inside Blank's condominium, the evidence had been frozen. When Dustin and Nadine walked in they found that the room had been gathering dust. On the floor chalk outlined the resting place where Blank's dead body had laid.

Dustin produced a packet of pictures, ones Nadine had examined too many times already. The pictures were successive enlargements of Blank's head, impaled below the right parietal lobe, actually below the ear, with a wood-handled screwdriver. After a cursory look at the stack, she nonchalantly commented to Dustin.

"I know how the Congressman was killed."

Dustin motioned for her to follow. He took off briskly across the room and through a door leading to the kitchen. The far end of that room opened to a small service porch. Dustin took out a tissue and used it to open a drawer. Inside were several tools.

"What do you see?"

"What do you mean, what do I see? I see what you see, a bunch of tools," Nadine answered unenthusiastically.

"Yes, but look at this picture again."

He handed her one with the enlarged views of the head decorated with the screwdriver impaling it.

"Look carefully at the screwdriver in Blank's head; then at the ones in the drawer," Dustin instructed her.

"Yes, they all match," Nadine, commented. "So it's a set."

Dustin would have exalted by jumping up and down and cheering with his arms extended, if he thought Nadine would tolerate his childishness—his pride was ungovernable.

"That's right. They're all from the same set."

"And . . . that means?"

"The killer let us in on a secret. It's his first mistake, at least the first mistake we've discovered: he knew Blank. He knew him well enough that he had previously visited. He must have taken the screwdriver beforehand, knowing at the time what its final application would be."

Nadine was for the first time Dustin's pupil. She played the role benevolently.

"Why?"

"He has to strike fast, right?

"He seems to," Nadine acknowledged.

"We've concluded that his victims know him; it's impossible for him to accomplish his mission otherwise. Yet we're fairly sure by now that he disguises himself before he kills—seems some very reliable witnesses have provided descriptions of the killer, and they're all totally different: red hair with beard, blond with mustache, black hair with goatee.

"I'm taking it as a working hypothesis until disproved that it's the same man and he's dressing up in costumes for the occasions. So you tell me, how does this man surprise Blank with his disguised appearance and then get his victim to wait while he goes off in search of a murder weapon?" Dustin proposed. "Does he tell him he's attending a masquerade party later in the evening? Or better still, that he's just come from an audition for a part in a play? Nobody is going to stand around and wait while he goes to get a weapon to kill them."

Out of her bag, Nadine found a lipstick. She turned away from Dustin. There was a wall mirror above a small desk. She stood in front of it while she dabbed an extra touch of the vermilion, choosing the color to fit the hot mood she was in when she awakened. Carefully, she sealed her lips for an even application of the pigment.

Intentionally she took her time, giving her an extra few seconds to assimilate the strong evidence Dustin has found. She didn't want to overreact. She'd learned how easy it is to be misled by an "obvious" conclusion only to spend endless hours working toward what proved to be a dead end. But if there was something solid in what Dustin was proposing, then every step that followed had to be meticulously executed to eliminate the killer's vital defenses, take away his castles, rooks and bishops in preparation for the ultimate prize of checkmate.

"I remember a case a few years ago," she shared with her student while still looking at herself in the mirror, "when I made a really great discovery. I determined that all the supplies this killer was using came from a well-known hardware store. Furthermore, when I discussed the matter with the manufacturer of one of the items used by the killer, he assured me it had to come from that particular store because one of the items was a new product and they were test marketing it at that outlet only. So what I did was make a public announcement that the surveillance films from that store were being analyzed and would soon lead to an arrest—a complete fabrication."

"So what did the killer do? Did he give up?"

Nadine smiled. "Like I said, I leaked the story to the press. Instead of feeling the heat, as I had anticipated, the killer called me up and laughed in my face. It turned out he'd never stepped foot in the store. He had a neighbor whose garage was supplied abundantly with the products he needed for his work. This happened to include the test product the manufacturer confirmed for me had to have been bought at that store. I didn't find out about the neighbor until two months later, when the man owning the home down the block from the killer discovered the pilfering and reported it. By then three more co-eds were dead."

She turned to look Dustin in the eye, knowing that it would take him years to learn what came to her the hard way.

"Dustin, you measure your closeness to an arrest not by clues you amass but by your talent to use those clues to instill fear in the mind of your prey. He must come to dream of nothing more than to know you, understand you, and hate you. You must come to occupy his waking and sleeping mind by reminding him you're as relentless, tireless and heartless as he, and he must come to know you can smell the odor of his flesh, taste the sweat of his brow, hear his unmerciful call and see into his ravaged soul. You must for the finale be his most treasured victim. He has to come to fantasize tearing the flesh from your bones," she lectured in a style not dissimilar to Larry.

"Then his killing of the innocent will stop—then he will be yours. For when he comes to suffer the unimaginable, that he cannot intimidate you, cannot scare you, cannot call you off, cannot even find you—and if he could, would lack the courage to take you—then, and only then, will he make that fateful error, subconsciously with intent; or he may willfully, eagerly, with unbelievable obedience and docility, surrender to you, knowing his torment is over and in your hands he will find peace."

All written like a poem by Nadine in the diary material I devoured one evening putting together this chapter.

That quote makes it understandable why she checked her reaction to Dustin's work. She appreciated what he had done, even later applauded his invaluable accomplishment, but understood it for what it represented, not what she wished it would.

"So?" she said to him indifferently.

"So what?" Young Dustin was still confused by her tepid response.

"So did you start checking to see if there's any way to know who visited Congressman Blank before he was killed?"

"Don't start salivating. It's a small world here in Washington. People are linked in ways you would never imagine. It's all about money, of course. Blank's district is in Virginia, bordering D. C., as it happens. Blank was getting some steam from a few important constituents about the trading of sex slaves, your favorite subject.

"The congressman knew the activity in his district was the prime supplier of merchandise seeping into Washington for use by various dignitaries and, my Lord, even our own politicians. How he expected he was going to get relief from our boss I don't know, but Lambert was over the day before the congressman was killed."

Wow! rocketed repeatedly through Nadine's head. She was lovin', lovin' it. She patted her hands together and formed her face like a child ready to blow out seven birthday candles on a vanilla frosted cake with "HAPPY BIRTHDAY, NADINE" in yellow letters neatly printed around the perimeter.

Lambert, a wolf…in wolf's clothing?

"I love this job," she exclaimed.

23

A MASERATI-GUIDED TOUR OF WASHINGTON

Washington, D. C. Remove the politics from the city and what do you have, a capital city that is a rival to any in the world? That's what Larry expressed to Nadine after picking her up in his midnight black Maserati.

"I think what is by far the most remarkable fact about our capital is that millions and millions of Americans have never wandered to their own Mecca. Imagine all the places that we go for travel, but how often people miss D. C."

He revved the engine, treating Nadine to a never-before-experienced treat of feeling a racecar grip the road so tautly it could negotiate a turn at freeway speeds and never stammer. Larry wasn't showing off; it was the four wheels and the purring metal under the hood boasting of its miracle and might. To punctuate the over two hundred- thousand dollar vehicle's intoxicating influence, the finely engineered specimen let Larry accelerate off a signal and make a sharp right a few blocks ahead, leaving Nadine with her head twisting behind her looking for an abandoned heart lying in the road.

She laughed, dangerously tempting the wheelman to let the proud innards of the immaculate machine titillate her to higher levels of delight, unaware that Larry had not even shifted out of second gear. This time he had the good sense to yell, "Whoa, Trigger," louder than she might have called out, "Giddy-up, Buttermilk."

The experience was grander than Nadine's fantasies as a kid of what rides at a theme park would have been like. She felt carefree, young, and wild for as long as the ride in Larry's fancy machine lasted. When it was over, she couldn't deny a touch of sadness.

Nadine was raised in Virginia, just beyond the border with D. C., but she rarely visited the capital before working for The Department. Then, because she was so busy with her work, she rarely had time to explore the city. When Larry mentioned sightseeing, Nadine was all for it.

"What I find unique about this city," Larry began, "is that you can come once and see the known sights—the Capitol, Washington Monument, Lincoln Memorial, Arlington Cemetery—and think you've seen the city. But all you've done is looked at the outermost skin of a fruit, without cutting it open to examine the complex biology, smell the fragrance, feel the texture, or taste the sweetness from its soul.

"You have to walk purposelessly—aimlessly—and let the attractions reach out to greet you. From an unnamed building, from a cloistered garden or from an obscured street will come an unexpected marvel welcoming you to share with it a remote memory, a proud history or wistful fantasy. Even when you think you know it, you don't. I discover something new each and every time I wander about here. I'll never outgrow this place."

"I'm sold," Nadine clapped her hands.

"We're just about at our first destination," the tour guide informed Nadine.

"You're a trip, Larry," Nadine remarked whimsically. "Thank you, really. Being with you is the only time of my life I feel taken care of, when I can sit back and let it happen. For a control cadet like me...I'm scared to say it, but its good therapy."

"That's what I do best."

"You wouldn't want me as a patient, I promise. I would probably send you into retirement."

"Have you ever tried?"

"Not for me," Nadine guaranteed him. "I've pretty much completed my own self-examination. Anything I haven't addressed, I'm probably better off not knowing anyway."

"What you're saying is the doctor prescribing a dose of denial may be the perfect remedy for some patients?"

"I hope that's not against one of your codes, but I believe so."

"I believe it too," he conceded earnestly. "Some types or levels of awareness for some people can be disastrous."

Nadine swallowed, the sensation alerting her that her throat muscles were tightening. With that feeling came an awareness that a bead of sorrow had dropped like a tear from a higher emotional brain center. Larry, busy parking the car, didn't notice her sudden tension.

"Well, I'm waiting," she urged.

"You mean for the first sight on the tour?"

She nodded. Larry tossed the psych talk into the bushes like a candy wrapper.

"Ask a thousand people who just returned from a trip to Washington if they've ever seen the Einstein Monument and of the two who say they have one is a liar and the other ran out of hotel money, had to sleep on the street, and by chance wandered in to a grove of trees near Constitution Avenue and plopped down only to discover by light of day that he or she slept with a 7000 pound, twenty-one-foot-high statue of Albert. The man is waiting for us right over there."

Larry pointed and led Nadine through a patch of trees on the grounds of the National Academy of Sciences. The location startled Nadine. It wasn't what she was going to see, but what she recalled having seen just yards away from the monument.

"Larry, why did you bring me here?"

"It's one of my favorite spots in Washington. I haven't had a chance to come here for some time now."

"Right along this path, just about a hundred yards from where

I presume you're taking me, is where Percy Hume was killed a few weeks ago. Didn't you know that?"

"I…well, I forgot," he responded awkwardly.

"Odd we'd end up here."

"If you want to leave…"

She looked at him curiously for a moment before responding. "No, I don't run. It's not like I'm squeamish about going to a murder site. I do that all the time. Besides, believe it or not, I never actually had occasion to go inside and meet Einstein."

"It's about time then." Larry signaled for her to follow.

After the Einstein Monument, Larry walked Nadine across the street to the Korean War Veteran's Memorial. He grabbed her hand in his, discovering a satisfaction he preferred more than talking. She was wearing thin baby kid gloves, but upon his advance she removed them, allowing the warmth of their skin together to do the work of the material.

Finally, he stopped to look at her adoringly. "You must be hungry. I know I am."

"If food is the way to a man's heart, call me Nathan," Nadine joked.

"Have you ever been to Nathan's?"

"Yes, but I don't eat pastrami sandwiches," her words passed to Larry through giddy laughter.

"Then I have someplace else in mind."

Stanouscci Tratorria on 19th SW: two o'clock.

24

FORTUNE COOKIES

Chitchat through lunch for the young lovers: all that was left on the table was a shared custard canola—what little there was of it. Nadine had shoveled in a healthy fork load and Larry surreptitiously, but lovingly, glanced at her as she sated herself.

"I'm glad we could spend today together."

"Me too," Nadine smiled proudly as she gulped downs her final allocation of the creamy sweet.

"I'm sorry. Mostly I watch what I eat, but this is too good," said the health enthusiast not shy about taking a day off.

"You don't let yourself have a lot of the light, bubbly you, do you?"

"I'm usually not the light type."

"Then I assume you'll need lots of drives in the Maserati to awaken your inner child," Larry bantered, his curiosity heightening about this enigmatic figure who chose to taunt and chase the lowest elements of society without offering a clue as to why.

"Inner child? You're not going to be happy until you start my analysis, are you?"

"One moment," he announced, sensing in her voice an objection to the thought of being psychologically stripped naked. He decided to employ a strategy to dodge the issue, at least temporarily.

He was carrying a case with him. He reached inside. There was no analyst's tool. Instead he extracted a never-opened, saved-after-dinner-for-a-special-occasion-like-this fortune cookie; that's correct, he had it with him. It was still fresh because he dropped it in his bag some weeks before, after a lousy, boring evening dining at a Chinese restaurant. He was so irritated during dinner that he swore if they served the traditional cookie, he'd refuse the fortune. The reason for his consternation is telling.

Truth is, he loved fortune cookies and always looked forward to them after a Chinese restaurant meal. It was the only form of sooth-saying he allowed himself because he knew all news would be good news—the Chinese knew it would be bad for business to stuff bad omens into the crispy treats. Other than the guaranteed positive prophetic forecasts, he had no use for any mystical revelations about his future.

His objection to opening the cookie the evening he received it, was causal to the company of the thirty-year-old spoiled "shit" he acquiesced to take out. Muriel had orchestrated the evening, selling Larry on the girl by promoting her not only as the daughter of an influential industrialist but also letting him know that the young lady was an accomplished writer on her own behalf.

The daughter proved to be a moron in Larry's opinion, the author of a few trash novels published only because daddy happened to own the media empire controlling the prominent publishing company. As he would explain to Nadine, had he read beforehand even the first two pages of one of this woman's books (which he did later) he would have passed on meeting her; the only negative consequence being he wouldn't have had the cookie.

That evening when he had the date, he took his good fortune to-ken and furtively placed it in his pocket while paying the bill, later transferring it to the case where it might have been forever forgotten. But now, sitting with Nadine, sensing a collision in the making and determined to avoid it, the cookie came to mind. He opened it. Then he stood to read it.

The tiny print proclaimed in the manner of a courier of the king delivering an edict: BE HONEST WITH OTHERS AND THEY

WILL BE HONEST WITH YOU.

Nadine's mouth opened in incredulity.

"I don't believe a word of it either," Larry said, tossing the fortune on the table. "My life experience has taught me exactly the opposite. But there's no escaping it now; my fortune has been told. This leaves me with no option other than to…be honest. So here we go." He took a deep breath, deciding to put his guts on the line. "No analysis. I'm interested in *you*, Nadine. I'm *very* interested," he announced.

Nadine rewarded him with an appreciative look. "That's really nice. You know, it's easy to say but sometimes people would just as soon not get to know another person too intimately."

"I'm a big boy. I can handle it."

"I'm sure. But we're talking about me; you want to know about me, right? As you know, things happen in people's lives, things they have no control over."

"Nadine, you've alluded to 'things' before, but you hold back talking about them."

"Of course, I do. Some parts of a person's past are best not discussed. That doesn't mean they're bad. They may be things that are frightening to us, like patterns that will repeat regardless of how hard we try to resist them."

"But those things can be destructive if kept to oneself. And why live with fears that may never materialize?"

"Because they may. Dr. Monroe. I'm sorry to be the bearer of bad news but we can't all will, or even work, our lives into bliss. Because of what we have experienced, we believe certain patterns have a greater probability of reoccurring."

"Yes, you're right. We can't fix everything troublesome in us, can we?" Larry agreed.

"No. But you'll be pleased to know that I don't let mine interfere with my life."

"Maybe when we get to know each other better, you'll feel comfortable enough to talk about them with me."

"Larry, it's just a little madness," she said dismissively. "We all have a dose."

Larry was still holding the cookie. Broken in half, he handed one piece to Nadine. The fortune with the word, "HONESTY," was face up, still daring both of them.

"Larry, all the private stuff aside, thanks for telling me you're interested in me."

"I want to see a lot of you, Nadine," he responded like a brave warrior.

Larry might have noticed a tiny concentration of moisture forming in Nadine's right eye. That damn cookie might have infected her with the Honesty Bug too.

"If I have anything to say about it, you will."

Fortune cookies can work miracles.

Well, it was a nice way to end a date. Made me want to cuddle up by the fire and read and read and read...about love. Sorry, we do have a serial murderer on the loose. Don't expect Nadine to let amour interfere with getting her man.

25

FOUR TIMES FORTY-FIVE

I'VE READ BOOKS ABOUT the horrors of mid-life crises, but not for these four boys. President Haley, forty-five; Dr. Monroe, forty-five; Chief Lambert, forty-five; and you can add Dustin's dad, Phillip, to the esteemed forty-five year old club. Is there anything other than age in common for these fellows? Now is a good time to find out.

The sun is out, the air is warm, and the ground is dry.

Hurrah! Yippee! Zippidy-do-dah!

This pristine day signals to the rich, or famous, or whoever has their own tennis court in the back yard—which, of course, is only the rich or famous—that it's the first opportunity in months not only to see the surface of the court clear of snow, ice or rain, but to play on it.

Hurrah! Hurray! Yippee!

Serve and volley.

Mid-forties is for some a sterling era. If blessed with even a par set of genes and the will to condition the machine, the man is fit. He can still jog a few miles, play light basketball with his buddies, ski Alta and play on a company baseball team. But can he compete in these activities with his twenty-five year old son?

Let me qualify the question: Can he compete with him if the boy is a professional quality athlete? The answer is no. If dad is foolish enough to test his ability, he'll likely be coming to work the next day with a brace on his knee; and that's if he's lucky.

Dustin, in addition to possessing looks that some women seemed to be willing to drop dead over, was a remarkable athlete. His love was football, but he excelled at several sports, including tennis and volleyball. He starred on his high school football team at quarterback and was accepted at a major university on a scholarship to play ball: his father talked him out of it, and Dustin proclaims he doesn't regret it.

Different from most of the young kids who would give their heart and soul, and if requested kidney, liver and spleen, for the opportunity to be the next Tom Brady, Dustin could have more than any of them regardless, and without the cost that his father knew first-hand was greater for most of the players than the rewards received.

Phillip Drake owned a substantial interest in a professional football team and had on occasion been called to represent key athletes who misunderstood that all their fame and star power actually didn't exempt them from assault, domestic violence, and if you can imagine, even murder charges. While all of Drake's client athletes were innocent of the allegations, some were dense; those in that category failed to realize they would be playing the next two years of their contract for Mr. Drake's bill.

What Phillip had learned through his intimate involvement with professional sports, in particular football, was that all the guys who got off on crushing the bones of their opponents discovered ten, fifteen or twenty years later that their own chasses were forever, irreparably, mangled. These vibrant, powerful, pit bull masses experienced a gradual metamorphosis from unbreakable, to weak, to brittle and crumbled. That's without steroids.

Phillip presented the case to his son: "The reason you see so few of these Atlas figures years after they retire, is that half of them can't walk. They can't stand well. Some can't talk or think well either. I'll do anything to keep you from destroying yourself like that. Dustin, you name it."

Some kids would have told their dad to stick it where the sun can't shine. Others might have gone along with their parent, but blamed them forever. Not Dustin. He didn't seem to care much one-way or the other. Besides, he defined "anything" for his father, and made him deliver. Both father and son were appreciative of having struck a mutually beneficial agreement.

Still, without the pro pursuit, Dustin was in top physical form. So when the rays were bright enough to make the tennis court fit for duty it wasn't father versus son, it was father and longtime friend and associate, Russell Foster, against son.

Many people's patience gets tested watching an entire match of tennis, even if it's the finals of the U. S. Open. Fortunately, we can pick up the tail end of this slaughter; Dustin was about to drive these pathetic dreamers to an early afternoon cocktail.

The boy served a bullet to his father, who returned it. The rally seesawed back and forth for a total of five full revolutions before Dustin smashed a cross-court winner past the outstretched reach of his father. Dustin strode to the baseline, ready to serve again.

"Match point," he charmingly announced the bad news.

Father's mumbling was short of faith, short of breath, but long on hope.

"Just serve; we'll see."

Dustin did, defining an ace by striking a serve smack on the centerline. Saving Phillip from further disgrace, his friend came to the rescue.

"That's it for me, Phil."

Without protest, Phillip started to move off court, attempting to save a morsel of dignity. "I see you've been practicing."

Dustin shrugged. "I was lucky, that's all."

This was not the first time his son had to back off in an attempt to soothe a bruise on father's touchy ego, and it wouldn't be the last. Someday Dustin would likely be taking licks from a son as unmerciful as himself.

The threesome walked along a brick path for a long enough distance to suggest an estate of several acres, ending up by the pool adjacent to an outdoor patio, which in turn entered into a wood-paneled den.

They put down their rackets. Phillip went to the bar. He took three tumblers off the shelf and poured shots of scotch in each. They tapped their glasses and took a drink, Phillip downing in one gulp what he called the smoothest finish since Shoeless Joe Jackson threw the 1919 World Series. He poured himself a second.

Russell, who had known Dustin since infancy, teased. "So, Dustin, still drag racing?"

Dustin had not, nor had he ever been, a car racer. But he assumed his dad had apprised Russell of the little scene Nadine took care of on his behalf. Further he presumed, though he has no interest in affirming it, that neither his father nor Russell believed the story Nadine fashioned. His father bought it hoping it would be a last violation of their agreement.

"Yes, sir," Dustin answered, "but only on racetracks these days."

While this exchange was transpiring, Phillip was kneeling down near a large cabinet, pulling out what looked like several photo albums.

"Lambert's been treating you well?" Russell continued. He intentionally changed to a subject he knew first-hand, Lambert's incapability to treat anyone well unless a handsome reward was coming his way. He wasn't at all surprised by Dustin's answer.

"He's a jerk to everyone. For some reason, he keeps a distance from me."

"You can figure that one out for yourself, young man."

"I think I have, Mr. Foster. He certainly has a hard-on for my boss, Detective Street. I think she's top notch, but Lambert detests her."

"It's the 'she' thing. Lambert's never respected women. And if this lady you're referencing is good at what she does," Russell paused to humorously preview his upcoming statement, "he'll devote himself to ramming a rod through her front privates and using it to shove her out on her ass."

"No sign of the rod yet, but most definitely he's shoving," Dustin quickly confirmed. "The only problem is, he has his hands full. She's not a pushover. I've never seen her on her ass yet."

"He'll keep trying. That's his style," Phillip off-handedly chimed in while flipping through the albums. "He doesn't want to discredit her now because she's a valuable tool for him. He'll wait until he's mayor and then find a way to drag her through the mud and into very early retirement."

He chuckled, knowing the path to power is littered with the carcasses of nothing but decent, hard-working souls charbroiled by the indelicate class of which he is the quintessential master. He thumbed through the pages of one album in particular and halted on a picture. He looked over toward Russell first, and then Dustin.

"I don't think you've ever seen these, Dustin."

He closed the book and walked over to a table, placing the volume on the top. Dustin and Foster came over to join Phillip.

"What is it?" asked Dustin.

"Russell and I are taking charge of our twenty five year frat reunion; should be quite a scene. This is a fraternity album I kept."

They all leaned over as Phillip slowly turned the pages. The pictures were what you'd expect from a frat house: lots of booze, party scenes, and prime, feisty college girls—some even with their clothes on.

Russell and Phillip shared a few memories, apparently ones they wish they could revisit. Then Phillip halted on a page, motioning Dustin's attention to one specific picture.

"Stanley Ringer."

"You never mentioned him," Dustin said with curiosity as he viewed what looked like a child more than a college age young man.

"Maybe it's about time you tell him, Phil."

Phillip seemed disquieted, apprehensive. "Do you notice anything different about him?"

"Only that he looks young for his age," Dustin replied as he inspected the picture.

"That's the point; he looks the exact age he is. He was only fifteen when we were all nearing or at…nineteen?"

Phillip went on to explain that Ringer was a national treasure, a genius equal to Einstein. Drake's parents had taken a role supporting the boy and Phillip had taken him on as a little brother. He graduated college at fifteen, overdosing the following day.

Recounting the story, Phillip was notably shaken.

"That's why your dad to this day, regardless of circumstances, has refused to defend anyone he knows to be a drug dealer," Foster embellished.

"I'm sorry, dad. I never knew about the boy."

"None of us could believe it," Phillip mourned, taking another shot to steady his nerves.

"While we're on the topic of sin, I have to tell you that young girls are being imported from halfway around the world through Mexico to America and then owned by some of our most reputable leaders here in our country. Would you defend them?" Dustin genuinely posed to his father.

Foster stepped in to field the query. "We know what's going on. But I'll promise you, if it's discovered that those ladies are being drugged…"
"I promise you they're not ladies. And since we're on the topic of Lambert, you both should know he's intentionally keeping a lid on what service these *little girls* are performing."

Staring straight at his son Phillip responded. "There are certain evils nobody is ever going to cure, Dustin. You have to pick your wars. Your boss was wise to back out of this one."

The album was still out with Ringer's picture open. Phillip looked at it. Then after a few seconds, he patted the backside of Dustin's hand before turning the page. The subjects of Ringer and slave trade were left to fizzle out, but Dustin's youthful outrage was still choking on the somber reality his father spoke to.

The new picture exposed in the album caught Dustin's attention. "Wait. Let me see that," he called out as he reached to bring the photo closer.

He was looking at a picture of three college age men with their arms draped over one another's shoulders, posing in front of a mountain peak. They were wearing mountain climbing gear. Each had their hats off. They were squinting partially to shade the bright sunlight. While Dustin examined the picture, Phillip and Russell looked blankly at each other. Dustin broke the silence.

"They look familiar."

The two grown men smirked knowingly. Russell volunteered to fill in the details.

"They should. When your dad and I were at Yale…

26

YOU CAN RUN, BUT YOU CAN'T HIDE

"Zach, do you know what's coming?"

These were the first words out of her mouth.

Nadine would usually sit in a small wood frame chair while disclosing material relevant to the unfolding of her D. C. case. This day, she leaned back in a tan leather recliner, staring at the ceiling, talking more to her God than me.

"You don't think I came here to brag about meeting Presidents, to share amorous outings in Maserati race cars, or recount how my boss was the most despicable asshole in the world, do you?"

I said nothing. Nadine was somber. Her mood had changed from our last meeting. She had no problem explaining what was troubling her.

"I could have done a crappy job of writing the book myself, at least up to this point. It would have been good therapy," she shrugged. "That's not why I needed help."

"It was because you couldn't write, right?"

"Hell, I could write," she yelled, her eyes beginning to tear as she pulled the chair upright to look at me. "I couldn't live through it again," she admitted with notable mortification. "I was too cowardly, at least until I came here and settled in."

"We'll all be here to help you," I assured her.

"I know. But I've decided I'm going to give you the unedited, un-censored version no matter how it hurts. Zach, we've reached the point in the story where things turn ugly," she cautioned. "I have to prepare you, this isn't going to be pretty."

Nadine was wearing a gold choker necklace with a pendant. It was just long enough for her to pull the chain over her bottom jaw and nervously nibble on the key that otherwise would have dangled on her chest.

As she finished her admonition, we heard commotion coming from the front of the house. It took only a minute before the nature of the ruckus was revealed. There was a sharp rap on the door to my study, followed by a frantic plea. In a moment of panic, Josea had committed a rare act of subordination of reason to emotion. What she needed to disclose, she knew better than to do in the presence of Nadine, but it was too late.

"I've got to talk to you, Zach!" Josea panted. Preeti, with Sousche in her arms, was standing behind her. "Look. Look!" she screeched.

In her right hand, was a piece of ordinary stationary, in the left was a matching envelope. The single sheet of paper was not unusual to the normal eye. There was only one line typed across it, the words each in all capital letters. Josea handed it to me, shouting for me to read it out loud. I took the note, but before I could even process what it said, Nadine shrieked an even more horrifying exclamation.

She stood up and grabbed the piece out of my hand, indifferent to what it said. Holding it with her right arm outstretched, she exam-ined it carefully. Then her face froze in an unimaginably grotesque stare.

I noticed that the cut was uneven along the bottom. It was a slight defect that at the moment I subconsciously dismissed as irrelevant. Nadine let the note slip out of her hand like a terminal diagnosis.

"It's for me," she said resolutely. "God damn it! God damn it!!!"

I picked it up and glanced. I read it as Josea had instructed: YOU

CAN RUN, BUT YOU CAN'T HIDE.

I looked over at Nadine. Her facial flesh had dulled to a flat white color, the blood spontaneously sinking from her head. It seemed to pool in bright red blotching cloud-like patterns about the neck and chest. The veins running laterally along the sides of the neck tightened to render the appearance of rods holding the head in position. Her eyes retreated into the sockets.

Her pose was steely. That single piece of paper had alerted her that it was time to dress for a battle with known enemies of evil intent.

"It's me they're after, Josea. You can tell Reuben he was being used temporarily; he's out of danger," Nadine insisted.

"I don't know what you're talking about," Josea shouted. "I knew it was too good to be true. Eventually some asshole would…oh, fuck it all," she exhorted as she ran out of the room before giving a thought to what Nadine had said.

Preeti had run after Josea in an attempt to console her. I was left alone with Nadine. She sat down, this time in her more customary seat, inclining forward with her elbows on her knees and her head resting on the palms of her hands, contemplating what to do.

"Some people don't like blood on their conscience, but they love to kill," she began in a melancholy tone. "They think they can break the spirit, weaken a person's will to fight, and leave them split open like a shell so the nut inside is left exposed to rot."

She stood up and took her purse off the table where she had placed it when she arrived. She extracted a thick envelope she intentionally brought with her as evidence for the next portion of her story. She held it in her hand.

"I'm not trying to be dramatic, Zach. I sat down last night to outline the next sections of the novel." She handed me the material. "Take a look. What a bastard."

"Okay, let's say you're right and this is about you," I proposed before examining what she was giving me. "Why Reuben? Why is he being harassed when it has nothing to do with him?"

"Since questions are such a hot item here, let me ask you one," she hurled at me defiantly. "Why was Josea terrified when someone hassled Reuben while hiking? Then she *thinks* she's seen a car snooping in front of their home?"

I was being trapped by a master hunter and knew of only one survival strategy, shutting up. I tried to look bemused, but I could tell she knew something she wasn't ready to reveal to me. Worse, I was certain she was aware I was holding out on her, that we at Kuruk were all blood bound together like a cult, and it was all about nothing of importance to her or really anyone else, simply the past fame Reuben had jettisoned—still, the shame I felt was only exceeded by sadness that I had no choice but to keep her at arm's length from our truly benign secret.

"Don't answer," she acquiesced. "But I'll tell you this, Reuben is not Reuben."

Nadine walked out. If there was triumph in her parting words, it was measured equally by defeat and dejection. I had no idea what she did know. I doubted I would get an answer from reading the packet of written material she had just given to me. Still, I opened it and began devouring page after page. By that evening, I was churning out writing at a record setting pace—it would continue like that for days.

27

I THINK YOU ARE GOING TO MEET ME—GOD HELP YOU

It was Sunday morning. Nadine was in the mood for a jog. She slipped on her tennis shoes, proud of her self-discovered trick of standing on one foot while she puts the shoe on the opposite one, then pulling her knee to her chest so she could make the tie. She did the same for both sides, fancying this a good method to practice balance.

It was nippy that morning in D. C. She had prepared for a cold outing. Gazing out the window in her dining room, she took in a deep breath of air to appreciate its freshness. After she finished tying the second shoe, she headed for the front door. Her large black and dark brown German shepherd dog, Horace, had blocked it.

The dog was a story of his own. Actually, he was more than one story, and they were unique and heroic ones—the tales of Horace will have their day, but not this one. There was a far more urgent matter that had come up. Horace was not only napping on the floor of the entry area with his backside up against the door, he was lying so that he partially covered a vanilla-colored folded envelope.

Nadine motioned for the animal to move. Noticing the stray item she picked it up, assuming it was an advertisement for a new download service for movies or a plumber who was trying to break in to the good graces of the owners.

With no more intent than to throw it on the floor after she opened it and trash it when she returned, she extracted the single sheet of matching paper folded neatly inside. This single typewritten letter read in all caps:

I THINK YOU ARE GOING TO MEET ME—GOD HELP YOU.

Her immediate thought was how on earth would the killer find out where she lived? Was she followed? She was always mindful of cars behind her that might be intentionally trailing her. Perhaps there was a leak at the office? Any secretary or clerk, someone in payroll or personnel, could have messed up and inadvertently given out privileged information. Could there have been a breach in the department computer system? There's never been a digital network that at some level couldn't be compromised.

Then she recalled the two events the other evening in the parking area and hallway of her building. Did she actually have occasion to stare into the eyes of the killer? Was it daring bravado on his part by testing Nadine for timidity, inadequacy or impulsiveness?

She thought back to the evening with Dustin, when Crow was killed—the movement in the open woods, the eyes she sensed was human and intently honing in on her? She couldn't dismiss all of this as coincidence. On the contrary, with the note she was staring at she had to assume that the investigator was now being investigated, that the hunter was also the hunted.

She rereads the message.

"God help you."

The words said "bully" to her.

He's threatening, wants to scare me. He thinks I'm a cowardly woman. Why else would he say that? If I were a man, he'd never have sent the same message. Warning me I'm going to meet him. That means he's probably already met me, and if not he knows he can any time he wants. But what's important to him is that I meet him. Still, he's indecisive and tentative about it because he phrases it he 'thinks' I'm going to meet him.

Then she altered the course of her thoughts. She was approaching the killer as if he was one of the common crazies she had been used to going after. He wasn't. It was probable that he came closer to what Larry had described, a deliberate killer with a rational objective who had an assignment to complete.

But if that were the case, what does he care about me? Unless, just unless, he does follow the progression Larry described whereby he comes at some juncture to love his new craft. Then he'd more and more assume the typical patterns and attributes of a rank-and-file maniac," she reasoned. *In essence, he'd be inclined to start behaving like every other deviant I've had to stop. Then again, he may simply not want anyone interfering with his work; he fears I may be the one to ruin the party.*

With her mind cluttered, moving back and forth, side to side, unable to settle one way or the other, and knowing from experience that the best way to filter out the juice from the pulp when confused was to drop the whole deliberation game, she decided to cease fire, go back to her original plan, get out for a run, try to relax and let the situation unfold to a logical conclusion on its own.

She took a last look at the note before putting it down. That's when she noticed that the paper was not an unusual color, it was off white, but what stood out was that the bottom had been cut ever so slightly shorter at the left side so that rather than a perfect rectangle, its shape barely revealed itself as a trapezoid. *Odd*, she thought.

She opened the door and made her way to the street. First, she walked down the block a short distance to warm up and then broke into a run. It was safe; there were lots of people out and she enjoyed a nice thirty minutes of exercise. As she approached her home turf, she slowed her pace for a cool-down walk. Her building came into view and she noticed a man sitting on the front steps.

Too far away to make out details of the figure, she casually moved closer. As she did, the man looked up, offering a full view of his olive skin and thick, dark hair; it was Dustin. He stood and greeted her with a smile.

"No girlfriends to keep you in bed this Sunday morning?" she lightly addressed him, offering him no clue that she was on high alert.

"Nope. Ever since I met you, I'm a new man."

"I presume you have something for me." She paused just long enough to reward him with a grin. "Why else would you be up before noon on a Sunday?"

"Y E S...I...D O...have something for you. I'm on a roll...big, big!"

A peculiar transformation abruptly creased his forehead, his eyes scrunched, and a frown jumped onto his face. "Nadine, if this goes where I think it could be headed, I'm excusing myself from the investigation. You can tell my dad, do whatever you want."

"Come in. We'll talk."

She led him to her unit, motioning for Dustin to take a seat on the couch. She pulled up a chair across from him. Dustin's usual bubbly tone was absent as he proceeded.

"I have something I think is pretty curious." Dustin produced the picture his father shared with him, handing it to Nadine to look at while he talked. "The three young mountain climbers you're looking at, know who they are?"

Nadine pulled the snapshot closer for a better examination. Her face grimaced with a faint recognition, followed by a stomach-gnawing sign of pain. It had been a tense morning already, and now she was looking at a picture that she knew was going to make it a tenser afternoon.

"In case you don't recognize all of them, I'll do the credits," Dustin offered. "From left to right, the future president, Howard Haley, our Chief Lambert, and Dr. Lawrence Monroe. I don't know if you know the last one? I checked him out with my dad. He's the president's best friend, since they were kids. He's also a world-respected psychiatrist. The picture was taken in 1979. They were young men on a trip together."

Larry lied to her regarding his association with Lambert. His dishonesty sucker punched her. She waited to catch a breath. Before the needed oxygen arrived, she was contemplating her plan for the rest of her day.

On a small end table to the side of the couch, was an envelope with several other pictures. She reached to pick them up and thumbed through the stack, deliberately pulling out two photos. One picture showed General Crow's head, the point of impact blown up. The other was of an atypical hammer. She tossed both over to Dustin.

"Forensics is still completing their examination of Crow's wound," Nadine reminded him. "Remember I said it looked like some sort of hammer that impaled Crow's head? Well, I went shopping. When I took this type of weapon down to the crime lab, they were convinced it was a perfect fit."

She reached to highlight the hammer with her right index finger. "It's a common mountain climber's hammer. They don't sell them in high volume. I had to buy this one at a specialty shop. Nobody would own one unless climbing was their hobby."

Dustin nodded he understood the point. "Nadine, there's something eerie here. I don't like it."

"We don't get to pick our killers. Let's not be rooting for this to turn out a certain way. And remember, a fact is only a fact after it's been determined it can't be anything else. There are lots of possibilities here and we have work to prove ourselves wrong about all of them."

During she short speech to Dustin, Nadine was staring mistily at the table where the vanilla-shaded note sat face up. But it wasn't the letter that was eliciting her attention. She had been summoned by a conversation she had on the phone with Larry after their date.

He called to discuss with her the packet of papers he gave her when he left her at her house. Among other materials, there was a concise but well-reasoned treatise. He had revised it from his initial assessment. He was now suggesting that there was a strong possibility that the killer had already had a tendency toward psychosis before the spree was initiated. He then postulated that it was the new occupation of murderer that brought the madness to full fruition. It was further incorporated into Larry's new formulation that "we" may be dealing with a multiple personality, one that likely had a very recent birth.

At first, she approached his theory with skepticism, much as she would any unfounded assumption. Then, as she followed his reflections and line of reasoning as he had outlined them for her, it began to make more sense. It was basically the same theme he had proposed earlier, except that instead of the killer discovering a new vocation through repeated acts of killing initiated as part of an organized scheme, it was a "functionally normal" gentleman who never could have been capable of doing what was assigned to him unless rallied by this previous unknown, undiscovered, unimaginable separate character within him.

Larry envisioned the personality of a deranged creature willing and able to do everything this regular guy could never have conceived. In other words, the killer personality would borrow temporarily the convenient body of the host solely for the completion of the tasks, and then return it with no wear or tear.

Nadine was far from settled on the concept. It was too...hokey, even synthetic, sensational and dramatic. But that was before Dustin arrived with the picture of Larry with Lambert, a revelation begging for her to add Monroe to the suspect list.

Now, her reluctance to accept his theory had morphed into distress over having been misled. She was troubled not only because this was Larry—a man she wanted to love—possibly intentionally formulating a fiction, but also because she detested a truth stretched, let alone a flat out deceit.

But why would he do it? The question repeated as if it were a lyrical line stuck in the groove on an old phonograph record: for what conceivable reason would he seek her out under the pretense of helping her and then attempt to lead her astray?

She had presented Larry's theory about the killer to Dustin only a few days earlier. Now she wanted his opinion—she had intentionally withheld from Dustin where the premise came from.

"I mentioned to you a potential supposition about the murders," she said at last. "What did you think about it?"

Dustin was flattered she had sought out his thoughts. Long before arriving at her home, he had prepared his answer. "Conjectural nonsense," he responded dismissively. "Good theme for a Hollywood script," he added flippantly.

"The way things are progressing we have a dandy of a film here, don't we?"

"I can't consider this theory you mentioned reasonable for a real murder investigation," Dustin continued. "This guy is calculating and exacting,"

"Yes, just what I thought. He has his wits about him all the time."

"And he's not going to take a chance that at any random instant, he's going to be called to the sideline and told the backup quarterback—some unpredictable personality within his being—is coming in for the next set of downs." Dustin took off his Rolex from the right wrist and playfully swung it several rotations around the left index finger.

Nadine paused before sharing further thoughts. "Along the same line of reasoning as you, what I was thinking was that if an individual had two personalities and one was a killer, there would be a risk that at any time something could happen and the master personality had to take over. I mean, what if something life threatening occurred while in the process of a murder and the killer panicked and quit, leaving the proprietor personality scary-assed and holding the bag?

"From what I studied of this human psychological phenomenon—multiple personality—the various personalities are prone to be somewhat fluid. They are discreet and separate, but the human owning them experiences them flowing from one to the other. The probability of what I'm describing taking place during a stressful event, a shift out of the killer personality, would be very high, and probably would have happened by now if the premise of a multiple personality were accurate."

"What we're both saying is that the whole thing is far-fetched and we're better off allocating our resources elsewhere." Dustin deduced.

"I believe so. But Mr. Investigator, since you're doing so splendidly on your own, I'll pose one more question to you. If someone were to propose this wild scenario about multiple personality as an investigative hypothesis, given its unlikelihood, why do you think they would do so?"

Dustin shrugged, uncertain what the answer might be. "Maybe as a diversion, to lead the investigation on a wild goose chase," he added as an afterthought.

Nadine responded with a grimace. She concurred. Dustin heard her mumbling one word: "Precisely."

Nadine was leaning forward from a seated position to stretch her legs. As she exerted herself, her demeanor turned gritty. Dustin, in the meantime, took the discussion a step further.

"Nadine, this multiple personality thing is way out. But do you think it may have worth in terms of alerting us to the possibility that we're looking for a team? That would make sense to me."

The picture of Haley, Monroe and Lambert as young men was on the coffee table between them. She picked it up, tapped it several times with the index finger of her right hand before holding it out for Dustin.

"That's a team."

A team? In reviewing the notes that Nadine provided for me after she and Dustin evaluated Monroe's advice, I found the following passages.

This whole line of reasoning about a team…I wouldn't even categorize it as reason—it's surreal. Presidents have people killed. At times law enforcement is corrupt. Police chiefs can be dirty. Psychiatrists can be crazy, demented killers.

What reduces the whole concept of these three working in harmonious partnership to near impossibility is that there has to be too high a likelihood that one of them will get scared or have an unanticipated dose of conscience. There are too many details to coordinate and too great a chance of making mistakes. Plus, the probability of one of the three betraying the trust is too great…too many people, too many people and too many people…

I can't recall any more than pairs of serial killers, and those are rare. More on the improbable side of the equation: these are three men who are very successful, very influential and very intelligent. None of them will take a chance on losing it all. The necessity of intimate involvement with others to accomplish these murders raises the prospect of failure so high that it would require the agreement of bumbling fools rather than men of this caliber.

On the morning of Dustin's visit, she recalled gripping down with the upper molars on the right side of her mouth hard enough to pierce the skin. The assault was triggered by her thoughts at the moment, ones she free-associated to me.

"Larry lied to me, absolutely. I distinctly asked him if he knew Lambert. There is no doubt about it. He said he knew *of* him' but didn't *know* him. I'm certain that's what he said. It was indisputably a brass ball lie. I'm one hundred percent sure. He had a reason for the deceit and I was going to get to the bottom of it." She showed no humor before continuing with her next statement. "I felt like taking my milquetoast Ford Fusion and running Larry—in his Maserati— off a cliff."

I chuckled but it didn't distract her from ranting.

"This multiple personality business…what kind of amateurish, idiotic profiling was that from a so-called expert? Did he think I'd go ga-ga over it because it seemed esoteric, out of the box, or some sort of innovative professional dialectics? What he was proposing was a ghost of a chance, a million-to-one formulation, and he was peddling it to me for my case?"

I couldn't blame her for letting off steam. When she calmed herself down, she admitted that after Dustin left, she went down on her knees to pray. She professed moderateness in her religion practice. Yet there was Larry, bringing her down in front of The Almighty, begging Him or Her to just make it all go away, make Larry innocent of any wrong for which she imagined he could be guilty.

Would her prayer be answered? We'll have to take a trip to the park to find out. Nadine was there. Larry was there. Horace was there. Nadine was about to be baptized.

28

HAIR HIDDEN UNDER CAP; NOT A GOOD SIGN

AFTER DUSTIN DROPPED BY with the picture, Nadine never divulged a detail to him about her dilemma with Larry. She thanked him for his diligence and then sent him away. In an instant, she was on the phone with Larry.

He was nearly ecstatic when she said she wanted to meet with him that afternoon. His day couldn't have started better; eggs Benedict, toasted English muffin, roasted potatoes and coffee stowed away on magical dishes that floated airily into his bedroom and landed right next to him on a tray. Katherine—that's his housekeeper—didn't forget butter and jelly, cream and sugar, and…real silver.

Nadine approached him so smoothly, that he couldn't detect a molecule of derision or consternation in her voice. That was her method, not giving away her hand by pricking with a pin when she knew she fully intended to impale with a cleaver.

She set the terms of the get-together. She wanted it on her territory.

If he had known her better, the moment he set eyes on her he would have turned tail and off for Siberia. Yeah, her hair was up under a cap…not a good sign.

There's a park not far from her house. She instructed him where to meet her: "A short walk north from the children's playground and sand box there's a large grassy open area with a perimeter of beautiful trees—you can't miss it." Since Horace needed a run, she took him along.

Nadine unleashed Horace, watching as her friend successfully made his way into the crotch of a female Golden Retriever. Larry, from quite a distance away, spotted Nadine. He waved excitedly and then hastened his strolling pace into a canter. To his surprise, only Horace greeted him as he came closer. Larry petted the dog perfunctorily while tilting his head upward to Nadine, encountering an incomprehensibly icy glare. He had no reference point for even wondering if she was mad at him so rather than confront her mood, he shifted his attention to Horace.

"What's his name?" No response. "Okay, you look upset. What is it?" he inquired, lured in by her unapproachable posture. "I'm not aware of anything I've done wrong, but I apologize if I offended you."

Harpoon, dart, javelin, machete; stone, bola, brick, tomahawk, spear, blade, baton; billy club, blackjack, brass knuckle, bicycle chain, two-by-four; bullet, buckshot, rocket, intercontinental ballistic missile, bazooka, spit, snot, sweat; all systems ready to fire. *To hell with rooting for outcomes,* Nadine muttered imperceptibly. Poor Larry.

"You're not aware?! You're a famous doctor! Didn't it ever come up in your self-analysis to be conscious of when you lie to another person?" she said with no intent to hide her asperity. "I was under the impression, falsely I guess, that people in your field, especially ones of your esteem, were a little more together than—"

"I'm sorry. But can we back up for a second?" he pled, still with no clue what she was fretting over. "What are you worked up about?"

"Goddamn it, don't play innocent with me," Nadine shouted, taking full advantage of a situation where she felt justified to let off steam. "You said you didn't know Lambert, didn't you…didn't you?! You don't need to answer. I'm not interested in hearing another barefaced lie. You were best fuckin' friends with him!"

The outburst was actually healthy, in that it helped her to restore emotional order. Larry, surprisingly, was tolerant and cooperative. Even more astonishing, he wasn't the least rattled, defensive or deterred—just bewildered.

"Okay, I don't know how this came to your attention," he said in a quiet, measured voice, "but I assume now I should be watching my rear. You've popped me up to number one on your list of suspects, right?"

Nadine sensed her level of indignation feverishly rising, but she let him continue.

"Lambert is an opportunistic, greedy bastard, which I'm sure is not breaking news to you. I'm embarrassed...I mean ashamed...to let people know that in my youth I had the flawed judgment to have befriended him. We all make mistakes growing up; we learn from them, and that should be my worst one. If you want to hold it against me, go ahead."

That was not what Nadine expected. In fact, it confused her at first and then maddened her even more than what she was initially. She hated being wrong. She turned around and walked off in a huff.

Larry took off after her, quickening his steps to catch up to her.

"That's wonderful," she glared.

"It's true I knew him. I didn't see any importance to highlighting my past relationship with him when it came up."

"And multiple personality?" she jeered. "What's the excuse there?"

With a "take-this" and "huh!" glare aimed at his face, she quickened her pace. But she went only a few feet before Larry's hand reached her arm and tried to pull her to a halt. The abrupt gesture won Larry no support from Horace. He declared his outrage with a growl and a mouthful of mean teeth. Larry didn't notice the dog, but he shook his head at Nadine in a signal of futility. Still, he didn't give up.

"You're right, Nadine. I've got to come clean. When—"

"Now we're getting somewhere." Nadine's voice chopping off his attempted explanation. "If you can't be honest beginning a relationship…I've been down this road too many times and I don't like where it goes."

"Nadine, just wait…please, just for a minute to hear me out. When I contacted Chauncy, I never had the opportunity to tell him why I wanted to meet you."

"You're just a nice guy who wants to help, right?" she spit at him with irrepressible sarcasm.

"I wish."

"This had better be good."

"Nadine, it's not good," he said in a tone suggesting fear.

"I believe I'm on the killer's list."

"You're going to have to do better than that."

"I'll do a lot—"

Larry's head jerked. His left hand instinctively reached upward to the side of his face. From out of nowhere came a softball. He was able to snatch it as it was about to whiz past him, within inches of his ear. Nadine stared in amazement as Larry's oversized hand grasped the ball. He winced from the contact. A small boy, unaware of the near mishap, ran over to Larry.

"I like my head the way it is," he quipped as he handed the ball to the boy.

The boy laughed. Then he took his baseball mitt and tapped Larry on the arm. "Good catch. Want to play?"

"Not a good time, but thanks for the offer." Larry turned back to Nadine as the impressed boy ran off. "I want to tell you everything. It's about my relationship with Howard. All the victims are his confidantes, friends or enemies. I'm not important like these people, but somebody responsible for this may see it differently."

Horace, now tethered, distracted Nadine momentarily, tugging on his leash toward where several children were playing. Nadine pulled lightly against the thrust of the dog, getting him to ease the tension.

Then she rotated to the canine's front, giving a hand signal for him to sit. He obeyed immediately.

"Go on with what you were saying."

"I thought if I could help you resolve the case, then I'd save myself at the same time."

"Why mislead me if you want me to help you?"

"Nadine, the moment I met you I knew I'd fall in love with you. If I'm right and the killer wants to harm me then he already knows about us…and your investigation." To be sure she fully understood that the situation was perilous, he paused before proceeding with the obvious: "He'll kill you too."

What Nadine took from this was that Larry was afraid, more for himself than Nadine. Her lover was a confident man, but murder was not his game. Nadine had seen murder, witnessed the consequences it has on the living, had transcended the terror that cripples most from acting when evil must be challenged.

She knew that Larry was out of his element; his fragility aroused a maternal compassion that had a settling effect on her. She took out of her purse the note she found inside her apartment and handed it to him. She waited for him to scan the few words.

While he read she wanted to observe the movement of his chest, the lines on his neck, the firmness of his mandible and creases of his eyes. If by some remote chance he'd seen it she wanted to know, needed to know, and was confident she would know.

She saw nothing resembling recognition on Larry's part. But the exercise clarified in her mind the challenge she now faced with him, that they might both become victims.

Larry handed the note back to her, covering his fear by expressing concern for Nadine's safety. "You're too close to this."

"My work is about getting too close."

Larry reached for her hands, holding them between his own.

"Don't lie to me again," she warned him, with tenderness as well as resoluteness.

Nadine was emphatic, sun-rises-in-the-east-and-sets-in-the-west certain before she left for the park to meet Larry, that this would be the end of their relationship. But he had answers that rang true to her.

Maybe she had lost all reason, her mind had been scrambled by emotion and she had been proven to be better-be-certain-a-fact-can't-be-anything-else-before-its-actually-a-fact wrong. That may be what falling in love is all about.

After completing this portion of the story, Nadine briskly pulled out a couple more pages she'd written from her briefcase.

"Are you interested in hearing the *Story of Horace* as I later told it to Larry?" she posed hurriedly.

"Is it relevant?"

"It is to me. You'll see why later."

With her encouragement, I agreed. Nadine explained to me that many hours of dedication and hard work went into the simple exchanges between she and Horace—she had every right to be proud of her success with her lanky companion.

THE STORY OF HORACE

Once upon a time there was a young lady all by herself with nobody to love. She wanted no more than to have someone to dote over, to speak kind and gentle thoughts to without being perceived as too needy, insecure or inadequate, to touch tenderly and lie with so as to feel their warmth and softness, to take along on errands, to feel safe with, to buy for them anything they wished or imagined with nothing expected in return other than loyalty, to hang out together watching a movie or listening to music.

One day while with a friend, our little lady wistfully voiced her longing. The friend promptly proposed an easy fix. "Why don't you get a dog?"

To most people, there would have been nothing extraordinary or

*surprising about the suggestion. But this girl was not like most peo-
ple. She never had a dog, or any other pet growing up. Such things
were never an option for her because there was hardly enough money in the family for the human members to eat.*

*But as a young adult, this girl had found success and could com-
fortably afford the luxury of a second mouth to feed. She praised
her friend's advice and went to the local animal shelter where she
instantly fell in love with a little puppy. She was told it was a German shepherd and was sure to grow into a large pet. That made no
difference to her, once she sensed she had found the most wonderful
dog in the entire world, one she knew she would have the most special bond with of any creature in her life. She took him home that
hour.*

*Parenthood progressed well. Dog and master became insepara-
ble buddies. But after a few months, as the pup grew and the time
for training arrived, she noticed a queer phenomenon. Horace, the
name she'd selected to pay homage to an uncle who had showed
kindness to her during a difficult time in her childhood, but who
was killed in combat, refused to respond when she called him.*

*He was sweet as maple syrup, but he'd stare dumbly as she in-
structed from manuals written by the great masters of dog training
such as Cesar Millan, James Silva, Dog Whisperer, Barbara Wood-
house; none of these canine gurus seemed to impress Horace. Nor
did it influence him when she'd lose patience and resort to pejora-
tives, calling him stupid, stubborn and retarded.*

*Then one day while lying on the couch, feeling as alone as before
she'd adopted Horace, and fearing an impenetrable wall between
them, she motioned with her hand for him to come to her. He got
up and raced to her side, laying his head on her lap—he was eager
to resume a courtship he never wished to interrupt.*

*Then a light started flashing in her head, yellow and slow at first,
then solid green: Horace could be deaf. She took him to the veteri-
narian for consultation.*

After a simple series of office procedures by the doctor, her suspicion was validated. While she seemed relieved to discover the problem, the doctor must have sensed she had despaired trying to train Horace. He was a kind man and took the time to comfort her with his own story of dog ignorance. It proved to be good medicine. With no gulf too large to cross for a dog and master, in moments the two were as close as the day they'd met. Mommy invested in a new set of books to research, and young son had a new set of lessons to practice.

Actually, what she did was study human sign language. She was able to take principles and apply them to her dog. It worked brilliantly. Now when Nadine signed for Horace to sit, wait, run, jump, retrieve or stand on his hind legs only, he did it. He had even developed language. Yes, Horace, the best-dog-ever-born-in-the-entire-world had acquired proficiency using several sounds all conveying needs such as feed me or else I won't stop bugging you, I'm going to shit on the carpet if you don't take me for a walk, would you mind getting me one of those doggie bone treats you keep in the cupboard or I'm going to kill that Larry guy if he puts another hand on you.

This was an animal that would prove to be a brave and fearless friend; there would be more stories of Horace heroics.

29

NEVER A DULL MOMENT

I WAS CONVINCED AFTER being apprised of the irregular cut of the paper used for the note delivered to Nadine at her home in D. C. that the ominous message left for Reuben had come from the same source. Was it from the same person, presumably the killer? I pondered the point but had no answer, and Nadine would give no clue. Nevertheless, it was unimaginable that these two events could be explained by coincidence.

Overall, the unanswered questions were piling up faster than I could intelligently contemplate them. Looming most troublesome was the possibility that the devilish person or persons indirectly trying to intimidate Nadine were at the same time privy to information about Reuben's personal history and trying to cruelly take advantage—like a two-for-one deal.

Yet nobody had contacted Reuben—as we would have expected if he were to be blackmailed—to discuss a price for keeping his secret, one that was not sordid, illegal or corrupt, instead simply a desire to remain incognito.

While all this unsettling material was lingering over Kuruk, the restaurant was operating with the throttle fully opened. In fact, the FBI agent, Gabe Kershaw, who had handled the investigation into the murders on the reservation some time prior, had followed up on his plan to leave The Agency to open an identical Kuruk with his brother in fancy Beverly Hills. It was a franchise deal that I never conceived, nor that my wife and I would be receiving monthly checks based on the success of the second Kuruk.

Periodically, Kershaw would come visit. He didn't have to but I think he loved Mescalero and used business as an excuse for his trips. In fact, I was working at Kuruk one afternoon waiting for him to arrive. Reuben was in his office, planning a few new menu items, when we heard the front door loudly slammed. We both rose at the same time to investigate. It was Josea. She was breathless, hardly able to talk.

"What's wrong?" Reuben said, running over to hold his distraught wife.

"Someone tried to kill me," she responded in disbelief. "I was in the car on the highway coming back from Ruidoso and this huge white SUV crawled up my ass within a couple feet, laying on the horn. I thought he wanted me to move over and I started to, but he kept after me no matter which way I went or how fast I drove. Then he pulled up beside me and started swerving intentionally, just enough to force me to the shoulder," she related anxiously. "He finished me off by slipping me the bone, smiling at me, and gunning his car like a bandit—his license was missing."

Josea was shaking.

"Josea, it makes no sense," Reuben challenged. "If they're after me and thought it was me in the car, what good am I at the bottom of a cliff—you can't shakedown a dead man."

"He knew it wasn't you. I'm only telling you he saw me plain as day and tried to kill me," Josea repeated.

"Reuben, what if we're wrong? What if all this has nothing to do with your past?" I whispered.

"Then what could it be?" he grimaced. "Josea has done nothing that might attract the attention of a sadistic, twisted monster like this man seems to be. Zach, I don't care what it costs. I want round the clock protection for Josea. I want someone damn good to find out what is going on. This stops now," Reuben declared.

Josea and I looked each other. In spite of her hassled state, she couldn't resist sharing a laugh with me, both of us imagining the same image. It was a slovenly dressed man in his sixties with long stringy grey hair diving off his scalp like aimlessly drifting vagabonds. He was a tobacco chewing, spittoon spiting smelly fellow smacking a pinball machine like his blubbered-rump lover.

P. A. Farley, Investigator, his door read. The man swore there was nothing he couldn't find out for a price. Farley had helped me with projects in the past, including exposing corruption of tribal funding.

"P. A. Farley," Josea and I called out simultaneously with a chuckle, the thought of him momentarily distracting Josea's fear.

Reuben was in no mood for comedy. "When can we see him?"

"Probably as soon as we want, hun," Josea responded.

"Why don't you call him and we'll go in the morning. In the meantime, stay here through dinner and I'll take you home," Reuben insisted.

Josea and Reuben went into the kitchen area. That's when Kershaw walked in. I noticed he still refused to give up his Stetson, the hat hugging his head like a mommy's embrace—he could bob, bend, fling, flip, flop, twist or twirl his head and never shake off the handsome endearment. The hat defined Kershaw. It was made of felt and was tan in color with a thin black silk band. The crown was rounded and rose precipitously above the wide flat brim, earning for the wearer an air of confidence and pride.

Kershaw sat down and as he always did, taking off the fine head covering and tossing it on the seat next to him. His hair was thick and dense, cut fairly short, retaining its shape without combing. There was no "ex" in his manner of speech, still retaining the authority of an FBI agent. But he was kindly and had a good sense of humor, and I liked him way over and above the fact that he kept bringing us royalty payments.

In fact, the first thing he did upon greeting me was smile as he pulled out an envelope and put it in my hand. I started to place it in my pocket but he halted me by holding my arm. "Aren't you going to look?" When I did I was shocked to find it doubled the last one. "What are you doing, running a brothel?"

"Nope. We're making money," he boasted. "New York here we come. Then we're going to kick Chicago in the ass with the best spot in town. After that…San Fran sound good?"

"I'd retire if I didn't have so many people depending on work here," I quipped. "By the way, we have room if you're staying tonight."

"Thanks, partner, but I'm already set at The Inn of The Mountain Gods."

"You fixing to lose some of that profit at the tables?" I poorly mimicked his subtle southern drawl. (The Inn was a hotel and gambling casino on the reservation.)

"Don't gamble. I just want a decent place to eat," he kidded. "By the way, how's Preeti doing with the pregnancy?"

"Nice of you to ask. Real good," I assured him. "But we have some major problems here. It seems like we can't get a break."

I proceeded to share with an ex-agent who had become a friend as well as business partner the tales of Reuben and Josea, and Nadine's purpose for coming to Kuruk. When I finished, I noticed I had added a consideration I hadn't consciously addressed up to that moment.

"Could it have something to do with Josea and her history with the Israeli affair?" I posed to him. "Could there be some angle she couldn't have imagined?"

"If you're asking me for a favor, you got it. I still have some damn good buddies at The Agency," he hinted. "Want me to see if they're aware of any activity regarding your friend?"

"If it wouldn't be too much trouble, yes I would," I answered resolutely.

"Can't promise we'll get an answer but at worst we can eliminate a possibility. To tell you the truth, I recall lots of operations I participated in or supervised where we scared the shit out of someone for no reason other than to let them know we were there watching them."

"If that's it she's scared, but trouble is she has no clue about what."

"Subversives. Gotta take 'em down before they multiply," he said flatly. "From what you tell me about her history, who knows what that girl knows and what she might do with it."

Later Josea came out of the kitchen and I introduced her to Kershaw. She sat down. During the conversation, I caught him several times probing her, unsuccessfully. If Josea was harboring secrets that might lead to the overthrow of the U. S. Government, there was no indication of it. She had definite political beliefs but she was a patriot as much as a devout Jew.

I listened to her free-associate many times (in front of Kershaw on this occasion) on the price paid by our forefathers to erect institutions of iron-reinforced concrete devoted to the protection of human freedom and decency. It was her opinion that no asset could ever compete in value with the foundations our country had sunk into the heart and soul of her citizens.

People from around the world would never cease to seek asylum in our land solely because we symbolized the highest regard for mankind. Likewise, wealth and capital would flow in the currents of our seas and then land on our shores because we represented the last bastion of safety and security for mankind's property —if people trusted our institutions and system of democracy, then they'd place their assets in America.

As he listened to her, Kershaw might have been wondering why her country would want to harm or threaten her. Then again, this was a man trained to look at deeds first and words...never. A man or woman was weighed by what they did, discounted by what they said. He didn't know Josea, but I did—her words were as sure as babies burping.

The following morning, I went to see Farley with Josea and Reuben. He listened to the story, a crease in his upper brow I hadn't witnessed in previous encounters with him alarming me that this was serious. What tipped him I had no idea, but his comment was shocking to all of us.

"That's government agency type behavior," young lady. "They've branded their own style. My guess, you've crossed the wrong person." Farley was sworn by oath of his profession to keep confidential information about his client's secret. He was aware of Josea's role in the crisis that unfolded in Israel—he didn't have a clue about Reuben's past history. "My hunch is it's not about overseas activities. No. This is domestic. There's knowledge you possess that is dangerous—but it could be what you attained over there."

"There were several projects I managed that left me with sensitive information," Josea admitted, "but I've never violated the trust. There are things I've never told my husband, Zach, or my family. It's not their business. Why should I burden them with knowledge that might pain them?"

"There you go," Farley swaggered. "Answered your own question."

"What?"

"It's not what you *will* do with the knowledge. It's what they believe you *could* do with it that matters," Farley surmised.

"If that proves to be the case, then what do I do? Can I set up a meeting with the Defense Department and assure them I'm not meeting with Chinese or Russian representatives?" Josea questioned.

"Let's see what we find first," Farley drooled out before launching a full wad of saliva bulls-eye into his filthy wastebasket. "I'll admit my contacts for this sort of operation are limited. But I have the right people to keep you safe. You can count on me having your security in place by the time you get back to Mescalero. I'll call you as soon as I have any information."

On the way home, we deliberated about the likelihood of our government trying to warn her, but it was all speculation because she really couldn't discuss the matters that she knew might be alarming to the powers of state.

Shortly after we were home, Josea called to let me know that Farley had arranged for a security person to be on duty watching their home and street.

The next morning, Kershaw phoned. He asked if he could come by the house before leaving for the airport. When he arrived he puckered his cheeks to signal he had it right. Josea Roth was determined a high risk to violate national security matters. She warranted on-going investigation and monitoring.

"What should she do?" I inquired.

"Nothing she can do…besides keeping her mouth shut," Kershaw advised. "Most likely what happened was that after she dropped out and ended up at some damn religious retreat, they feared she might have had a hundred-percenter; you know, turned commie or some shit like that. They're probably keeping an eye on me too." He minimized his concern by flipping his hand in the air.

"But they nearly got her into an accident," I countered his indifference. "They might make a mistake and she will be hurt or killed."

"There was one strange thing," he remarked, dismissing my concern as he pondered a point he hadn't thought through. "It appeared that the Defense Department was handling the operation. But oddly the case was red-flagged with a note that all interventions had to be cleared first, and then reported afterward, directly to the President's office—that's not typical," he admitted.

"What could it mean?" I quickly asked.

"Somebody has a huge hard on for her."

"But why was Reuben followed as well?"

"Mistake. Thought they were together. I wouldn't make much of it," Kershaw answered.

"What about Nadine being involved," I added to my wish list for him to answer. "She insists the target was her."

"You got your hands full. That's sure as hell the truth, isn't it?"

"Great. Never a dull moment at Kuruk,"

Kershaw had no solution.

The answer would literally be blowing in the wind. It would land as a torrential storm from the whimsy of a paranoid lunatic's mind.

I called Farley after Kershaw left, telling him he could cancel the investigation into possible government involvement but to keep up the surveillance of Josea. He sounded relieved, expressing openly that he had "hit a brick wall and bounced off." Farley didn't like to fail and I saved him from an embarrassing defeat.

Unsolved mysteries were rolling around Mescalero like pool balls on a billiard table. My day was just beginning. I now had the unfortunate job of informing Reuben and Josea that she was being targeted by the Defense Department as a possible saboteur to her country. Josea would first take the news as a terrifying exclamation mark, then as a cruel insult.

After I informed them, Reuben immediately called Farley, instructing him to double the troops protecting Josea. He was ready to do battle with the U. S. Government to defend his love. He had enough money in the bank to enlist his own army, if necessary.

It was not long after that when I remarked to Nadine what I had learned about Josea. Her reaction was hardly what I would have expected.

"Bull shit; it's all a diversion," she adamantly insisted. "Lousy bastard."

"Who?" I asked urgently.

"You ready to work?" is all she'd say. "You'll find out in due time. Believe me, Josea will be fine."

"And you?"

"Where were we?" She was standing at the entrance to my office. "We need to get this book written soon…just in case."

Nadine mumbled something about somebody not wanting her to tell the story. She refused to embellish on the point when I confronted her. That aside, there was no doubt that the case-hardened Detective Nadine Street was back on full-time duty. Her head was down. As she made her way to sit in her chair, her feet shuffled back and forth at the ground. She looked like a kid kicking the daylights out of fear.

30

DOC, CAN'T YOU TAKE A JOKE?

SIGHTSEEING WITH HIS NEW girlfriend on Saturdays, taking her out to dine, unexpectedly getting called to the park by her on a Sunday to be grilled like a chop; Larry had his hands full. But there was also work to be done for the busy Dr. Monroe. Monday was a full day of patients in the office.

Monroe ran his sessions like a master horologist. He started exactly on the hour and ended with equal exactitude ten minutes before the next hour. Arrive late and it was the patient's dime. Actually it was four hundred dollars a session, so every minute the patient was tardy cost…let's just say patients with punctuality issues might need only a brief series of sessions to get over their bad habit.

If a person had arrived at precisely four-fifty in the afternoon at his office Monday afternoon, they would have seen Dr. Monroe escorting out an old man with a cane. It was his second-to-last appointment of the day; the last patient would be scheduled at five o'clock.

Dr. Monroe behaved kindly to the man, patting him on the shoulder as the old fellow began ambling down the hall. As the patient reached the end of the walkway, he opened a door—not the regular exit, but the one leading circuitously to an interior stairwell frequently used by Larry to leave through the rear of the building into the alley—and disappeared.

With a large grin on his mug, a composition of amazement and delight, Monroe went back to his office and sat down to check phone messages. Relieved to find that there were none, he leaned back to doze a bit before the last session begun. He wasn't looking forward to his next fifty-minutes. Each time the detestable man arrived (the one previously introduced during a heated session with Dr. Monroe) Monroe cursed his having been conned into taking his case. His waiting list was long but this patient found a way to be waltzed past the whole group like a celebrity.

None too early, Dr. Monroe saw the arrival light brighten. He went to the door to make the formal greeting and when he did, his face froze in a shocked expression. The man was holding a replica of Nadine. He must have worked long hours making it, because it bore a frightful similarity to her in size and feature. The reproduction alone would have been tolerable, admirable even for its artistry and craft. However, the man had grotesquely impaled a long pick through the entire head of Nadine's look-alike. He was holding it up with both hands, lifting the metal spike and grinning proudly at the effigy.

Larry would have grabbed him by the neck and squeezed the life out of him, if he didn't know the capacity for brutality and savagery this patient possessed. He might also have broken down crying, if he were not concerned about maintaining his clinical posture.

"This is going too far. I won't have it!" he shouted.

"Relax, I'm a patient," the man mocked. "Aren't I allowed to act out my feelings, if I'm not hurting anyone?"

"Your behavior is intolerable and inappropriate."

"Inappropriate? What diagnosis do I get this time?"

"That's not what's important."

"Is to me. Think I'm in this for a lousy character disorder or obsessive-compulsive neurosis? I deserve better. I thought of schizophrenic at one point, but no, you're not putting that one on me. I'm one complete guy here, just me and me alone. I'm not some ordinary type of madman, so I deserve a special label."

"It's your behavior, not your diagnosis that we're dealing with in treatment."

"Okay, then." The patient strode into the office. He placed the copy of Nadine on the floor by his side as he sat. "Let's talk about women."

"What about them?"

The man smirked. "You have a new lover, don't you? I'm trying to help."

"We've already discussed the fact that my personal life is not what we're trying to resolve through your treatment," the doctor explained with forced tolerance to his patient. "I appreciate your concern for me, but in the future we have to limit the therapy to what is happening between you and me here."

His speech fell on dead ears.

"Being involved with the wrong woman can be disastrous."

Any reasonable person would conclude Dr. Monroe had every right to toss the vile wretch out on his butt—he wouldn't get the chance. The man beat him to it. Seeming to have accomplished his purpose, he strutted out, grinning delightfully. The only plus for Monroe was that the patient left a few hundred dollars in unused therapy, "treating" Larry to nearly a free full session.

What crossed my dizzy mind was why Monroe didn't confront the patient with how he knew about Nadine in the first place. His antics were proof that he'd had an eye on her. Then again, I'm not a renowned doctor of psychiatry.

31

HILL, THAT BASTARD

RAYMOND'S. THAT'S WHAT THE sign above the solid oak, double doors said. The restaurant had a loyal following, attested to by anyone lucky enough to get a reservation, elite enough to believe they belong there, and—needless to say—prosperous enough to afford the dining fare: no corkage fee, don't bring your own unless pre-approved.

The proud owner was Winky Lori from Los Angeles, who, by the way, had never stepped foot in the place. Instead of worrying about food service, Mr. Lori devoted his time to a porno movie company and chain of massage parlors that brought in so much cash that he needed legit businesses to make his lifestyle look reasonable to the taxing authorities.

Since Winky knew nothing about fine food, he employed a maestro of the palate, Jean Pierre, to ensure that the establishment maintained its superiority and exclusivity. Jean was the name used by his close friends, a collection of esteemed people numbering in the hundreds, perhaps thousands, who, despite their wealth and position found it to their gustatory advisability to place themselves on his good side, hoping it would favor them a better table or reservation on short notice.

This evening a black limousine—most patrons arrived in limos, but there was no shame in wheeling up in a Rolls or Bentley—pulled in front. A chauffeur opened the door to drop off the important package he was delivering.

His name was Senator Daniel Hill, representing his home state of South Carolina. He was esteemed for his influence over, of all things, money. The Senator was considered essential for bringing appropriation bills to the floor of Congress. He came to *Raymond's* this evening to attend a very important meeting. Decisions were about to be made that might influence the future of such important matters as Medicare, defense spending, government employee benefits and… limo allowances for congressional leaders?

The senator was no stranger to Jean. A witness to their greeting one another would imagine they were best of friends. After the warm embrace, Jean donned a look of puzzlement.

"Good evening, Senator. I don't have you—"

"There's no security here?" Hill barked.

"I beg your pardon?" Jean countered, taking Hill's apparent puzzlement to the level of bewilderment.

The senator seemed preoccupied, taking hold of the phone at the reception stand without asking permission.

"This is Senator Hill," he spit out at the person on the other end of the line. "Is President Haley in?"

Hill had called Haley's personal secretary. She was not at her desk but her assistant was. The response to his query was that the president was attending a reception for the ambassador from Afghanistan. She notified the senator that if it were an emergency she'd get a message to him immediately.

Having nothing to say, he hung up the phone. He hesitated to think the matter over. Something screwy happened. While he was deliberating what to do, he felt a sudden, urgent need to visit the men's room.

"Jean, would you be kind enough to tell my driver to stay put? I'll be right back."

Hill walked toward the rear of the establishment, familiar with the location of The John. There was no reason for him to notice, as he passed the bar just to the left of the hallway leading to the bath-rooms, that of the several people drinking only one was alone. And at any rate, from his angle all he would have been able to see of the individual would have been the back of a brown herringbone sport coat and a dark brown fedora.

The man at the bar shifted his head. With a narrowly discernable eye movement, he was able to catch Hill on his way to relieve himself. He reached for the glass with his left hand and took it with him, his other hand toting a large case. Then he followed the same path as Hill, guzzling the remainder of the contents in the glass.

He was about to enter the men's room. Before he did, he looked over his shoulder to be certain nobody was around to witness him take the glass and awkwardly cradle it in the same hand as the case, allowing him to open the door with a coat-covered hand.

The senator had already gone to the urinal. It was a relatively small lavatory and by squatting the man wearing the fedora could survey the complete floor space and confirm what he hoped would be the case, that there were no other occupants but himself and Hill.

Hill was attending vigilantly to his duty, never looking up from the urinal as the man put down his case and extracted from his pock-et an angled rubber doorstopper. He jammed it in place, preventing the door from opening inward. He knew his work would be speedy. Any customers needing the facility would assume it was full and ei-ther wait or return in a few minutes.

He moved to the sink, ostensibly to clean his hands. He waited patiently while Hill completed his business and zipped his trousers. Hill then proceeded to the sink to wash. He was now standing next to a man who, unbeknownst to Hill, was not just splashing water on his face, but contemplating murder—Hill's murder, in fact.

Men on death row are granted a choice of a last meal before ex-ecution. This killer had allowed his target only to be fully relieved before his assassination.

Hill took a linen towel off a small table and wiped his hands. Then he dropped the soiled cloth in a bin and reached for the door.

The killer extracted what appeared to be a long, thin wire from his pocket. As Hill challenged the door's objection to being pulled open, the instrument was wrapped around the senator's neck. With a quick and decisive tug, death was delivered. As Hill was gradually let loose to fall to the floor, the killer cursed him under his breath.

"You asshole."

Little time remained for the fedora-capped man to go into detail of his disdain for Hill. With the victim on the floor, the man took the wire and ran it under the water to eliminate any blood. He dried it off and put it back in his pocket. Next, with the water still running, he cleansed the glass of any hand or lip prints and put it in his pocket. Then he wiped off the faucet handle and pulled Hill into the corner so that the door, when opened, would block the body from view.

He picked up his case, used his free hand to take out the door-stop—which he pocketed—then with the same hand, now covered with his coat, he opened the door. He couldn't take a step before another man came to enter the bathroom. The killer offered him a polite nod, held the door for an instant with his heel so the man could enter without being hit. He then turned briskly and walked through the restaurant, depositing the glass on a busboy's unattended cart before exiting to the street.

Poor Nadine. The killer was making chopped liver out of her detective skills.

32

NADINE AND BRENT – BARBIE AND KEN?

FINDING NADINE IN AN antique shop is not unusual. When time permits she'll browse for special gifts to brighten her condo. On this particular day she made one of her favorite finds, a stained glass piece she had in her hand as she proceeded down the block for a lunch engagement. She reached a small café with an outdoor patio area on the sidewalk. She made her way toward the front. Then all of a sudden an arm reached out and grabbed her.

It belongs to a tall blond man, overweight a few pounds, but muscular above the waist. Brent stood to greet her. Nadine responded with a warm smile. He motioned for her to come around the railing separating them for a proper welcome.

She swiftly made her way through the entrance and then to his table. They gave one another a tight embrace and while they're holding each other, Brent pulled backward momentarily to look into her face. He released her with a sign of pleasure and then arranged the chair opposite him for her to sit.

"Got your song book?" he asked with a pleasant smile.

"No, didn't know I'd needed it," Nadine laughed.

Nadine was a crafty investigator, knew how to be invisible if necessary, and could drop a tail like spitting in a bucket. Today, however, she had no reason to believe she was being followed, no reason either to look across the street to a parked car that was partially obscured by passing traffic. In the car sat her boss, Chief Lambert. No stranger to surveillance, he knew how to stay out of view.

He was holding a camera and had been snapping shots of Nadine since the second she met Brent. Even when he exited from the car he was undetectable to her, parading himself as the consummate pain-in-the-ass tourist. Unfortunately, this man was no tourist. His proofs were going to change the course of history. Well, I'm exaggerating. What they were going to do was hurt Nadine, which is exactly what they were meant to do.

It was the type of mean-spirited act that Lambert was best equipped to pull off. The motive was not hate—he would have never undertaken the assignment for that alone—but his detestation of Nadine did sweeten the pot. The real goal was to impugn her character before Larry, although Lambert would never be aware of this. He was blindly carrying out an assignment.

The project had to be important for the boss was making a full afternoon of it, and that is a lot to ask from a man who knits a well-tailored schedule. He waited for the meal to end and then followed Nadine and Brent to a small women's clothing boutique down the block, Gigi's. Through the camera lens, Lambert zoomed-in on Nadine while Brent was holding up a sweater to Nadine's chest to preview it. Nadine then slipped it over her head and positioned it so she could model it. He stepped back to take in the full view and then nodded approvingly.

Next Brent touched Nadine's elbow to softly lead her to a rack where numerous hats hung. He took one he seemed to fancy and placed it on Nadine's head. She adjusted it and then moved a few steps to a mirror, pausing to form her own opinion.

Lambert made sure not to miss the shot of Brent hugging Nadine a second time. Then, abruptly, he threw the digital camera over his shoulder and walked back to his waiting vehicle, leaving Nadine with Brent to settle their business with the storekeeper.

33

NADINE PUTS HER LENS ON REUBEN

EVERY OPPORTUNITY PRESTON HAD—A day off during the week, a cancelled concert date—he'd come to visit Nadine. I knew the affair was serious to him because he never arrived without those dead-give-away Lucchese ostrich boots. They would also frequently take off and Nadine wouldn't return until the next day. Preston displayed his reverence to her by never mentioning their obvious intimacy.

Each time, Nadine would return in a merry mood, indifferent to the potential dangers she was facing. Her only apparent relatedness to the threat she perceived was that she became increasingly eager to move the story forward. As a result, she kept at me with a slave whip—Nadine was a persistent woman when on a mission and I was getting exhausted between all the pursuits and responsibilities on my plate.

Unknown to me was that Nadine was hardly wasting her time between her sessions with me. She was a woman whose nature demanded she work feverishly to find an answer when confronted with a mystery. In this case, it was Reuben. Preston lit the pilot, raising questions regarding Reuben's background. What tweaked Nadine's interest was not Reuben per se, but instead her curiosity if by chance our chef had some remote involvement in the troubles now closing in on her at Mescalero.

Nadine knew precisely how to proceed in investigating him.

The first task she undertook was to review everything Preston had researched on Reuben; she concluded that there had been no such person meeting his description before a man of that name wandered upon Mescalero. Establishment of social security identification, drivers' license, credit card and bank account had been arranged just prior to his arrival. The fact that all this identification material was set up at a late age in life alerted her that something was amiss.

Nadine, like Kershaw, retained a vast network of friends and associates she could call on for favors. It was a simple task, therefore, for her to obtain Reuben's phone records. There were very few calls, but one in particular was repeated. It was to the office of a prominent Beverly Hills attorney.

She had also taken note of one man in particular who attended the opening night musical at Kuruk. He was an elegant looking gentleman whose stylish dress contrasted with most every other person present. She had no problem confirming that the gentleman was the same Jay Weiner of Beverly Hills whose phone number was on Reuben's cell bill.

She attained Weiner's home phone number. Then when she had one of her contacts with knowledge of phone systems make a call at the early morning hour of three to Jay's house using Reuben's number, she had her answer.

"Why are you calling me at home," Jay's weary voice called out in panic. "You okay?"

Nadine said nothing to a soul about what she had discovered. She dropped the matter with Preston, telling him that he had made a mistake and she found Reuben to be legitimate. Since Preston had expressed concern only because he worried that Reuben, who was a stranger when he arrived at Mescalero, could have a criminal or deviant background and, therefore, be a threat to my family and me, hearing an "all-is-clear" from Nadine relaxed him. He never mentioned it again. She also didn't bring up the topic with me—at least not at that time.

34

CHEERIE'S

Nadine has a da-ate.

Nadine has a da-ate.

Nadine has a da-ate.

She's a grown lady but I would have loved being her younger sibling, teasing the hell out of her. This evening would have been my chance because Nadine was going out with a guy. She wouldn't be dressed in any of the luxurious items she was trying on earlier for Brent; she wasn't going out with Brent. She was going out with Larry.

Nadine has a da-ate.

Nadine has a da-ate.

Nadine has a da-ate.

Larry was due momentarily. Nadine was standing by her kitchen sink, peeling and slicing a couple bananas and dicing a mango for a dessert. She mixed the two fruits together in a ceramic bowl, drizzling lemon on top to keep the banana from discoloring.

The lemon squeeze was nearly completed when the phone rang. Quickly, she washed off her hands and grabbed a kitchen towel as she reached for the phone.

"Hello." Pause. "Hello." Pause, then louder. "Hello!"

Annoyed, she placed the phone back in its cradle. *Probably just one of those calls wanting to leave a message on the answering machine,* she mused as she went back to the counter. As soon as she picked up the lemon a second time, the phone rang again. No need to dry her hands this time; snatching the phone, she refrained from speaking.

Silence. She heard no voice and no recorded message.

Finally she broke the stalemate. "Could this be a little prankster?" she posed, as if speaking to a child playing phone games.

No response. She hung up.

Nadine's kitchen sink, and the adjacent counter where she was preparing the fruit, were directly in front of a large window offering her a view of a verdant area behind her building. She never pulled down the window covering. She preferred enjoying the natural scenery that was partially lit at nighttime as part of the landscape her building had installed. Having been hit with a series of thunderstorms a few nights earlier, the area was exceptionally green, lush plants spilling across a thick expanse of…mud.

Just as she finished with the lemon and dropped it down the disposal a powerful beam of light, almost laser-like in its density and intensity, blinded her. It was aimed from the field in front of her and seemed to originate from a location far back in the grassy area, on the perimeter of a tree line.

Nadine ducked, at the same time covering her eyes with her hands. Immobilized by the shock, she quickly recovered her senses and ran to the living room, where another window looked out onto the same area—the top center portion of the window was home to her recent purchases, a lovely stained-glass face with glowing pink lips. She scanned the darkness, but before she could reach full focus, the light located her eyes again, blinding her to any movement in the area from which it was coming. She ran to the side of the room and drew the curtains, then hurried to do the same over the sink.

In the drawer of a small end table near the kitchen she kept her handgun. She opened the drawer and took the pistol out to check that it was loaded and ready to fire. Satisfied that it was operational, she set it down.

On the same table was a phone. She picked it up and dialed quickly, deciding it was not too much of a disclosure to make Dustin aware of an evolving situation.

"Dustin, somebody is following me. If you can, once in a while check around my place."

A few seconds passed as Dustin said something to which she responded simply, "Okay."

She hung up. She sat down with no purpose other than to compose herself. Minutes passed by, five or ten of them. The buzzer at the front door to the building rang. She took a deep breath and answered the intercom.

"Hello."

"It's Larry."

"Your timing is perfect," she responded with a sign of relief.

A few seconds later, she opened the door to let him in. He was dressed casually; navy blue slacks with a blue pinstripe dress shirt under a maroon cashmere sweater. He was a handsome sight, not to mention one of relief. She wasn't looking bad herself; she never did. They faced one another as if they both had winning lottery tickets.

"Sit down. I'll be ready in a minute."

Her plan was to take Larry out to a little local joint she liked to visit. After settling him in the living room, she yelled out to him from her bedroom. "I'm taking you to a bar, okay?"

"I think I can handle it," he called back merrily.

"We'll see. It's not your normal club. It's more like a saloon," she hollered. "But the good part is you don't have to drink and drive; it's only down the road a piece. Give me a minute."

In the living room was an upright piano, a gift of a friend who recently left the state and offered it to Nadine free if she paid the moving charge. Larry sat down at the instrument, the first to do so in years and, therefore, the first to discover it was badly in need of tuning. Nadine couldn't play but adopted it thinking, hoping, that someday…

He started playing a Chopin piece, which Nadine could distinguish from Beethoven as well as most people a wasp from an American white-faced hornet; unless one had the misfortune to be bitten by the latter, in which case they'd be eternally aware that Chopin is sweet but could never deliver the wallop of Beethoven.

Nadine came back into the room. So engrossed was Larry in his performance, despite the poorly tuned instrument, that he hardly noticed she was wearing a colorful, wide feather necklace accenting her long, narrow nape. She reclaimed him from his recital.

"You play piano. I sing."

His eyes widened as he inspected her. "Hey, I love that neckpiece."

He noticed. He also noticed upon arriving at the club near her place that lots of people know her, some waving across the room, some approaching to say hello. She and Larry sat at a small table.

The place was a neighborhood tavern with a menu limited to drinks, sandwiches, and a few hot dishes. Its specialty was performance by the locals. To give these amateurs a proper platform for their singing—karaoke mostly—and dance routines, the owners constructed a small stage. The patrons signed up and were free to do their thing.

The fans were a tolerant crew who knew full well that if somebody was horrible, they themselves might be worse. Nobody was booed off the stage, even if they deserved it. And while some of the numbers were top notch, the raves for those were hardly distinguishable from the ugly.

Every night the place was bustling, and the entertainment was pretty much non-stop. The owners had a fine deal in that they didn't have to pay for live acts. They expressed their appreciation by passing on the goodwill to the customers in the form of cheap drink prices: everybody was cheery at, yes, Cheery's. The evening of Nadine and Larry's date was to be no exception.

Nadine loved coming to Cheery's. It wasn't because she was a dipsomaniac; she could never be mistaken for any type of maniac. Truth was that the happy spot was a core part of her social network—and she was a singer. She was untrained but people who listened to her were encouraging. They often used designations such as "polished," "classy," and "melodic." Like I said, the patrons were gracious to everybody. Nadine made no mistake thinking of leaving her day job to pursue a career as a recording artist.

When Larry and Nadine first sat they watched as an African-American couple onstage rocked to a hip-hop piece. The twosome said they had discovered the song they were performing to have been written by a pathetically unknown songwriter, whose work they figured would be ideal for a pathetically unknown team of amateurs singing to a pathetically unsophisticated audience in a pathetically run-down dive.

The tune was called *You've Got Lines*. The lyrics and beat were catchy enough that most of the customers were actually listening. Some even put down their drink, and a few appeared mesmerized: maybe the songwriter wasn't so pathetic after all.

Every time the situations arise, you've got lines, you've got lines, you've got lines and you've got lines.

Apparently, the driving theme of the song was that when it comes down to commitment, it always draws a B.S. line.

This couple was not only singing, they were acting out their interpretation. It was clear they knew a thing or two about lines of their own. No doubt that's what made their rendition of the song so engrossing.

When the couple finished, there was lots of soused applause. If some of the spectators found alcohol a tad sedating, the music was clearly an antidote. Nadine and Larry, just settling in, had yet to order anything.

"Ever do karaoke?" Nadine queried her date.

"No."

"That's hip-hop, what they just did. Of course you can do any style," she explained while waving to a friend.

"You said you sing. Are you going on stage?" Larry asked.

"I'm not sure when, but—"

Through the mass of inebriates a hand was seen rushing toward Nadine. As it got closer, it was evident it belonged to a tall blond figure—none other than Brent. Her friend was so excited, he dispensed with the full greeting he displayed when they met for lunch. In fact, he barely took time to tap her on the shoulder to be sure he had her attention.

"Nadine, where were you? We're up next," he uttered from his nearly out-of-breath chest.

"We've got five minutes. Relax," Nadine said to her exuberant buddy. "Hey, I want to introduce you to a friend of mine. This is Larry Monroe." She turned to Larry. "Larry, this is Brent Daniels."

Nadine was so casual she might have just introduced Larry to her accountant. Brent, still tense about the pending performance said a friendly "hello" and shook hands. Larry stiffened slightly, unwittingly lifting his spine a notch higher as he reached for Brent's outstretched hand.

The formal greeting satisfied, Brent shook his body freely, a gesture of preparation for a contest, like any athlete about to confront an unknown adversary. "Ready, ready to go, darlin'?"

"Wish me luck," Nadine playfully called out to Larry as she stood to go onstage.

The performance platform had been vacant for a few minutes. There was no MC but an informal system has been worked out by the entertainers whereby whoever performed last, announced the next act. Larry watched as Nadine and Brent walked to the platform. The couple completing *You've Got Lines* moments before met them. They chatted briefly; then to loud applause the male pulled out a bugle to call the audience to attention. The couple stepped back up to the microphone.

"Are you ready?" To arouse the crowd, the twosome call out louder. "Are you ready?'

Whistles, foot stomping, glass pounding, whooping, cat calling, grunting, screaming, you name it, no rules except that nothing gets thrown and nobody gets hurt; a track record so exemplary that one would have more likelihood of getting beaten up or assaulted on a nursery school playground.

The noise level sunk a few decibels, just enough to allow the couple to try and introduce Nadine and Brent. But they were interrupted again. This time it was a zany but cherished tradition that precluded the couple's announcement. Randomly a bell sounded. When it did, it was time for the entire audience to joyfully sing together, *Cheery's Anthem.*

Performed to the tune of *When You're Smiling*:

When you're drinking, when you're drinking, the whole world drinks with you. And when you're tipsy, when you're tipsy, you do what you care to do. But when you're sober, you kill off them dreams, so jump the wagon; you can barf at Cheery's. When you're drinking, keep on drinking, and the whole world drinks with you.

It was crude and raunchy, hardly what you'd expect Nadine to enjoy, but she was revealing herself as a lady of diverse tastes. She coveted secrets like most everybody does, and *Cheery's* was one of hers. Finally the couple with responsibility to make the introduction brought the pandemonium under control.

"You all *think* you've heard *6th Avenue Heartache by The Wallflowers?* Well, you're about to hear it the way it was supposed to be done. Listen up for Brent and Nadine."

Larry was ninety percent listening with the remainder of his awareness wondering: Nadine, Brent? At the same time a particular line in the lyrics struck him. It was about the cries of strangers, the force of the world against one's back, and knowing how to laugh.

Nadine crooned her part, enough to impress Larry she had a gifted voice.

"Not knowing how to laugh?" he rehearsed the phrase again in his mind.

No, she does laugh. But he was deliberating what he was aware was beneath the surface, sorrow. He listened to her sing the words as if she were the author of the regret the lyric spoke to. He knew there was something in her past that harmed her and that her moments of girlishness were only a thin membrane gauzing pain beneath, an artificial layer superimposed…like the sheet over the Ghost Clock? But what could it be inside asking permission to escape, to come out of hiding?

He hoped there would be plenty of time to get answers; he hoped she would get to where she could confide in him. But beyond his curiosity about the psyche of this enrapturing woman was a deeper question about whether there is, or had ever been, a romance between Nadine and Brent. His concern was not put to rest when after the performance Brent warmly embraced Nadine. Then as she was heading back to the table where Larry was sitting, Brent called out to her that he was leaving.

"Where are you going?" she yelled back over the boisterous crowd.

"I'll explain later. Just cover for me, okay?"

"Sure. I'll take care of it."

"Hey, excited about next week?" Brent added with a wink.

"Can't wait; wouldn't miss it," she gleefully assured him.

"Good, I'll see you there."

Brent acknowledged Larry only with a dismissive wave. Nadine made her way back to Larry. She could see he wasn't happy.

"We sing karaoke in competitions. That's it," she assured him.

Larry was not about to cop jealousy at this early stage of the romance, and what right would he have to in the first place? Playing it cool, he responded casually.

"Sounds like fun."

But the distrustful inspector sensed black mamba venom racing through her lover's veins. She snuggled close, resting her head against his arm. "I'm happy to be with you."

That Larry liked.

"I'm going to announce the next act. Then what do you say we order something?"

"Here?"

"You'll be surprised. It's not at all bad. Oh, and I prepared dessert for us at my place."

"Sounding better."

"Come on," she said cheerily. "If you're going to hang with me you need to learn to live like a plebian."

"I have to admit I'm not looking forward to that."

She laughed and moved to the stage to complete her duty of announcing the next act.

Between sandwiches and a few beers, it was a good hour before they left. They went out to the street hand in hand. It could have been a lovely stroll home, could have been, but...

35

MOTHERLESS CHILDREN

It was brisk outdoors. There was no rain but the air was heavy and wet. The cool gushes of wind were invigorating. Larry led his darling along the back streets to lengthen the walk and enjoy the more relaxed setting.

Little by little they strayed from the road, following a sinuous course through several trees before stumbling onto an old concrete walk Nadine had long forgotten was there. Partially covered with dirt and leaves, it was not easy to spot but Larry strode on it as if he had journeyed along the footpath many times.

Nadine hadn't had anywhere near enough alcohol to dull her senses; she never did. Her thoughts immediately jumped to the unlikelihood of Larry being so familiar with the landscape. Quickly she came up with a plan to question him in a non-threatening manner.

"How did you know this path was here? An old girlfriend live nearby?" she jested. "Or…magic? I'll bet that's it. That's probably what makes you such a great therapist."

Larry chuckled at the thought that she'd endow him with clairvoyant authority. Indeed, he'd gladly take credit for it, if he possessed a seed of prophetic power. His explanation fell far afield from metaphysics, but it was the only one he could offer in honesty.

"If you'd had the kind of back country experiences I have, you'd understand. I always know what direction I'm headed. Your building is just through the trees. How far off could it be? Then with the moon giving us ample light, I knew something like this would happen. There had to be a trail across."

Her next question was more confrontational.

"So you knew a path might be here?"

"No, how would I know there was a path? I said I knew we'd get through."

"Okay, but it's rained for days. It's a muddy marsh in some parts. You were going to take me into that mess?"

"I planned to lift you past any conditions we encountered unbecoming a lady," Larry responded gallantly.

"You're serious."

"Nadine, I would take you on my shoulders to the pearly gates of heaven if you were called and had no transportation."

"Okay. Then…carry me home."

He did, all the way. Nadine was laughing. Larry showed the initial signs of his age. By the time he was into the condo—where Horace rewarded him with a wet lick on the cheek—and placed Nadine on the couch, he was breathless. Nadine was giggling, both due to a private admission that once again she had unfairly doubted him, and due to the reward she had planned for him that evening.

Tired after the fireman's carry of his love, Larry also leaned back on the couch. To his surprise—and it's not surprising he'd be surprised because in all his years he'd never had the experience of living with a dog—Horace jumped on the couch and rested his head on Larry's thigh.

Nadine noticed his awkwardness with Horace. Curious about his apparent discomfort with the dog, she felt it was time to tell Larry, *The Story of Horace*; and she did, nearly as she'd disclosed it to me.

"I know he's rather large, but he's never bit anyone," she promised after edifying about Horace's birth defect.

"Oh, it's not that I'm afraid of him. I'm just not used to dogs," he confessed.

"You never had one growing up?

"I never did."

"They are man's best friend, you know."

"So I've heard. And maybe that's why I never saw the need. I always had Howard."

"How about dessert?" Nadine offered, making note of the odd comment about Haley. "You sit; I'll get it."

On her way to the kitchen, Horace jumped up to follow. "Don't be insulted. He thinks he's getting food. And that's one drive the U. S. Marines don't want to try and stop."

She took the container of fruit from the refrigerator, setting it on the countertop along with two smaller bowls with spoons. On her way back to the couch, she surreptitiously tossed a few pieces on the floor for Horace.

She sat back down at the table with a vague plan of initiating a conversation, but unsure how to approach it. She wanted to find out something about Larry's background, other than that he has a friendship with Howard Haley and Chauncy knew of him as an outstanding profiler.

"So when do I get invited over for dinner with your family, Larry?" she posed in a light-hearted manner.

Yet when he winced as if the subject was painful, she quickly backed off. "We'll save that for another conversation."

"No, that's all right," Larry, assured her. "It's just that there's not much to meet. I never knew my mother, and my father died when I was nine."

That was not what Nadine wanted to hear. She had her own history and when she heard Larry's background, she began calculating the probability of bad begetting bad. *My god, we're both motherless children,* she mused, thinking back on a song she found in a music collection left to her by an uncle. The piece went by exactly that name and every time she played it, she heard the words, "I'm a long way from home," and she'd weep uncontrollably.

"I'll listen if you want to tell me what happened to your mother?" she offered, suppressing the sorrow gripping at her throat.

"She died when I was born."

"Then who raised you?"

"My uncle."

"Well, where's your uncle now?"

Larry swallowed, the same horrible throat squeezing feeling she was experiencing that instant.

"Larry, some other time we'll talk more about all that family stuff."

What she wanted to do is to hug him, mother the motherless child, but instead she opted to shift gears entirely.

"You like funny movies?"

"I love to laugh."

No sooner said than Nadine was pulling a DVD off a shelf. She put it in the player and turned on the TV.

"Let's laugh," she said as she cuddled next to Larry on the couch.

Horace was accustomed to the movie viewing, but not the seating arrangement. Typically he'd occupy the part of the sofa where Larry now sat, his head in Nadine's lap. What to do? Horace took up a position in front of Nadine, studying the dilemma. Then he hopped up, swirling his frame in an attempt to settle between them.

The dog didn't understand that it was too early for a child; they hadn't even had sex. Nadine set her priorities in order, at least for the evening, shoving Horace off the couch and then signaling for him to lie. He did, but not at the base of the couch where he'd be expected to rest. No, that wasn't Horace. He moved to the side of the coffee table and sprawled out so that he had a fully unobstructed view of the screen—got any popcorn, Mom?

Nadine and Larry were watching the remake version of *Little Shop of Horrors*, progressively nestling closer together. The hilarity of one of the scenes temporarily postponed the fun, Larry wondering why they had to select such a funny flick.

He wanted to kiss Nadine, but she was hysterical. The patient, Bill Murray, was sitting in the dental chair with the dentist, Steve Martin, performing an extraction. She was slapping her hands on her knees and shedding tears of humor, and Larry couldn't help but join her. It was a therapy session with Dr. Fun, the head of research at the newly established Laugh Therapy Institute.

Once she'd recovered from the guffawing, Larry picked up the remote. Click, off goes the television. Nadine sensed what was coming and offered no resistance. Horace was pissed that he couldn't see the rest of the flick.

Larry started kissing Nadine. Gradually he assumed a position on top of her, using one hand to unbutton her blouse. Neither he nor Nadine noticed Horace who had shifted to attention in a sitting position off to the side of the couch from where he could absurdly and vigilantly witness the act unfolding.

Good night, kids.

36

IT'S A LOVE AFFAIR, NOT AN IN-VESTIGATION

IT SHOULD BE EVIDENT by now that when Nadine has an unanswered question circling in her head, she won't surrender it even if she's pricked, prodded, poked and pulled it, threaded it through the eye of a needle, shaved it naked, acid bathed it…until she's satisfied she has an answer. It drove her teachers mad when she was growing up, and as an adult she's maintained the same indomitable drive for certitude.

Why doesn't she believe Larry's disclosure about his parents? She does…except her gut isn't satisfied. She assumed that over time more light would be shed on the subject but in the meantime, a short inquest was in order.

A large parking area serviced the members of a private tennis and golf club. Any improvement in the weather and the place bubbled over with member activity. Today was another of those pleasant early spring days that left Nadine sorting through rows of vehicles to find a parking spot. She finally succeeded about halfway between the tennis courts and gift shop.

When she started to get out of the car, she scanned the lot. God knows she hadn't forgotten that vigilance was the rule. What she noticed about two car rows behind her—going away from the courts—was a pair of eyes peering at her through a the rear window of a car.

She locked her vehicle and walked to the right toward the edge of the lot. She casually glanced back to notice that the figure hadn't budged. She turned to go on her way, hastening her pace and then shifting further to the right on to a landscaped area with a stepping stone path leading to the club. But instead of proceeding forward as she might otherwise, when she was sure she was out of sight of the person she assumed was staring at her, she doubled back into the lot, just behind the row where the eyes were seen. She now secured from her bag her hand weapon, flipping off the safety. Slowly she crept along the row. As she approached the place where the man was still standing, she noticed him jiggling a key stuck in the trunk lock.

Her eavesdropping favored her hearing a couple choice phrases aimed at the man's vehicle. "You f—er. God damn you, son of a bitch." The outburst ended with the frustrated fellow pounding his car's trunk.

Nadine slipped her gun back into her purse and walked away, feeling just a little sheepish. Part of her was hoping it was the killer so she could put a bullet through the bastard's head and end the whole crummy ordeal. But her wish would not be granted this day. Instead, she headed into the club to take care of business.

She went into a food stand and asked for a fruit drink. The clerk told her they couldn't take cash, so she put the charge on Chauncy Meyer's account. Then she walked out with her drink, taking a seat at a table on a patio that was slightly elevated above a tennis court. Chauncy was in a match but expecting her.

"We're almost finished," he shouted up to where she was sitting.

Nadine waved. She leaned back to rest. She contemplated the benign non-encounter she just had with the man trying to extricate his key. She recognized that she was under strain, no doubt about it.

Had she the ability or the inclination to peer into Chauncy's mind at the moment, she would have found him equally or more distressed than she. He'd never tell her what was wrong. He was hopeful he'd be dissolving his stresses at a single meeting he'd be attending in a few days—with our national leader, President Haley.

He interrupted Nadine's reverie with a gentle touch on her shoulder, unintentionally startling her.

"Something wrong?" he asked, noticing her seeming deep in thought.

"No, I'm fine," she responded, though unconvincingly.

"Let's go inside. I'll treat you to lunch."

She raised the drink in her hand. "You already treated me to this."

They sat at a table and Nadine perused the menu—she liked what she saw, no prices. She settled on a tuna salad sandwich. The waitress, close to Chauncy's age, greeted him warmly; they seemed to know each other well, very well from Nadine's perspective.

The woman took the order and was about to leave. As she glanced over her shoulder with a warm smile to Chauncy, he patted her on the behind. She didn't smack him a good one. Instead, she beamed as joyfully as if he'd just slipped her a C-note for taking the order.

"Your generation, it's a lawsuit. My generation, it's a compliment. Nadine, mine's more fun." He motioned for her to talk, knowing she had contacted him to discuss business. "How's the case going?"

"Still slow," Nadine admitted. "I've been working more on two of the strangulation murders in the series, Percy Hume and Nolan Flannery, and the stabbing of Hank Owens. The Owens killing is interesting because there are several hesitation wounds on the arms, wrists and abdomen, along with the fatal stab that cleverly severs the aorta."

"You think the killer wanted to make it look like a suicide?"

"No. You know that the hesitation wounds only happen when someone is frightened before they finally slit their wrists. I think the killer put those wounds there intentionally to tell us he knows everything we do, and possibly more."

"So he's talking to you."

"I think so. Now on the strangulations, something kept bugging me as I examined the pictures and the medical examiners' reports."

She took out a stack of photos and placed them on the table. "There's usually excessive force, petechial hemorrhages of the eyes, fractures of the Adam's apple and hyoid bones. But the crush here seems more massive than I've ever seen. In my opinion, it's in excess of what was commented on in the reports. So I went back and met with Lucifer, who did the original post-mortem."

She glanced at Chauncy, who was leaning back in his chair smiling proudly at his star pupil. He pointed to the pictures. "Let me see what you have."

"Chauncy, the exam was so straight-forward they failed to notice that in both cases, the killer snapped the odontoid clean. Look." She handed him the shots. "It was not only the strength that intrigued me, it was the precision with which both fractures were accomplished, as well as the spread of power. We're talking about going down to the second cervical disc," she revealed with sufficient amazement to catch his attention.

"You're right," Chauncy said. "These are frontal strangulations. For Christ sakes, he's probably using the baby fingers to induce the odontoid fractures. The head is damn near hanging limp from the spinal damage."

"I know. Big hands with lots of power."

"I'm surprised the medical examiner's report didn't address it."

"It's an inference," she shrugged. "He just didn't see it."

Nadine now prepared to proceed to the other issue on her mind. She wanted more data on her new fling.

"Tell me what you know about Larry."

"You have a romance going?"

Little blush; it's like talking to dad. "Working on it."

"I've known him for about twenty years. His profiles on serial killers are the best."

"Sure. But what do you know about him, the person and his life?"

"Graduated Yale; then Harvard Medical School."

Chauncy threw up his hands, an acknowledgement that while he'd known the man for all these years, he really couldn't offer much in the way of intimate detail.

He helped himself to a roll. Heedlessly, he put a piece in his mouth. "Don't expect too much from the meal; the bread will be the best part. They have pros here for golf, pros for tennis, but for food service, forget it."

Nadine remained on track, wondering if she might tweak some recall for Chauncy that would lead to other associations he could share with her.

"He told me his father died when he was nine."

"The only comment he ever made to me about his father was that he was away a lot on business."

"He never said anything about an uncle raising him?"

Chauncy shook his head to indicate he hadn't.

"His mother—what about her?"

"It never came up," he answered nonchalantly. "Nadine, I don't recall telling him about my mother, either. Have I ever told you about her?"

"Actually, you haven't."

"There, we'll have something new to talk about. What's all the urgency about Larry's family?"

"I noticed he was uncomfortable talking about it, that's all."

"Nadine, it's a love affair, not an investigation," Chauncy laughed. "Enjoy. That's why I'm so pleased you finally met each other. I'm delighted I was right that you'd find something worth pursuing. Listen, when you get older, loneliness can be a cruel companion; take it from me. I could have married—at least had a live-in—a hundred times after I lost my wife. I'm going to tell you something I've never said to anyone: I should have let myself love one of those women.

"I loved my wife. I swore my loyalty to her, but when she was gone and I thought I was being honorable by refusing to give my love to anyone else, I was wrong. Now I understand that she wouldn't for a second have wanted me to grieve endlessly for her; she was never a selfish person. I was the selfish one, fondling my high values and morals like they were a sure trip to heaven."

He paused, readying to make further disclosure.

"And let me tell you, dear, it's not too late. No excuse that I'm too old and all that crap. If the right thing comes along, I'll do it. And in the meantime, I'm trying to have some fun. You should do the same."

She listened attentively to the man she knew at the time was the only living person on earth who loved her.

"Okay, I will." She still plowed forward about Larry. "Do you still have access to the Bureau files?"

"Everything…why?"

"If it's okay, I'll come by and look at Larry's bio."

Chauncy got the picture. As a gesture of unconditional acceptance, he stroked the side of her face with the back of his hand. Then he proclaimed matter-of-factly, "If he hurts you, I'll kill him."

37

DR. HALEY?

THE MAN IS THE President of the United States. We can understand that it is not the easiest thing in the world to get a private meeting with him. But what was happening this day was ridiculous. His personal secretary was inventing excuses to use on the congressmen, ambassadors and foreign leaders lining up to confer with him.

What was up? President Haley was in his sitting room apparently doing some sort of role-playing, role reversal therapy with none other than his chum, Larry.

What brought Larry to see him? It was plain to see that the president's friend was down in the dumps. Haley was concerned as he listened to Larry. At the same time, he was drawing on one of those prime stogies he'd allowed General Crow to sample. Still, so engrossed was he in Larry's blahs that when his buzzer went off--again—he ignored it.

"Things are not good," Larry said dismally.

"I can see that. What is it, Larry?"

"Your patient! I never should have let you talk me into taking his case."

"You did the right thing. You're his only hope."

"I could never discharge him; you know how I am. But, honestly, he's scary. I've felt that from the beginning."

Biding time, Haley walked toward a window overlooking a garden. A group of children had been honored to visit the presidential home. They brought with them a choir performance. The teacher was standing in front of the students and leading their presentation to a small audience. The select group of ladies, including Muriel, was seated on a patio.

Haley stared down to watch. As the music came to an end, he waved to his wife, who in turn directed the jubilant children toward the president. In unison they jumped up and down and pointed excitedly to have caught a glimpse of their leader. In turn, he used both outstretched arms to show them a sign of welcome. Not moving away from the window, but turning to Larry, he addressed him.

"Soon he'll have nothing to come for; you'll be finished with him. I promise."

"He's more dangerous now. He's aware that we both know about his perversion. And I'm worried about Nadine's safety; he's concerned she'll uncover him." Larry's response played like a plea.

Haley moved closer to Larry, leaning down to speak softly into his friend's ear. "If I step into this…"

"He'll just make it worse on me."

"You need to get perspective. Sure, he'll be punitive if you try to force him out. But when the time is right, he'll disappear like a mirage."

"I don't see how you can be so sure," Larry retorted dubiously. "Think about it. Hasn't he really been there all along with me?"

"Actually, he's never been there with or for you," Haley said bitterly. "When the time comes, you'll shut him out and that'll be the end. Have some faith."

"I'll try," Larry consented half-heartedly. "I just hope I don't lose the tenuous grip I have over him."

Haley hugged his friend. "Lighten up on this. It will pass. You have to trust me on this one."

Maybe Haley was more of a therapist than either Larry or Nadine gave him credit. Larry seemed to buy his words…or did he?

No time to dwell on that. An important appointment was scheduled for the following morning around nine at *Pour It Hot Café*. The locals say they have the freshest brew of coffee in town. Must be something to it. The president goes there…but nobody knows it.

38

COFFEE WITH THE COMMON FOLK

POUR IT HOT IS a downtown D. C. spot where anytime in the morning you can meet two elements of the city. The first, some would argue, are the most elite in town. These are the people responsible for running America; they're called the bureaucrats. They operate divisions of the Justice Department, administer the Smithsonian Institute, run the Bureau of Weights and Measurements and manage accounting for the Small Business Administration.

The second group that makes *Pour It Hot* their haunt is your common working people. They may be guards at the Capitol or at the Washington or Lincoln Memorials, construction workers at a renovation site for the Senate Building or clerks at a pharmacy.

Pour It Hot is not where a tourist hoping to snap a furtive picture of a Congressman or Justice of the Supreme Court would go—for that they'd need to go to *Raymond's*. So an elderly looking man strolling in to *Pour It Hot* with a cane that appears more of a figurative than functional aid is not going to attract much attention, except of course if one knew what only one other man, Miles Denton, knew.

If a random person arrived promptly at nine that morning, they might have watched the disguised President Haley go directly to the counter, take a pot of hot coffee—fully caffeinated—pour it into a ceramic mug, add cream and sugar, then proceed to the cashier and pull out two one-dollar bills; a buck generously dropped in a tip jar earned him a kind smile from the cashier.

Today is a big day. *Pour It Hot* is being honored, not only by a presidential visit, but the esteemed company of the Chief of their own Police Department. To what do they owe this distinguished duo's company? Better get seated quickly. There's every reason to believe that this is due to be an extraordinarily brief meeting.

Lambert was already far off in a corner sitting alone. His coffee cup was full and there was a paper plate with the remnant of what looked to have been some variety of a Danish sitting on it. Haley moved in his direction but never looked straight at him. Lambert gazed at his watch: the hands formed a perfect ninety-degree angle. He didn't look up as Haley sat to the right, and adjacent to him. Instead, he withdrew from the inner pocket of his coat an envelope. He casually placed it on the table. Then he glanced left, intentionally avoiding eye contact with Haley, stood up and walked out, leaving the envelope in place.

Haley lingered to sip his coffee. While holding the cup in one hand he used the other to shift the envelope so it rested in front of him but slightly to his left. After a couple minutes enjoying the rich brew—*Pour It Hot* was known for fine flavored coffee at a low price and has even managed to stay in business despite two Starbucks within a block that charged twice the amount for a product any of the regulars would tell you was inferior—Haley put the envelope in his inner jacket pocket and stood to leave.

Did Lambert even know it was Haley? To this day of writing the tale, Nadine has doubts. Lambert may have been nothing more than an errand boy and thought he was giving the envelope to the president's clerk. It makes sense. If Lambert were working for Haley, the last thing the president would want would be a direct link back to him—especially if murder was the business they shared.

39

MONICA RUSSO, SEXY CRIME INVESTIGATOR

SOME GUYS HAVE ALL the luck. It doesn't take much to figure out Dustin is one of them: star athlete, rich kid, and handsome stud with women chasing after him—he even works for a fox. Men like Dustin don't know of a world where plain, plump, damn-why-couldn't-I-be-born-with-hair-like-Heather-Marks and I-wouldn't-wear-a-bathing-suit-to-the-beach-if-my-life-depended-on-it women live. So should work be any different? If there's a pool of secretaries, be assured Dustin's will be the prettiest. And if he needs work done in the crime lab, presto, a beautiful crime analyst will appear.

There she is. Meet sexy crime investigator, Monica Russo. She's adorable and petite. This morning she has her brunette hair tied in a long ponytail. She's wearing a ravishingly bright yellow blouse that accentuates her blood-red lipstick. With a pair of designer black jeans, she hardly fits the standard image for a person in her capacity. But it turns out that Monica is Cornell bred. She's used her energy and intellect to earn a shockingly good reputation based solely on her professional skills.

Dustin had parked himself on a stool and was sipping a cup of coffee. Monica was sitting on top of an investigative counter and appeared to have done everything she could to look devilishly erotic before leaving home. She knew the night before that she and Dustin were due to talk.

"What do you have for me, Monica?" our young investigator asked.

"Hair samples or otherwise?" Monica answered seductively, her reply a dead giveaway that there was a failed history between the two.

"Otherwise we've already tried," Dustin responded with a smile. "So how about the hair samples?"

"All of a sudden, it's all business is it?"

"I've had to get more serious."

"I'm so happy for you." Monica's voice was a soupy mixture of sarcasm, sadness, contempt and grief. "Let's get on with it then. First of all, the sample from Blank's place was not his. It was definitely human and there were still fluids; it's not from a hairpiece nor was it dead hair. I'll keep it safely put away so we can make a match later." Monica then seized the opportunity to punish Dustin with ridicule. "You're going to bring me in a suspect's sample soon, aren't you? I mean, now that you're a real grown-up detective."

"Come on, Monica. We all have to move on."

Monica jumped off the counter and went to her desk, a gesture indicating that is precisely what she was about to do. She took a pile of pictures and dropped them next to Dustin for him to view. Several of the pictures were of victims' skulls, most displaying injuries in the same region, near the right ear, slightly below. She stopped at one of the shots and commenced a mini-lecture.

"It should be obvious to an amateur that these killings are not accomplished by a female, right?"

"We've ruled that out pretty much on our own," Dustin assured her.

"Well, if I were new to this case, unaware of any other facts, I wouldn't be so sure. In fact, I'd be more inclined to say you are looking for a woman," she rebuked, joyously extracting a couple grams of revenge. "You see, almost all stab wounds inflicted by women have an upward trajectory, which is the case in all of the killings of the cases you're looking into. The reason this is fairly consistent for women should be obvious: women are usually shorter than their victims. So why in this situation with the penetrations having upward motion would you be looking for a male?

"I'll explain, because I'm sure you don't know." Monica let Dustin stand mute, allowing him sufficient time to stew on her ongoing castigation. "If you look carefully at the pictures you'll notice that none of the wounds to the head are linear skull fractures; they're not skull fractures at all. But the angle of penetration is what contradicts the theory of a shorter woman. Also, I'm betting heavily on a male because of the amount of strength required to accomplish these murders.

"This guy is very smart. I mean, why go up against the resistance of dense skull tissue when there are so many more vulnerable sites of entry? There are weak spots in the skull itself, called diastatic sites, which are like suture lines between the bones of the head. I doubt you've been around infants much, but if you ever stroke one's head you'll feel at the top, an open area called a fontanel. As the child develops these gaps close and the bones adhere, leaving a fault line, which is the path of potential diastatic fractures.

"But to nail these dead on target, even if you know their approximate locations, would be very difficult. If he goes for the base of the skull to attempt a basilar skull fracture, it's more predictable. But what he does is much smarter; he comes from slightly beneath the ear, avoiding the jaw and skull base. Now he drives his object up into the base of the brain, fixing his aim—which is damn good—on the medulla oblongata. That's the center for a human's most vital functions like respiration, heart rate, blood pressure and swallowing." Monica takes a sip from a cup of tea before proceeding.

"The damage is so gross that the brain goes into what is called an ischemic cascade; a predictable series of mortal biological events based on lack of oxygen and diminished blood supply." She chuckles. "I assure you, nobody lives through a trauma like that. Especially when you consider that it's usually hours before any of them are found. It's not as if they could get up and dial the phone if they were still legally alive after the attack. The damage to their functioning is so gross that life from the moment of impact could never for any of these victims be more than a vegetative state. Look at this one of Blank. See the black and blue under the ear? That's called a battle sign."

"I never knew that," Dustin responded inquisitively.

"Gee, how shocking. Better do some reading."

"I see that I'll have to."

"Now look at the pictures again. Not all the killings in this series involve head trauma, but for now let's focus on those, only because the exceptions involve profiling issues that I can't address. Notice what I just talked about, the similar, almost identical entrance wounds; I'm talking about the initial contact only.

"No signs of slashing, banging, pounding or twisting. These were done by someone, in my opinion, with knowledge of anatomy, especially cranial. Dustin, every single case you sent me involves a brisk, powerful, precisely positioned impalement that killed the victim immediately or left him so disabled as to not really classify as human. This means that all of the secondary wounds from slamming and hammering have to have another explanation."

Dustin is feeling pounced on by Monica, and rightly so. She's been sharpening her fangs, using her superior knowledge to immobilize his pride. Now, finally, he takes a large gulp of air and proudly exhales an insight about the killer's motive. He knows that the thought he is about to deliver is not his, but his wounded pride encourages him to borrow it.

"Got that covered, girl. The man likes the business. You see, killing is a job, but the butchering and brutalizing following the killing is like a well-deserved meal after a vigorous workout."

Today is not Dustin's in terms of ego. He's playing on the enemy's court. Monica is not in a mood to dispense mercy.

"I wouldn't be so sure of that."

"Why not?"

"Think about it. If you were a person in possession of the information this killer has about the head, brain and microanatomy, wouldn't you know damn well that an act like shoving a screwdriver into the head was going to kill the person?"

"What's the point?" Dustin asked.

"You should consider all the possibilities before definitely drawing conclusions. This killer may not want anyone to know the extent of his knowledge. He's sort of in a catch-22 here. The pattern of penetration I've outlined is—at least for now—his favored way to kill. But it places him in a dilemma. He starts off using the approach, unconscious of the fact he's created a noticeable style. Then when he realizes that he's potentially offered a clue—because let's face it, how many people possess the knowledge he does—he tries to cover it up, to leave doubt in the investigator's mind. That's when he starts all this hokey pokey about knocking around the victims, hoping by chance it will confuse whoever is working the case. If I were you, I'd be keeping an eye on some medical specialists in fields related to the brain."

Dustin stood up to go. "I'll be back."

Satisfied she had inflicted a sufficient beating on him, she dismissed Dustin coquettishly. "Oh, and when is that going to be?"

Dustin picked up his coffee cup, took a healthy gulp, and coolly motioned goodbye. After meeting with the apparent ex-girlfriend, Dustin went back to his office. If any man were in need of a primer on *How to Shake Off the Prick of an Angry Woman's Pungency* they might line up outside Dustin's office—he left the unpleasantness of Monica like a wave does its crest. Why not? If you had an orchard full of ripe fruit would you fret over a single tart plum?

Dustin had more important matters to focus on. As soon as he was back at his office, he received a call that provided him with an essential piece of information, one that lifted his already high spirits higher. The problem was it would not do the same for Nadine.

40

MEANWHILE BACK ON THE RANCH

IT HAD BEEN PEACEFUL and serene for over a week at Kuruk, which was a miracle. Josea was left unmolested by the FBI. Nadine rode me like a pack mule—but was pleasant about it. Reuben was inspired about new musical material. Most important, Preeti was in the stretch run, about to enter the final month of her pregnancy.

Nadine had set up a yoga program designed for Preeti during the pregnancy. Every morning, she came over for a private session after which they would take a walk. It seemed to me Nadine was most at peace when she was with Preeti. She took every opportunity she had to be around her. My opinion was she wanted to smell, feel and sense what pregnancy was like. She really had no experience with the state she yearned to experience it at least once in her life.

The mystery note on the irregular sheet of stationary remained a taunt. Nadine took it as no more than that, refusing, up to this point, to allow it to interfere with her life.

Then one afternoon when I was at Kuruk working, one of the waitresses, Camille, asked if she could talk to me.

"Zach, I didn't think anything of it at the time but as the day went on, and then I talked it over with my mother, I realized it was odd," she explained with a strange tone of apology. "See, this man I had never seen before ordered lunch and started talking to me; just small talk. Then he mentioned that he recalled that a writer owned Kuruk.

I told him you had published two books—we're all proud of that, you know."

I didn't but it inflated my ego to hear it despite the fact that my grand successes as a novelist had earned me less money than literary respect—I had been under the false assumption that both rewards would come equally.

"He asked me if you were writing now, real innocent, like he was curious for no reason. So I told him Nadine was here from D. C. I didn't know the details about what you were working on but I told him you had a project together." Camille paused to take the blame for what she estimated to be an error in judgment on her part. "I wasn't thinking, Zach. I shouldn't have said anything, should I?"

"This isn't top secret," I assured her. "He asked and you answered. I don't see anything wrong with that."

"I talk too much; mom always said so," she continued to admonish what she saw as an unpardonable lapse of prudence. "I guess I was excited to say I know you."

"Thanks, Camille." I was standing and about to leave but I thought I might at least ask what he looked like, which I did.

"Nothing unusual," she said, and then giggled, "'cept I could tell he was wearing a hairpiece—my step-father has one and you can always tell."

I walked back to my office and frankly thought nothing more of it. Then the next day, I was working again at Kuruk when Nadine walked in. She stood looking at me. She was composed but I could tell her gut was churning.

"Come," she demanded.

I followed her. She led me to her apartment at the rear of the restaurant. It was a mess. Someone had ransacked every room. Not one item had been damaged but the person who had done it made it clear he was looking for something and willing to tear into every drawer, cupboard and crevice to find it. There wasn't an article of clothing that hadn't been strewn helter-skelter or an item of food or decoration that hadn't been toppled, turned or tossed.

Immediately the man Camille had mentioned to me came to mind. I brought it up to Nadine.

"They know what I'm up to; they just wanted to validate I was formally documenting the story," she deduced. "This is just the beginning. The intimidation will get worse and worse…but fuck 'em. They're not ready to kill me…yet. I'm not stopping unless they do," she said with resolute defiance. "Bullies."

"Nadine, who are they?" I asked again, entreating her to let me peek ahead into the story.

"It'll ruin your writing if I tell you the ending out of order. Trust me. We just have to work fast." Then after a moment of reflection, she asked for a pledge, which she just as quickly retracted. "No matter what happens, I want you to publish the story…that's not fair. I don't want you to be endangered"

"You're telling me that whomever *they* are, that they would try to stop me?"

"If they'd kill me, don't you think they'd do the same to you?" she said lamentably.

"If you're committed to finishing this, so am I," I informed her.

"They can kiss my royal derriere. This is not Iran. How many Americans perish in war each year fighting to protect our freedom? The least we can do is to live it to the full letter of the law," she said devoutly.

Nadine was similar to Josea when it came to patriotism. It wasn't blind faith for an abstract set of beliefs; she loved her country. Plus, she had a story to tell, and "God Damn It" she'd be willing to be killed executing her right to do so.

No wonder her stomach was in an uproar. That organ was her heart, her spine and her lungs all in one, drafted in the service of defending life, liberty and "pursuit of any darn thing I want."

I thought about my friend Preston. How on God's earth was he going to handle this dynamo? So far, he was doing it. Shockingly, they both seemed all the better for it.

That afternoon Josea and a couple employees helped Nadine clean up the mess in her cottage. I stopped by to check on her before dinner and she took me aside.

"I want to have some work done, you know, very private. I don't want to be associated with it and I don't want anyone I know to be involved."

"I'll help if I can," I offered. "But I really don't know what you're talking about."

"No, you can't help with this. But I remember you mentioned you had used an investigator—"

"Farley," I chuckled. "I'll make the man rich."

"He's good?"

"There's only one thing he had difficulty with and he openly admitted it."

"Just leave me his name and number before you go, if you wouldn't mind"

The following morning we met to work on the next sequence in the story.

"I loved teasing Dustin," she mused fondly. "I'd let him report to me brilliant findings and then gently let him know I had already figured them out. But I still never trusted him…I was alone, too far out there. Other than Chauncy, I trusted nobody. But even there, look what happened?"

"What did happen?" I coyly tried to trick her into an early insight.

"Stop it," she laughed. "You're the most impatient person I've ever met."

"That's what my mom always told me. I think it's more about excitement—like a kid, I can't wait."

"All impatience is childish, I believe," she surmised. "You didn't invent it."

Nadine asked me to wait. She went to her room and in a moment returned. She had a tiny key in her hand and a small piece of paper with writing on it.

"Take this," she said as she held it out both the key and paper. "I've put my notes outlining what happened in a safe deposit box in case something happens to me. You'll get your curiosity itch scratched one way or the other."

"You're really worried about these people?"

"I don't think they're scared as much as they're angered. If they want to bad enough, they'll take me out. Killing means nothing to these people."

I looked into her eyes. My urge was to caress her, make it all go away like a good daddy would. Nadine sensed my foolish wish. She moved close to me and smiled. Then she hugged me.

"I'm not giving up without a fight," she whispered.

Had she known she was being called on to go to war against the full power of The United States of America, she still would have raised her weapon.

41

THE DOCTOR WAS A NO SHOW

DUSTIN MET NADINE JUST as she was exiting her office. The sight of her elicited a burst of excitement that necessitated him taking two quick steps down the hall and then leaping up to touch the ceiling. His descent landed him at Nadine's side. He playfully tapped her on the shoulder.

"I just got off the phone with an… I'll just call him an acquaintance."

"I'm listening, Dustin."

"Okay, he kills Senator Hill in the bathroom of a public restaurant. What did you say about that the other day?"

"I said, how is that for chutzpah?"

"Right. Whatever that means," Dustin quipped dismissively. "Anyway, as we discussed, the killer had to be confident that Hill was going to relieve himself. How would he know it?"

"Hill is diabetic," Nadine answered playfully.

"How did you know?"

"I guessed," Nadine said with a straight face.

"That's a good guess. But I don't believe you."

Nadine couldn't keep it straight and began laughing. "I have my sources too. You think I'm going to let you get too far ahead of me?" Dustin still seemed a bit deflated. Nadine was feeling kindly toward him. "You did well. That's sophisticated investigating. Now go ahead and tell me the details."

"You know the night that Hill was killed, he was scheduled to meet with Haley. But the President couldn't have had any intention of seeing him," Dustin reported. "Where was The Man?"

"He was at the White House entertaining the Afghani ambassador," Nadine mumbled to ease any potential insult.

"The ambassador's visit had been scheduled months earlier," Dustin continued, brushing aside her showing him up one more time.

"How did you find out?" Nadine questioned him pleasantly.

"Direct quote out of the President's own appointment secretary's book. And how did you find out?" Dustin queried his partner.

"I won't tell you."

"Nadine, you're terrible today."

"I'm terrible every day. You just don't notice it all the time. Now, I think it's time we coordinate more carefully, if you're ready to fly on your own."

"I like shooting from the hip," Dustin admitted.

"It's good for you, Dustin. You'll never get anywhere in life following orders." Then Nadine changed gear. "Okay, so let's go way out and assume that Haley set up Hill. That still doesn't answer how he knew he'd be able to get to him in the bathroom…and also, why do we see a change whereby the killer is strangling his victim rather than striking the head?"

Dustin was momentarily distracted by the figure of a uniformed officer who had entered the hallway from an adjoining one. He was walking ahead of them. Dustin jumped in front of Nadine and caught up to the officer, flipping his hat off his head. The startled man turned. He quickly understood the nature of the act, pure horseplay. They exchanged a few guy-talk phrases, the conversation ending with Dustin motioning as if throwing a football pass to the would-be receiver as he raced down the hallway.

"Frisky today, aren't you?" Nadine commented breezily.

"Football buddy. We're playing Saturday."

"They're letting you play quarterback?"

"I was pretty good." Dustin complimented himself. "So you figured out the business about Hill suffering from diabetes. I guess you also know he had to use medication, but relied a lot on diet and health techniques to limit drugs." He waited for an affirmative gesture. "He was an avid exerciser and a nut about food and beverage. He was constantly drinking water. Well, get the picture?"

Nadine smiled, inviting him to continue.

"Mixing diabetes, which causes frequent urination, and a steady diet of water is like milking a cow while it's grazing," Dustin instructed. "Hill was known by his friends to never go more than twenty minutes between visits to the latrine. People who knew him well would joke by reminding him it was time."

"Now we have that settled," Nadine said matter-of-factly. "So the killer must have known Hill would arrive, learn there was no meeting and then head out to relieve himself before having his driver take him home, right?"

Dustin hesitated to proceed. He had planned to reveal at this point a delicious fact to Nadine. Now he was concerned it was redundant, but he took a shot.

"The reason this was the first ligature strangulation was because *Raymond's* had just installed—" Dustin smirked, realizing that Nadine was being generous letting him brag about another fact she had already discovered. "You know all this?"

"No, I don't," Nadine, said, having a difficult time containing the humor. "Checking at *Raymond's* was the next thing on my to-do list."

"Promise?"

"Swear on my life." Nadine held her hand over her heart.

"Cool. Well *Raymond's* just installed a scanning system that's fairly sensitive to any large metal items, like guns. A shooting in a place like *Raymond's* and you might as well close the door and put a lock on it.

So the killer didn't want to take a chance that a knife or some other object would be discovered on him and set off alarms."

"Is this public information, about the metal detection?"

"Only for those who like to dine with their hand gun or an Uzi."

"Makes sense," Nadine off-handedly commented as she deliberated on the point. "I found out it was not a metal cable that strangled Hill. It was a very tightly woven towrope that was as strong as wire. He aimed it just below the bifurcation of the carotid artery; damn near sliced the thing in half."

Nadine stopped to collect her breath. "The killer might have known all along what to expect about the scanners at the door, just as you said. Haley then could have orchestrated the whole thing to have Hill killed. He could have done it himself, if he wasn't at a reception...I'm assuming he was there."

"He was, for sure. But—"

"Was he there or not?"

"He was, Nadine, but he excused himself for business and didn't show up for an hour and a half. I can't get any information on where he was during that time."

"Dustin, we have to start checking to see if by chance all these victims were enemies of Haley."

"That's a president whose shit list I do not want to be on."

They both moved down the hall. When they came to a door on their left, Dustin held it for Nadine to go in, then followed and took a seat. Through a one-way mirror they saw a Latino male. He looked like a boy more than a man, but he was twenty-three. Covering both arms and around his neck was blue and red tattoos. He was slender, with long, braided black hair and a short, scraggly goatee. He was seated at a table, pensively.

"He was picked up running away from the scene only moments after Hill was killed. His name is Rogelio Humberto, a petty crook and junkie. Obviously he's of no interest to us other than whatever he may have seen," Dustin briefed her.

Nadine, followed by Dustin, went into the interrogation room where Rogelio was sitting.

"I'm Detective Street and this is my partner, Detective Drake."

The man tentatively shook with them. He had to be more concerned with what they were about to accuse him of than making their acquaintance. There were innumerable crimes for which he was guilty, but he was confident that once he heard the charges, he'd be able to figure out what line of fabrication to use to confound them.

Nadine knew from experience that his relaxed and indifferent persona was a façade; he was nervous. If she was going to get anything out of him, she realized she had to assure him that he was not under investigation and would be free to leave after he answered a few questions. But before she could approach the subject, he started talking.

"Look, lady, I'm on parole, so I'm keeping clean. You got nothing on me."

"We don't. Did anyone tell you why we brought you in?" Nadine gently asked the man.

"Hell, no. They brought me in like a lousy criminal. I didn't do nothin.'"

"Look, Mr. Humberto, you have my word. All we want to do is ask you a few questions and then you can go. I don't care what you did or did not do. You are not being accused or charged with anything."

"That's cool."

"The other night you were stopped running down the street. The officer took your information and let you go, remember?"

"Just like I told the man, I heard a lot of sirens and cars racing and wanted to get away as fast as I could."

"Okay, now I'm not going to even ask you why you were there—"

"I told the officer, I was looking for a job."

"Most people don't look for jobs at that time of evening, but that's not important. What I want to know is what you saw."

Now Rogelio started to get excited, talking quicker as he entered a here-and-now experiential state. "Right before I was picked up, I was running. I come to this alley, so I turned sharp into it. Then just as I do, I almost tripped on this briefcase lying right on the ground. There was this man, seemed like he was about to tear something off his face, like his hair. Weird."

"What can you tell us about the man?"

"That's it. I was scared. When I saw him, I turned around and went back out the alley and up the block. That's when they picked me up."

"So you can't picture anything about the man?" Dustin broke in.

"I swear. I'd tell you, but I was flying out of there."

"You said he was possibly pulling something off his face, like hair of some type. Can you recall which hand he was using?" Nadine continued the interrogation.

"I guess…wait, I get confused about my left and right." The man stopped to mentally walk himself through the experience. "I'm moving as fast as I can and I turn… this way into the alley—he's holding up his right arm. Yeah, I go right. Then the man is over by a trash barrel, one of those giant ones behind businesses. So he's to my right, and he's using…this one, for sure—he's now holding out his left hand."

"Left hand?" Nadine questioned.

"Definitely, like he's pulling off…crazy man, he's pulling off his beard. I can see that but I can't see him."

"Now think carefully if there is anything else you recall, no matter how insignificant you think it might be."

"There's nothing, really."

"I told you as soon as we finished, you'd be free to go. We're done. But Mr. Humberto, I'm giving you my card. By chance if you remember anything else, anything about the man, I want you to call me. Now you may get home and all of a sudden remember, for example, he was wearing tennis shoes or had a scar on his forehead.

"I know how it is, if you did remember something you wouldn't want to call a cop. I understand that, but this is very important. So if you do call me and by chance have more information, then sometime in the future you may need help with something and you'll know whom to call. Do you understand what I'm saying?"

Nadine was not dishonoring her profession by misleading him. She had performed many acts—all legal ones—to assist those who helped her with a case. Her tips typically came at a cost, but she paid her debts.

"I hear you, miss."

"Thanks, Rogelio." Then she motioned him to leave.

He began walking out, but was seized by a thought. "There was one other thing, Miss."

"What?" Nadine asked, trying to restrain her impatience.

"He didn't actually talk. It was more like a growl but I heard him say, "How do you like that, sonny boy?"

"That's all he said? You sure?"

"Absolutely."

"Anything you remember about his voice...face."

"Only that he sounded angry, like a demon."

"Call me if you want to talk more," Nadine reiterated as he left.

A second later, Nadine and Dustin were making their way down the same hall.

"That's the first person to definitely confirm the disguises, Dustin."

"And that he's left-handed."

"'Sonny boy? How do you like that?'" Nadine parroted the words while she tried to decipher their meaning. "Like he's proving something? Wants to show off, build himself up to someone he sees as beneath him?" Then she jabbered so only she could hear. "He tried to intimidate me with his note."

Dustin reached in his pocket and hesitantly took out a piece of paper. His uncertainty was due to the fact that Nadine had disclosed to him that she was seeing Dr. Monroe socially and that he had offered to help with the case.

"Nadine, this isn't going to thrill you," Dustin cautiously prepared her. "I know you'd want to see it but I wasn't sure when to give it to you."

He handed her the paper. It was a log sheet. She examined it quizzically, noticing a line in bolded print.

LECTURER WAS NO SHOW.

Dustin explained. "You asked me to examine Blank's phone calls the day he was killed."

"So what did you find?"

"That's the schedule for the class that Dr. Monroe teaches on Tuesday nights at the university. As you can see, he's a reliable professor. There is only one session he missed, the one designated as a No Show. What is unusual is not so much he that couldn't make it but that he never called to say he wouldn't be there."

"What does Blank's murder have to do with Dr. Monroe's teaching?"

"Nadine, the No Show was the night Blank was killed…and I hate to say it, but the telephone records show the doctor called Blank earlier in the day."

Nadine exhibited a flat, expressionless stare, heralding no sign of the inner drama fomenting. She kept moving along the hallway.

"I'm sorry." Dustin spoke as if he'd misbehaved.

She addressed him nonchalantly. "There is no reason for you to have the slightest reservation about delivering to me any relevant information."

Her head was pounding and pulsing. By chance, at that instant, Lambert was approaching, from the opposite direction along the hallway. Seeing him reminded her that she needed to discuss allocation of funds for informants. In spite of everything Dustin was bring-ing to her attention, she needed to arrange a time to debate what she knew would be a testy matter with her boss. She deliberately moved into his path.

"Chief, I wanted to talk with you about—"

"I'm busy, Street."

Lambert whizzed by, no horn tooting, only a blast of dark smoke stinking up the hallway. Nadine had only Dustin to hear her conster-nation. "Asshole."

Dustin thought he could soften the blow. "If the Chief is involved, you'll get his job."

"That is a definite N O."

She then resumed a calm detachment. She felt she needed to put to rest any doubts Dustin might have had about his boss sacrific-ing objectivity in favor of romance.   "What if the college chums had some secret pact that they would forever support one another regardless of the consequences? Could they're all be working togeth-er to plan and execute these murders?" she posed ponderously.

"My dad would make a bundle defending them," Dustin smirked.

"Let's be realistic. It would never get to that."

"It could. Look what happened to Nixon."

"This is different, Dustin—this is murder. They'd probably try to kill us before they'd be taken down."

Dustin rolled his eyes to punctuate his response: "Oh, great."

42

BAD GENES

NADINE ARRANGED IMMEDIATELY TO go to Chauncy's office at the university. She was not the type to leave her curiosity on hold for long. When she arrived as scheduled, she ran into him scooting out with not one, but two, cute little ladies, one on each arm. He was giggling like we would expect he should be, and the students looked happy too. He didn't notice Nadine until he had a near head-on collision with her. His comment to her was of similar revelatory order as a man discovering that cars have engines.

"The young ones find me irresistible."

Nadine, a bit startled, wondered if she needed to play mommy. *Great, Chauncy. Just make sure you card them before serving drinks.* But her words reflected astonishment more than practicality. "So, I see."

"Nadine, just go in my office. I logged under my code so do whatever you want. When you're finished, if you don't mind, shut it down." He paused to begrudgingly permit a moment of reality, looking side to side at the girls. "Don't worry. We're on our way to class."

"Thanks, Chauncy."

Nadine entered his office, a small room cluttered mostly with books and files. The only pictures on the walls were standard issue prints that had likely been there since the last professor occupied the space. Behind his desk on a table was a computer. She swiveled his rocker around to face the screen, easily accessing Dr. Lawrence

Monroe's dossier.

It began with a standard introduction: age, marital status, level of education, professional associations and licenses. The next section highlighted specifics regarding colleges and universities, as well as fields of expertise and specific work experience. So far there were no surprises.

Nadine mumbled as she perused the material. *So he did graduate from Yale. Later received his medical training from Harvard, going on to residency at Columbia School of Medicine... Psychiatric license... valid in several states including New York, Colorado and California.*

Professional publications, hospital staff assignments and research specialties—wow! Federal and state agency consultations and legislative advisory panel assignments: he's good at what he does, that's for sure.

Interesting outline. Summarizes, evaluates, and rates his involvement with Bureau assignments. "AAA" rating; must mean your cases are as safe with him as your money in U. S. Treasuries...we hope, anyway. Holy crap, he's consulted on the most extreme serial cases...Jeffrey Dahmer, David Berkowitz, Richard Ramirez, Ed Gein... and Theodore Bundy. But there's no reference to his relationship with anyone outside The Bureau. No mention of Haley, Lambert, Drake or anybody else.

Then she clicked on *Final Summary*. The screen switched to a page entitled, *Sensitive Material*.

As she scanned the contents her stomach sank. It stated that Larry was raised in Mississippi up to age nine, when his father murdered his mother. Custody was given to industrialist Calvin Monroe, Larry's paternal uncle in Virginia. Larry's father, as of last update, was in Mississippi State Penitentiary serving life without possibility of parole.

Nadine aimed the cursor to darken the section she wanted to print. She pressed enter. A single page printed. She folded it and placed it in her purse. Then she shut down Chauncy's computer. She left after completing what she was hoping would be step one in a one-step process.

Her first stop was the library. I'll summarize what she uncovered; it was quite extensive:

Winona, Mississippi is a small town about twenty-five miles east of Greenwood and is considered to be the eastern entrance to the Mississippi delta. Other than that distinction, a claim to fame of no significance to anyone other than those immediately proximate to the region, it had no distinction until...until years after Tyler and Maggie Monroe started their family.

In rapid succession, the couple had two boys, first Calvin and then Bobbie, only one year apart. One might say—years after relatives and friends did—that the dearness of Calvin rushed them into a second child, and with the same degree of dismay, Bobbie sealed their resolve to never have another.

It's not uncommon for fruit from the same tree to vary in sweetness. Calvin and Bobbie differed in every quality of temperament, attitude, intellect and behavior about as much as a dove and a python.

Calvin was easy to rear, cooperative, eager to please, and on top of that hardworking and quick to learn. He was caring and likeable. Bobby was everything negative that Calvin was positive. From birth he was a grumpy, irritable and colicky baby. As he developed, he rebelled against the disciplines of parental and community authority. At first, his antics landed him in principals' offices and later in local police stations and jails.

His social network was a handpicked crew of coarse and profane types. His appetite for the most elite level of miscreant forced him to travel distances to other communities to find the worst of the worst. While he was acquiring the fine arts of crime, drug and alcohol abuse, and violence, his brother was lining his wall with awards and degrees.

By the time that the brothers were in their early twenties, Bobbie had a long record of arrests and convictions. Conversely, Calvin was on his way to a stellar career in business. In fact, he had already opened the first of what would be many successful enterprises, Monroe Sand & Gravel. By that time, he was also working on Can't Miss Catch Catfish, a line of luring gear that would shortly attain national recognition in the fishing sport industry.

When Bobbie was only sixteen he hooked up with Sissy Gandry, the daughter of a local farmer. As a father, Mr. Gandry was a stern, strict and rigid man; and his wife was as religiously predictable as a tape measure. Unfortunately, a year after the birth of their daughter, the mother suffered acute vaginal hemorrhaging requiring a full hysterectomy, precluding the couple from having a second child.

While Sissy was never abused, she would have fared better to share the oppression of parental love with siblings. Being an only child is arguably a choice situation to inherit in that there is no apportioning of love and money. However, it can be a great disadvantage should there be negative traits and patterns on the part of the parents because there's nobody with whom to divvy up the suffering.

Sissy, a quiet and docile child by nature, sucked the subjugation from her home like the delta drank mud from her beloved Mississippi. Bobbie must have donned a charismatic veil the day they met. In Sissy's eyes, there was nothing that Bobbie could do to remove it.

She defended him from any guilty verdict regardless of evidence to the contrary, turned away from acts of disloyalty on his behalf when she must have known there would be new affairs following the long line preceding them. She believed his promises that he would redeem himself for misbehavior toward her when she knew he was morally bankrupt. She was an old, sad, pathetic story replaying itself for no sake other than attesting to man's undying devotion to hope.

She was only fifteen when pregnant with her first child, Lawrence. From deep in the swampy land of Mississippi, her life sunk to unfathomable depths. Bobbie was absent most of the time. When he did show up it was with no spendable loot, but lots of booze. He drank himself wild and then started in on his wife.

She tried to pacify him with sex, which would only infuriate him—no doubt he had already had his fill. As little Lawrence grew, the sight of him drove Bobbie to rage. Beatings for the boy were commonplace. When mother protested or tried to defend him, Bobbie delighted in whipping her with a birch switch as well.

All this was spelled out in the numerous articles Nadine reviewed from the Greenwood Mississippi Commonwealth Newspaper. Based on the history, the outcome was as predictable as dirty water squeezed from black earth. It was to be the biggest news story the region covered in several decades.

Nadine scanned a series of pictures. First, was a desperately-in-need-of-repair shack of a house where the family lived. Second, was a shot of Bobbie Monroe, a man whose picture reeked of evil. Next there was one of Sissy, her body lying haphazard on the floor. The final picture was a little boy noted as Lawrence Monroe, age nine, expressionless in a rocking chair.

She gritted her teeth. This was exactly the type of stink hole many of her killers came from.

The revolting tale of the Greenwood trauma ended unceremoniously for the media, with a simple, dismissive headline: "BOBBIE MONROE CONVICTED OF MURDERING WIFE."

Nadine searched further, but little was ever mentioned in the paper again about what the community considered a shameful episode that was best forgotten.

The article did say it took the jury no more than an hour to deliberate his guilt for brutally beating and then strangulating his wife to death.

Bobbie Monroe was known as an alcoholic and had a history of violence, including threats with guns and physical abuse toward his young son. A powerful man, rumor has it that in a bar fight he immobilized a large man by grabbing his arm with so much force he crushed the ulna and radius bones, causing compound fractures. In murdering his wife, he caused multiple broken bones in the neck.

Nadine felt a jolt. *Multiple broken bones in the neck.*

There was one final statement of great interest to Nadine.

The boy has been turned over to state officials.

Reading this information was as painful to her as meeting face-to-face with family members of murder victims. She wept at the screen, stood up, went to the bathroom, and vomited.

After she composed herself, she went back to the screen and made the copies she wanted for her file. Then she searched for any later additions to the story. There was nothing until two years before her meeting Larry, when a newspaper in Jackson, Mississippi, over a hundred miles away, published a very short clip: *Bobby Monroe, convicted murderer, died in prison yesterday. He was fifty-nine years old.*

Nadine sat immobilized in front of the monitor. It might have been hours before she moved. She had warned Larry not to lie to her. Had he not believed her that future acts of betrayal would be terminal to their relationship?

She also deliberated if what she had found would qualify as a punishable deceit? No doubt he withheld the truth about his family history, but who wouldn't? Come on, if any sane person were applying for a job as a youth counselor would they put on their resume that their father was a convicted child molester?

Larry came from a rotten father. Should he wear a sign: MY DAD IS A CONVICTED KILLER? No, but…and there is a legitimate "but" she couldn't dismiss like a mistaken weather forecast.

He's a grown man, an accomplished analyst, she reasoned. *Presumably he had a life of opportunity after the tragedy, not to mention the reviews of his history suggest his mother delighted over him, as did his grandparents, so it's not as if it was all torture and hate. Why does he have to covet a sordid piece of his past? If a man can't face yesterday openly and cleanse his heart of shame or regret, then can he live with truth today, live a life of courage and integrity?*

As she sat with these crushing thoughts zipping ungovernably in her head, a new image was born. It was one final character in her silent script; it masqueraded as a question mark, taking a position in line in her parade of the absurd. When the haunting image passed, she tried cursing it out of existence, but failed. This surreal, yes emblematic, devout homage Dr. Lawrence Monroe had for the sick and incurable mind must have found its tributary stream in the soul of Bobbie Monroe.

There was only one course of action our heroine would permit for herself. She knew she had to take the great load she now carried and land it on Larry's doorstep. She wondered if dreams of make-believe worlds made up of sunny beaches and warm skies ever came true for people like Nadine Street, motherless child.

She was digesting the inevitable direction she needed to travel when her mind shifted to…guess whom?

"I'm looking at myself, Nadine Street, strong, resolute, self-assured, nothing like the meek, timid, fearful and hopeless Sissy Monroe, the girl who found love for a hellhound sinner, but I'm being swept just as helplessly into a love that might kill me," she admitted to me.

"If this slogan of mine that I'd sleep with a killer to solve the case is about to be tested, I'm getting a little nervous. But I'm still not ready to prosecute this man because of the past. I'm going to have to play this out a few more moves and then make a decision."

She loved him. She loved him. She loved him.

That delirium stirring, frenzy concocting, abracadabra state can sock a being in the belly like a meteorite. Love can mimic the condition of madness. In that state, even the greatest of our American leaders, athletes and outlaws have found ruin.

Nadine left the library to be ominously greeted by a dark, windy night. She felt comforted that her fate would not be similar to that of

Sissy Monroe. Then again, Sissy Monroe's suffering ended.

Tomorrow afternoon it's off to Dr. Monroe's office. The famous psychiatrist has a hidden aid he employs in treating his patients. None of them, not one, knows, and none ever will. But it's still a big deal.

43

NO, MRS. PURCELL, I DON'T
TAKE NOTES

LIKE FATHER, LIKE SON? Maybe Dr. Monroe sitting at his desk this afternoon was contemplating the idea in spite of his objections to its truth. He was gazing at the opposite wall from where he sat. The allotted few minutes between sessions had been a restless time. He was anticipating *That One Patient* he wished not to see. Knowing he had to schedule an extra treatment session because of something deemed "urgent" by the patient, added to his unpleasant mood.

He stood up and paced, walking to the window, perhaps to get an early sighting of the scoundrel crossing the street. He glanced over his shoulder in the direction of the arrival light, still not lit… reprieve. *And may it last forever,* he whispered to himself. No luck. Precisely at the stroke of five the light cast a dreaded command for him to walk to the waiting room.

"Come in," Monroe said perfunctorily to the arriving patient.

Dr. Monroe is no different from most serious analysts. He has a selection of patients he routinely sees at least once a week at a specified time for long-term treatment. Understandably, each of his patients is a complex story with a vast history, static and dynamic plots and themes, characters interacting with and acting upon one another, and rhythmic, circuitous, progressive and converging events. His job is to log all of the information, store it for future use, and be able to readily draw on it as the need may arise.

Of course, there are challenges in attempting to be effective at collecting this mountain of facts. To take copious notes distracts a doctor from noticing the subtleties of the patient's non-verbal communication and listening attentively to his or her story. Monroe decided long ago that the return from scribing notes was not worth the cost to the therapeutic process.

Finally he hit upon another process whereby he would always have a perfect running record of every patient's chart in the event he needed it. He decided to install a recording network. Whereas, at first, it was a cumbersome process handling the tapes and cassettes, over the years as technology advanced, greater levels of simplicity were achieved, up to the latest generation of a fully digitized recording system.

No, he never informed his patients they were being recorded. He rationalized that he was doing them a favor because he could devote to them his undivided attention. He assumed the discs would never come into the hands of anyone else. He also concluded that as long as he concealed the equipment so nobody knew of its existence, and then locked it safely to protect its security, there was no harm done.

He would end up badly mistaken on all accounts.

Dr. Monroe's system was housed in a closet in the corner of the office. If one were to open the door leading into that secret area, they would notice besides the jackets, office supplies and stereo set, a compact piece of equipment, similar to a small computer, with a hard drive that stores every word spoken in his office. Even his end of phone conversations, from the moment he arrives in the morning to closing in the evening was preserved.

In this way, he could house in the cabinet a living transcript of his work for years running: he labeled the drives by date and kept them in chronological order. After the last patient left each day, Larry's habit was to make the appropriate backup and then shut down the system.

Following the therapeutic session, Dr. Monroe had completed with his reviled patient on this particular afternoon, he felt distressed. So before shutting down the system, he allocated time after the patient left to listen back on what transpired.

I was privileged to hear selected recordings that Nadine handed to me (the conditions of her betrayal in attaining them to be divulged shortly), allowing me to make verbatim presentations.

"You called me and insisted on an extra session. Why?" Monroe confronted the patient.

"We—that's right, doc, *we*—have a problem," the patient shot at Monroe.

"You insisted you had a matter of urgency you needed to see me about. Now you're saying it's my problem also, but I don't know what it is."

"Oh, let's not get back to the games," the patient spoke derisively.

"You know the rules. I'm available for emergencies, real emergencies only," Monroe admonished.

"I'll decide when we have an emergency," the patient struck back.

"I can assure you it's not an emergency for me, so it's not 'us' having a problem. Why don't you tell me what's on your mind. If I can help you, I will."

"Okay, we'll do it your way," the patient jeered. "She's a woman. Now you see the problem?"

"No. And I believe we agreed your sessions would be about you and not me."

"That would have been the case except you can't seem to handle your women."

"She has nothing to do with any of this. Leave her alone." Monroe was half pleading and half warning.

"I can't. I've been instructed to take care of her, if you can't. It seems you don't get it." The man continued invectively. "Women are bitches and have a way of doing things to men, especially men like you who can't control them."

"What are you so worried about? She knows nothing about you and never will. Just leave her alone."

"Beautiful, doc. Her job *is* to know about me. She's not gonna' stop until she finds me. And you could lead her right to my door."

"I would never—"

"You're so far gone with her you don't know what you would do."

The piercing, propelling sound of a helicopter dimmed the voices momentarily, the pause no doubt offered Dr. Monroe reprieve.

"She's a cunt," the patient screeched, louder than normal to overcome the residual thumping of the blades. "I'll tell you what I would do. If it were up to me, I'd get rid of her...NOW!"

"That's your style, isn't it?" Monroe fired back.

"It's our friend's style too," the man countered in a cunning manner. "He's as cruel as I am. If you don't get this right, I think he'll turn me loose on her. Wasn't too happy with General Crow or Senator Hill and look what happened to them."

There was a gap of time on the tape after the last comment, about a minute. During this period a rustling was heard, as if someone was pacing the office. Then the patient's voice burst loudly from what was clearly a different location. "I'm very worried about her, and you should be too."

The next sound was a door slamming.

A passing glance at Dr. Monroe would have surprisingly found his appearance about the exchange apathetic, but as he lifted his arms backward to stretch, profuse moisture under his arms revealed his agitation.

Monroe knows absolutely who the patient is and what his capabilities are. He also knows it's a pig-faced lie that the patient been instructed about anything pertaining to Nadine. The only genuine issue is that he hates her, period.

To make matters worse, Monroe knows he's pathetically caught in the middle of something he can only hope and pray will end soon.

His only saving grace is that he does firmly believe, as Haley assured him, that the patient would end treatment soon and then remove himself from Dr. Monroe's life.

The back line phone ringing interrupted his lamentation. Monroe was able to achieve composure and answered in a relaxed voice.

"Hello."

"It's me."

"Oh, Nadine. I'd like to see you."

"Good. When?" she chirped, eager to keep her agenda hidden until they were together.

"Tomorrow night. I don't think I ever mentioned it to you but I act in a theatre group. Come see the play. We can go out after."

"I'd love to," she replied. "My lord, you are a busy man. How do you have time for all this…and me?"

"We only do two plays a year and I'm afraid our limited rehearsal time doesn't do the outcome any good," he laughed.

"I'll still come."

Larry urgently needed to talk to someone, Nadine especially. He yearned to spill the rotten beans, exorcise the evil teeth nibbling his toes, but there were reasons he wouldn't. To himself he lamented his sorrowful plight, the silence long enough to gain Nadine's attention.

"Larry, you there?" Nadine shouted into the phone.

"Sorry. I was thinking about something."

"You must have just finished an interesting session—care to share?"

"No, actually it was a disturbing call on my back office line that came in a while ago," referring in truth to the patient he had just seen.

"Well, what was the call about?"

"I told you we could both be in danger. The voice insisted I tell you to be careful."

"Is that the first contact you've ever had with him?"

"Yes," he responded, seeing no option but to lie.

"Did he say anything else?"

"No, that was all."

"Well, could you tell anything by his voice?"

"It was very fast. No, there was nothing I noticed. Nadine, you've got to be careful!"

"That's exactly what I'm doing. I'll see you tomorrow evening."

Perhaps an off-off-off, far-away-from Broadway production might be the perfect mental massage to ease her tension.

44

PSYCH THEATER

EVERYONE LOVES BROADWAY; IT's a national treasure. Like Washington, D.C., it makes us proud of the masterful artistic creations for us and from us over the last hundred years. But there is a big difference between D.C. and Broadway. That is, you can never find what characterizes D.C. anywhere in the world. However, what Broadway offers can be discovered in various colors, sizes and shapes in many other places around the globe.

Take for example, Los Angeles. There are more theatres in the greater L.A. area than even New York. And around the whole United States, there are literally thousands of live production houses lit up to provide dramas, romances, comedies and musicals year around. These range from venues with thousands of seats and $100-plus tickets to store fronts with less than a hundred seats charging under $10 per performance. The best part is that the size and price is not predictive of what you're going to experience.

The most elaborately designed, lavishly funded and extensively marketed pieces, with famous and renowned artists, can flop; while evenings of unimaginable joy can be harvested from productions put on literally with a shoe string and staffed by unknown actors and directors.

You have to love it…it's a grassroots free-for-all in live theatre, for it represents everything democratic and liberating, it nurtures and cradles artistic freedom; it's the best of what America is, has ever been, and will ever be.

It's cocktail waitresses playing Cleopatra, truck drivers playing Caesar, shoe clerks playing card sharks, lonely widows playing wives and mothers, penniless welfare recipients playing princes, disabled construction workers playing Supreme Court Justices, prostitutes playing...prostitutes.

It's more about the love of acting than anything else. The greatest of Hollywood talent—actors, choreographers, directors, producers, stage directors, lighting directors—who make a bundle more in TV or film cannot resist at least once in a while the thrill of doing it live, for a breathing, sneezing, tearing, cheering theatre audience.

Larry's opinion was that if the theatre-bug bit, you were infected for life. Then, a person might sacrifice great opportunity for the delight to act, even for a half-filled theatre that only has a hundred seats. Which takes us to Larry's production in a theatre with about that many seats, but fortunately filled.

There was standing room only in the rear. The end of the production was near. Nadine arrived early for the first-come first-serve performance and was sitting dead center, her face fixed with a contagious smile.

The actors were dressed in costumes suggesting a twentieth century English period; they all had appropriate accents. The scene was a festive atmosphere highlighted by a couple—the male Larry—on one side of the stage holding one another in a state of exhilaration, joyfully dancing and prancing. On the opposite side of the stage was a king on his throne. A loyal subject approached his master.

"Your Highness asked that I find the secret to a happy marriage."

The king nodded to acknowledge he indeed did. Then he addressed the lowly one.

"You have found the answer?"

"My Lord, I have been by land and sea for three years searching for a couple that can answer the question."

"Then you must reveal what your journey has produced," the king ordered.

"This couple," the subject pointed to the still rejoicing twosome across stage, "has been together for over thirty years and they never disagree, fight or argue."

"Send for the queen," the king called out with the imperial demeanor reserved for kings.

Several attendants from off stage were seen ushering in Her Royal Highness. She was seated next to her mate.

"Once again we shall find peace in our union. This good fellow has traveled the world by ship and foot to find, my love, that elusive ingredient for a long and happy marriage."

The Queen begrudged a skimpy nod. She appeared more amused than optimistic. The king directed his wife's attention to the couple frolicking together.

"They have been together three decades and more, yet are as content and compatible today as when they met." Then boldly he queried to his subject. "Humble one, what is their secret?"

The lowly citizen bowed deeply to the king, then in turn to the queen.

"Royal Ones, they are each married to another."

The king looked quizzically at the queen who was quick to deliver a rebuke for her husband having blundered again. The audience laughed and clapped. The music began. The entire cast of characters joined with the royal and not-close-to royal couple: traditional bows were followed by traditional applause.

The best things in life are often free, or so close to it they might as well be. Larry's performance charged a mighty five bucks a seat; no wonder no empty seats. Most remarkable was the faces of the audience; nobody left the performance in other than a cheery mood.

Nadine, along with the rest of the group, headed out to the small lobby to enjoy another of the amenities of theatre-of-the-unknown.

With productions on this scale, the actors come out after the house darkens and bathe their starving egos in the audience's accolades.

Larry was one of the first to appear. He hustled excitedly through the small crowd to give Nadine a full embrace. Nadine, holding a bouquet of flowers, handed it to him. It was likely the only gift of flowers he'd ever received in his life. He faced Nadine with the flowers awkwardly held in front of him. Nadine assumed getting flowers set off some "silly male reaction" Larry would have to get over if he was going to be a fixture in her life—she loved giving gifts that were alive.

"Let me hold them for you. I love that play. I didn't know you were such an accomplished actor."

"I keep it to myself," Larry said as his mouth widened with joy.

"I hope soon there'll be no more secrets," Nadine said, her tone slightly ominous.

"We'll see," Larry, answered, oblivious to her warning.

"How did you get into this acting thing?"

"Like the rest of the people here. We're all psychiatrists: the actors, writers, directors, set designers, costume directors, lighting people, even the ticket sellers. We rotate jobs, but we all perform. Didn't you notice the little placard when you came in, *Psych Theatre*?"

"I did but I guess I didn't pay attention to what it meant."

"I'm not the only doctor who would abhor going for treatment. It's common knowledge amongst us that we have a stressful occupation, yet we have few options to relieve our own pressures. So the theatre idea naturally came about. It was our way of trying to deal more effectively with our feelings. We opened about five years ago. This little place has never broken even," he expressed delightfully.

"Clever."

"Every bit of material is one-of-a-kind written by us. The play you watched...yours truly is the playwright."

"I'm impressed. Really, I am."

"Come on, we'll get a drink and something to eat."

It had been a short time since she and Larry were last together, yet much had happened. While Nadine rejoiced in the festivities of the play, at the same time she was agitated over the interrogation soon to come.

It's a romance, not an investigation. Chauncy's words circled through her mind. With the information she now had, it was looking a lot more like an investigation...and Larry was going to be interrogated once more.

45

INVESTIGATING A ROMANCE

LARRY AND NADINE WERE strolling along the street. She wasted no time employing the tactical plan she devised to approach Larry. The Blank killing would be the bait. She'd relax him into the role of being her consultant by feeding him information about her investigation, and then...

"We're turning up some interesting material now on some of the murders," she said casually. "Take Blank. We're now certain the killer knew Blank and that he had been to Blank's place before the murder."

"How can you know for certain?"

"The murder weapon. It was a screwdriver that was part of a set that belonged to the congressman—the matching pieces were found in a drawer in the kitchen."

"I don't understand what that means."

"The killer has to strike fast, right? He comes disguised, yet he's easily recognizable to the victim. Any time allotted for the person to react, and the scene could turn unpredictable. Now that means the killer had to have possession of the weapon when he arrived, so he had to bring it. In order to do that he had to take it on a previous visit."

"I hate to weaken your finding but isn't it just as likely, or at least factually probable, that he possessed the same tools and by chance brought with him one that matched Blank's set?" Larry proposed.

"Two reasons that's improbable. First, the size of the tool missing from Blank's kitchen set was the one used to kill him. Second, Blank's fingerprints were on all the tools, including the one used to kill him. I doubt the killer is that clever, to put Blank's prints on the screwdriver in anticipation of somebody concluding that the killer had visited Blank before the murder." Nadine stared oddly at Larry before proceeding.

"Would you propose that the killer decided to use the fingerprints to create a false truth for the purpose of throwing off the investigation? And if so, how would he have known Blank had the exact same set of tools in the first place? You're raising probabilities in the one out of one billion range," she argued.

"Then I agree. That's big. Now all you have to do is figure out who was at Blank's house during a reasonable span of time prior to the murder, and you have a suspect list. I'm sure you're already working on it."

"I'm not certain we can get a complete listing, but I will tell you we have the name of someone who was there just three days before Blank's death." She paused to inspect him before continuing. "I have to ask you something."

"Nadine, I told you I want to help with this."

"I'm not asking you to help. I want you to answer a question about you."

"Sure, anything."

He took her arm and aimed her down the block.

"The day Congressman Blank was killed you called him. Do you remember that?"

If Nadine expected this direct line of inquiry to ruffle him she was plainly wrong. Monroe was entertained.

"Am I still a suspect? Really, have I ever not been?" he laughed. "Let's see, I'm left handed, refused to disclose my prior friendship with your charming boss, sought you out on my own to help, and now called one of the victims on the very day he was killed." He holds his hands straight out and together, inviting a cuffing. "I'm all yours."

"Larry, this is not a joke."

"I'm not making light of it. I…am…all…yours," he repeated play-fully. Then he spoke more earnestly. "Nadine, I can't apologize for my connections. I know most people in this town. If you checked, I be-lieve you'd find I knew every one of the victims. That does not make me a killer—I know you're a better detective than that. But I do get the feeling you have some interest in damaging something special we have together. Why can't you enjoy us? Why are you trying to destroy what I think is love between us?"

"I'm looking for a murderer. You keep popping up in my investi-gation. I have to follow every lead. I'm not going to let my relation-ship with you interfere."

"Fine. Then let me explain about Blank," Larry responded indiffer-ently. "He heads—headed I should say—a congressional committee that controls the funding for mental health research. I do everything I can to support my chosen profession, especially when it comes to scientific endeavors.

"I lobby. I'm on the payroll of several organizations, including the National Institute of Mental Health and American Psychiatric Asso-ciation. I'll show you all the records to substantiate this. They use me to influence legislation impacting particular areas of experimental research. As you might understand by now, I'm able to talk to the right people…and get them to listen."

"So you're saying you called Blank that day to talk about money?" Nadine questioned dubiously.

"If you examine the records you'll see I've called him several times and even visited with him at his home and office during the last month. You can check with his secretary, Marley, and she'll have not only the meeting dates, but also the agenda of what we talked about. Recently when we met it was getting down to crunch time because voting by his committee was due on two crucial pieces of legislation.

In fact, the vote was scheduled for the day after his tragic demise."

Nadine stood mutely as Larry continued.

"Now, can we go have a drink?"

"There's more."

"Well, let's get it over with now, please," he said tolerantly.

"Fine. On the evening of Blank's murder you were scheduled to lecture, but you never showed up for class. The next day when the school contacted you, it was reported to them that you forgot; you never missed a class before this."

Larry was bullet proof, a comic book hero holding up his hands to repel rockets, missiles and grenades, all the while with the attitude of the Jolly Green Giant.

"What a disappointing evening for you, Nadine. You were really hoping to make an arrest and wrap up your case. Instead, you and I are going to have a drink, a great meal, and best of all, snuggle with each other."

"I'd like that, believe it or not."

"Oh, I believe it. You can't keep yourself from questioning me. That's what I adore about you. If it were me who was your killer you'd put me away before I could scratch an itch. If it came to it, you'd shoot me dead on the spot. It's a professional code, and honorably I share it with you; we're very much alike."

"We do have a few traits in common, don't we?" she admitted.

"More than one. Now, can I answer your question about not showing up for class?"

"Please do."

"Howard called and said he needed me. I went to the White House. It was last minute. Shamefully, I did forget to notify anyone at the school."

"What was so important?"

"That, I cannot discuss. Please, he's the president and there are personal matters it would be inappropriate for me to divulge. But I want to put you at ease about the circumstance of my whereabouts when Blank was killed and clear myself once and any suspicions that you might have." Larry reached into his pant pocket. "I look forward to us spending our time together in ways other than you conducting interrogations of me. Now, one call should clear this up."

He tapped on the keypad of his cell. "This is Dr. Monroe. Please connect me to the president's scheduling office." Larry punched in a special code to verify his identity. "Dr. Monroe, this is Anne Tranton."

"Hi, Anne. I have a favor to ask of you. My friend Nadine Street is with me. We're having a little disagreement about plans we had the other night—you know, I said this, she said that. I think you can be the objective third party to settle this for us. I'm going to put her on."

"If I can help, of course, Dr. Monroe."

Larry handed the phone to Nadine.

"Hi, I'm Nadine. I'm sorry to bother you but if you have the records for the evening of March seventeenth this year, could you check if Dr. Monroe was there?"

"Ms. Street, could I put you on hold for just a moment so I can find it?"

Nadine waited only a few seconds, during that time she watched Larry stroll a few paces down the street.

"I have it right here, Ms. Street. On the seventeenth of March, I show an entry by Melva Marks, my associate, that Dr. Monroe was called at the request of the president at six thirty to come to the White House. Dr. Monroe arrived at seven ten. He logged out at ten twenty-eight. Is there anything else I can do for you?"

"No, you've been very helpful. Thank you."

Nadine flipped close the phone. She called to Larry who was a full store length down the block. He came to meet her, beaming with confidence. "Just ask me in the future if there's anything you doubt."

"Okay, then tell me about your family."

Larry's confident smile was still plastered on his face. "I'm glad you mentioned that. I thought we'd talk about it tonight."

This should be interesting.

46

WE'VE GOT THAT LOVIN' FEEL-ING

CECIL'S PLACE WAS LOCATED a few stores up along the same street. The couple sat at a small table toward the rear of the restaurant. Nadine later recorded in her diary in that moment she felt the most peaceful, secure and relaxed she'd experienced since meeting Larry. The coincidences, clues and inconsistencies dissolved into the appetizing aromas coming from Cecil's kitchen, leaving her freed for the moment from the awful sensation of being harshly tugged in two opposing directions simultaneously. Larry would be her man, if not for eternity, at least for that evening.

Their hands reached out across the table and clasped. They gazed at each other, bonded as tightly in sight as touch. The time they were embracing passed in an instant but might have been a long duration because twice the waitress approached the table but sensitively backed off from disturbing them. Larry's play ended at seven forty-five; they wouldn't order dinner until ten-thirty.

Larry had an unresolved issue of his own he hadn't had time to bring up to Nadine due to him being under her investigation. At the first opportunity, he approached the subject.

"I called you today. Didn't you get my message?"

"I'm sorry that I didn't get back to you," she smiled. "I was busy preparing for our meeting tonight."

"Honestly, it makes me feel badly if you ignore my calls. You've done it a couple of times before, but I haven't said anything."

"I know. I get so wrapped up in what I'm doing that I shut everything out." She pulled him closer and kissed him tenderly. "I promise, it won't happen again."

"Does this mean we're going steady?"

"As soon as I get to wear your ring around my neck."

"Sounds like Elvis Presley; the fifties." Larry held out his hands. "No rings today." Then he casually reached into his jacket and took out a small box. He held it toward her. "Will this do?"

He handed it to Nadine and she opened it. It was a gold necklace with a heart-shaped pendant. It was common in theme but elegant in design. Nadine was taken back.

"For me? Larry…"

Larry opened the clasp and placed it around her neck, admiring the facets of the diamonds as they sparkled from the candle flickering on the table.

"I feel like I'm in high school. Going steady is great," Larry said merrily.

"I'll tell you the truth. I never went steady in high school. I never….let's save this one for later. I'm really touched you would do this."

The waitress did come to the table a third time and they ordered a drink to celebrate. Larry then volunteered to provide Nadine the background she'd been waiting to hear about his family. There were no discrepancies as he recited the story, but he did offer many additions she'd have preferred not to know.

"Bobby Monroe was a vicious father. I wish he had abandoned my mother and me. Long before he killed my mother, he took sadistic pleasure in torturing us. From my earliest recall, I have nothing but graphic images of the horrors he put us through." Larry's recounting of the early years of his life seemed dispassionate.

"There was a time he locked me in a closet with the water heater and left me there several hours. He thought he was the master of the house when he was there. I didn't call him properly by 'Sir', so I was punished. Another time I threw up on the floor because I had the flu. My father hit me in the head raw-knuckled. He knocked me out that time. When I came to, I remember that my stomach was fine. However, my vision was clouded by small black spots that didn't clear up for months.

"But the worst was the day he killed my mother." For the first time, Larry's tone turned somber. "I wasn't allowed to leave the room and had to serve as witness to a beating my mother 'deserved' because she had been seen at a market talking with another man. It turned out he was a clerk who happened to be a borderline retarded fellow. She was helping him find an item he couldn't locate and had taken him by the hand to assist him. My father passed by an exterior window at that moment.

"He stormed into the store, threatening. My mother was embarrassed to the point that she told him to get out. He said she'd be sorry. I was forced to watch when he actualized his threat." Larry was able to maintain composure, but his eyes turned glassy.

Larry proceeded to explain about his uncle. The man was probably as hard-hearted in business as Bobby in his street life, but at least he had a heart. In fact, many times he'd drop off money for Sissy when Bobby was neglecting his responsibilities. He offered to spend time with the young Lawrence but Bobby not only refused him contact with the nephew, he threatened his brother to stay away or he'd inflict a beating on his son. Thus, it was very rare when he'd see the uncle.

"After my mother was murdered, all I remember is a lot of strangers taking me away, but then my uncle came and took me to his house that night. From that evening forward, my life took a radical turn for the better, except of course that I grieved for my mother.

"I recall falling asleep crying for months. But my uncle made sure he was there with me each and every evening he was home. The man had never married but must have had a secret yearning to have a family. I became the son of his dreams.

"He was actually well-suited to the parental role. He cared for me like a baby. After I settled in, if he had to travel or be away for an evening he always called. There were servants in the home and one woman, Tonya, had nearly full responsibility for looking after my needs.

"With what I know now, I can say that I was lucky in another respect. Had the tragic events of my early life actually occurred when I was twelve, thirteen or fourteen, the negative consequences would have likely been nearly irreversible. But I was a young boy during the traumas and in a relatively early stage of development. Also in my favor, I think that I possessed a generally strong character. So, with the support and love of my uncle and Tonya, I was able to overcome most of the ill effects."

Once adjusted to life in his uncle's home, he started to excel in his studies and outside activities. He proved to be a fast learner and physically he inherited from his father an athleticism he was able to channel into organized sports rather than street violence.

His uncle introduced him to the world of money and business. As Larry grew up, his uncle would take him on business trips and on visits to his factories and properties. While he wished the best for Larry, offering him an opportunity to achieve his potential, he never placed expectations on him. It was his belief that everybody possessed a unique pattern of interests and skills that should determine their career path. Larry would have to discover this on his own. However, if it proved to be in the business world, then he would have a privileged place from which to start.

"I think it was fairly obvious to my uncle as time went on that I was not destined for a life similar to his. My intellect steered me toward science and philosophy. Business required a capacity to analyze a situation and formulate decisions on the spot, and to be ruthless, if necessary. That was not how I operated.

"Nevertheless, he educated me well on affairs of commerce. He explained that the essential characteristic of a businessman is a pure love of making the deal. The wealthiest people in the world—and he was certainly part of that group—were not driven by a desire for wealth and power as the majority of people believe, but by the sublime thrill of making things happen.

"He had a gross mistrust and disrespect for government, especially the elected officials whom he believed were no more than swindlers playing with other people's money and lives." Larry paused and passed a devilish smile to Nadine. "I know what you're thinking. My uncle would detest me being so close with Howard, the leader of the leaders?"

"Is it rebellion?"

"No. Howard's interest in politics came long after our bond was sealed. I don't judge my friend's decision. I also don't disagree with my uncle in his general assessment of public leaders. Anyways, the bottom line is I was never cut out for the world of commerce but it didn't negatively impact my bond with my uncle. He remained unconditionally accepting. He encouraged me to follow my instincts in seeking a career. He also paved the path fairly well for me.

"He set up trust accounts that have made me a very wealthy man. I'm not bragging; that's just the way it is. If I choose never to work another day in my life, I'll still not be able to spend what I have... and to be honest I limit my patient list because I have so many other interests and commitments. As you can tell, in spite of my assets, I've thrived on hard work. My uncle was correct to allow me the latitude to explore on my own terms."

"Where is your uncle now?" Nadine's interest was piqued. "Is he alive?"

"He's aging. Truthfully, he's not in good health. I'm his only living relative, so I have to take care of his business affairs for him. Most of it I've handed over to agents that I supervise. He lives about an hour away. I visit him every couple of weeks."

"Maybe someday, I'll meet him."

"You will, soon," Larry assured her.

"That's the dirty secret of my life," Larry summarized, ready to wrap up the discussion.

"Did you ever go to the prison to see your father?" Nadine asked, eager to drill Larry with as many questions as he was willing to answer.

"My uncle never said a bad word about my father. I knew he hated him. He had shamed the family since they were boys. After the trial, he never mentioned my father again. I never brought it up, although I thought about my father many times. I wondered why he not once wrote me."

"And that was it? All those years you never talked to or saw your dad?"

"Two years ago, I was contacted by the Department of Inmate Relations and told that he had died. I didn't even ask about the cause of death. I took the news about as hard as I'd take it if you told me this table is made of pine instead of cedar."

"You really weren't upset?"

Larry winced. "At first I wasn't, or at least I didn't think I was. Then it all started to come back, as if I was reliving it for real. All those years after it happened, I forced myself to put it away. My uncle—and believe me he was well-intentioned and would have bought me a hundred psychologists if he thought it would help—must have believed it was best for me to shut my father out of my mind.

"I succeeded fairly well, so I had to conclude he was right. But when a dog buries a bone, he always remembers where it is. After he died, rain clouds settled over my psyche. First, they showered my mind with pelts of nervousness and worry, about what I had no idea. Then the pounding of water, like bullets, went on the attack, exposing one after another the memories that answered the confusion of why I was a wreck inside.

"The attacks were intermittent at first, but over time they wouldn't let up. Lakes of horror formed from the rivulets of toxic memory racing through my mind like satanic time capsules. At any moment from the depths of the troubled water, monsters would rise upward and then outward like prehistoric creatures, roaring in terrifying harmony.

"Nadine, I was sinking into a depression that was dragging me forward to a sewer of recollections I thought I had disposed of like the garbage they were. Every single whip of a belt, every welt on my body; every blackened eye of my mother, every swelling I saw on her face, it all came back like a dark skeleton. Had it been like a dream, I might have found relief. But no, it was as real as if it were happening that moment."

Larry paused for a thought. "Depression is terrible. I'll tell you, though, what I learned firsthand. It's exactly like quicksand. You fight it and it sucks you deeper and deeper, eventually drowning you. It can kill you. There is only one way to deal with depression. Do you know what it is?"

"No, I can't say I've ever been depressed like that to know," Nadine remarked. "I know most doctors use drugs."

"Yes, they do. But I believe much of the time the drugs dress the depressed feelings in a costume so it can masquerade unrecognized at a surreal ball. Nadine, most of the time you can overcome the depression by surrendering to it, by accepting the power it represents, by understanding that depression is your strength, your will to survive and heal. So, you make friends with it. That's right, it is nature's remedy to heal you.

"If I could spend my entire practice being a light beam for man to see the inherent strength that depressions empower us with, and then teach people not to run away from that inner force, not yield to the fear—because the dynamic potential dormant in the depression is indeed frightening—I would be a giant in my field."

"I thought you were already," Nadine joked in an attempt to lighten the moment.

"I doubt it."

"Well, at least you cured your own depression."

"You say cured," Larry shrugged his shoulders. "I don't think the term as we understand it, is applicable in psychology."

"You're not cured?"

"I'm not dysfunctional from the depression like I was for a while."

"Then it would seem to me you're cured."

"It may be an esoteric matter, but I have a hard time with the word 'cure' because I don't subscribe to the theory of 'illness' of the mind."

"Larry, what matters is you had the strength to stop it. You're healthy now."

"That is true. I'm grateful."

"But, Larry, did you do it all alone or did you go to someone for help?"

"I did it myself—and I talked with Howard. I told him about my father when we were kids. He's the only one I disclosed it to. Come to think of it, that was probably what bonded us. He never told a soul. I'm not even sure if Muriel knows about my past."

"So, it might only be Howard and I?"

"I guess so," he admitted, eyeing Nadine as an inductee into an elite club. "But I'm not finished. I'll let you in on another secret—something you may have already figured out. I came to realize through my battle with depression that I actually became a psychiatrist to avoid anything bad inside me. Obviously I was concerned about having tendencies similar to my father. I had repressed all those worries that I could be just like him and end up as a violent, hateful man. My profession had become my unconscious protector. Psychiatrists are good helping souls, not monsters like him.

"But his death unleashed all the fears. Like wild dogs they came at me ready to tear flesh from my bones. The depression was born from the fact that I believed they could, that I was weak, that they had me dead to rights because I was just like my father. The good profession-al façade couldn't defend against these savages who could claw into my psyche with me offering no more resistance than the little piggy's house of straw to the exhalation of the big bad wolf."

"But you did it," Nadine complimented. "Aren't you proud? You're not your father."

"No, I'm not him. And sure, I am proud. But my past horrors still linger on me in ways I'd rather be free from."

"Like what?"

"I take cases and work with patients that I probably shouldn't." Larry shook his head to acknowledge what he realized was a fool's journey he had traveled too many times. "There's a part of me that's hoping if I can help any of these so-called monsters and murderers to grow, then there could have been hope for my father.

"It's terrible to think of him as all bad, but that's all I ever knew. I get tired, Nadine, tired of trying. It may be that some people are nothing but bad and never will be anything else. But that's my Achilles' heel. I have to persist in trying to make good out of evil."

Nadine took his head and rested it on her shoulder. She cuddled him.

"Chauncy was right. We're perfect for each other."

After dinner, Larry dropped Nadine off at her home. He knew he was mentally exhausted and had to get up in time for work. Nadine cleansed her face and applied whatever creams and lotions she used, brushed her teeth, gave Horace a biscuit, and fell into sleep as serene-ly as if a light in heaven graced her.

47

COME AND TELL DADDY WHAT'S WRONG

IF I WERE A cameraman, I'd suggest shooting this scene in black and white film. That's how I envisioned it when Nadine described it.

An early nineteen-eighties Volvo is winding along a dark and lightly traveled mountain road during the early evening. The driver is not speeding. It's a man at the wheel, and beside him is a woman who is no doubt his wife. In the rear of the car is a young girl, about nine years old.

It's a family. They're all smiling and having a good time. Maybe because she's an only child, or perhaps because these people enjoy one another, it's not like a car trip with whining, stubbornness and protestations most parents recall with young children. In the dash is an old eight-track player, and blues is the music of choice. The song is *"Mama Talk to Your Daughter"* by J. P. Lenoir, a jumpy, smooth-guitar driven tune.

The vocalist is a female, but it seems to be the type of piece that wouldn't matter what gender sang it. The theme is that the daughter is not behaving and needs firm instruction. The verses are few and simple, but the chorus is the key, repeated over and over, an order to speak to your daughter.

The father and daughter are handling the chorus line, directing the admonishment toward the mother. Father is teasingly leaning toward his wife, instructing her, *"You should talk to your daughter,"* while from the back seat the daughter is pointing an insistent finger at her mother, craning her neck toward the front and close to her dad to make a nicely harmonized duet.

Just as the third chorus is ending, out of the darkness, as if suspended in space, like the fairy tale "cow jumping over the moon," a figure leaps in front of the windshield. The deer's face reads tragedy as quickly as does the man driving. The impact from the deer being pounded by the front grill of the hood thrusts the vehicle out of control. First shooting into the guardrail, and then through it, the car tumbles down a thirty-foot embankment.

The shattering of metal, glass and rock mixes with human screams into a deafening cacophonous explosion as the vehicle descends, first rapidly, then appearing in slow motion, downward. As the declination nears its end, a large, bright red banner flaps in the wind, the letters streaming across it nearly indecipherable. A ringing now attunes with the slamming of the vehicle's frame, becoming louder and more distinct from the crash itself as the car approaches a final resting state.

The ringing, louder and louder, persistent and invincible, startled Nadine out of her dream. She snapped her head upward and back against the headboard, locking it in place.

It's the phone, phone, phone, she finally realized. The clock on the nightstand reads two-fourteen. Her breathing was still heavy as she searched in the darkness for the receiver next to the clock. Dopey, she answered.

"Hello."

Silence. She waited several seconds while listening to a rustling sound.

"Hello."

Louder.

"Who is it?"

Silence still. Then a few seconds later a click. She hung up, threw her feet over the side of the bed and contemplated heading for the bathroom. It rang again. Still seated, she stared at the phone. She leaned forward to flip on the light to bring herself further out of the sleep trauma, then she jumped fully out of the bed, marching to the front door to be sure it was double locked.

She noticed Horace—who has been sleeping in his usual spot—with his head up and looking at her, likely confused as to why at this ungodly hour his master was wandering about and disturbing his sleep. Outside his realm of awareness was a fact that was dreadfully disturbing to Nadine. Horace was partially covering a vanilla piece of paper that had been pushed under the door. She snatched the dreaded intruder and hastily opened it.

I'M GETTING TO KNOW YOU WELL, NADINE. IF I MAY SPEAK CANDIDLY, I DON'T LIKE YOU.

The phone stopped ringing. Then it commenced again. Nadine ignored it. She went to a small drawer in the table and took out the first note, comparing them to be assured that her memory was correct and they were the same stationery. It returned to her attention that the first note had been shaved for some reason on the bottom. Now as she put the two pieces next to one another she realized they were identical samples of irregularity.

She folded the two together and put them in her purse. She went to the bathroom and groomed herself as if it was time for the day's activities. After she'd dressed, she checked her weapon to be sure it was ready to fire, placing it back in her handbag when she was satisfied.

Carefully observing the area around her, she opted to use the stairwell to descend to the parking lot. When she reached the bottom floor, she opened the door into the parking area. It was quiet and she saw no movement. She made her way to her car.

As she unlocked the door, her senses alerted her that she was being watched. In that same microsecond of time, she heard the sound of a leather shoe rubbing on cement. Conditioned by the number of times she played over the first sighting of the man in the parking area, her reflex was to eye the precise place she first saw him.

She wasn't shocked when she glanced that way and found him standing in the same place, identical in pose but very different in appearance. He was now sporting long, shaggy dark hair, a full dangling beard of similar color, and an old khaki army jacket. He looked like a Vietnam War protester or street bum.

This time her reaction was without hesitation. She grabbed her revolver and ran across the structure to where he was standing. He smiled a taunting grin as if he cherished playing with her. He then leapt out the door.

In good physical shape from jogging, Nadine was ready for a full marathon. She wouldn't get the chance. By the time she reached the exit door leading to the street, he had disappeared into the dark.

This entire sequence in the parking area unfolded in an instant. The tail end of the tick introduced a Porsche racing full speed down the street and then demonstrating the trick of accelerating the car while flicking the steering wheel left to execute a nifty, steady ninety degree turn all in the space of about ten feet…at sixty miles an hour. Dustin had schooled Nadine on how to recognize Porsche models— she knew this to be a turbo. A simple nanosecond was all that was required for a brain pulse to inform her there aren't many of these in her neighborhood—in this bright red one had to be Dustin.

The adjacent street he turned left on was actually a dead end cul-de-sac. From where Nadine stood she could see the short distance to where it came to a stop. Dustin brought his car to a halt and in an instant was out and running; the engine was still purring. But only a few moments later, Nadine saw the world-class athlete wandering back toward her, looking defeated.

It took Dustin a few seconds to reclaim his breath. As soon as he was able to speak, he related his tale. "Great speed…sharp movements…he really tested me."

"Dustin, wait. What were you doing here at two-thirty in the morning?"

"Remember you told me to check around your place? Well, I was here this afternoon. Then I stopped by after dinner. You know I don't sleep that well. I fell asleep and had this dream. No idea what it was, but it woke me up and I couldn't fall back asleep, so I thought I'd take a ride and do an early morning inspection.

"I drove past a couple times. I thought I saw somebody entering the garage area, but I wasn't sure. It seemed late to be getting home on a weeknight so I thought I'd double check. I was parked just up the block when I saw this guy burst out the door and take off running. I didn't know if he had anything to do with you, but I was going to find out."

"Brilliant timing."

"He raced around this building and I thought I had trapped him in a closed area. There's a concrete wall about nine, ten feet tall behind that building. I'm going straight for him, ready to take him down; I didn't want to use a gun—what if he's a petty crook and I kill him?"

"Go ahead."

"While I'm going at him he's still running...like a flash. Then he charges right into the wall and *scales it*. The dexterity was amazing. On my third try, I got up to the top too, but by then he was long gone into that field behind the building."

"Good try."

"If that was him, it's the closest we've gotten."

Nadine knew differently but is not going to disclose the other encounters.

"Thanks, Dustin."

He was still excited by the experience, shocked at the physical capability of the man and his own inability to match him.

"The guy went over the wall like...well—"

"Like a mountain climber?" Nadine proposed to an astonished

Dustin who nodded his agreement. "Dustin that was a snazzy bit of driving. I'm impressed."

"Porsche driving school," Dustin remarked, still trying to conquer his breathing. "Five hundred buck option when you buy the car."

Her gut instinct told her Dustin would never, could never, betray her. But was it conceivable that he could have shown up at precisely the moment the presumed killer was stalking her? She needed Chauncy.

Her mentor had always invited her to call anytime she needed him. In fact, on a few occasions in the past when matters of great urgency arose, she took him up on the offer. He was sensitive to the risks and dangers of her work. He also knew that frequently she operated in secrecy, especially when turning for home in a case. He wanted her to know she always had someone to talk to.

She excused Dustin, but with a humorous comment she knew would make him feel treasured. "Your driving has improved since the night I slammed your car into the tree. I'll see you tomorrow."

She had a fifteen-minute trip to Chauncy's. While in the car, she called to notify him that she was coming. On her way, she repeatedly checked for any vehicles behind her. The affairs of the evening had placed her on high alert. She was in danger, the killer upping his attempt to intimidate her.

When she arrived at Chauncy's complex a short time later, the moon was dimly lighting the tree-lined street, the leaves shaking off rainwater like a frigid light shower. She made her way up the stairwell to the second story unit and knocked. Chauncy, dressed in old sweats, opened the door and wrapped her in his arms. He then stepped back to survey her troubled face before leading her inside.

"Come. Lie down on the couch and you'll talk to me."

Nadine dropped supine on the sofa, her head propped at an angle by a pillow at the base of the neck. She gazed about the room, noticing the clutter and unkemptness as distinguishable from the neatness and order of her own dwelling. She also noticed the warmth and fullness of his space.

Chauncy's hobby was electronics. The room has been ordered around several mini-workstations where computers, cameras and infrared devices were in various stages of assembly. Scattered more randomly was an array of other gadgets. The room was very large, obviously where he spent most of his time.

A wall covered with bookshelves was home to what appeared to be thousands of novels, a collection of mystery and crime stories that someday would make a sought after jewel for an estate buyer if it were not for the fact they had already been promised to Nadine.

Chauncy left the room, but in short order returned with a knitted quilt that he draped over her. He then took a small cushioned chair and moved it closer to Nadine, positioning himself in an analyst's pose—but without the pipe. As soon as he was settled, Nadine started to brief him about the purpose of her visit.

"Chauncy, I'm probably no better, no worse—and you're correct—no different than Larry. It's not that I lied to you about my own family history. I just never told you the whole truth. I wanted to deceive you, but only for the purpose of making sure you would never pity me.

"I worried that if you did, I'd never know if you respected me, cared for me, took interest in guiding me and my career because of me, not because of what happened to me. So I think you could say I told you a half-truth.

"My father and mother were like a pair of wild hares. My dad was a musician, played any type of guitar you could think of, and my mother was a singer. Before I was born, she had a good deal of success, and a prosperous career awaited her.

"My parents met at a recording studio; my mom was singing and my dad doing backup instrumentation. After they married—it was only a brief courtship—they were traveling around the world performing in one venue or another. Seeing the world appealed to them, and why not, they were young, talented and had careers that paid for their wanderings.

"Things changed after I was born. Mom insisted there was nothing more she wanted than a child. She chose of her own free will not to try and do the mommy and career thing simultaneously. So she stayed home with me. We did all the things a mother and daughter might do together, and our family was genuinely full of love.

"Dad traveled some but tried to limit most of his work to local gigs. Whatever he did, he was able to support us nicely. What they retained from the free and restless years was the spirit of exploring. So any chance that came up, we'd take off. It didn't matter if it was a two- or twenty-hour drive. Where we went depended on how may days we had to be away and what there was to see within that time: mountains or lakes, any small towns in Vermont, Connecticut or Rhode Island. These destinations were all choice spots for picnics, outdoor carnivals or festivals, concerts or rummaging through antique stores.

"It was on the way to one of those getaways that it happened. I told you I lost my mother when I was nine; it's true. A deer ran in front of the car on a slick, twisty mountain road. The car went out of control and down a cliff. My mother died on impact.

"You may recall I told you I did have a father, but not really. My father suffered severe head trauma and was in a coma for several weeks before coming to. After that he came home, but he couldn't write a check let alone know if there was money in the account to cover it. I wasn't hurt except for some bruises and a broken heart.

"The only person who could help was my grandmother, my mom's mother. You can imagine she was devastated about losing her daughter. She was a nice lady but old. She'd had my mother at a very advanced age and by the time she came to stay with me she was not particularly fit. Frankly, she kept me out of a county placement but I'm not sure when I think about it if I might not have been better off being orphaned and my father placed in a facility where there were people to look after him.

"As it turned out, I ended up a nine-year-old parent to a nine-tenths brain-dead father, as well as a mentally and physically crippled grandmother. Thank god the only thing my grandmother did bring with her was enough money to feed us and make the house payment. We'd have been on welfare if not for that, and even so we lived on a razor's edge.

"I know my childhood warped me. Some of it was good. I knew what responsibility was, long before my peers were having sleepovers. Anyway, Chauncy, I thought I needed to clear it up with you."

"I'm sorry to hear that. It's terrible for a child to lose so much of their youth." He hesitated before posing an obvious question. "What happened to your father?"

"He had many strokes. The medication wasn't working toward the end. About five years ago, he had a massive one and died. Honestly, I was relieved. My parents were decent, fun-loving people who I know loved me and would have cringed at the thought of my suffering. I remember them as healthy, creative and full of life. And I'll tell you, Chauncy, I had enough nurturing from them in nine years to get me through the rest of my life."

He leaned forward to hug her. "I appreciate you sharing this, but it's not why you called me in the middle of the night."

"No, it's not. The reason I wanted you to know about my family is so you'd understand what I'm going to tell you. Ever since the accident I've had nightmares; not all the time, but every so often, and they're always nearly identical. We're all riding in the car, my father behind the wheel. We're singing and enjoying ourselves. Then a deer races in front of the car windshield. Following that is this screeching sound of twisting metal and a slow motion tumbling decline. The dreams are simple reenactments of the accident.

"Then this evening I had the dream again, but for the first time there was a different element. Near the end of the crash, this large, bright red banner appeared. It was flapping wildly in the wind. I could see letters at first but couldn't make out what they said. But then the air calmed and they became decipherable."

"What did they say?"

Nadine hesitated. "It said, 'I KNOW WHO IT IS, DARLING.' I knew as soon as I was conscious what it meant."

"Which is?"

"Larry knows who the killer is."

Chauncy had taught himself to be a skilled listener. He knew not to interfere before she completed her revelation.

"I think the killer is a patient of his," Nadine said.

"Nadine, if that's true, why wouldn't he just have the lunatic arrested?"

Nadine sat straight up, tugging the blanket to cover her shoulders and front side. "You don't know some things about this man. He has laws that govern his practice. He holds them as immutable, no different than the basic protections and rights of our constitution. And that's not all. If I'm right, Larry believes he can bring about growth and healing for the maniac. Even if he can't, he still believes it's his duty to give him every chance for redemption."

Chauncy was too old and too wise for this type of adolescent nonsense. He shook his head in bemusement at what he considered Larry's foolishness. "This may be your most thrilling love affair yet."

Chauncy went to a small cabinet. He took out a bottle of rum and two glasses. He poured a healthy shot in each and walked back to where Nadine was seated, placing one glass in her hand and holding the other. He tapped his to hers.

"Have a drink and go to sleep. We'll talk more in the morning."

She did as instructed. Chauncy secured the cover over her and dimmed the lights. As he was exiting, Nadine yawned her question. "Will you help me with this one?"

There was no need for a verbal reply, but a nod assured her she wouldn't be alone—unless she chose to be.

48

THE SECOND NOTE

IT WAS POURING. SMALL, thin shreds of organic material were dropping from big mamma trees that for days had been joyfully shedding green, brown, rust and yellow matter that would be nourishing the earth in a never ending cycle of creation. Everywhere one looked the colored snow blanketed, so thick that the padding of leaves warmed the ground and protected it from the cooling air above.

It was fall in Mescalero—the outdoor festivities left no doubt that at least the name of one season of the year made sense.

I watched as the sky darkened from grey to black. The cloud cover on this morning was low, doming the land like a capped cathedral. The leaves showering down might have been blowing in a pattern ordered by The Composer's symphonic masterpiece. They oscillated, fluttered and wavered to the string section's plucking and bowing as they made their delicate descent. They gusted, flurried and floated as the brass instruments tooted and bellowed at them. Percussion instruments taunted and bullied the little tree deserters to pay attention.

I loved putting on Count Basie and dancing with Sousche in the front garden once the wet showers quit—we were waiting for our chance. It was not until the next day that we had the break we were looking for. Then a dry downpour of tree matter replaced the storms; the leaves seemed to be giggling with us as we rolled on the ground.

Time was more precious to me than ever. I recognized that I wanted to inventory the moments of my existence like fine wine in a cellar and then allocate them judiciously. I can't say I preferred life under the authority of a stern timekeeper but it was the best I could come up with. After all, it was my choice in my new role as adult to impose duties, schedules and timetables on myself.

While I was sharing the moment with Sousche, Preeti came out to tell me that Kershaw was on the phone. I presumed that he wanted to brag about how much money he was about to send us. She brought the hands-held unit outside and handed it to me.

"I wanted to tell you I've had my friend keep an eye on that matter you mentioned to me," he related in a coded manner. "It was called off. No explanation why. It was odd, but abruptly the operation was cancelled and they were told all information was to be deleted after copies were sent to the other party I mentioned to you (alluding to The President's Office)."

"That's good news, isn't it?"

"For one of them, yes," he noted.

"One of them?"

"The person who looked into this didn't know it when we first talked but the operation actually was directed toward two people, both are ones you know—both are there with you."

"What are you talking about?" I asked with understandable bewilderment.

"There was a companion order which was to simply monitor and gather information about the activities of the second one," he continued in cryptic style. "Then when the instruction to cancel on the first was issued it was stated that the second one (obviously referring to Nadine) would be handled internally—meaning by people accountable only to that entity."

"Were you able to find out why the thing happened in the first place?" I further queried him, now talking like an agent myself.

"No idea. But I'll tell you that the whole matter is strange," he admitted. "My hunch—and it's just my opinion—is that the first one was merely collateral damage. She might also have been a decoy to cover up the prime target. Whatever it is, the second one has enemies you don't want to have."

In a timely manner, the storm thundered with the vibrations shaking thousands of leaves loose from an elderly oak. Sousche screeched excitedly as she watched nature's show. I shuddered. Kershaw's words caused me to take my daughter by the hand and lead her inside to shut off the music. There was about to be another downpour—the party was over.

"She could be in danger?" I concluded as much as asked.

"I don't know physically, but legally, for sure. Do you know much about this person? Do you have some information that could give you any clues what this is about?"

"Vaguely. I think I have some ideas but I'm not sure yet."

"I'll let you know if anything else develops," Kershaw offered.

After ending the conversation, I immediately received a call from Preston.

"I don't want to get you in the middle of this," he noted. "I do want your opinion on what I should do."

"Of course. What is it?"

"All of a sudden Nadine's avoiding me. Zach, it's not that she won't talk to me. She wants me to call her all the time," he carried on with anguish in his voice. "Nadine won't see me. I had two days off and wanted to fly in but she insisted that I not come. I asked for an explanation and all she would say was, 'It is better if you don't come right now.' I don't know what to do. Zach, I've been true to her. I can't figure out what I did wrong."

"You did nothing. I'm not placating you. It's not about you," I absolutely assured him. "I'm going to tell you something but only if you swear on our relationship you will not show up here before she gives you the okay."

"You have my word."

"She thinks she could be in danger and doesn't want to risk you getting hurt. I can't tell you much more than that because I really don't have the details. It's all tied in to the story I'm writing for her. The problem is we're getting close to the ending but we're not there yet. She refuses to give me a preview of what's coming, which if she would, might allow me to answer your question better."

Preston finally hung up, sounding dejected, unsatisfied and...worried. I didn't blame him but there wasn't much else I could do. The day before the call from Preston, the day of our most recent meeting, Nadine insisted that instead of getting together as we normally did at my office, we go to the park. When we got there, she handed me another piece of paper, the stock identical to that used for the first note delivered to Josea. The words were a perfect duplicate to those of the second note she had received at her condominium in D. C.

I'M GETTING TO KNOW YOU WELL, NADINE. IF I MAY SPEAK CANDIDLY, I DON'T LIKE YOU.

She was being sent a message. It was delivered with the express intent of letting her know that "they" knew everything that had happened, and was happening, and she needed to call off the writing of the story...or else.

After I read it, she folded it into the envelope it was delivered in. Then she looked at me and smiled. When she reached down to put it in her purse, I glanced down. I couldn't help but notice...she had a pistol.

"Farley, he's quite a character. He's very efficient. That said, I'd suggest a haircut and new suit," she jested.

"Let me guess. Pale blue and white stripe suit—laundered last in 2004?"

"It might be his pajamas as well. Still, he gets the job done...quickly. I have him monitoring something critical for me," she revealed. "They'll come after me first to scare the crap out of me. If that doesn't work…they'll kill me; they may want to kill me regardless."

"Farley can help. He knows how to provide security."

"I'm not hiding. I want them to know they can come to me any time. Then we'll settle this," she proclaimed like a prizefighter. "In the meantime, Zach, I think it is best that I keep my distance from Preeti, Sousche, Josea and Reuben. As far as our meetings go, there's not that much left. I can arrange for us to get together without being followed."

"Real cat and mouse stuff." I tried to make light of a situation I knew by the item in her purse was anything but that.

"We'll see if this little mouse gets a chance to roar like a lion," dubiously streamed from her lips. "Zach, did I ever tell you that I hope someday to have a child?"

The question seemed so oddly misplaced. Yet that was Nadine's way of bucking up to the pressure—I prayed that night she did have a child, and with my friend Preston. She proceeded as if she never made the disclosure. "Well, come on. I swear, you'd chatter all day and never get a thing accomplished."

She was right. I was prone to bouts of indolence. I yearned for the beach. I wanted to go on holiday with Preeti, Sousche and my soon coming baby. I couldn't wait to visit my mom and her husband. I wished Reuben and Josea's next musical would open soon. I thought of going to New York for the opening of the next Kuruk. I fantasized that soon I'd be honored to cut the ribbon at the grand opening of Kuruk, London.

I dreamed of becoming a famous author. I went back to my favorite childhood fantasy, whizzing through space so fast I could outrun bees. I wanted the sun to warm my cool bones as I swam in a bathtub as large as the ocean. I thought I was a great ballroom dancer bowing as I accepted winning prize in a contest.

I wondered how it would feel floating in an air balloon.

I felt like crying. Nadine was probably going to die right here at

Kuruk. There was nothing I could do about it.

Then it crossed my mind for the first time, a demonic thought I should have smacked across the face for smirking at me in the mirror that Nadine was holding to refresh her lipstick. Some ideas have no propriety. They come uninvited, sit down in your favorite reclining chair and refuse to leave, race to get into your snug bed before you and then toss and turn all night keeping you awake, even try touchy-feely with your wife until she offers you the choice of a Xanax or a muzzle, haunt you by invading your dreams and then have the indecency to be waiting for you when you get up in the morning, asking if you might have forgotten them.

This specimen of my imagination raised the specter of Nadine having done evil. My dear Preston had worried sweetly that Reuben could bring danger to my family. But he was the one deliriously in love with a lady nobody knew much about except she had an amazing story that had to be told and had been a top detective in D. C.

Was the great reveal—the culminating act—the flabbergastation of this drama to be that she, the innocent, darling, lovable, durable, tasteful, heroic star was a murderer? And now those who knew of her treachery, those with power to act beyond the law—are the law—were coming for justice, unwilling to rely on the fickle nature of courts of law?

"You're daydreaming again, Zack," Nadine picked at me. "You'll never get answers to all those questions buzzing in your head if you play silly mind games." Was she now reading my mind?

"But you have a gun in your purse," I wanted to say. Instead I towed the line. "Right, go on. Fingers tapping computer keys; I'm on duty."

49

MEETING AT THE RED-HOT REDHEAD

It may have been a wild analytic interpretation of her dream that Larry was treating the killer, but with the intimate understanding she was attaining about the inner workings of her lover's mind, the logic seemed flawless. Ever since she thought him treating the killer might be true, her mind (what she labeled "intuition"), focused on what information might be in Larry's office. And from that irrepressible, nagging consideration she knew that, right or wrong, no matter how unpleasant, unethical, immoral mistrustful and even illegal, a snoop operation had to be conducted…and the assignment was going to Dustin.

It had taken her most of the day to formulate an action plan designed to prove her either right or wrong. She knew what she was about to do wasn't nice, pleasant, respectful, ethical, moral, or even legal. But it was crucial. So, yes, IT was going to be done. For good reason, Nadine was hesitant to handle the job on her own—too bad for Dustin.

When she called her partner to discuss it with him, he suggested they meet at nine that evening at The Red Hot Redhead, a joint with a history Dustin delighted sharing with Nadine.

It turns out there is a real Red Hot Redhead who was professionally called Red. It's not hard to guess she was a renowned call girl, famous for…red-hot sex, as well as for her flaming hair. What wouldn't be a slam-dunk would be discovering that while Red may have been a fallen woman, she was also bright and wily.

She had early in her career worked under the supervision and protection of an overseer, her pimp. She was the favorite of many clients so, of course, he awarded her the best assignments. Where she differed from your average prostitute was in her values and perceptions. She realized she was fortunate to be born with a gift that, even if she took care to nurture, would still only have a limited period of utility.

Thus, she needed to milk the career for all she could while she was on top, mindful of what would happen when her tools rusted. So she decided early on to live modestly, abstain from all drugs and alcohol, save and invest her money, and have goals for her future. Her peers would fantasize what it was going to be like when they were no longer working girls. She never shared her personal dream, didn't have to because she knew it was going to happen—she was going to run her own business.

When she opened The Red Hot Redhead, she was thirty-seven and still pretty hot by most men's standards. She took a lease on a small store on busy Elm Street in downtown Washington, about four doors from the corner. Within four years, she had grown the bar and dance club all the way to the corner. With no first-hand business experience, one might question her secret to rapid success. Dustin explained it in terms of ambiance, and Red always being mindful of her shop. Well...let's see.

The Redhead ran into trouble with the city shortly after opening. Seems that because of her well-known history of prostitution, an assumption was made that her establishment was a front for her to operate her own network of call girls. Was it true? Let's put it this way, Phillip Drake stepped up to defend the charges and she was cleared of any wrongdoing. The city ended up paying her an undisclosed amount for her counter-suit, which covered Phillip Drake's legal bill as well.

The moral of the story is you're only as guilty as your most powerful friends think you are. The Redhead ended up becoming the most happening joint in town, making a fistful of dough. Dustin was treated like a prince whenever he showed up.

He had already arrived by the time Nadine came in the door at precisely nine. The noise level made Cheerie's seem like it was playing chamber music. Given that she told Dustin she needed to discuss something important with him, she found Red's place an unlikely choice for having a conversation. The crowd was packed so solid you could pass out, be unconscious on your feet for ten minutes, come to and be ready to order your next drink without ever hitting the ground.

There were tables. Our silver-spooned boy had already been taken to "his." He'd been keeping an eye looking toward the entrance to spot Nadine. When she arrived, he jumped up and made his way toward her. The density of flesh and the volume of the music blinded her. She did sense a hand grabbing her arm. Then she saw Dustin, even noticed his lips moving. Holding on to her he carved a path through the mob and to his table. Now she could hear, she thought.

"How are we going to talk here?" she shouted at her highest possible decibel range.

"This is perfect. You said it was important. We can scream and nobody can hear what we're saying."

"Ah, I see."

"You'll get used to it in a few minutes."

"I think it will do me some good. My brain needs a proper ablution."

Dustin turned to notify the waitress they wanted to order. Nadine watched as he motioned to a lovely-looking girl with long auburn hair and a bust worthy of commencing World War III. Nadine also observed as soon as the girl made eye contact with Dustin, and next looked at Nadine, a frown creased her face. She approached the table but seemed irked.

"Connie, this is Nadine," Dustin yelled merrily, knowing he had a problem that was best quickly defused.

If a lady has suspicions her man may be two-timing with Sally, Sue, Sandy or...Bob, and then he brazenly confirms it smack in front of her face, she'd probably shoot first and ask questions later. Connie was cocked. Thank god Dustin's ability to read her mind was faster than the speed of a bullet.

This is the first serious involvement he'd had in a long time. In fact, he'd just asked Connie to live with him. He didn't want her to misunderstand his feeling for her. A lot had changed since our young detective started working with Nadine. He was settling, maturing, and probably his father's instinct was correct, he would be in law school in due time.

If one surmised Dustin was dredging deep to suck up a crawfish like Connie, they'd be sorely underestimating this young lady. The Redhead, being no fool, decided when she went into business she was going to hire girls not only with bodies, but also with brains. Connie had been working for her for two years and was her quintessential employee.

Connie's only shortcoming was that she wasn't born rich. She had the misfortune of having to put herself through school and was finishing a degree in, of all things, biology. She had recently applied for a graduate degree in biological computer science; a field she believed was cutting edge.

When she heard the words, "This is Nadine," the unpleasant scowl was replaced by an effusive smile? She didn't hear Dustin, as he proceeded with the rest of the introduction.

"Nadine, this is my..." He looked at Connie and realized that omitting adjectives under some conditions might spell disaster. He corrected what was going to be a grammatical catastrophe. "Live-in girlfriend."

"Dustin talks about you all the time," Nadine said warmly as she shook Connie's hand.

"I'll hope I've left him with something positive to say."

"Oh, you have!"

"This is a heck of a place for a business meeting," Connie's scowl chastising him for poor judgment.

"Top secret stuff," he responded, making himself seem important to his gal. "We don't want anyone to overhear us."

"Good thinking; no chance of that here," Connie commented farcically. "Now, what can I get you two to drink?"

Nadine answered she'd take a rum and coke. Dustin wanted "my usual." When Connie left, Nadine stared off in a reverie before addressing her partner. "What would you say if I told you Dr. Monroe may be treating the killer?

Nadine had already briefed Dustin about what transpired between her and Larry regarding him knowing Blank and the missed class. That convinced him that Larry was not Blank's killer. But he still questioned, as did she, what involvement he might have in the overall spree of murders. When Nadine offered the possibility of Larry treating the killer, Dustin was intrigued.

"If that were the case, it would definitely make our job a heck of a lot easier."

"Would it?"

"Do you know it for sure?" Dustin asked.

"No, I'm saying he *may* be treating him. We need to find out."

"Assuming you're right…that's a big maybe…does Monroe know it's the killer who is one of his patients?" Dustin asked.

"It doesn't matter right now," Nadine said dismissively. "We have to find out first if it's true."

"And we do that by—?"

"It's simple. We get his appointment book, run a background check on all the possible patients; and while in the office we search for any other materials that may help answer my question. If there's nothing…bad hunch."

"We'd need a search warrant," Dustin clarified a fact he knew she had to have factored in. "How are you going to manage that?"

"I'm not."

Dustin's face registered alarm. At the same moment, Connie approached with the drinks and deposited them on the table. She pinched Dustin's butt, winked at Nadine, and left.

"Dustin, do you have another suggestion on how we do this?"

"Wait. Before we go any further with this, why do you think it in the first place?"

"I'm just following a hunch."

"It's hardly worth risking our skins then. Besides, we could stake out his office, couldn't we?"

"I thought of that. But do you realize how much of our time it would take? Weeks. Then we still wouldn't be sure if somebody had missed sessions for a period of time because of illness or vacation, or we simply confused his patients with different clients coming to the building for other offices.

"I checked the place out. It's almost impossible to be sure who is going to his suite unless you park yourself outside his door and obviously that's too risky. Besides, even if we took pictures of all the patients coming in and out of his office for a month, we'd still have to figure out the identities of each one. It's too big a job; I'd have to have half the department on it. I don't want any of them cluttering up my work."

"Nadine, you can't just break in."

"I've already decided."

"What do you care if we attempt to do it legally?" Dustin argued.

"No judge would order a search based on a hunch; I don't blame them. Besides, it would ruin my relationship with Larry, regardless of whether I'm right or wrong. I don't want to do that."

"Then how do we do it?"

"*We* don't do it. *You* do it. If I go there the chances are too great that he'll see me. He doesn't know you. Dustin, you owe me, you agreed," she said flatly.

"Oh, I didn't know I agreed to risk getting thrown in jail."

"You won't; I promise. Besides, if anything happens…"

The inference is obvious to Dustin's dad.

"This is crazy; you know that," Dustin protested.

"Dustin, I can't explain to you why but I have a feeling this may save lots of lives—Dr. Monroe's and mine included."

Nadine instructed him on the layout of the office and the details that would allow a swift entry and exit. He could use the camera on his cell phone to take pictures of the pages of Monroe's book for the last six months' appointments. She reasoned that would be more than sufficient to see if there were any potential hits.

"Tell Connie it was a pleasure meeting her," Nadine smiled after they had hashed out the details. Then she waved to let Dustin know she was leaving.

50

WHAT ARE FRIENDS FOR?

IT'S WORTH MENTIONING AGAIN that there was one person with a special privilege allowing him to maintain anonymity by avoiding the waiting room if he were to come visit Dr. Monroe. In fact, if he wished he could bypass the entrance to the building entirely and come through the alley directly into Larry's inner treatment room. That individual with exclusive accommodation was President Haley.

With this information a tourist, or assassin, or any person for that matter could take a post in the alley behind Dr. Monroe's office this afternoon to see the disguised figure of Haley on his way to his friend's office. The adventure of spying on a president could be made even more interesting by befriending the interloping pigeon that loved loitering outside of Dr. Monroe's office. If the flying creature could be enticed to hoist the individual up to the ledge, they might perch themselves and listen in on a conversation between buddies.

Howard was seated across from Larry. Larry was in his customary treatment chair.

"This second term is crucial," Haley began.

Haley, a proud man, was well aware of the infamy of the number two—coming in second in his run for re-election was objectionable. He took an unusually long, deep breath after he uttered the most obvious truth since someone proclaimed that napalm smells: he wanted another term. He looked intently at his friend.

"I'm going to need help with this one." He stopped to be sure Larry was fully attentive. "Just a couple of more things before the election."

"I know."

"I would have never made it this far without you," Haley complimented him before moving on to a potentially very contentious matter. "By the way, I did some checking on this lady you're seeing."

"Why?"

Haley reached to take an envelope out from the coat he had draped over the back of a chair next to him. He handed it to Larry who spent the next several minutes scanning photographs of Nadine with Brent, the ones taken by Lambert. Haley had placed them in order, aiming for maximum impact. First were the ones most suggestive of intimacy. Any person asked to comment on what they saw in the pictures would be inclined to say they were looking at a couple dating or married.

A picture is worth a thousand words. Larry wasn't interested in nine hundred and ninety-eight—just two: guilt or innocence.

More likely what happened cognitively in Larry's mind as he was processing the pictures was that he went back to the night at the club with Nadine and Brent singing karaoke. He probably recalled a slight tenseness in his physique when he was first introduced to the man in the pictures. Naturally, he would have attributed it to normal emotions that any male would have when he had invested his heart in a woman and saw her with another man. Silly, juvenile feelings, but still ones well within the realm of the expected.

Now, with the evidence he was scanning, his mind's imagination graduated to concern that Nadine was a woman capable of acts of deception he wouldn't have suspected. Haley, who knew Nadine to be the most promising match ever for his friend, gave him plenty of time to work over the painful reality that he may not have his lover's heart all to himself.

After a few silent moments, Haley went on in a paternalistic tone. "I worry about you. I didn't want to see you go back into that depression."

"I appreciate that. I don't want to either."

"Larry, you're still fragile. That's why I wanted to see about her background. The wrong woman can be devastating to a man."

"The wrong woman can be devastating to a man?" It registered with Larry that this was the identical phrase used by the patient rampaging against Nadine at his office.

Haley continued. "My concern is not just this man and what appears to be an intimacy. After I received the pictures, I had further inquiries made. She's been around, Larry. In the last two years, she's had at least three relationships ranging from three to six months. It seems she's the type who easily attracts the attention of men. It excites her to conquer, and once she's accomplished that she's rather heartless in unloading them. Larry, it's usually through an act of unfaithfulness."

"Are you sure about—?"

"Larry, I have no interest in this other than your well-being. Whatever issues she has are of no concern to me. Frankly, I don't care to engage in an analysis of her character. All I can say is she is conflicted and confused about love. That makes for a dangerous liaison for any man. You are not just any man. Don't expect me to sit by and watch her trash what you've accomplished over the last two years."

"Where did you get these?" Larry was stunned.

"I have people who can find out anything," Haley reminded him.

"I know. It's just hard for me to imagine her...we never talked about anything exclusive. Maybe I should wait and see what happens."

"Well, do what you want but my advice would be to get out of this with as little suffering as you can. The longer you wait, the worse it's going to be. Larry, even if she's in the process of ending it with this man, can't you see what I'm saying? There is a pattern here. She's not going to break the habit as easily as she does the hearts of men."

"I'm just surprised."

"I knew you would be. I don't blame you. I'm hurt for you Larry. I know what this meant to you. I could tell seeing you with her that it was serious for you."

Haley hesitated for a moment, not one hundred percent sure he should continue with what he'd calculated to say at this point. Then he decided to proceed.

"I'm concerned this is the type of woman who will try to come between us."

Larry was tapping his fingers on the table in an unconscious ritualistic practice used for soothing himself. Haley prepared for the final instruction.

"Your friend, this Nadine, works for Harry Lambert—you know that?

"She told me all about it, including how she thinks he's subverting her investigation."

"It appears things are not going the way she'd like. You know how it is, somebody has to be blamed."

"Howard, she's not stupid. Besides, Lambert's not the most supportive man in the world."

"I know how you feel about him. But what I'm getting at is whatever happens to your connection with her, it is better that she doesn't know anything about the nature of your relationship with Harry right now."

"Believe me, she won't. She already confronted me about knowing him. I was able to put it to rest."

Larry hoped his current involvement with Lambert would never come to her attention. He knew fireworks would be sparking if it did. But did it matter now? Would it be of any difference after he finished talking to her about…Brent?

51

A FACT IS A FACT ONLY WHEN...

DUSTIN, THE FAITHFUL AND still indentured servant, unable to find an alternative to gaining Dr. Monroe's patient list other than stealing it, had tucked his resistance under his arm like a football en route to the wrong end zone.

Several hours earlier, at a precise time orchestrated by Nadine, when Larry would be under her visual supervision, Dustin gained access Larry's office. Once inside, he found the setting exactly as she had described. The top of his desk was swept clean of any unnecessary papers, books or journals. All that was visible was a phone system, small lamp, pen and pencil set with notepad, and the appointment book.

The sought after book was on the right side halfway up the desk, just where Nadine recalled it being placed. In a matter of twenty minutes, Dustin was in and out, calling Nadine to apprise her of the operation on both ends of the espionage. "Breeze," "snap," were the only two words exchanged until they were able to meet later to determine what to do with the information.

Dustin had already taken the digital images and made copies, one for him and one for Nadine. Before they met, he volunteered to take a crack at the list, already having broken the patients into groups based on age and gender. His initial screening was as expected: between the women and those too old or weak to physically carry out a murder, three quarters were eliminated.

The remainder seemed a manageable number. Dustin took it upon himself to conduct the initial background checks so that Nadine would be free to work on other leads. When at last they met at Nadine's office sometime around nine at night, Dustin tossed a large stuffed envelope on the desk and sat down.

"What did you find, Dustin?"

"Look it over again yourself. I left all my notes and sources. Your suspicion is wrong," Dustin said with undisguised relief.

"You believe for certain there are no killers in his stable of patients, and you found no other evidence that might yield fruit?" Nadine seemed far from disappointed herself.

"No killers; no other findings."

"I'll double-check everything," she assured him.

"It's all there. Go ahead. Most of these people can hardly leash their dogs for a walk in the park. There'll be one surprise for you, but let me leave you with a little suspense. It'll give you a kick."

"I don't think anything will surprise me. Most of the people you would least suspect needing help, are the ones who need it the most."

"There's a hell of a lot of action going on in his office that *People* magazine would die for, that's for certain. But I think you'd be better off keeping this list unofficial. Burn it as soon as you're finished. I have nothing left of it at home or in my office. It's all in your hands."

"Great. Dustin, I'll take care of it."

If, as he proclaimed, Dustin had done due diligence to his job it meant she needed to reinterpret her dream. Her curiosity on the subject had already led her to read an article on dream analysis and wish fulfillment. Was the whole "red banner message" nothing other than a clever wish that her unconscious invented to lead her into a blind alley? The author had written that the content of dreams might be "tricky" and the wish element might rankle the dreamer who denies the underlying motive.

Dustin's cell rang. "Drake here." After listening for a few seconds, he responded.

"I'm with Street now. We'll be right over." Dustin waved his hand for Nadine to follow. "Monica over in the crime lab said to come over immediately."

When they arrived, Monica greeted them at the door, ushering them into a small office. She appeared troubled.

"I decided last night I'd work more on the Blank hair sample. There were a couple of other tests that I wanted to complete. They were long shots but just the same I wanted to try. When I arrived this morning, I ordered the box to be pulled off the shelves and put in my lab.

"Then about ten minutes ago, I finished up another job I was doing for Detective Ball and went into the Blank material…no sample. I know it was there because I put it on top the last time I used it. I checked and nobody has had access to it since—you have to sign in to look in any of the evidence containers. Very strange, right?"

Now she took her computer screen and turned it around to face Dustin and Nadine. She started typing into it, urging them to watch. She typed in Blank's name. When the file came up she went to the "Evidence" section and clicked. The notation for the hair sample was gone.

"It's evaporated. Somebody erased that sample out of existence; it's not in the backup, nowhere is there reference to the sample. Anyone going on into the file would be listed but there's no link for that."

"Monica, we all know the security procedures around here. How do you think this could be done?"

"I really don't know, Nadine. It's not just about erasing a portion of a file and stealing evidence, it's about rewriting the security codes for our computer network for this case. I'm not even sure Chief Lambert himself could do this."

"Somebody can do it because it happened, right?" Nadine grimaced.

"We need to report this immediately," Monica responded.

Nadine had concerns about Monica's plan. If this were brought to light, it might alert the wrong people, the possible conspirators, that an act of sabotage that they were already aware occurred had been identified. The guilty party or parties would be more comfortable believing what they had done was undetected. Nadine surmised that by leaving it alone she might be able to use it to her advantage down the road. Thus, she posed a careful appeal to Monica.

"When do you suspect it might have happened?"

"Within the last four days, since I last used the file," Monica calculated.

"Does anyone else know about this?"

"No. I called Dustin the second I confirmed what I'm showing you."

"Monica, can you pretend…just for a few days…that you don't know about this?"

"I'm a great pretender," Monica glanced at Dustin, who had been voiceless through the entire conversation. "Ask, Dustin, he knows how good I am."

Nadine got the point. But Monica's bruised ego was not the issue for Nadine. "One other thing. Did you ever mention the hair sample to anyone else?"

"No, why should I? At this point, it has no special significance."

"That's correct, it doesn't. Monica, I need your word you won't do anything until we talk. Is that a deal?"

"You have my girl scout's honor."

Nadine couldn't imagine how it was possible that someone had walked into a storage room inside the Crime Investigation Laboratory—where shelves upon shelves of boxes are held that house background data, samples of tissue, saliva, clothing, fibers, anything pertaining to a particular case—and taken a box marked CONGRESSMAN BLANK, opened it, removed a plastic baggie containing a strand of hair, put the box back in place, and…left with the hair sample.

"This was one hell of an artsy job," Nadine muttered.

"What was?"

"Dustin, you thinking about Connie or Monica?"

"Sorry. She really hates me."

"Ladies get mean when relationships end, especially if they didn't end it."

"For sure. She was the angriest I've ever had."

"Don't press your luck. Connie is very serious about you."

"Nadine, you can tell?"

"I'm warning you, yes. It's best to take your ladies one at a time, Dustin. Infidelity is the worst crime in a woman's mind. Sticks and stones will break your bones, but a revolver will kill you."

"Okay, I get it."

"I hope so. Now, can we get back to work?"

"Of all the evidence, why take that?" Dustin mused.

"The 'why' should be obvious, Dustin. It's a match they don't ever want made. It would incriminate somebody very important. To me the more relevant question is how did anybody know that it was there? Monica never said anything. Are they routinely going through the files and case materials for all of our investigations, looking for anything that might be contradictory to their interests?"

"They! It keeps coming back to the same theme," Dustin commented reflectively. "A team?"

"We'll see. For now, I'll buy that it's not one of Larry's patients, but we're warm. I feel it," Nadine said as she popped her chin forward in an affirmative gesture.

She feels warm. She feels warm. Is she? She may be hot, and if so, she will bust open this case. Then shrapnel is going be flying like candy out of a piñata popped by an Albert Pujols home run swing.

52

I THOUGHT WE WERE GOING STEADY

NADINE HAD RISEN EARLY to attend a seven o'clock yoga class. When she exited at just past eight thirty, she headed to her car. Her plan for the morning was to drive to Baltimore to meet with an associate of Lacey Reynolds—one of the victims—to interview him about Reynolds' relationship with President Haley.

The connection between Reynolds and Haley wasn't the agenda she presented to Tyler Warren, the associate. Still, it was her aim in interviewing the man to see if there was aspects of the relationship that might help her understand why Reynolds was killed. If it were the case that all these victims were tied into Haley in some way, she needed to find the link; Reynolds was as good a place to begin as any.

On her way to her car, she was carrying an exercise bag in her right hand and keys in the other. Her left arm reached out toward the car door. Just that instant she sensed swift movement coming from her right. A rush of panic caused her to reflexively swing the bag as a defensive measure. Her body rotated right as it followed the upward trajectory of the airborne sack. Upon reaching its apex the bag was blocked in flight by an arm.

She stood nose to nose with none other than…Larry. By now she was passing oxygen like she just completed a hundred yard dash—it was Larry who looked like he had just finished pranayama. It was surprising he was as calm as he was, because he had rehearsed his anticipated acrimonious encounter with Nadine repeatedly earlier that morning; each time the thoughts riled him.

"What are you doing?" Nadine said, pulling back the bag while she stepped backward instinctively. "You scared me."

She was standing by the driver's side front hood of the car. Larry was holding the envelope with what he feared would be potentially damaging pictures. He'd prepared for a showdown.

He had deliberated if it might be wiser to let some time pass and see how their relationship progressed. He thought about waiting to see if there were hints of Brent lingering in her background. But as he ruminated on what Howard had said to him about Nadine, he found himself fuming about the possibility she was playing him for a fool.

He let the pictures drop in front of her on the hood.

"I thought you might want to keep these in your scrapbook."

The calm, slow, shallow in and out movement of air through his nose present when he first approached Nadine, was now replaced by a heavier, pulsing chest and a mandible joint locked down tight.

The scene would have been humorous to a detached observer. That is, Nadine in an instant had swapped attitudes with Larry. She was now the one looking content, actually merry. A smirk gradually spread across her lips as she examined the contents of the envelope. She took her time. Slowly, picture after picture, shot by shot, she examined them.

She said nothing until she completed a full review of each item. Then she placed them lightly on the hood and turned to face Larry.

"Okay, wonderful investigative job, Larry." To highlight her approbation, she lightly slapped him on his arm.

"I'm not looking for your compliments."

"Good, because I'm not applauding you," she retorted sharply. "You wouldn't know where to start an investigation of an inanimate object, let alone a human one."

"You're avoiding the issue. It's plain and simple."

"Oh, and what is that?" she challenged.

"That while you're supposedly with me, you have someone else in your life."

"If this is the way you do your analyses, God help your patients."

"My patients are doing quite well…and let's not change the subject."

"Look, until you tell me where you got these, this conversation is over."

Her smooth, self-assured and aggressive response agitated him. He expected a bloodletting, but Nadine was so cool she'd have had to be thawed before he'd earn a drop.

"We have a damn large problem, Nadine."

Nadine couldn't resist a grin. "Sure. You're like a little boy who thinks he just dug a hole to China. I hope you have a way to climb out."

"I can't believe you, Nadine. I show you evidence of unfaithfulness on your part and you refuse to explain it until I tell you how I found out. That's like one of your criminals looking at evidence that they embezzled from a bank but refusing to admit it until you explain how you amassed your facts."

Nadine looked puzzled. She was trying to decipher if the analogy fit. "I think I have a right to know where your evidence came from. What if these pictures were falsely generated on a computer?"

"So you're saying you're not having an affair with Brent at the same time you're sleeping with me?"

"Larry, don't make me regret the intimacy that I've shared with you." Contrary to the opinion of the big-shot president, Nadine did not ever take sex casually, and promiscuity was not a practice she'd know any more about than hunting little dyed eggs on Easter. "No, I'm not saying a thing until you talk about why these pictures were taken, and by whom."

Larry must have sensed that something had been miscalculated;

he might as well have been standing on a greased platform and about to fall on his face. There was a trace of a plea in his voice as he spoke. "This is not a joke. Nadine, we're not in high school."

"I wonder. It seems classical high school insecurity to have me followed, wouldn't you say?"

"That's not the issue here. If you're involved with this man, then I find your behavior reprehensible."

"Larry, I don't know where all this came from or who might be filling your head with these ideas about me. Did you ask yourself, great mind doctor, if I seem like the deceitful type? Is there's anything I've done that has given you cause to mistrust me? Is there?"

"Yes, this."

Nadine was getting frustrated with the gaminess of the exchange. She was irked that she had no idea why these pictures were taken and couldn't get a straight answer from Larry. In the end, she decided to step back from her demand and answer his question.

"Let me put this into a deep sleep for you. Brent is not my lover, nor has he ever been. If he were, then I would be guilty of a deceit I would rather die than own. But it has nothing to do with you." Her words were strongly condescending. "I have a best friend, Lori. I believe I've mentioned her to you once or twice, the one with two children whom I am godmother to. She's been married for fifteen years to her high school sweetheart, who by an amazing coincidence is a man named Brent, the same man in these pictures."

She picked out two of the pictures. "This picture shows me hugging a man who genuinely adores me as a friend. Look." She pushed the photograph directly in front of his face. "Do you see lust? Does this look like he has the hots for me? Does he look like you look when I walk into a room?" she sneered.

The second picture was of her and Brent shopping. She placed it next to the other—they rested on the hood of the car in front of Larry like fraternal siblings.

"Just to leave no unfinished business, yes, he is checking me out in these cool clothes. Lori's having a fortieth birthday party in two weeks. I had intended to invite you. Brent is making a major fuss over it. Since I'm her exact size, who better to model the potential purchases?"

"Well, I guess…"

"I guess you screwed up big. Now, you don't want to tell me why you had me followed? You don't want to tell me who took the pictures?"

"It's not—"

She was steamed. "Go ahead and have me followed. Go ahead. You want to threaten me? Do it if you have to."

"Nadine, these were mailed to me," Larry said at last, choosing deception over disclosure. "I don't know from whom or why. Why would I want to have you followed?"

"You are going to look me in the eyes and swear to me, to God, to whomever you pray to, or to your friend Howard, you have no idea where these pictures came from?"

"Yes," he answered without hesitation.

"I don't believe you."

"Then you're going to throw our relationship out because you don't believe me, but you don't have a shred of evidence that I'm lying?"

"I don't want to end it. No, actually I don't, but this is getting too uncomfortable."

"I told you I got a call warning me about you. Obviously someone is trying to destroy us. Please, let's not help them."

He approached to take her in his arms. Nadine couldn't bring herself to return the gesture. "If what you're telling me is true…"

"Why would I lie?" Larry pled.

"I don't know, but I'm concerned for both of us."

"I am too. Nadine, before I received the pictures, I had an idea.

What if we could get away from this, even if it's just for a short time? "

"Why a short time?" Nadine bargained.

"Because neither of us would leave it forever."

"I know that."

"I have a place on the beach at Martha's Vineyard. What do you think about spending the weekend there?"

Nadine contemplated the jack-knifing of her emotions over the past few minutes. What really had happened? Larry was guilty of nothing. Once again, she had sentenced him without a proper trial.

"Why not? Maybe getting away from all this will do me good."

Martha's Vineyard? A world she had heard of but never seen.

During the summer, the tiny island located about three miles south of Cape Cod is home to the most well-to-do along the eastern seaboard, along with some flashy names of Hollywood celebrity. If Nadine had concerns about fitting in, it wouldn't be a problem. It was springtime. No self-respecting Martha's Vineyardian would be caught dead anywhere other than skiing in Chamonix, France or the like.

"Yeah, might not be a bad idea," she concluded.

"You sure know how to sharpen your sword, Nadine. I just hope you don't use it on me."

"You'll survive me. This question is if I'll survive you."

Helter skelter. Mercury's in retrograde!

53

HE'S A PATIENT?

WHAT A DAY! MERCURY must have petered out—the weatherman had been knocked on his rear. Early spring on the island of Martha's Vineyard should be biting cold, windy and wet. Not everything was coming up weeds for our couple. While the night before when they arrived it was predictably raining, there was no residual sign of the storm in the morning. Outdoors it was sunny, still and mild.

It was probably the only brief run of inviting weather Martha's Vineyard would see until well into the summer. Larry had in mind warm coats, walks along the deserted beaches during the day, and a fireplace-warmed cottage—it's not easy to call a home with over three thousand square feet a cottage—to cuddle in at night. He did get the deserted beaches.

Upon arriving at his place, Larry couldn't resist filling Nadine in on the history of this small island. This time, however, Nadine trumped him. "I never knew much about the island until something interesting happened," Nadine began.

"What's that?"

"When I discovered Horace was deaf and I began studying sign language, I came across a code system that I liked. It was the one I chose to use with him. It was started here. It was called Martha's Vineyard Sign Language."

"That is interesting," Larry commented. "By the way, the weather sure went our way here today. We deserve it, Nadine."

"Oh, we do? For what?"

"For suffering, but not losing hope." Larry's tone was sentimental.

"If you don't mind, I'll take the not losing hope without the suffering. Is that possible?"

Larry was resting on a lounge, wearing shorts without a shirt. He knew her question was rhetorical. He was holding a book. Next to him was an iPod and speaker. Nadine was also on a chaise, sitting sideways, a bit edgy, as if she couldn't relax. She walked a few short feet to the water. Larry resumed his reading.

Having lived her life on the East Coast, she wasn't unfamiliar with cold water and freezing temperatures. Her thick skin allowed her to submerge herself in the ocean at fairly cool temperatures. However, as she waded knee-deep into the smooth coastal waves she noticed her feet, ankles and calves numbing. She splashed herself to wet her body and cupped her hands to cradle a small amount of the sea.

By the time she made it back to where Larry was lying, most of the ocean water had dripped into the sand. Still, there was just enough for her devious act. She came behind his head and reached her hand out, shaking the droplets of almost freezing water so that they bounced off his unsuspecting fleshy chest, face and head.

While the air was pleasantly warm, the frigid water more than earned his attention. After ascertaining the origin of the attack, he leaned his head further up to the sky and then stretched his neck a few degrees further back to meet her eyes, smiling adoringly.

The Eagles' "Desperado" was playing. While Larry was enjoying the moment, the chorus repeated a line about letting somebody love you, and doing it sooner rather than later.

Nadine was in the mood, kissing his cheek and then moving around to seat herself next to him on the chaise.

"You're blessed to have a place like this to get away to."

"I'm doubly blessed then. I get to share it with you. I hope we'll be able to do this lots of times."

"I do too."

"Nadine, if I could stay here, I mean for the rest of my life…"

"Why can't you?" she earnestly wondered.

"I have responsibilities. You see what I do."

"People who have the means can make changes in their responsibilities," she argued

"But I like my life. The only thing bothering me is some of my patients," he chuckled oddly.

Nadine was in an unusually playful, gamboling mood. Her next comment to Larry seemed innocent and off-the-cuff. "Patients like your friend, President Haley?"

"How would you know I treat him?"

Nadine was stunned. Her flippant comment never anticipated Haley as a patient. "I didn't 'til now."

"Just forget about it."

"I was joking, Larry. It's none of my business."

"I'm his best friend. Wouldn't it make sense that he'd talk with me if he had a problem?" Then he added in a manner that might have been interpreted as naughty. "I even make him come to my office."

Nadine's lips parted but her mind bit down on a question: If he was a patient, why didn't Haley's name show up in the appointment book?

She kissed him on the forehead. Then she grabbed her towel off the lounge and wrapped it around her bottom, slipping on her thongs. She had a piece of urgent business needing attention.

"I forgot my book in the house. I'll be back in a few minutes," she informed Larry, intentionally feigning disinterest in his comment about Haley.

She followed the cobblestone path set out in the sand to the back door of the cottage. Once inside, she went to her purse to get her phone. She keyed in numbers and waited. It rang several times.

"Drake here."

"Dustin, it's me."

"Where are you?"

"It's not important. I have something of highest priority for you to do."

What Nadine couldn't see was that Dustin was home in bed, at eleven thirty in the morning. Connie was by his side and his two Blue Seal cats were traipsing across the comforter. Connie's eyes were blurry. They had stayed out after she finished work. Connie was staring quizzically at Dustin because his tone snapped to attention at the sound of Nadine's voice. He was looking at Connie as he responded to Nadine.

"Do I have to do it this minute?"

"No, any time before I get back."

"You didn't tell me you were going away."

Nadine finds his interest endearing and treats it lightly. "Geez, I'm sorry I forgot to tell you."

"Got it. Now, how do I know when you'll be back?"

"That's the right question. I'll be back tomorrow, early evening."

"I'm on it as soon as you let me know what it is."

"Go back to Dr. Monroe's office—"

"Please, Nadine. I did it once. I don't want to risk it again."

"I promise there's no risk. You can go anytime, but it would be best to do it early tomorrow because it's Sunday and nobody is around. Listen carefully. Double-check the appointment book and make sure you didn't miss any entries for patients being treated." Her voice was hushed but firm.

"Maybe something is written in a margin or as an entry on a separate page, even initials or an anagram. Also, do another look-around, just in case. Look for notes in his drawers. Look at the calendar on the desk for scribbling of names or times. Find anything you can about other patients."

"What happened?"

"Nothing happened. Just another hunch that I'll explain later."

"I could live without these hunches."

"You won't have a problem. I'll call you the minute I get home. Make sure I can reach you tomorrow night."

In the afternoon, Larry took Nadine on an excursion around the island. He rented an off-road vehicle so they could drive to some of the less accessible areas he'd explored in the past. Nadine recalls loving the sand dunes.

"I had a blast whirling through the silt-like material. It was even more fun when Larry ran the wheels by mistake into a sandbar and had to knock on the door of a local farmer to use his tractor to pull us out."

Nadine said it was her perfect level of danger for a nature adventure. She had no qualms about mixing it up with the most audacious of human desperados but would cower at the thought of facing a night alone in the wilderness. Larry would never let that happen to her.

54

WHO'S CLOSING IN ON WHOM?

FORTUNES MOVE QUICKLY IN island living. Sunday was hardly a replica of the day before. The couple spent the thundering morning indoors and then set off for the airport.

When they arrived back in Washington, Nadine asked Larry to drop her at the of-fice so she could look into a couple of matters. She told him she'd cab home when she was finished. It wasn't until about eight-thirty when she arrived at her condo. She had first stopped by the unit of a neighbor who looked after Horace for the weekend.

As soon as she started to make her way to her condo, Horace was atypically unrelenting as he pulled on the leash. At the same moment, Dustin called. She put down her overnight bag to retrieve her cell.

"All I found new was an invoice in one of his drawers from Efron Tech Services; it appears they made repairs to his in-office recording system."

Horace, all the more energetically was tugging at the leash. Mightily, she pulled back on him, her force reflective of her being stunned by the unexpected discovery Dustin had made.

"Horace is going nuts on me; I'll call you back."

Taking a moment to processing the new information, at the same time she tried to calm her pet, assuming he missed her and was just excited. Yet even with her effort to reassure him, his mood shifted to agitation. She decided to let him free, knowing he'd make his way to her place. She followed as he bolted down the hall and as she took her key and inserted it into the front door lock she noticed that the door released with only slight pressure.

She pulled backward, almost forcing a fall, watching as Horace darted inside ahead of her. He ran through the rooms, sniffing anxiously. By this time, Nadine had armed herself and was waiting at the threshold for the "all-clear" from Horace, an animal deficient in hearing but not smell.

Glancing through the open door, she was able to see her home was in a state of slight disarray. It was nowhere near thoroughly vandalized, yet there was enough disorder to let her know she'd had a visitor. After his vigilant inspection, Horace scampered back to Nadine's side and wagged his tail.

Once inside, she made a quick assessment of the damage, leaving the door open in case she needed to make a fast exit. There was no broken furniture or cracked glass. The signs of entry were limited to items misplaced, personal papers taken out of drawers, and closets disrespected.

Minimizing the situation, she was about to close the door when she heard footsteps approaching in the hallway—the sound brought her back to a state of shock. She stepped out of sight behind a wall. The noise came to a halt just outside her door. Breathless, with her weapon drawn, she peeked out.

"Oh, I'm sorry. I was looking for my aunt's apartment, two fourteen," said the boy who was about fourteen years old. Nadine ventured out from her hiding place. The boy's mouth froze in an open gape and his eyes had widened. Nadine was pointing her weapon at his chest. She quickly dropped it to her side.

"It's okay. I'm a police officer. Somebody broke into my house. Look, you turned the wrong way off the elevator; she's just down the hall."

There are times when we as human beings can feel, literally feel, a dramatic shift in an environment when, in fact, no physical factors could account for it. It's a sixth, seventh or even eighth sense that picks up on extra-normal phenomena.

Nadine described this type of experience once she was alone with Horace in her home. The rooms were chilled as if a polar storm were crushing sheets of ice against the floor, walls, and ceiling to force them inward. All sound froze, leaving a deadly quiet space. From the stillness, a pair of threatening eyes reached out to command recognition before disappearing into the walls, furniture…and finally…silence.

After a few seconds, she closed the door. She had already turned on the heat. Later, she unpacked, made a light meal and went to bed, noting that she would decide in the morning what, if anything, she would do about the recording device. She recalled sleeping surprisingly well.

It was earlier than normal when Horace wagged his way into her bedroom the next morning. He had staked out the entire entry area as his kingdom when he was still a pup. Nadine learned long before not to buck his wishes and placed his soft bed each evening next to the front door.

Typically his highness was still sleeping when Nadine awakened, sometimes even as she put on the teakettle. The explanation for a breach of habit this particular morning was that he was awakened only seconds earlier by another piece of paper being delivered under her door. Thus, he'd served the role of a good messenger.

Horace tugged her to the door. When she saw the delivery she left it in place. The contents might be important, but not as important as her processing the recent events. She told Dustin they were getting warm; now she knew it would soon be sizzling.

The letters were increasing. Threatening gestures toward her were more frequent. She knew from experience that whoever was the maker of these overtures couldn't wait much longer to bring about a direct confrontation. All she needed to do was be vigilant and wait.

Nadine was not required to keep a schedule at the office. With outside investigations, meetings, and working at home she really couldn't. She had taken care Sunday evening to clear her desk at work. She was in no hurry this brisk, sunny Monday morning.

After feeding Horace and having a cup of tea with lemon slices, two dates and a handful of raisins, she shoved the unopened vanilla note in her purse and put the pet on a leash in preparation for walking to the park. She passed a wooden bench and sat, while Horace squatted for his morning bowel movement. Waiting for him to complete his task, she surrendered to the lingering curiosity of what the third in the series of letters had to say.

The seat marked a perfect spot to open it. The task took all of two seconds. She placed the note on the bench next to her and called Larry.

"Larry, there was another note for me this morning."

Why she called Larry was inexplicable to her. She said it was the first thing that came to her mind. The wonderfulness of the weekend together, feeling a mutual trust and genuine caring again had to have inclined her to seek his companionship.

"What did it say?" he asked urgently.

She picked up the note again, reading it silently a second time.

YOU'RE GETTING CLOSE ENOUGH THAT I'M GOING TO HAVE TO DO SOMETHING ABOUT YOU.

She then reads it out loud to Larry. *You're getting close enough that I'm going to have to do something about you.*

"He's going to kill you," Larry shouted frantically.

"No, he's not," Nadine insisted.

"How can you say that? Each of the notes is more threatening."

"He wants to scare me off the case. I don't know why, because if not me somebody else has to take it over. Maybe he has an issue with women. That's happened before but I've always been able to use it to my benefit."

"Nadine, this doesn't seem like your other cases."

"You're right, it's not. Look, I'll see you tonight and we'll talk."

She had only a few words to write in her journal that night on the subject of the killer ratcheting up his warnings to her.

"Yes, I knew what I was doing was putting me at the highest danger level. But I held on to this thought I couldn't get rid of, that he had opportunities to kill me but didn't. Instead, he puffed his chest and pointed daggers."

Nadine sat a while on the bench. To the right of where she was seated was a large children's play area with a sand-filled playground. Moms were talking to each other while watching their little ones on the slides, swings and other apparatus used to crawl, climb and jump.

Only fifty yards of physical space separated her from these specimens of womanhood, yet light years of distance would have to be traveled for Nadine to join their actual universe. A sad yearning filled her heart as she stared, wondering when and if it would be her turn to push one of those swings and talk of mommy-and-me classes.

She halted the blind chatter of her imagination. What good could come of it? Her here-and-now existence was about death, violence, crime and perversion, not pregnancies and birthing, burping, pooping, peeing, diapering and strolling.

She stood up to find a more isolated location; where she'd be hidden from what you knew was a farfetched dream. She called Chauncy. He was in the middle of a morning exercise on his elliptical machine. At the same time, he was watching the news on television. He carried on the conversation with her while pumping his legs.

"Chauncy, I need someone to talk to."

Breathing hard. "I'm your man for a talking head."

Nadine took a sip of water from the bottle she carried with her. Horace leapt on to the bench to position himself with his head on her lap. In the brief time she'd been at the park, the clear sky had clouded up and a mild rain began falling. She didn't move. She was sitting where large trees canopied high above her.

"While I was away with Larry this past weekend, he revealed a stunning piece of information," she informed Chauncy. "It turns out that his friend, our President Haley, is a patient of Dr. Monroe."

Chauncy's stride was in harmony with his passionate speech and symphonic hand gesturing. "What's wrong with that? There are no laws preventing it."

"I know. Based on the dream I told you about, we checked the whole patient list and concluded I had been mistaken. Then I found it strange not so much that Larry would set sessions for Haley but that we had the appointment book and his name never showed up."

"He is the president," Chauncy cautioned. "Monroe may be protecting him. You know how crap like this can be distorted by the press."

"True. But Larry is a precise person. There would have at least been entries in the appointment book with a code or fake name but it's not there. There are a lot of other things that concern me about Haley."

"Are you suggesting that President Haley is streaking out and killing all these people?"

"I'm not saying anything…yet."

"Let me know if you need anything."

"That's why I'm calling. Larry told me that he doesn't like to be distracted during sessions by taking notes. Fine. But now I find out that he has this recording system in the office…since he doesn't like to write during a session would it not make sense that he'd record every treatment session? He claims that he needs recall to all details of his patients' treatment sessions, so what better way to assure that than to record? He might have discs from years back."

"It's plausible. But that does not tell you where, if there are recordings, he keeps them."

"It has to be someplace in the office because the note Dustin found referenced repairing the in-office system. It's worth a try finding them; those transcripts could clear up everything."

"Then you want me to see if I can find it and then make copies."

"I already sent Dustin into the office twice and he's not happy about it."

"Poor boy."

"Plus, he's not expert on these recording systems, and neither am I. Look, all I need is the last year."

Chauncy still hadn't slowed down his routine. "If they're in the office, it's done."

"I'll get back to you with either details about the office and when it will be safe to go." Then she added. "Chauncy, did you get me someone to talk to about the vanilla stationary?"

"There's a man I know who's an expert on these things, owns a store not far from here and he's looking into it."

"Let me know."

"One more question. What are you going to do when you find out that President Haley is the killer?"

"Arrest him."

Chauncy broke into full laughter, shaking his head because he could imagine her doing just that. "You better check with me first."

55

PLAYING WITH FIRE

PREETI HAD OVER TWO weeks left until her due date. Josea and Reuben announced that Josea was pregnant. The soft theme of babies that had laced its way through my journey to Israel was popping up all around my life again. Why not? Isn't birth where the cycle of life starts? If it doesn't begin there, it's for certain that without it existence, as we humans know it, screeches to a dead halt.

There was no question that Nadine wouldn't be making a similar announcement. She remained in a voluntary sequestering. She'd call Preeti daily to check on her but refused to visit or meet her. Nadine would promise to help babysit as soon as she could. What she didn't tell Preeti, and I didn't either, was that she wasn't sure she would be alive to follow through on the pledge.

Her behavior was becoming increasingly irregular and unpredictable, precisely as she wished it to be. She would call me and tell me where she wanted me to be and then pick me up, driving us to a remote location where we would talk about the story. She would be constantly checking and re-checking to be sure that we weren't followed. She knew whom she was dealing with and I didn't.

One afternoon we were about to work but Nadine wanted to walk a few minutes first. As we started, she handed me a third note. It was short: PEOPLE WHO PLAY WITH FIRE GET BURNED. SOME ARE MAIMED FOR LIFE AND OTHERS DIE.

She grabbed the paper back, focusing my attention to the nearly indiscernible watermark.

"I have several others that are identical. But you know that already."

"I believe you," I said sadly.

"This will be over soon," she instructed me.

"What makes you so sure?"

"Can't you tell? He's losing patience…"

"He? You've been talking about 'they.' Now it's 'he.' You're confusing me."

"Zach, it's he, but in order to do this *he* has to be *they*. You'll understand in due time. Now, they…he…act like he's trying to be humane, giving me a chance to live. He wants me to think that if I go back to D. C. and forget the writing, all will be forgotten. All he really wants is to get me on his turf where my death can be more easily made to appear to be an accident."

"But what if you could go home and be safe?" I hypothesized. "Would you do it now rather than risk dying over a book?"

Nadine smiled, aware that I was making a logical proposal that could save her.

"It may sound foolish to you but I owe this to someone. *Childish honor. No principle is worth dying over.* Sure, I've considered all that. It's not Nadine Street to back away. If my life was different and I had other people to live for, I might not see it that way. I have nobody."

"Preston loves you," I unwisely yelled at her. "We've all come to care for you here and certainly Chauncy must still care."

"If this works out the way I'm planning, I'll never put myself in this position again. How's that for a promise?"

I kept thinking what Preston might want me to say but realized it was senseless. She hinted at having a debt to collect and deputized herself into a posse-of-one. The main problem I saw was that all of the messages so far were coming her way and she already knew that the sender had a final one earmarked for her.

We had been gone about fifteen minutes, ambling through a wooded area. We had put our materials on a table with benches in a picnic spot. When we turned to go back, Nadine received a call on her cell. She glanced down and then motioned to me that she had to take it. The conversation was short.

"What is it?" She paused for a few seconds. "You're sure?" she responded to the unknown caller. "Then he's here still!" she stated with alarm.

Nadine abruptly flipped the phone shut.

We walked the rest of the way back. Nadine was eerily quiet. As we reached the clearing coming out of the trees where the bench with our work on it waited, something seemed to alert her. She scanned around us. I noticed her reach inside her purse and begin to draw out what I was sure would be her handgun. What happened next took place in an instant, before I had the opportunity to factor in that my life was also in danger.

"I'll be right back," she shouted, racing forward toward where we had parked the car. She screamed back to me with urgency. "Don't move!!"

56

OUT OF THE FRYING PAN, INTO THE SKILLET

NADINE DISCLOSED TO ME that the more she thought about the risks she was facing, the more she considered excusing herself from the case. In fact, that evening when she met Larry for dinner, she was leaning strongly toward taking that unprecedented action.

But she never had the chance. The poor kid was taken by an undercurrent and sucked helplessly below water. Then a riptide dragged her deep into the open seas and swallowed her far from shore. Now, there would be no choice. She'd have to gasp for air and swim for her life.

If this sounds bad, it was very bad—then it got worse. Here's what happened.

Under the pretense of allowing Larry and Horace to get better acquainted, Monday evening, when she went to Larry's home for dinner, she brought the dog. The truth was she felt better having Horace around as much as possible, and Larry genuinely seems agreeable to him coming over.

The evening was uneventful. Nadine appreciated the escape because she was feeling drained. In fact, it was fairly early when she was on the couch with her eyes shut in sleep. When Larry saw her fading he put down the book he'd been reading and helped her into the bedroom.

If the excitement of young lovers requires constant sexual satisfaction then it has to be assumed this evening's festivities were already past. Nadine was drifting into a slumber as his guiding hands tucked her in. By the time he was lying next to her, she was deeper in sleep. The room, as Larry preferred it, was pitch black. The shutters were drawn tight. The only radiant light came from a tiny night reflector.

The conditions were perfect for a restful night of uninterrupted sleep. Unfortunately, the stillness and silence were sharply challenged by several quick, deep breaths, in turn producing an anxious guttural shriek as Nadine bolted physically upward and out of her sleep state. Her eyes opened, unfocused, but tenuously she witnessed another set of eyes moving out of the darkness. She screamed as she rolled to the right off the bed, which she instinctively used as a barricade to peek out from while yelling in terror.

"I've seen those eyes!" she bellowed terrifyingly.

Instantly, the lights illuminated the room. Larry was naked, standing by the switch. With Horace deafly unmoved at the foot of the bed, Larry quickly rushed to Nadine to cradle her in his arms.

After several minutes, during which time her state of hyperventilation syndrome was arrested, her capacity to move restored, her senses returned to normal, and her respiration stabilized. She stared dumbly as if just arriving out of an epileptic fit, still on the floor and in Larry's arms. He lifted her back on to the bed.

"I got up to go to the bathroom. Then you were yelling."

Her spoken affect was flat. She babbled a few incoherent words. Then as she tried to talk, the flow of air through her throat again was restricted and her lungs heaved slightly. Finally, she formulated a narrowly intelligible stream of thought. "I get bad dreams sometimes; the eyes, the forest. I must have been dreaming; the garage, my house," she mumbled.

"Just wait, you'll be fine," Larry said as he gently comforted her. "You got scared, that's all. You're safe."

"I know, Larry, but it was so real."

"I'm sorry that I scared you. I'll stay up with you until you're ready to go back to sleep."

"No, just turn off the lights and rest. We have to work tomorrow. I'll be okay now."

Larry did as instructed. He held her securely as he fell asleep. Nadine was up a good hour more, too agitated to achieve a restful state. Finally, she drifted back into what she would recall was a profound sleep, waking after Larry had already groomed.

They spent another robust hour in bed enjoying each other. Then Larry dressed and left the room. Soon after, she recalls the sound of loud music, a fast-paced piece she appreciated as a needed a picker-upper.

Larry, meantime—his housekeeper had been given the night off—could be found in the kitchen pouring glasses of fresh orange juice while synchronizing to the bluesy, rock sound. His spirits were high. Why not? The nightmare for Nadine was over. He could still smell the juices of her body on his flesh.

At one point, he walked into the bedroom and asked if she was ready to eat. She told him she wanted to clean up first and would be about half an hour. Larry went back to the kitchen.

Nadine had gone into the bathroom and was preparing to shower. She yelled out the door of the bedroom into the adjacent room where Larry was. "Larry, where are the towels I should use?"

No response. She waited a few more seconds and repeated the question. "Where are the towels?"

No answer. What would be the big deal if she took the liberty to find them herself? Normally she wouldn't think of searching through a friend's personal effects, but this was not a violation; she only wanted a towel and washcloth.

Nadine described the bathroom being as large as her living room. To one side was a walk-in closet that was the size of most people's sleeping quarters. She opened the door and entered, immediately noticing ample towels to select from on a shelf. Naked and eager to get into warm water she reached quickly to grab a set of lavender linen.

By mistake, her arm firmly hit the wood shelf. A spontaneous "shit" conveyed that it was a knuckle bruiser, but what was unexpected was the impact was strong enough to cause the entire unit to swivel about an inch.

Noticing the movement, she did what any Curious George would. She pushed to test the purpose of the rotating unit. Expecting it to be nothing other than a clever swing design, she was shocked to find as she revolved it ninety degrees that there was enough space to pass left or right from the closet to a hidden room beyond it.

The secret space proved staggering to Nadine due to the contents. Hanging in long rows were clothing; jackets, suits, coats and shirts, spare items that could be dismissed as insignificant. But then there were cabinets housing sets of eyebrows, mustaches, beards, goatees and wigs.

Shoes were lined up on shelves, row after row of boots, loafers and then tie dress shoes in every color followed by hundreds of hanging neckties. Then finally, and most distressing, was a large built-in mirrored unit with innumerable small cubbies filled with vials, jars and bottles containing various types of makeup, plus the necessary brushes and applicators to do the job.

As she was marveling at the incriminating discovery she'd made, her eye was drawn toward the back of one of the shelves. Simultaneously she registered recognition and terror. Directly in her line of vision was a small piece of paper, crumpled up. It was vanilla shaded, identical to the color of the notes she'd received. She grabbed it. As she examined it, she froze. The bottom line was a replica of the "hidden trapezoid," a perfect match, with the three samples in her possession.

Overwhelmed by the discovery she had made, she hadn't noticed the sound of music diminishing in volume. Unexpectedly, she was interrupted by Larry's voice calling out to her from inside the bedroom. She could count the jackhammer blows of her heart pounding.

"Honey, you okay in there?"

"Fine, just wrapping myself in a towel," she called out, trying to sound casual.

"Let me know if you need anything. I'll be in the other room."

She heard the door to the bedroom gently close. She peeked out from the bathroom to make sure he was gone. When she exited the bath area, she heard the musical tone increase again—she ran back to the closet. After snatching the piece of paper she rotated the cupboard back to its original position.

Nadine's slacks were hanging on a hook. She stuffed the paper into the pocket. She walked to the shower, turned on the water and stepped back hesitantly. Then she ran to lock the door to the bathroom.

Her only thought was getting out of the house and to a place of safety, where she could think. She already knew it was Larry who had sent the letters, it was Larry who had been stalking her, and it was Larry who had been trying to terrorize her. As the thoughts cascaded in a sick progression she halted on the worst: it was Larry who was the killer, dressing himself in a choice of costumes to accomplish the murders.

But what about the Blank murder? Larry couldn't have killed him; he was with Haley. Together, two, three of them, they're orchestrating the murders of innocent people, key leaders? Was it all motivated by a need to remove obstacles to Haley's precious career? *Hell, maybe Haley lied to protect Larry and he wasn't at the White House at all*, her mind considered.

While showering, she wondered if she was up to a cameo role; if she could control her wits to pull off dealing with the rest of the morning without allowing Larry to detect a garbled syllable, slip of the tongue, forgotten line or…fear.

The goal, the goal, the goal; get out without arousing any suspicions.

Keep your mind on that and nothing else. She rehearsed the instruction over and over.

She dressed, gathered her belongings and went to the kitchen. Larry had prepared breakfast and had the table set. He came over to hug her and she reciprocated the gesture. When he tried to get playful Nadine was prepared.

"I'd love to, but I need to take Horace home and get to a meeting I'm supposed to have with Riley," she said sorrowfully.

"You had a terrible night. I'm sorry."

"You would know more about this than me but I notice I tend to get the nightmares when I haven't been sleeping, when I'm overtired."

"Could be. Now don't forget we're going to see Howard and Muriel Thursday night."

"No, I'm planning on it," she responded enthusiastically.

She managed to eat, leave, and keep Larry unsuspecting, which is all she could have dreamed of doing under the circumstances.

As soon as she arrived home, she went to a drawer of her nightstand and took out a small hand-held micro-cassette recorder. She loaded a tape and began speaking.

"Chauncy, I'm making this tape in case anything happens to me. I have to follow this…wherever it takes me."

In this first recording to Chauncy, she spilled each bean she had collected, one by one; it was an up-to-date detailed progression of events similar to the account of this story I've outlined up to this point.

When she was finished, she took off for work, but not to the office as she had told Larry. Her plan was to have every detail of her investigation documented and in the event harm came to her, know it would be released to the press. They could kill her, but they were not going to snuff out the truth.

Larry's going down; so is anyone else responsible for these murders, she babbled to the walls of her room. *In the meantime…I'm going to have to stay close to him.*

57

I'M ONLY TRYING TO PROTECT YOU

DURING THE NEXT COUPLE of days, Nadine's activities were routine. Then Thursday arrived and Larry picked her up for the scheduled date, the meeting with "his friend" and Muriel.

It was damn near a repeat performance: same sitting room, same staff, same snacks and cast of characters. This time the seating arrangement had worked out differently, with a diagonal conversation whereby Nadine and Muriel were talking across the discussion between Larry and Howard.

The merging of voices likely created no distinguishable pattern until Muriel suddenly turned to her right to square off the pairings, addressing Larry directly. Knowing Larry's fondness for modern art she had it in her mind earlier to get him alone for a moment to show him some of the new pieces she had purchased.

"Come, Larry. I want to show you these new treasures I picked up for my office." Then she addressed Nadine. "Would you mind if I borrowed him briefly?"

"No, it's fine."

"Howard, this will give you some time to get to know Nadine better," Muriel rejoiced to the president.

She led Larry by the arm out two large doors, Haley smiling dutifully at his wife. However, Mr. President's use of his time with Nadine was not what Muriel had in mind. First he sat mutely, deep in a thought that ultimately required him to make a note. Nadine observed him use his left hand to reach for a pad on the table. He then transferred the paper to the right hand and reached inside his jacket for his pen—with his left hand. *Lots of lefties*, he thought.

After Haley completed the task, he dropped the pad and pen on the table and leaned back into a more relaxed pose. He examined Nadine, more aptly an undressing. It was likely a tactic Haley was accustomed to employing to weaken females.

Tact? Haley dispensed with it. His background check on her had already uncovered Nadine's provincial roots. He knew when dealing with a common lowborn like Nadine, that if he indelicately burned the bridge she crossed to get where she was, she wouldn't make a second showing. In other words, insult her and let her be gone.

Tact? Haley was merciless.

"I'm glad we have time for a few words alone…and if I'm too blunt for you, I apologize. But my advice is to run for cover before you're left heartbroken. Larry's not who you think he is."

The words of the president she understood as obvious mischief, but why Haley felt threatened by her relationship with Larry remained a mystery to her. It crossed her mind that it may have been pure and simple selfishness. Howard wanted Larry available to him. If Larry were to marry and have a family he'd venture away. Howard might lose him. *This is as sick a relationship as I've even seen. No medicine can cure it*, Nadine concluded while The President continued his assault.

"Sorry to be the one to inform you, young lady. Larry's a different man than he appears," he repeated a second time.

"Not to worry. I've witnessed what an accomplished actor he is."

The sarcasm didn't go unnoticed. It actually seemed to alarm him and Nadine regretted immediately she'd let it dribble out.

"Do you see something that disturbs you?" asked Haley curiously.

"Oh, no. But I'm sure you know he belongs to a theatre group. I had the honor of watching him perform," she proclaimed, relieved she had an opportunity to erase her carelessness.

"Yes, I see what you're referring to," chuckled Haley.

"Good."

"Well now, the reason I bring it up is that I hope you can appreciate my warning. Larry's gone through a fan club of ladies vying for his affections and in the end they all were tossed by the wayside. It would be a shame if an upstanding woman like yourself met a similar fate." He paused to reflect. "Come to think of it, I always thought of him as the consummate bachelor; lucky fellow in a way."

"As long as he's happy that way," Nadine replied.

"That's my point. I think he is," Haley said, pausing this time to interject the next dose of poison. "Oh, he gets all worked up and excited each time he's in love, but by the time the curtain falls he's tickled to have escaped free again."

"I promise you, sir, I'll make your friend a very happy man."

The last comment delighted him. He glanced up and noticed Muriel and Larry coming down a hallway.

"I hope we'll keep this little talk to ourselves," he said in a hush.

Softly, nearly mocking the president, she retorted. "I wouldn't even disclose to my best friend the fact that I've met you, Mr. President."

"We had a nice talk while you were gone. Another lovely specimen you've selected, Larry," Haley said as he welcomed his friend and wife.

"Is everybody hungry? I am. I'm afraid I was so busy I never stopped for lunch today," Haley disclosed.

"Dear, you do play the martyr. I can't believe the president can't send out for a sandwich," Muriel gently chided her husband.

"Then I simply forgot." He led the foursome to the dining room. He hadn't finished with Nadine. "I hear you're quite the investigator. I talked with Chief Lambert about you."

"The Chief and I have a history," Nadine responded—she had in mind to assess how much Haley would lie. "Do you know him well?"

"Strictly business," Haley answered.

Nadine ever so elusively glanced toward Larry. He knows Lambert but is ashamed he was a friend of his: that's what he told Nadine after the first of several confrontations. Now Larry's best friend is openly talking about Lambert, the third of the mountain climbing team, saying they know each other but it's "strictly business."

Larry knew he'd been uncovered as a deep-in-a-sea-of-shit liar. The whole affair made her want to vomit, but she restrained the urge to uncover Larry publicly.

"He tells me you're as aggressive as he's seen when it comes to closing an investigation." Then in a reviling tone Haley continued. "So, any progress on the case?"

'Not much," Nadine answered curtly.

"Dear, I hope if Harry moves into politics you can put in a good word for Nadine in the department," Muriel interjected.

At that moment, a suited man entered the room and walked up to Haley, whispering in his ear. Haley walked out with the man. He never said a word and never returned.

Nadine was astonished by his rudeness. She hoped to wake up in the morning to news that India and Pakistan finally decided to end the stalemate over the mutually claimed beautiful territory of Kashmir by nuking each other. She really didn't but something on that order would have had to take place to justify Haley's disrespect. President or not, Haley was now moving to the top on her "puke list."

The evening ended with a goodbye to Muriel.

After a long, silent drive toward Nadine's home, she was unable to endure the pain of a clenched jaw any longer. "Is that your idea of a friendship?" Nadine tersely posed to Larry.

"What are you talking about?"

"If you don't know, I'm more disgusted than angered."

"Look, I heard what he said but he just has a thing about me…like a parent, nobody is good enough. He'll get used to you, you'll see."

"Oh, I don't think the issue is whether or not he likes me or thinks I'm good enough for you. The point is that he would insult your judgment and then insult you right to your face…and then you would ignore it."

"I didn't ignore it," Larry passively responded.

"You said nothing to defend yourself. It makes me sick to think that a man of your stature would allow himself to be degraded and then believe the person doing the disrespect is a…'cherished blood brother'?"

"Nadine, you don't understand everything. He's under a lot of pressure. It's not a good time to create added stress for him."

"If that's how he handles pressure, I'm not going to be sleeping too well tonight. He's the president! Does he get to blow up a couple of countries because he's under too much stress?"

Larry laughed as if she had made a terrifically funny joke, but Nadine was at the point of exasperation. Larry tried one more attempt at appeasement. He reached across to the glove compartment and opened it. Inside is a stash of both caramel and chocolate See's suckers Larry had just bought to surprise Nadine. He took out two, one of each flavor.

"Chocolate or caramel?"

Nadine was shaking her head rapidly back and forth, her anger increased by what she saw as an idiotic gesture. "Are you out of your mind, Larry?"

"I'm just trying to lighten things," he said as he peeled off the wrapping of a chocolate candy and put it in his mouth.

Nadine had reached the end of her tolerance. From her seated position, she rotated left. Holding out the palms of her hands toward Larry chest high she signaled to keep him at a distance. "Take me home. Just get me goddamn home, now!"

When they arrived at her building Nadine shoved open the door and leapt out, not even looking behind to close it. Larry thought it was just Nadine overreacting...again. "Look I'm sorry. I'll call you tomorrow."

Twice after she was in her house the phone rang, but she refused to answer. As she was falling to sleep, it dawned on her that all that was left of her relationship with Larry was to seal his criminal fate. Further, she realized that there would be no future visits to Haley's White House, no other encounters with Haley—she was sadly mistaken on that point.

58

GETTING CLOSER

Not long ago the average city-dweller could go down the block near where they lived or worked and walk into a stationery store: Valley Stationers, Pat's Office Supplies, Livingston's Paper & Pen or The Onionskin. Then the industry was monopolized by giants like Office Max, Office Depot or Staples: the little, independent guys were nearly all wiped out…nearly.

Bob Houston of Houston's Stationary in Georgetown is a surviving champion of the keep-it-small-and-intimate spirit. He's been in the business since carbon paper was ten sheets for a and fountain pens came with real inkwells. Earlier in Bob's career he worked for International Paper, where he learned the production and distribution side of the business.

You might say he's an expert, and having just passed his eighty-eighth birthday, he's not insulted with the "old" guy reference. He'll tell you he's the happiest man on the planet because—as he explained it to Nadine—the alternative didn't seem like such a hot deal; and he's been in business long enough to know a deal when he sees one. In his words, "I'm tickled to still be here," Bob proudly announces.

Chauncy agreed to accompany Nadine to the store since he knew Houston personally. He and Nadine entered close to the old-fashioned opening time of ten in the morning. Bob was there to greet them. He had the samples of the vanilla stationery given to him by Chauncy lying on the counter. He wasted no time conveying the research he had done after Chauncy gave him the items.

"This paper was made twelve years ago by a small company called Mayfair Paper Products out of Baton Rouge. I remember it because I carried their line at the time."

"Did they stop making it, Bob?"

"Mr. Meyer, they got washed out of business here a few years ago; big fellows sucked em' all up."

"Can you tell us anything else?" asked Nadine.

"Sure. Mr. Meyer told me to call after I looked into it. Mayfair was merged into a division of Weyerhaeuser. The ex-owner of Mayfair, Todd Brooks, works over there now. I called and talked to him. He recalled the product and remembered they ran the production in a host of very unusual colors, this one probably the only shade that was fairly common. It didn't go over well, so they discontinued it. What he told me was that the runs were very small, demand was low, and there was no second production."

"Mr. Houston, what about the irregularity on the bottom?" Nadine queried.

"Oh, yeah, I forgot. Todd remembers that they had a problem with the cutter on the last run, which was this vanilla color. Most of the end of the run was damaged and they wholesaled it out. Kind of like finding a mint error on a coin, but the coin is worth a fortune. Sorry, but the paper has no value other than to write a note."

"Could any other companies have made it or still be making it?"

"If you wanted to place a special order you may find somebody willing to produce a small lot, but it would be price prohibitive. Besides, you could never get it to be a perfect match, if that's what you're aiming at. You'd have to know the paper industry, but I can tell you that these pieces you gave me are aged fairly well: they're several years old for sure. So how can you duplicate them?"

Nadine reached into her purse and took out the creased piece she found in Larry's closet. She placed it next to the other samples.

"What about this piece? Could you tell if it had any association with the others you were given?"

Bob glanced blankly at Nadine. He walked away to what appeared to be a storage area behind the service counter. He pulled out several drawers before finding what he was looking for. He returned with a ream of bright orange stationery, not dissimilar to her vanilla paper.

"Miss Street, when Mr. Meyer brought me these I knew immediately where they came from. Like I said, I sold this line. But if we want a scientific look at this..."

He reached for a magnifying glass from a drawer under the counter. One by one he held up the original pieces he was given by Chauncy. Then he displayed them to both Nadine and Chauncy.

"That's a water mark. Every company has their own, like a trademark, and it shows on every piece of stock so their product is distinguishable from the competitors' line. Now we know for sure these samples all came from Mayfair, and since the production was so small and brief they had to be from the same production run."

"Obviously there's no way to tell if they came from the same box," Nadine mentioned off-handedly.

"I think that's impossible. Now let's look at this other one you just put down."

He held it up and the mark was the same. "It's definitely Mayfair too. Since it's got the same defect in the bottom cut, no doubt it's from one of only a small number of boxes."

"Mr. Houston, I'm the one who asked Chauncy to talk to you. I want to thank you personally for your time. You've been very kind."

"I just hope it will help you in your investigation."

"Believe me, it has already," Nadine assured him.

Nadine walked out, followed by Chauncy, who trailed her all the way to her car before speaking.

"You want to tell me what this is about?"

"Not this part yet."

Chauncy laughed at her evasiveness. He was also concerned. "Okay, but just answer one question. You're getting messages from this killer, aren't you?"

Nadine acceded through a facial acknowledgement.

"Home or office?"

"Home."

"Do you know how he knows where you live?"

"I think so. You didn't look at the notes, did you?"

"You asked me not to."

She didn't want to unduly alarm him, yet at the same time she planned to inform him that morning about the recordings she was making.

"Chauncy, you're the only one who'll know this. I'm making tapes documenting every detail of what's happened to date, and what I'm doing from now on. I'm keeping the tapes in my nightstand drawer."

"There's a lot more you're not telling me." Chauncy recognized this atypical procedure as an obvious indicator of trouble.

"If this pans out like I think it might, it's better this way."

Chauncy had learned not to challenge her tenacity. Yet at the same time, blindly riding shotgun didn't rest well with him. "You be careful," he said grimly. "You need anything, I want to know immediately. I need your word on that."

"I promise. Don't worry."

"I promise too—I'm going to worry on this one. Oh, you still want me to copy the discs in Larry's office, don't you?"

"That's what I was going to go over with you. I figured out when you can do it."

She explained to Chauncy that the office would be safe that evening because Larry had a dinner meeting. A friend he went to medical school with was in town for one night only.

Early in the evening, Nadine went home and recorded the pertinent matters of the day. She was leaning back in bed against a large pillow. After completing most of her material she found herself suspended in a physical pose. The recorder was between her palms, her hands were facing upward with her elbows out and her head was tilted slightly to the ceiling. She looked as if she were praying. Her final words for the evening were recorded into the machine: "I can't think of a happy ending."

She let one hand drop to her side while the other held the recorder close to her mouth. She rolled over to her side, ignoring a single tear journeying down the left cheek. She had no conscious memory of getting up to turn off the overhead light or flipping off the nightlight on her stand.

59

LIGHTS OUT

WHILE NADINE SLEPT, CHAUNCY worked; long into the night.

It was a good thing Larry's dinner meeting lasted until late in the evening and he had no reason to stop by the office. Chauncy found the recording system and stored discs with no problem. Unfortunately, his compression apparatus failed and rather than abort the operation entirely he decided to go back home and replace it with another that worked. He knew Nadine was eager to get her hands on what he was "borrowing," which contributed to the potentially risky decision to return that night.

He had dined earlier at Madame Wang's Chinese Restaurant not far from his house. Unlike Larry, who stashed his fortune cookie for later use, Chauncy opened his. The message enclosed was one of those optimistic deliverances promising gold from whatever he touched. He felt so secure after reading his fortune that he had no fear going back to Larry's office a second time—despite the fact that his luck has been running bad.

When Nadine received the call from Chauncy, it was later in the morning than she expected. His tardiness had produced a dab of worry, but he reported to her the good news that he has completed the task. She wasn't able to go by his place until much later in the afternoon. By the time she arrived, she was on a mission to get to work on the recordings so she kept the conversation brief. In fact, after knocking on the door, she refused his invitation to visit. They stood on his threshold.

"These are a piece of cake to use. Just be safe," he mentioned as he handed her the discs.

"I'll call you soon. Thanks, Chauncy. Really."

It was already almost seven when she arrived home. She planned to eat a light meal and begin on the recordings. She pulled into her parking spot and took the elevator to her floor. As she inserted the key into her front door her sentient power alerted her that something was amiss—but she had no time to process the impulse.

The door opened suddenly of its own volition. An arm lacerated the space in front of her face from left to right, striking her across the right parietal lobe just above the ear. The blow was blunt, but acute and authoritative. Nadine fell unconscious to the floor.

Had Horace been there to witness this assault, he would have seen an unrecognizable man with rubber-covered hands and shoes step over Nadine's limp body and disappear down the stairwell across from her front door. By chance, however, the woman who looked after Horace when Nadine couldn't was taking him for his evening constitutional. At the precise moment when Nadine was being attacked, the woman and Horace were climbing the alternate stairway on their way back to the woman's apartment.

Horace became atypically agitated, pulling furiously on his lead as the woman was being dragged upward. Nadine's neighbor literally lacked the strength to hold him back; his signature terrifying bark had transformed to a siren. Finally, the woman let loose of Horace's leash. He broke into a full rush upward, still bellowing an alarm as he passed her level and proceeded up to Nadine's.

By chance the door at the top of the stairs was ajar. Horace burst through like an attack animal. Down the hallway, he found his master lying unconscious on the ground. The woman rightly hit the panic button, rushing down to her unit to call an ambulance, leaving Horace guarding Nadine.

All the way to the hospital, she remained unconscious. Fortunately, after looking at her purse and seeing her badge the paramedics hauled everything on the ground with them, including a separate large sack with compact discs. They also noticed the "in case of emergency" name and number with Chauncy listed. From the ambulance, they called him. He arrived before she was put in a room. The necessary tests were performed and fortunately proved negative, despite Nadine's prolonged somnolent state.

When she did come to, she was being wheeled out of the ambulance. Then by the time she was placed in a room, the swelling had already reduced appreciably. Moments later, Chauncy was by her side.

"Where's Horace?" was her first comment.

"Your neighbor said she and Horace were out for a walk and he went crazy when they got to the building. She told me she's never seen a dog as ferocious as he became. He might have saved your life."

Nadine's eyes welled up as she thought of the dog's devotion and of the danger she faced. "Where's my purse?" she blurted out frantically.

"I have it right here," Chauncy said as he held up the handbag. "And no need to worry about Horace. Your neighbor said she was pleased to keep him."

"The bag with the discs, did he get them?"

Chauncy pulled the tapes from the bag where he had originally placed them and held them up to assure her nothing was missing. "The person who did this clearly had no idea what these discs are. He never touched your purse or the inside of your house. This was not a robbery, Nadine."

"He didn't kill me. He doesn't want to."

"I'm not so sure. Your neighbor was fairly convinced by the way Horace behaved, especially his loud barking, that your life was in danger," Chauncy warned her.

A doctor accompanied by a nurse came into the room and asked

Chauncy to step out. Only a short time passed before they exited and Chauncy went back in.

"What did the doctor say?"

"They'll do a couple tests later tonight and then if I'm feeling better, send me home tomorrow."

"Nadine, I arranged for officers to be stationed at your place round-the-clock for a while."

"It's probably a good idea."

The nurse re-entered. "Sir, Ms. Street really needs to rest. You know she's had a concussion."

"I'll leave right now, nurse."

"Let me keep the discs here."

"What, you're going to start working already?" Chauncy said with comical astonishment.

"No, but I want them with me when I leave tomorrow."

"I'll bring them in the morning. One other thing, Larry called," Chauncy mentioned.

"How did he know?"

"He didn't. He said he had been trying to reach you but you wouldn't return his calls. He said he felt like an adolescent calling me to intercede on his behalf, but he didn't know what to do. He sounded pretty upset, and more so when I told him what happened."

"You didn't tell him where I was?"

"Nadine, if by some outside chance he's involved with the treatment of a killer that doesn't mean you have to boot him out of your life. This man has treated known killers for years."

"It's more than that."

"Look, I'm sorry if I got myself mixed up in the middle of your relationship with him. I didn't think anything of telling him."

"It's fine. You did the right thing."

"Get some rest. I'll check on you later."

Chauncy moved to the side of her bed and brushed her cheek gently, kissing her on the forehead before leaving. At most five minutes passed before Larry, not looking his terrific self, his brow furrowed, rushed into the room.

"I came as soon as I heard."

"Look, the nurse said I have to rest…and I can't deal with you now."

"What are you talking about? One issue with Howard and even after that great weekend we had, you want to end it? I don't understand you."

"I think you know well what I'm talking about."

She had ventured far from her normal state of mind. If she were she would have never lost control and revealed the thought contained in her next comment.

"Did you do this to me? Did you have somebody do this to me? Did you know somebody was going to do this to me? Don't lie again. Just one time, tell me the truth."

"Nadine, you took a hard blow. Your head is messed up from it; you're not seeing things clearly." Larry appeared astonished by her accusations. "Get some rest, and by morning you'll feel better. We can work this out."

"I don't think so. You had something to do with this."

"I'm going to tell you this one thing, so listen to me. I'm the one who has been protecting you, in ways I hope you'll never know."

"You know what this is about, don't you? Do not lie to me," she gritted.

For the first time, implicit in his response was an admission he did know something. Nadine, even in her compromised state, never missed it. "Give me a little more time."

"I can't," she bitterly shot back at him.

The nurse walked into the room, surprised to see yet another visitor. She looked at Larry but spoke to Nadine. "Ms. Street, really, you must rest."

"I'm leaving, ma'am. Nadine, I'll call you tomorrow."

Not a word. Her stare was cold and detached.

Was Nadine going to be baptized again, her second submersion in a sea of innocence—could he prove himself to be blameless, guiltless and sinless? Poor Nadine. She said it: a fact is not a fact until it's proven that it can't be anything else.

60

PERFECT TIMING

THE GERALD CHAMPION REGIONAL Medical Center in Alamogordo, New Mexico is the closest fully staffed hospital to Mescalero. It's located on Scenic Drive North. On those few occasions I visited the medical facility, my upper lip would snarl wondering how they had the nerve to employ the word "scenic" to a road about as spectacular as a traffic-clogged freeway.

Then there was the facility itself. I hated the standard anemic rust, jaundiced yellow, lifeless cream and bilious green colors mixed distastefully on an architectural design equal to what they toss out freely in Cracker Jacks boxes. Physical presentation of colossal public buildings directly sheds light on a culture, and it was my opinion that this institution was giving my region of the state a black eye.

Still, there were no published statistics indicating they were killing people with their care. To the contrary, the reputation that the doctors and staff earned was stellar. Thankfully, there was no delay getting into Gerald Champion on the afternoon Nadine Street was admitted. I should know. I was with her.

I was damn lucky to be by her side, luckier still to "be" at all. It seems that the still undisclosed assassin dispatched to come-back-with-Street-on-a-slab had no conscience about causing potential collateral damage. If someone like myself were to be lost as part of a kill-Street operation, he or they seemed the type that would announce unapologetically: "It was nothing personal, sonny; it was simply business."

I was shook up. I'll admit it. I wasn't nearly as shook up as Nadine.

What happened was that when something caught her attention before we went to work at the picnic area, and she went running, gun in hand, she was sprinting toward her rental car. What she didn't calculate was that the mechanism that was being used to kill her—and myself as well—had already been set in place. It must have been her instinct that the person that had responsibility for the execution, hadn't yet be able to flee from the area.

Thus when she took chase after the man, past the car and into a wooded area beyond it, she had come up empty-handed, returning with a grimace on her face. I had no idea what she was seeking as she approached the car but I saw her aim the key and press. She was within twenty feet and what I saw next was a horrifying sight. The car exploded, lifting itself into the air like a rocket launch, blowing out fire and gas as vengeful as a menacing dragon. The carcass thundered angrily and the detonation thrust Nadine backward like a wisp of straw, landing her on her rump.

I ran to her and saw she was nearly unconscious. Her eyes were open. Visibly, she presented without sign of injury. But she didn't move or speak. She was expressionless. I called for emergency assistance. It was only ten minutes before the ambulance arrived. I accompanied her to the hospital.

Physically, she checked out unharmed. But she couldn't hear. She had been distressed when she first arrived at Kuruk; still troubled by the experience she had endured in D. C. Yet as I looked back, she never seemed frightened. This was the first time I knew her to be scared. As I would discover later, her fear was not for dying or that she was in a state of mortal danger. It was because she was alive and damaged. The thought that she could be living and deaf, lacking her independence, terrified her—she cried on and off for two days.

When I gathered up her possessions at the site of the explosion, I carefully put her weapon back in her purse and collected her cell phone. I noticed that the last call she received was from Farley. He had informed her that "somebody" was still there—I presumed in Mescalero.

I called Farley while I was still waiting for the ambulance. He immediately arranged for her to have guards posted outside her room around the clock. Thus, her hospital suite was like a fortress, the second that she was placed in it.

It really didn't matter to any of us. Nadine wrote me a note that she didn't want anyone coming to see her—she feared they might not be safe. That included me. I was to leave and she'd get in touch with me regarding the final acts of the play I had not finished crafting.

I routinely called the hospital. Through the staff, I learned of her condition and the anguish she had suffered for the first two days. Fortunately, by the third day her hearing was beginning to return. Gradually, over the next two days, it came back to near normal. It did mountains of good to elevate her spirits. With her full faculties available, she could fight. That was all that she cared about.

She checked out of the hospital, took a room somewhere she refused to disclose, and went into hiding. It was only Farley who she was keeping in touch with. Every flight out of D. C. and every flight coming into Albuquerque or El Paso airports had to be checked for passengers. It was Farley who was handling the job.

As far as my writing was concerned, she had a courier service sending material to me. Over the next few days, we communicated through an intermediary.

Preston refused to listen to my instructions to stay away. He arrived the evening of the incident but when he went to the hospital, the gorillas guarding her room refused to let him in. When they checked with Nadine, she sent him a note.

You have to give me a little more time. If all this comes out the way I want it to, you will be the man of my life. I believe that I'm ready for love. For now, you must go away. If something were to happen to you,

I couldn't live with myself.

Preston was confused. He did the unimaginable, he cried.

Before Israel, I had prided myself on not having shed tears since I had been a little boy. The experiences I endured caused me to set records in that area. I even became a certified expert in self-pity. Now, at the prick of a pin, I can weep like a faucet. Preston produced tears pitifully—he was a rank amateur, actually reminding me of Josea. I reasoned that, if by chance, Nadine survived and they were to be together as a couple, being with her would provide opportunity for him to improve his skills.

I received the first delivery of material the day she left the hospital. It was back to work for me. I couldn't wait to see how all this would end—I wanted it to end, period.

61

OVER A HUNDRED THOUSAND?

"Ms. STREET, REALLY, YOU must rest," urged Nurse Reid.

"You need to rest," moments later Nurse Carlson insisted.

That's what nurses are always telling the patients under their charge in the hospital, but…

"Good luck."

Who can rest in a hospital? Forget sleep, when the activity level, day and night, approaches the track at the Indy 500, "restful hospital" becomes an oxymoron. Blood pressure and temperature checks, medication administrations, meals, doctor consults, interns and residents prodding and peeking, visitors, respiratory therapy, lab tests, gurneys shuttling about to X-ray, MRI, EKG, CAT, ABC to XYZ tests, kids running down hallways, pick-up-the-spirits canine visits, fire alarms, Code Blue, Red, Orange, Yellow—in the more fashionable "medical centers" sometimes Mauve, Magenta, Salmon and Chiffon Codes—bed pans and telephone calls, for what?

You didn't think you needed a speech therapist for a hernia, upper GI for a fractured femur, infectious disease and endocrinology specialists for a tonsillectomy or codeine, Vicodin and Zoloft for acid reflux?

Checking out of the hospital after the assault, Nadine perused her bill—over fifty-five thousand dollars for an overnight stay? She nearly collapsed. Instead of doing so, she did the only sensible thing that came to mind…she raced home where the rent was a lot cheaper.

Nadine had nothing on her mind other than those discs. By late that morning, she was setting up her equipment on the dining room table to give herself ample space to work. She flung a ball across the room to Horace every few seconds. Each time he'd retrieve it, nudging her hand to remind her he was ready for more play.

That first day she didn't get far. She was admittedly too fatigued. She fell asleep early that night and felt slightly more refreshed and eager when she awoke. She decided to again try to tackle a very large project.

She selected the sessions of interest she needed to listen to, intermittently making both written notes on a pad and verbal ones into the recorder. She had already come to grips with the likelihood of every scenario imaginable regarding Larry and his role in these killings. She included the distinct chance that he was simply a bastardized version of his father, crafting an opposite, seemingly peaceful rather than violent persona, but a sociopath just the same.

Her first meaningful finding was made early that evening. She immediately recorded it. "Chauncy, I was right all along. He is treating the killer. My only relief is it's definitely not Larry or President Haley." There was a long pause on the tape before it continued. "You'll meet the killer in a moment."

Again silence while Nadine was preparing the disc player. "The following is a sequence during a session with President Haley and Larry, and then the killer has a session two days later. This goes back a ways, to before Arnold was killed. Chauncy, you have to imagine Larry in his treatment chair and the President either on the couch or in one of the chairs across from Larry. Notice how the tone is so matter-of-fact and casual."

"What's wrong?" asked Larry.

"I'm having a big problem," the president answered.

"About what?"

"Larry, it's about Arnold."

"I thought he was handling the fund-raising in Hollywood."

"He is, but it appears he's got his own agenda. He's been drumming up support from his entertainment buddies for Quinlin, to have him run as an independent in California and New York." The President was vexed. "That's going to draw me down in the primaries and overall make me look weak. Then he'll move to have me replaced on the ticket. In the end, they'll encourage me to decide not to run again due to whatever I'm told I should say is the reason. I can see what those scoundrels are up to."

"That's really bad," Larry commiserated.

"It's worse than that. Those are critical regions for me. This is very, very big. We've got to do something."

"My god…"

"Larry, I think we know someone who can help."

"I'll see what I can do."

Nadine turned off the recorder and walked into her den. On the TV screen was a picture, but the sound was muted. She saw a lion trainer with several animals in a cage. The man was prancing about proudly and confidently, his beasts under the dominion of a snapping whip that he hurled through the air to caution the deadly felines to behave. The way the tamer's role harmonized with that she perceived the president to be doing did not go unnoticed. She pressed the recorder to "on" again.

"The president is not asking Larry for help," Nadine said breathlessly. "He's master orchestrating a trio sonata with Larry as first violin. Listen to Larry treating—if we can call it that—the killer. Every sound in the office can be heard. When a patient sits, burps, or farts, when a chair moves, a phone rings or a pen drops on Larry's desk, you hear it. This time the killer walks in to begin the session, but never sits down. It seems like he's speaking as he enters, because his voice is definitely moving through the room."

"I can see it in your eyes. You need me for something, don't you?"

said the patient.

"Look, I don't want to be involved in this."

"Just spit it out; you can whisper it if you're too meek to say it like a man," the patient disdainfully spoke to Monroe.

"All I know is that Wesley Arnold—you remember him, don't you?"

"At the station last year?" the patient retorted sharply. "I remember. Something about security for that affair?"

"Right."

"Asshole-pompous-arrogant-greedy-phony-pretentious-superficial bastard if I recall," growled the patient.

"That's what his friends would say privately."

"Doc, I think this is going to be fun."

"Maybe for you," Monroe said with obvious disgust. "Anyway, he's been sermonizing to some of his important associates, lots of damaging ideas about our friend. I guess what's important is he controls a lot of what happens back in Movieland and has decided to work for another man to…be a replacement," Monroe explained in a business-like manner.

"I'll take care of it," the patient deviously assured him.

Nadine paused the CD and continued talking into the recorder. "Chauncy, everything for the next two days was as normal as you'd imagine any therapist's office. Then the killer arrived again for a session. It's very short. Listen."

"It's done. You place the order and, presto, I fill it." The patient blew his nose. He sounded as if he might be ill with a cold. "By the way, I'm not sure how much longer I want to come for therapy."

"That's something you have to decide. Personally, I think it would be fine for you to discontinue but I'm not sure there won't be more for you to do. You might want to wait a bit longer," Monroe mentioned as if he had no personal interest in the matter.

"Just said I'm thinking about it, doc. Or is it Mr. Big Shot, Dr.

Monroe?" the patient jeered. "You may not be getting rid of me that easily."

"I don't get rid of patients."

"I'm one you'd like to," the patient mocked in a bullying tone. "I know that. Too bad though, isn't it? I'm the only one you really can't dismiss. Besides, it's my job to do the getting rid of, isn't it?" The patient fell into open laughter.

"Chauncy, can you imagine any doctor allowing a patient to talk like that? He's got something over Larry," Nadine said with astonishment. "If this man is not in the mood to talk, he picks up and leaves. His sessions otherwise are quite diverse. There are times he takes up the full fifty minutes and seems motivated by his analysis. Other times, he's threatening and abusive to Larry."

While working on the tapes, the days seemed to roll one into the other. She hardly noticed that she rarely left her place or that the calls from Chauncy, Dustin and Larry were either ignored or responded to with short answers notifying them that she was still recovering. She did inform Chauncy that she was making progress but gave him no details. Every so often, one of the officers guarding her home knocked on the door to see if she was all right or needed anything. Generally, she invited them in for a soda before resuming her task.

One afternoon, just after she had spent a few minutes with one of the guards, she was leaping athletically, jumping on her couch like a trampoline. Horace couldn't hear it but he had no deficiency of sight. He joined in the festivities with her on the couch. When she calmed down, she picked up the recorder to document another chapter for Chauncy.

"I found the cycle," Nadine panted into the recorder. "The pattern repeats for each murder. Our dear president points the camera's lens at an enemy, so Larry can get a shot of him. Later, in the presence of the killer all Larry has to do is mention the name of the next intended victim within the context of "our friend"—which means Haley—and the killer executes the target.

"They really are executions," she added. "Seems President Haley has crafted a weapon to use for a chain of perfect crimes. He's the true killer but could never be held accountable. Now, that's good politics, I guess."

Nadine switched off the recorder and gave Horace a belly rub. "I'm almost home," she shared with her friend. "But I still have a few questions left to answer."

Questions indeed. Why does Larry have a hidden room full of costumes and supplies at his house? He's clearly not the killer, but he appears to be serving as a conduit between his friend and the murderer.

Nadine had been in sweats and t-shirt tops for days. But she had business now that was going to require her going back out into the world. She showered and put on makeup. Then she dressed as if she was going to a job interview. One more time she reached for the recorder, this time to make her final entry before leaving.

"Chauncy, I'm going out but you have to hear this last bit between Larry and the patient. This is a recent session. Something was happening in the dynamics between Larry and the patient, but I don't understand it."

"You used me. I'll end up dead over this." The patient's voice was flat of affect.

"Who used you?" Larry countered defensively. "You did exactly as you chose. I couldn't have stopped you if I'd tried."

"I'm thinking of shocking everybody and giving myself up, get in touch with the top police bigwig. I'll go to your lady, tell her everything," the patient threatened.

"Nobody will believe you. Besides, I didn't know you were bothered by this."

"I'm not bothered by what you think I'm bothered by. It's personal. I think I've been a sap. In the end, you guys will go on your merry way and I'll be worthless—I'll have nothing. You'll both have each other like old times."

The CD went silent for a long period, conveying an interruption in their communication. Then it went live again.

"From what I understand, there's not much more to do. One or two jobs, real soon, and that's it," Monroe said calmly.

"Oh, fuck it. I'm leaving, doc."

Nadine turned off the CD.

"This is all coming to a boil, Chauncy," she spoke into the inanimate object. "I've got to go and take care of something important. I might still be able to save a life or two."

Wishful thinking.

62

I QUIT

NADINE HAD BEEN AWAY from the house for the entire day. If she had possessed the power of precognition, she might have posted herself on the corner of "L" Street and 15th in Washington, D. C. at about two in the afternoon. She would have seen a tall, elderly man with a trimmed gray goatee strolling carefree down the block with the use of a cane. A short distance from the corner, he would have turned to go into a small diner.

Then if she had tailed him inside, she would have noticed him going directly to the rear of the establishment where on the wall between the men and women's room hung a pay phone, one of those rare artifacts left over from the period of Cro-Magnon man. To overhear the conversation, she might have positioned herself in the lady's room and cracked the door a tad. She would have been surprised to recognize the distinctive voice of President Haley.

"Annie, hi. It's me. Sorry you're not well to go out. Don't worry. I'll have my driver bring me later. We can talk about it then. (Short pause) Bye."

Then she would have watched him amble for about an hour before arriving at the White House.

Possessing the same blessed power of telesthesia, Nadine would have also known beforehand that the killer had another five o' clock session that day in Dr. Monroe's office. In one afternoon, she would have gathered enough knowledge to if not change the flow of the mighty Amazon, definitely change the destiny of one more poor soul who was about to die.

Inside the office of Dr. Monroe, the therapist was in his chair talking with the killer. To the side of the desk was a large sack. Monroe picked it up and placed it in the center of the tabletop.

"As always, I've included everything you'll need"

"No dresses or skirts I hope," jested the patient.

"No, not this time. You don't like being a woman once in a while?" Dr. Monroe mocked.

"Don't fuckin' joke with me about that." The patient let Monroe know he was on a dangerously short fuse. "That's for perverts like you. I've been accused of a lot of things, but not that."

"Take it easy," the doc exclaimed to calm him. "You'll be wearing pants."

"Why does he hate Solomon so much?" asked the patient.

"All I know is, I'm to give this to you."

In a few seconds, Dr. Monroe would be sitting by himself again.

During the actual time the session was being conducted, and Monroe was outfitting the killer, unfortunately, Nadine did not receive a psychic S.O.S. She was in her office miles away, working on a plan.

"I decided I was going to make an unscheduled visit to Larry's office after his sessions were over. I had already informed the officers at my house that I was leaving that morning and wouldn't be back until early evening. I insisted that I leave alone.

"My last stop before Larry's office was a bookstore at the corner of Church Street and 14th. I was passing time, reading the paper and having a tea. When I left, I noticed that I was moving at a rapid pace. I wasn't in a hurry; it had to be nervous energy. I waited purposefully until a half hour before Larry's class that evening to enter the office, assuming he'd grab a bite to eat and go directly to teach.

"When I exited the store, I turned right and walked along Church to the first corner. Then I proceeded up 15th Street until I reached a small three-story building. I took the elevator to the third floor and proceeded down the hall to Suite 302. The name on the door read: Lawrence A. Monroe, M.D. Psychiatry.

"I was able to unlock the door without any sign of damage. I entered through the waiting room and locked the door behind me—thank god I did—and then I went directly into the treatment room. I wasn't in a hurry, but I never liked to dawdle when I was where I wasn't supposed to be.

"Still, I needed to feel the space. For what, I had no idea. Perhaps it was to see if I could smell the aroma or sense the presence of the killer I now knew by voice only. I sat on the couch and surveyed the room as if I'd never seen it, taking a few added seconds to put myself in the mindset of the murderer.

"Then all of a sudden I was startled by a sound. Somebody was fiddling with the latch on the treatment room door. I froze in terror. The room received some light from the street. Fortunately, I hadn't switched on the interior lights. When I scanned the area, I noticed a large cabinet off to the corner of the room.

"I calculated that I'd be able to cram myself in between the cabinet and wall and not be seen, but at the same time not have a view inside the office. I had no choice. I made a quick leap and prayed, my hand in my purse gripping my gun…just in case.

"A few seconds passed before the door lock was opened by whoever was there. I steadied my breathing, concentrating on silencing the alternating inhalations and exhalations, a trick I'd learned in meditation. So while I'm as silent as mist, I can hear clearly what's happening in the office.

"Then I see a dim artificial illumination from a flashlight. From my position, I could only look out across the office. But I noticed the lighting instrument the person was holding gave off a wide glow. Now the glass covering of a picture offered me a reflective image of a left shoulder, arm and hand. I could see it was holding a piece of paper—in the left hand.

"I could hardly make out what was happening. I dared not try to look out from my hiding place. In the mirrored glass, I saw the hand releasing the sheet of paper on to the top of the desk. Then the image disappeared. The event ended with me hearing footsteps, followed by the door opening and then closing.

"I waited in the dark silence for a few minutes. The last thing in the world I wanted to do was to be caught. Explaining what I was doing breaking into Larry's office was not my concern. I feared I could be forced into a deadly confrontation right there.

"When I finally perceived it safe to come out of hiding, I came into what was now the same empty space I entered moments earlier. I went to the door that had been opened and checked to be sure it was locked. Then I double-checked the alternative door I used to enter; all was secure.

"Chauncy had given me detailed instructions on how to copy the most recent discs. He wanted to do it, but I insisted that I could handle it since it was only a relatively small volume of sessions that had accumulated after Chauncy made his initial visit to Larry's office.

"Getting everything I wanted for the last three days of sessions went smooth and fast. In no time, I was able to place all the items I had touched back so that no signs of disturbance would be visible to Larry. I closed the closet and then realized that in my anxiousness about nearly being caught, I had forgotten to look at the piece of paper I saw the intruder drop on the desk.

"I stopped on my way out to look at the perfectly ordered desktop. A single sheet of paper had been randomly tossed on it. I leaned over and read the typed message."

TODAY WAS THE LAST TIME

Nadine describes herself quivering from fright. "I knew then that the action I had taken out of urgency, was probably for naught. The message was clear. I dreaded the phone call I was sure I'd be getting in a few hours, informing me of a person who could have been spared a brutal death had I been able to get to Larry's office a day earlier.

"I let myself out of his suite and used the stairwell to go down the two flights to the ground floor. When I arrived home, the guard gave me the 'all's fine' sign. I went in. I threw down my purse and mindlessly let my fingers sort through my mail. I noticed the red message light blinking on my answer machine and listened, expecting the worst."

Message one, three twenty-nine p.m. Hi, this is Stanford at Cleaning Hut. We finished the alterations on your pants, and you can pick them up; we'll be open until seven this evening. Message two, six fifty-one p.m.—

"A loud rapping on the door scared the crap out of me. I knew the guard was stationed outside, but just to be safe I grabbed my gun. I went to the door. As I looked through the peephole, I couldn't see anything. But in an instant the knocking resumed, louder and more intense. In the meantime, the message machine wouldn't shut up. Then on the machine, in the midst of the pandemonium, I heard a recognizable voice."

It's Dustin. Pick up! It's urgent.

"The problem was my hearing was confused because I was listening to Dustin's voice simultaneously inside on the answering machine and outside assaulting the door. I opened the door and he rushed in."

"For Christ's sake, what is it?" Nadine shouted as her partner barged into the house, out of breath from having leapt the stairs that he knew would be faster than the elevator. "I kept calling. Why didn't you answer your cell phone? Where's the guard?"

"He was just there. Maybe he took a break."

"Put on the news," Dustin blurted out.

He ran to the set and switched it on, using the clicker to go to Channel 4. Nadine pressed the stop button on the answer machine, now on Dustin's third message. The newscaster was speaking from a chaotic scene inside a building.

> *For those of you just viewing for the first time there's breaking news. Federal Reserve Chairman Annie Solomon was brutally murdered earlier today. She had served in the highest monetary position in the world for twelve years and was the first female to hold the job. Her recent policy decisions had brought praise from leaders around the world for her handling of a tenuous global economic environment.*

Nadine clicked mute. She felt badly as she stared at Dustin. She had excluded Dustin from the latter phase of the investigation only to learn that he had been an honest, loyal and devoted partner all along. Nadine went and stood in front of him. Then in an unprecedented display of caring, she hugged him.

"I really appreciate you. But right now I need a couple of more days to get myself right. Everything okay between you and Connie?"

"Uh...yeah, really good. What about you?"

"I promise, I'm well."

"This Solomon thing, should I get on it?" Dustin asked.

"You can handle it without me for now. A couple days and we'll be back in business together. I'll see you then."

With a reassuring look, she ushered him out. She needed to be alone, to suffer by herself the burden of a murder she could not rationally have prevented but would blame herself for just the same.

The tape recorder and discs were in front of her at the dining table. Early the next morning she'd still be seated at the table, breaking only a couple times to pet Horace or get a snack.

"If I had gone one day earlier, I'd have been able to warn her," she admitted into the recorder. She paused to gain control of her voice and then recorded another message. "Chauncy, Larry is not a cross-dresser. He makes disguises for the killer. It appears Larry's so devoted to Haley that he's willing to help him kill—up to a point. I can't believe he'd let himself be an accomplice to murder, but if you see him and Haley together you get the feeling their bond is very unusual.

"Here's a man with strong ethical and moral principles in his practice that he professes he'd die for rather than violate, yet he's willing to participate in murder. He rankles his friend, Haley, by refusing to disclose privileged information about patients, yet he colludes with Haley to exploit a patient's psychotic impulses."

She stopped for a moment and then continued to free-associate philosophic chatter into the recorder.

"The greatest figures in human evolution are made of contradictions. Human history can be better understood by its dissimilarities rather than its consistencies. It's the exceptions to our mores, rules and laws we witness in people that thrill, defy, intrigue, fascinate, revile, disillusion, excite and despair us," she postulated enthusiastically.

"What would any man be without that exception, his unique exception? The human species would not survive on this planet if all people followed the same ordered and predictable path. Invention, creation and imagination are the tools upon which man has evolved to be king of the jungle. Those capabilities are born out of man's exceptions, not his uniformities.

"But what if a man is not allowed the privilege to in some way establish his exception? A dear man has been a pillar of respect, dedication and integrity for thirty years in his community, volunteered to help neighbors, never missed a day at work, paid his bills on time and never cheated on his wife. He lives void of deviations, prohibited from variations from his personal norm, forbidden from divergence from the norms he believes—probably rightly—others expect of him? He lives straight, perfectly and predictably...except...we find out he's killed fourteen teenage girls and buried their bodies in the marshes near where he lives.

"The average person might accomplish a piece of their identity by driving an old Volkswagen, shaving their scalp bald and riding a motorcycle, putting a tattoo on their breast, hiding a package of cookies in a box in their closet or changing the price tag on an item in a retail store. That's a rich being, a person who can afford a benign exception.

"Poor men can't say 'fuck off' when insulted, can't tell their wife they hate their job, can't tear a page out of a magazine at the doctor's office when they don't have paper and pencil to write down a number, can't tell a neighbor that their barking dog is bothering them, can't tell their children they're sad, can't miss church on Sunday to go to a football game, can't stick a piece of chewed gum under a theatre chair.

"But they can kill, because that is, thank god an exception, the only privilege they grant themselves in their demented world.

"Jesus, Chauncy, I lost myself. I'm not sure what Larry's exception is but I don't think it's going to be pretty," she lamented as she fell asleep on the couch in her living room.

She had only a few hours of rest before she woke. She dressed immediately and prepared to go out. She knew things would be over soon and insisted to the guard she'd be fine going down alone to her car. She had no business doing so. When she reached her car, she opened the door to the back seat to lean in and grab a book.

Then before opening the driver's side door, she glanced around. Her eyes followed an imaginary path on the concrete floor that led to the door where she had witnessed the killer twice before; his figure was standing there. The stare was familiar to her. Nadine didn't even reach to take out her gun. Instead, she recklessly dashed off in that direction where he was standing.

"Who the hell are you?" she shouted.

The figure stood motionless. As she approached her face read ghost. She was looking directly at Larry, relaxed and smiling.

"What are you doing here?" she railed accusatorily. Then without giving him opportunity to respond she defiantly repeated her words, all the more forcefully. "What are you doing here?"

"You never returned my calls. I needed to see you."

"I've been recovering."

"Please, just listen to me. Nothing is the way you might think it is."

"I sure as hell learned that from this relationship."

"From the beginning you've accused me, doubted me and mistrusted me," Larry said excitedly. "I never did anything to deserve it—I proved that to you each time. I've done nothing but be loyal to you and try to protect you. I don't understand why you want to destroy us."

Nadine's lips were quivering. Her head was quaking side to side like it was on a spring. She viewed Larry with mixed pity and contempt. No longer did she fear that he was dangerous to her. Through her secret listening to his office sessions she'd learned of the killer's resentment toward her and Larry's pleas for the killer to excuse her from the whole mess. She knew Larry had feared at times that the killer could perceive him as a threat, turning his deathblow toward Larry, no different than other victims.

She also determined that Larry was weak and deficient of character, sadly not the variety of man with whom she was looking to settle down. As far as she was concerned, it was over. It was Larry's inadequacy that prevented him from challenging Haley. It was Larry's inadequacy that put him in the position to be a conspirator in multiple murders.

If things could only stay the way they typically are at the beginning of a romance, she lamented, she would have married and had a family fifteen times over. However, real human encounters take time to play out. It's during the mating game that all these idiosyncratic patterns emerge and each party gets a wide-angle view of the person they're dancing with—and what life might be like in the long haul with he or she as a partner.

She couldn't blame Haley for Larry's shortcomings or the demise of their relationship. All she could do was be aware that life was about making choices. Larry would never choose her over Howard. She would never choose a man who would choose anyone or anything over her.

Oddly, the words she heard that ceased her musing were the ones she most wanted to hear, if only the circumstance justified them.

"Nadine, I love you." Larry's declaration was as much a plea. "Can't you see that?"

"You could never love anyone as long as your friend is in your life," she heartlessly responded.

Larry wiped away her comment. He had anticipated her being upset over Howard. Plus, even at this time he had no reason to believe the problem went any deeper than Nadine suffering an insult she needed to get over.

"You're wrong. I know how you feel but don't forget what we've shared."

"I won't forget. Some of it is what I'll look for in a real man."

"I'd do anything to put this behind us, to have you."

"Look, I have business to take care of. I have to go."

"All I ask is one thing. Then if you feel the same way, I'll leave you alone."

"What?"

"Meet me Wednesday night at six fifteen at Chester's, at the corner near my office. I know I've had a lot on my shoulders for a while but…just meet me and I'll tell you everything and then you can decide."

Nadine rotated away from him, still more tormented than she'd care to admit. As she walked away, her voice was nearly inaudible. "Sure, I'll be there."

Nadine doubted she'd make the meeting or that Larry would care to see her Wednesday evening if everything went as she suspected. Her intention was to have a meeting with a killer instead. It was time to end the murders, stop the terror.

She knew it was improbable she could go after Haley. She also understood that most likely Larry would go free, too. Her goal was to remove any one point along the triangle. Once she shorted the circuit, the power would fail and the lights would extinguish. Whomever it may be that Haley was employing in his service could never be replicated—the killing was about to end.

63

SETTING UP FOR THE LAST SCENE

THE FINAL SET OF discs informed Nadine that Larry had agreed to see the killer for his last appointment that Wednesday. The way the dynamics had been twisting during the most recent sessions, along with the note left on Larry's desk that the killer was quitting, suggested to Nadine not only that this might be the last session but that it could be dramatic. The animosity on the part of the killer had heightened to an unprecedented level during the last couple of meetings. Larry seemed to vacillating between fear, antagonism and prayer.

On Tuesday when she awakened, she glanced at the clock. The time had come for her to call on Chauncy.

"I hope I'm not disturbing you."

"Nadine, you're never disturbing me."

"Are you free later this evening and tomorrow afternoon?"

"Unless one of my new girlfriends call me," he jested.

"I wouldn't want to interfere with that but in case you are available, Larry's office has to be bugged. Can it be done?"

"I looked over the building when I was visiting for you the other evening. Handling his treatment room is a piece of cake," he assured her. "Also, it's perfect. There's a tiny attic area; in fact, it sits just above Larry's office. It's cramped, but for a few hours it'll do. I'll get everything set up this evening."

"There's a bit more I'll need you to help with."

"Name it."

"Can you be at the building—around the lobby area—by three thirty tomorrow afternoon?"

"You want me to call you when I get there, right?"

"You read my mind."

"Nadine, there's a door going into that attic. It says *Maintenance*. You can pick the lock easier than your nose."

"I'll talk with you tomorrow, Chauncy."

Nadine slept soundly Tuesday night. She woke with a euphoric feeling. After her morning grooming and a round of calisthenics, she tidied up a sadly neglected house. She put in a load of clothes, filled the dishwasher and assigned floor cleaning duty to the broom and mop. She had nothing planned until that afternoon—hanging about taking care of her household chores and paying needed attention to Horace was the best use of the time.

Later that morning, she delighted as she deliberated what she should wear for her long-awaited get-together with the killer. *Let's see,* she joked to Nay, *he's seen me in my black jeans with caramel colored sweater and in my dark brown suit with chocolate boots. He's seen me in probably most all my outfits...but wait, I bought that tan camelhair sweater that I can wear with those new black linen slacks; black boots and I'm set.*

The humor helped calm the jitters that were beginning to grip her gut as the hours passed. There was a strong likelihood she could find herself in harm's way. The thought that the surprise killer could be Lambert gave her the quivers. It didn't matter. She had the means and knew her duty was to put the murderer out of commission, at whatever cost.

Just before leaving the house at two fifteen, Nadine cleaned and loaded her weapon. Performing a task she had done hundreds of times, she suddenly realized that in all her years of work in law enforcement, fencing with some of the most violent and insane criminals, she'd never had to fire her weapon in action—the only time she used it was when she went to the range for target practice.

She timed her arrival at the building to avoid the possibility of running into Larry. At twenty after three, she went directly to the maintenance room. Chauncy was correct: the attic was located directly above Larry's office. Nadine realized as she crept in that she could come down the nearby staircase in a matter of seconds into Larry's office to make the arrest.

Inside the attic room, Chauncy had thoughtfully left for her a small folding chair and a tiny desk with a set of headphones and a receiver resting on it. When she switched on the machine the audio came in perfectly. She might as well have been sitting next to Larry in his office.

Her phone vibrated at precisely three-thirty. She picked it up. It was Chauncy. Old habits don't die. He always preached that tardiness was the sign of a poor work ethic.

"I'm off the foyer, just out of sight down the hall."

"Great," Nadine whispered. "Can you mull around and alert me if anyone is coming up?"

"I'll call you."

Nadine waited, poised for action. At three fifty-five, her cell vibrated again.

"A blond woman about fifty, very attractive and dressed in a black coat, purple skirt and black leather boots just went up," Chauncy reported.

"Do you know who it is?" asked Nadine.

"No, but I'd like to."

"She's not for you. It's Chief Lambert's wife. I assume you never met Becky."

"No. How did you know she was coming?"

"I don't have to tell you all my nasty tricks, do I?"

"I had a few of my own, too."

"But you never told me all of them, did you?" she said playfully.

"I wanted you to do it right," Chauncy chuckled. "You know how idealistic us parent types can be."

"Don't worry. I followed most of what you taught me."

"I'm sure, but that only helped you solve half of your cases. It was the part that was left over after most that solved the other half. We can never do it someone else's way and be great."

"We'll see how I come out on this one."

"I'm with you, Nadine; you'll be fine."

"Thanks."

"So what's with Lambert's wife?" Chauncy asked to cure his curiosity. "You must have listened to her sessions."

"Just a few."

"Don't be coy with me. An affair? I wouldn't blame anyone married to Lambert for having a backup."

"Actually you're wrong. It's mostly about his sexual preferences," Nadine giggled. "After hearing her talk, I have a whole new outlook on my boss."

"Then you don't think he could be the killer?"

"No, I'm not sure if or how he might be connected. I'm going to tell you everything when this is over. But for now I'm not dismissing him being in of a partnership of sorts. But let me tell you about the therapy."

It was a good topic. It offered the perfect tonic for Nadine to laugh off her nerves. Becky's problem may not have been all that uncommon, but it was not something Nadine had encountered in her romantic escapades. In a movie or at a comedy club, that would have been her only familiarity with the kinky side of sex for Nadine.

"She doesn't get revved up over what turns him on. He likes to be tied up and hit with a belt or strap. If he's in a more imaginative mood, some extra humiliation...outfits, wigs. Look, he's got all sorts of fantasies…the guy is not what he looks like on the surface."

Chauncy saved her by interrupting. Nadine was so hysterical she couldn't have continued if she wanted, near wetting her pants.

"Stop!" Chauncy yelled out. "You're ruining my image of the man."

She tried to respond but the words wouldn't come out.

"Nadine, I wish to god you could play the session over the loud speaker at the office. The tyrannical bully begging for mercy at the hands of his wife. I like those boots—she could be good."

"Her problem is moral; she says she doesn't think it is right."

"Her hang-ups were likely the curse for lots of innocent people. If she'd have let him have it his way, he might have calmed down to where he was only a normal mean son-of-a-bitch instead of maybe a killer-mean son-of-a-bitch."

"You might be right, Chauncy, but up until today he's not getting it."

"Well, maybe Dr. Monroe will perform magic this time."

"Doesn't sound like it's going to happen. The worst problem is that Lambert knows, of course, that Becky comes to Larry. But from what she tells Larry, she denies to Lambert she's told Larry anything about his fantasies. Lambert doesn't believe her. Can you imagine the underlying tensions between Lambert and Larry, especially when you consider the relationship between Larry and Haley?

"Lambert has to face Haley all the time. If he even suspects Haley was laughing his head off imaging Becky taking her belt off and using it on him, you can figure out for yourself where that goes."

"Won't it be charming if he ever finds out you know?" Chauncy said wryly.

"God help me."

"You'll need more than God on your side."

"Actually, it might be charming. I could give him a studded belt on his birthday. That might earn me a real hug. Hell, he might even ask me to use it, which, of course, as much as I hate him I'd refuse, just to get even."

The clowning between the two wasn't a bad comedy club routine. The spell of humor was broken by sounds coming from Larry's office.

"Okay, they're starting the session. I'll talk to you shortly."

Nadine had no visual of Larry, except in her mind's eye. It was better that she couldn't see him at that moment. He'd never looked worse, like a puppy in need of petting. His hair was curiously out of place, he had passed on his daily shave, and the coordination of his dress, a cornerstone of the status of Lawrence Monroe M. D., was in disarray. One might have concluded that Howard had dumped him, which was not the case.

The real cause was that Larry's influence over the killer patient had gone into terminal eruption—the man may need electroshock therapy, a lobotomy if that didn't work, or a bullet through his head as a last resort. Larry was not equipped to administer any of these.

When Becky Lambert arrived on this particular day, she was feeling especially hyper. Dr. Monroe, a medical professional likely involved in murder, was a stingy fellow when it came to prescribing psychotropic drugs. He had warned her about the downside of Diazepam. Still, she had a three-year habit of using the anti-anxiety medication that she secured from her generalist.

The night before her session with Dr. Monroe, she had drank a bit too much and forgot to take her little yellow helper. She was up most of the night. Then she shoveled in too many bigger white ones and nearly couldn't get out of bed to make her appointment…at four in the afternoon. She was jittery and self-consumed, hardly attentive to the compromised state of her therapist.

"Becky, come in. How are you?" he greeted her unenthusiastically.

"Terrible night. I'm miserable today," she answered without looking up, speaking in a presto-paced, plucking manner, "and Harry… he's been unbearable, simply an animal. Something is going on with him. It's not just the normal sex stuff. Now he won't stop pestering me every second. I swear he acts like a condemned man wanting his last meal. Thank god he takes some of my sessions and talks with you. If he didn't, I swear…he might be worse. Too bad he's too embarrassed to admit it helps him."

"Becky, can I ask a favor of you?"

Becky looked up at him for the first time.

"My Lord, doctor, you don't look well if you don't mind me saying."

"Something urgent has come up. I wonder if you would mind if I cancelled the rest of the session and made it up to you another time."

"I won't pry, but I hope you'll be okay. I'm not doing too well myself, but I'll make it until our next session."

"Thanks for being so understanding."

His body was limp, like melting ice cream about to drop off a stick, as he dolefully proceeded to open the door for her to exit.

"Doctor, you take care of yourself."

Nadine's mouth was hanging open. It was one thing for Becky Lambert to be a patient of Larry's; it was another for Lambert to take sessions himself. While she knew in her heart after listening to Haley discuss Lambert that Larry had lied to her about him, this was firm confirmation of deceit as far back as the beginning of their relationship.

All along she suspected the triad of Lambert, Haley and Monroe, the three mountain climbing chums all committed to the common cause of keeping Haley in his presidency. They all had an interest, Haley for his ego, Lambert for his greed, and Larry for his blind devotion. She picked up her cell.

"Chauncy, anything doing?"

"Nothing."

"Larry lied again to me. He told me he detested Lambert, but the truth is Lambert has at times been his patient. We never picked up on it in the book because the appointments were all in Becky's name.

I only listened to a few of her sessions; I felt funny since she couldn't have been the killer—and the nature of the sexual material..."

"So you did it just a little out of good monkey curiosity."

"That's a nice way to put it. But if I'd listened to them all and been more careful, I would have recognized Lambert coming for sessions."

"I'm sorry about all this, hon."

"Chauncy, just stay where you are. Something is wrong with Larry. He ended Becky's session early. I want to listen to what's going on in the office."

"Nadine, you know Lambert's been my first choice all along."

"Remember, we don't go hurrah or hurray."

"Okay smarty pants, I'll be here."

"Chauncy, if by some chance Lambert is the killer, he'd have to have been disguising his voice when he was with Larry"

It was now twenty-five after four. For the last fifteen minutes Nadine had been listening to prolonged silence inside Larry's office. Finally, it was lacerated by a clicking sound, alerting Nadine to get back to duty. Larry must have lifted his phone. At precisely twenty-six after the hour, Larry's voice was heard.

"Is Chief Lambert in?"

Larry was using his speakerphone; Nadine could hear both sides of the conversation.

"He's not available right now."

"Just tell him it's urgent, please!" His rising voice revealed his frustration.

There was a silence of several seconds before Lambert's voice was heard.

"I told you not to ever call me at the office."

"I have to...tell you something important," Larry, said, his voice stammering.

"I'll come by when I get the chance."

The abrupt hang-up terminated what would scarcely qualify as a conversation. Again there was silence. The last session of the day would not be for some time now. Nadine contemplated a lengthy duration of empty time. Mounting feelings of dread, curiosity and excitement suffused the small room.

Under such conditions, mind-time is characterized by a crawling tedium. Every second drags through a needle head as if guided by the unsteady fingers of an old lady seamstress. The minute hand hangs for what seems like an eternity working its way to a straight down direction; the only consolation is that it will now pass the "after the hour" reading and head home on the "before the hour" path—the last session will begin at five, now less than half an hour in the future.

Nadine checked her pistol before placing it on the desk. She ran through the possible outcomes again and again, unable to quell the chatter of her mind.

She leaned back. Then effortlessly, she was whirled off for a magic carpet ride, launched for no known reason other than her being there, in the here-and-now—all consciousness turned to pure *thought*. Now, a budding philosopher, she zeroed in on our most precious resource, time.

The seminal thought she sprouted was a question. What might life be like for most people, and for the whole of mankind, if each individual were to treat every kernel of time as if they were jewels containing opportunities to learn and understand? Further, what if, based on the knowledge they attained from those exercises in thought, they made informed decisions about their life instead of sitting back and letting an army of professional advisors or advertisers define life for them?

After posing this inquiry, she was struck by the first stroke of awareness. It is an epidemic. The blind are leading the blind, and even the seeing-eye dogs have lost their mind for reason. Time, the kind of time she was enduring, had ceased to be an opportunity for free association and exploration, a philosophical experience setting in place the wood, concrete and steel that would be used to construct a world view, a working belief system to find if not peace and comfort, at least confidence and resolution in a usually confounding world.

WOW, she said to herself as she forged bravely, deeper, into circumspection. *If we took all the thoughts, their energy, force and weight, from every person who was willing to allow an awareness of how important these mind specs are, and we bundled them like pools of monetary instruments what might become of the world we know?*

Would all men embrace their innate love for humanity? At last would the world be free of oppression, hatred, discrimination, slaughter, war and genocide? Or, would the depth of perception acquired from the victory over ignorance and blindness empower men with an irrational exuberance whereby proposals, plans and projects of unattainable magnificence would implode upon him with a meteoric force leaving life in irreparable chaos and destruction?

Then, her mind's gymnastics produced more insight: Awareness comes with a price, and it's a big one: Blind hope must be surrendered. Attachment to false deities must be terminated. Living in a world of egocentric illusion must be ceased.

The plight of most all of mankind, those who have lived in the brightly illuminated realm of hoping and wishing at the expense of truth, has always been powerlessness, victimization, insecurity and insignificance. A small minority of the strongest, most intelligent and richest of possession have reigned supreme and inflicted their will on the less fortunate majority solely because they were able to separate reality from longing. These few in power know that the downtrodden will never stop to think their way to attain knowledge, will never sacrifice their hopes—history demonstrates they never have. It's this understanding of the plight of the masses that affords the rich a liberal, duplicitous pulpit from which to preach the needs of the less fortunate.

That's why the average human doesn't think, why they are so easily educated to not think. They are the first to know—the first to admit—it's a futile endeavor: not every person is going to have riches and au-

thority and equity.

Only the intelligentsia and the artists are foolhardy and naively idealistic enough to believe the pyramid of those few at the top who have, and the masses at the bottom with nothing, can be altered in the world we call reality to a near infinite flat rectangle. And for their childish views, how is this group of visionaries rewarded? In the end, they are free to smash their heads into walls of concrete, attempting to change the flow of an immutable human destiny—they're certain to wind up getting bad headaches.

Surrendering. Relinquishing thought. The pattern is etched into the cellular structure of modern "civilized" mankind with only a fraction of the species custodial to the mutant gene permitting them to test their mind close to its capacity. Yet it is upon the backs of those few, that the destiny of humanity rides—it's back to exceptions.

This enlightening philosophical commentary on the history of mankind wasn't where Nadine wanted to end her internal dialogue, especially after beginning with pockets stuffed with inspiration and excitement. But as she passed the waiting time, she began to feel rich. She also realized that it was likely her destiny to be one of the few who would battle to the last instant of life to retain thought.

If that were the case, that she was ordered by her unique makeup to contemplation and analysis then she owed it to herself to begin taking the necessary time to stretch and expand her mind, for no purpose other than discovery.

The few minutes of waiting while her brain had floated into unexplored regions had served to partially calm her. The hands of the clock that minutes before seemed to be pushing through tar had sped ahead; the angle had shrunk to a mere sixth of its previous size.

She looked up. It was five minutes to five.

64

THE SHOWDOWN

IN HER MENTAL ABSENCE while deliberating intellectually, an event of great significance took place. It was not inside Larry's office and not accessible to her awareness. President Haley left the White House and was strolling in the direction of Larry's building. He would have been seen turning a corner only seconds away from where Nadine was stationed, and then disappearing out of sight at five to five. At that precise moment, Nadine had picked up the phone to call Chauncy.

"Anybody there?"

"Not a soul. It's been extremely quiet."

"Right after I talked to you, Larry called Lambert at the office. It's been silent here since. Keep me posted, and…" Nadine halted mid-sentence. She heard a door open in Larry's office. Briskly it closed. "Wait. I have to go. You're sure nobody came up?"

"Absolutely."

"Call me if you see anyone," she instructed Chauncy.

It was five on the dot. The voice of the killer was heard. She listened to a sound she had heard on the recorded material but had no face to match with it; was it actually a foursome rather than team of three she was confronting? She had no idea who had reached the office without going past Chauncy.

"You decided not to turn yourself in, I see. You did the right thing," Larry commented.

"I'm not so sure you'll think so after today," the killer voiced angrily.

"Why is that?"

"Because I have some last minute business to take care of and then...I don't care what happens."

"You should. You can simply retire. All this will have never happened for you. It's not the type of thing that would ever eat away at you. But for me, it's different. I have to live with..." Larry's voice sounded mournful.

"That's your problem," the patient retorted bitterly. "Right now I'm setting things right. Betrayal can only be vindicated through punishment, and all punishment must be proportionate and appropriate."

"Punishment? For what; to whom?" Larry sounded infuriated.

"Oh, stop with this pitiful display of self-righteousness. Will it make you feel better if I forgive you?" His words were delivered with scorning disgust. "I don't give a crap about your moral hang ups about murder. Your punishment is for what the two of you did to me. You made me...you called me to duty...you urged me to kill. Now that you're done with me you think I can go back to...what? Nothing!" he bellowed. "You want me to go away so you don't have it on your conscience. You want me to simply disappear. Well, now I'm here and I don't want to go. You should have thought this through before. Now he'll pay, and so will you." The finishing touch to the killer's speech was fiendish.

"You stop this now. You're going too far. You don't call the shots."

"Too late, Mr. Great Success, Dr. Monroe. You're the one who has gone too far, you and that friend of yours. I should have known all along as soon as I wasn't needed you both would terminate me."

Larry had a back office line. Only those who know him well would use it, and only with discretion during working hours: its ring was perfectly timed to the last insulting comment made by the killer. Larry used the call as an opportunity to break the killer's rhythm.

"Please excuse me. I've got to answer this," he said with an insincere apology.

Larry picked up the line and listened. It seemed forever as Nadine waited for Monroe to speak his end of the conversation.

"Absolutely not! This is not a good time," Larry vehemently object-ed to whatever the caller was requesting. There was another pause. "I don't care if you're coming in only five minutes or five seconds, don't!" There was another silence before Larry spoke. "No, I have a patient here and he can't be put in the waiting room. Do you under-stand? This patient won't wait."

During this short interlude, the killer was pacing back and forth, his rage escalating with each turn. Then he directed himself to Larry, as if he'd all of a sudden become mindful of the nature of the call Lar-ry was dealing with. With an evil, tooth-brandishing, eye-tightening devilish smirk, he whispered, "It's him, I know it. Let him come."

Larry was in a pickle. The killer was tugging at him for atten-tion. At the same time, the caller persisted in his intent to visit. Lar-ry breathed in deep and then held the air in, hoping the inhalation would calm him while he tried to negotiate between the two forces.

"Please, it's just not a good time to come," he pled to the man on the phone.

Standing with the receiver to his ear, Larry's body appeared to melt; his elbows dropped to rest in supplication on the desktop. Leaning down he spoke to his God; it sounded like a bewildered weep. *He hung up. He hung up!* Still leaning in the same position, he twisted his torso toward the killer. "Please don't do anything. I vowed my life to protect him."

"You should have known better, sonny."

Nadine was listening from her perch atop the theatre of action. Her plan was to let the session play out and then make the arrest of the killer. She sat and waited but fragments of the conversation she was hearing confused her.

Who is coming, she wondered. Haley? Were the three conspirators coming together to have a little spat? Wouldn't that be the time to burst in, gun drawn, cuff all three of the boys and book them in one clean swoop?

She assumed Chauncy would be the first to know if it was Haley. She called him. "Anything going on down there?"

"Nobody at all. It's as dead as a morgue."

"Have you seen President Haley?"

"Sure, he stopped by to say hello to you but I forgot to call you."

"No, really. I know it sounds bizarre, but keep a close eye."

Chauncy glanced to his right and saw a black limousine with the windows down. There were several people inside. "I do see a limo, but the people inside are not presidential material. They look more like criminals." He couldn't refuse a dose of humor. "Well, maybe they are presidential material."

Just then Nadine heard Larry answer to the second ringing of the line inside his office. He responded frantically. "You're coming up now? You can't! It's not safe."

Again there was a moment of silence. The caller to Monroe had hung up.

"Chauncy, do you know where the rear entrance to the building is?"

"Of course. I told you I inspected the building. They keep it open during business hours."

"I'm staying on the line. Can you run around to the back and see if anyone is coming?"

"Run, no. But I'll waddle as fast as my old bones will move. I'm on my way."

In the background—while Chauncy was changing his post—Nadine was hearing commingled muted and hostile sounds both from the killer and Larry. Monroe spoke first.

"Wait, you don't want to do anything you'll regret," Monroe entreated. "We can all talk about this."

"There is nothing left to talk about. You wanted me to kill and I did. That's the only purpose you gave me. It's the only thing I can do to stay alive."

"You were always a killer; it came naturally. Nobody had to want you to do anything."

"Oh, you did. You do everything he wants, like a good little servant. The two of you have always been like Leopold and Loeb. Monsters separate and monsters together."

"Chauncy, you there?" Nadine called out.

"Yeah. All I see is an old bearded geezer with a cane. He just went through the door to the stairs."

"Did he look like Haley?"

"Definitely not. But do you want me to follow or detain him?"

"No."

"Nadine, I don't know why but I sense that you don't need me anymore."

"There is one more favor, Chauncy."

"Just one?"

"Please. Promise me you'll go directly to your car, *now*, and go home."

"Only if you promise me you'll be okay."

"I promise." The tension of the moment, her awareness she may not be okay, evoked sentimentality. "Chauncy, thanks for being there for me…always. I'll call you later tonight…I promise."

And there she was, in her birdcage by herself. It all came down to her alone against the world. She was the lame duck, underdog, possibly soon to be scapegoat or even prey. Where's Dustin? Why send away Chauncy? Why battle the president, her boss and her lover… alone?

Theoretically, it wasn't too late to go home, but practically for Nadine it could never happen that way. She created the end and she'd have it as she determined it to be, by herself.

At the instant Nadine hung up from Chauncy, two events occurred almost simultaneously. The first was her phone vibrated. When she saw it was Dustin she started to put it down, but then decided to take the call.

"Nadine, I'm at the office. That computer guru you were working with to figure out who broke into the Blank file and who took the sample was looking for you."

"What did he say?"

Dustin was silent. He nearly couldn't speak the words.

"Damn it, Dustin, spit it out," she ordered impatiently.

"It was Chauncy who took the evidence and deleted it in the system."

"You're sure, Dustin?" her voice muted.

"I'm sorry, Nadine," he said apologetically. "This is a fact proven a fact because it can't be anything else."

"Do nothing until you hear from me. Do you understand?" she shouted.

The second event was a loud knock on a door, coming from inside Larry's office.

"It's him, okay, I'm telling you," Larry disclosed. "Now we'll all work this out, right?" There was begging in his voice as he moved to open the door. But in an instant the scene drastically altered.

"Oh, no. Just put the gun away," Larry screeched to the killer.

Gun. Kill. Death. Murder. Trigger words that propelled Nadine into action. She flapped her mighty eagle wings and set flight out from the safety of her high nest. No need for thought now; she knew the shortest distance between her location and Larry's was through the floor she stood on, but the quickest was down the staircase. She leaped several steps at once.

When she reached one floor below she opened the door to the hallway and turned only a few feet to reach the entry to the waiting room of Larry's suite. Now she placed her weapon in hand and made a change in temporal perception, from standard to atomic clock—every second would be subdivided into tiny units and within these spaces of time she would think her way to the best course of action.

She approached the door, but first she placed her ear against it to test if she could hear inside. There it was, the voice she'd heard a hundred times over now, the voice of the killer.

He spoke in his classical cold, cruel, coarse tone. "So, finally we meet for the first and last time, face-to-face. My pleasure to kill you, sir."

GO!!!! Nadine heard two letters in her mind and they amalgamated into a single command. She burst into the office with her gun forming a perfect line extended from shoulder to arm to hand. As she entered she visually fixed on another weapon, pointing directly—from only a few feet—at the heart of an old man with a cane who just entered and was standing with a puzzled and disturbed look by the back door.

The owner of the weapon was looking deranged, foaming at the mouth, eyes crazed. He cocked with the index finger of the left hand with the intent to fire rounds from his pistol into the inert old fellow. He'd never get the chance. Nadine showed no hesitation as she discharged three accurate heart-guided shots in rapid succession. The killer, propelled by the impact, rotated slightly in her direction, eyed her hopelessly—with a wisp of apology, and she believed a sliver of familiarity—and keeled over dead.

Before the decorators could arrive and stream the place with miles designer yellow ribbon, a guided tour of the room would be helpful. The killer was on the floor with blood soaking his shirt, the disguised President Haley hadn't moved an inch, and Nadine was still holding her arm straight enough to unload the bullets remaining in the clip at the fallen man if necessary.

Slowly she glanced toward Haley. She made eye contact with the old man. Their silent stare was a portion of a lousy second. It was one of acquaintanceship from Nadine—antipathy, contempt and infuriation by Haley.

Abruptly, the President turned away and exited the door he entered. Not a word passed between them. Nadine rushed to the fallen, breathless body, crouching to her knees to tearfully embrace the man.

"I know you loved me, Larry."

He did. But big pieces of Lawrence Monroe, world famed psychiatrist, had been hijacked by his father and best friend.

Nadine had little time to dwell on psychodynamics. Her remorse was cut short by a rational drive. She walked over to the closet where Larry stored his recording equipment and the discs. She gathered up everything and carefully inspected the office. She didn't lock it, but exited. She used the elevator to go down to the ground floor and then left the building and walked the short distance to where she had parked her car. She opened the trunk and deposited the machine and discs and then locked it. She retraced her steps back into Larry's office. Now she picked up the phone on the desk previously belonging to Dr. Lawrence Monroe.

"Hi, Maggie. This is Detective Street. There's been a shooting. I'll need backup."

Nadine hung up. Tears were freely streaking down her cheeks.

Meanwhile, only a short distance away, an old man ambled meditatively along the north side of 16th Street, heading west, toward his home, a dwelling owned by his loyal subjects. He turned as he approached the security booth. He entered the grounds of the White House and went directly to his office. His desk was covered with documents. He sat pensively. He sighed, whispering under his breath.

"Damn the bitch. I will make her pay for this."

EPILOGUE, PART I

IT SHOULD BE APPARENT by now Nadine loves good food. One evening shortly after her shooting the father-in-Larry killer, she was dining with Chauncy at a small Italian trattoria. Most of her food sat untouched; she had lost her appetite. The bottle of Pinot in the middle of the table was three-fourths empty and there was no sign of liquid in either of their wine glasses.

"Nadine, I'm listening when you're ready to tell me the details."

"This is going to be really hard for me." Nadine's pain was evident as she paused several seconds before continuing. "You know how important you are to me. I have nobody closer in my life. But I have to do this."

"I have no idea what you're talking about."

"When you were helping me at Larry's office, you know, at the end…I have to know the truth, Chauncy. Did you know what was going to happen? Did you know about Larry and the others?"

"If I did, I never would have left you there alone."

"But when you went around to the back of the building and saw the old man you said, 'I guess you don't need me anymore,' didn't you?"

"Right. I know you. I could hear in your voice you were targeting on whatever it was you were after. I anticipated you didn't want me involved. That's all." Bemused he added. "What I don't understand is why you're questioning me in the first place."

"Because I know you're the one who took the hair sample on Arnold and deleted reference to it in his file."

Chauncy leaned back, a man condemned of a crime far more heinous than the one Nadine was charging. He noticed the glassy sheen in her eyes, not from alcohol but fright and sorrow. He shook his head back and forth in solemn resignation.

"I'm getting old. I don't know how you found out but it took everything I could think of to cover my tracks."

"Just before the investigation ended, I had Monica confront Lambert about what happened to the evidence. He brushed it off like dirty linen. So I brought in an outside computer technician. Look, Chauncy, it was just one keystroke you shouldn't have done but it was enough for him to figure it out."

"We all make mistakes, don't we?"

"What was yours?" she painfully posed to him.

"You want to know the whole story, I suppose."

"Might as well. I've lost everything else," Nadine despaired.

"Nadine, it's not what you think. The evidence I took had nothing to do with the investigation and would have done you no good. I know a lot of people here in Washington. They know what I've done in the past and what I'm capable of doing. It was Haley, probably upon referral by Lambert, who contacted me."

Chauncy let the point sink in before he continued. "Arnold had a long-term mistress. That lady is the mother of his youngest daughter. The only ones living who know this are Arnold's wife and the mistress. The true mother of the child, the mistress, won't say a word because she's well compensated for her silence. Arnold and his wife were very good friends of Haley's. After Arnold was murdered, his wife went to Haley because she knew the mistress had been there at Arnold's place. She feared that if any evidence were to come up implicating the mistress, an embarrassing and possibly damaging secret would come out.

"For Christ's sake, Nadine, she didn't want to crush her daughter of eighteen by finding out her mother was not really her mother. They told me the hair sample belonged to the mistress. Then Haley gave me some information to help with the task and I did it."

Chauncy stopped. His head dropped and he rubbed his eyes. He was straining to hold back tears.

"And," Nadine urged him to continue.

"Of course, I would have told them to shove it, but I had a problem. Some months before, I had made a large investment and it went sour, really rotten. I lost almost everything. Without harming anyone, I had the opportunity to get back even, and I took it. I'm sorry."

"Are you okay now? I mean financially, are you stable?"

"I'm fine. I never would have imagined you finding out. All I can do is ask for your mercy."

"I have one thing to say and then I hope we'll never mention it again. I can let this go if you can. You're too important to me. Don't we all do things we regret?"

"I don't know if we all do. My recommendation is don't grant yourself the right. Here I am at my age, learning the hardest lesson I think I've ever have."

"This is between us only, that's it. But what I want to say is the odds are strong that you were used this time. I believe Haley was lying. It may be true about Arnold's wife and mistress, but he would have never lifted a finger to help her once Arnold was dead. The chances are far greater that the hair sample would have revealed the killer." She stopped to reflect before going on. "To tell you the truth, Chauncy, you probably did me a favor. If the sample proved what I think it would have, I'd have been in a worse predicament."

Nadine stood to hug Chauncy. She sat back down and from her purse took several micro cassettes. She handed them across the table to Chauncy.

"It's all there. The killer seduced Larry to avail himself of Larry's genius mind. It was the killer who broke into the *Avenue Grill* and taped over the cameras during the night so he could meet Rita Tully there the next morning. We checked on her romantic involvements and Larry's name never showed up. Why did she keep her affair with him secret?" Nadine asked rhetorically. "I don't know. One person who did know about it was Dustin's father. But he had no reason to suspect Larry, so he never mentioned it until it was too late.

"You'll also find that Haley did a lot to cover for Larry. I know that because Larry never could have been at the White House the night Blank was killed. Yet Haley had it entered in the log as if he were there the whole time. He had to have told Larry if anyone ever questioned him about it to say he was there."

"When did you know about Larry...that he was the killer?"

"Larry wasn't a killer...and I didn't know his dead father had reincarnated himself inside Larry until...that last second."

"Damn crazy thing why the father came to life," Chauncy commented.

"No, it wasn't. There was one person who knew the seeds for the rebirth existed and if it was nurtured carefully would come alive."

Chauncy placed the tapes on the table next to him. "I can't wait to hear the whole story."

"It's about time you do. Sorry, I couldn't tell you everything while it was happening."

"I would have played it the same as you did."

"If I ever try to tell the true story, the luckiest thing would be that nobody believed me."

"Why?"

"Because if I'm not lucky, I mean if Haley takes offense, my life could be in worse danger than it was before."

"We don't want that."

"No. I think I'm better off keeping it here."

She pointed to her heart. A lone clear pearl from her right eye landed on the same spot. A moment later, both eyes are dewy. She was imploring Chauncy for an answer about what to do with the unimaginable, yet true, experience.

"Write it as a novel," he suggested. "At least then you can make a buck off it."

"I might. I'll need the money because I've decided I'm not going back to the department, at least for a while."

"Good for you."

"I think I figured something out. Ever since I was a kid and lost my parents, all I've been doing is proving myself. It hasn't been to any single person, but to everybody and anybody. I've had to demonstrate that I can face anything, no matter how gruesome, terrifying or horrible, and survive on my own...and that I don't need anybody.

"I've done it. I have nothing to prove and nobody to prove it to... and I'm tired. There's one thing I learned from Larry and that's that I can love. If it's not too late, I'd still like to start a family."

Chauncy picked up the bottle from the table. He poured the remaining wine in their glasses and downed a large gulp in honor of her wish.

"To love. To babies." he toasted.

EPILOGUE, PART II

AFTER I FINISHED THE final chapters, I wanted to call a psychiatrist and discuss how such a freak phenomenon of mankind could have occurred. What might I have accomplished? As Nadine had expressed, it was exceptions that defined individuals and the same applied to the whole of mankind. The entire spectrum of human conceivability had to be filled, with the tiniest space on the outer reaches of the Bell Curve serving to remind us we are creatures of infinite potential, we can use our exceptionalness for love or hate, and act it out it at the furthest points of imagination in the spectrum of human capability.

Larry might have earned a title—possibly a new diagnostic category—never held by another member of the human species. Deliberating that point zeroed me in on the fact that it placed Haley in an equally unique position. He was sanely crazy. I considered that to be the most dangerous state a person could own. Frightfully, he had attained a position of unimaginable strength and had no qualms using it to maintain a cruel advantage over both friend and foe.

Nadine knew he hated her but had no idea how much—nor that he had cause to fear her. The thought of her attempting to disclose what she knew—even in a fictitious account—haunted him; plus he hated her and wanted revenge. During the months after Larry's death, she was crushed. She had retreated to her home. He had no way of knowing that she was attempting on her own, though failing telling the story as fiction. Still, he had kept an eye on her and had never forgotten his vow to punish her—he was waiting patiently for the best time to strike.

When she came to Kuruk, his suspicions peaked. Why would she come to this remote location, and then stay? After his investigation uncovered her intent it must have been close in time to when the FBI was doing routine checks on Josea. He took advantage of that, leading to the fiascos with her and Reuben. But then he must have had second thoughts about outsiders—even within his trusted FBI—getting involved with his real target operation. So he ordered the project dropped by the FBI and took it back internally. That's when he handed it over to...

I froze when I reached this juncture in my thinking. It was a Monday morning. I was in my study looking over the last few pages. That's when I realized I would never see Nadine again. Haley would never allow her to live. She had gone too far and he employed somebody he knew he could squeeze to terminate her. It would be a bullet in the back of the head, a car bombing, or a fire in her hotel room with the doors and windows sealed shut.

Who was coming to kill her? Could Chauncy look her in the eye and shoot her?

With these theories unimaginably earning factual status in my mind, I never sent my final notes by courier back to Nadine. There was no use. The story was told. I knew it would be my call what to do after her death.

What would I do with it? I concluded Haley was not going to let a story be told that could infer to those on the inside that he had a role in murder. Reflecting on what was a true fact, that there were people who loved me who would die a thousand deaths if I sacrificed my life for a novel—a mere fiction written with the purpose of not being believed—I sadly decided I had written it for nothing; it would never be published.

Poor Nadine. Motherless child, I kept mumbling. *Poor Nadine.*

I sat that morning mindlessly entertaining myself with glum speculations while unbeknownst to me Nadine was fighting for her life. She had stuffed her just-cleaned weapon in her bag and hailed a cab to take her from the hotel she was staying at to the airport. The registration at the hotel had intentionally been placed under her real name. She had even gone out of her way to drop the information to a couple of associates she kept in touch with in D. C. to make it simple for the right people to find her.

She waited for United Flight 416 to arrive from Chicago at 2:15 in the afternoon. It was the second leg of a flight that left earlier from Washington D. C. Farley had attained the flight list and confirmed that the man she knew was coming to thirst on her blood was on it. It was assumed to be a short assignment because he had booked a return flight that evening.

Nadine knew he'd have no luggage. She had the cab driver pull up and wait for her. As the passengers were exiting from Flight 416 at the Albuquerque airport, she stood in the distance by a phone booth. She spotted him and watched as he went to the cab line. He was carrying an oversized briefcase. She ran back to her waiting cab, slipping her driver a twenty-dollar bill. "Do not lose that cab," pointing to the one the man entered. "A hundred more if you stay with him."

The driver was about to make his daily earnings in an hour and latched on to the other cab like a barnacle on a whale's belly. Nadine observed the route that the other vehicle was traveling; she could predict every turn on his way to the Hyatt Regency Hotel.

"Stop here." She instructed her driver to pull over a distance behind the other cab. She handed the driver the promised tip and got out.

Before she left the Hyatt Regency Hotel that morning—she had up until the evening before booked at another hotel—she called the front desk to inform them she was expecting a package. She instructed them to have it sent to her room. She further advised them that she would be out until five-thirty, so if it came before she returned they could hold it for her.

The man coming to murder her went first to the house phone in the lobby and made a call to the front desk. It was then that he found out his task would be handled uninterrupted since Nadine wasn't expected back for hours. He then placed a call to Room 817. There was no answer. He sat down and picked up a newspaper left by another guest. After ten minutes, during which time Nadine was monitoring his activities, he called the same room a second time, with still no answer.

Nadine watched from the lobby as the man stood. He went to the elevator area and waited. When the door opened, he entered alone. She noted that it stopped on the eighth floor. She took the next elevator to the seventh floor and exited. At the end of the hall was a stairwell, which she used to walk to the eighth floor. She saw nobody in the hallway. Slowly she proceeded until she was outside Room 817. She put her ear to the door, pausing to listen. Then she took her gun out of her purse and flipped off the safety.

She had a more severe punishment than death in mind for the man. Carefully, she slipped her key card into the latch and opened the handle, her weapon drawn and ready to discharge if necessary. She had taken a suite and the living area was empty. Silent as a mouse she closed the door and started the short but endless trek to the bedroom. When she came to the threshold of the room there he was, as expected, fiddling with a gadget that was ready to be positioned between the mattress and box springs.

He had his back to the doorframe. He was about six foot and his hair was buzzed short, silver in color. Watching him caused Nadine a feeling of nausea, the sickly sensation she battled mightily to subordinate to her will to live.

"I suppose I'm going to sleep comfy this evening," she said dispassionately, her pistol pointed at his head. "Put your fuckin' hands on the bed—don't even flinch," she instructed while pushing him with one hand and pressuring the barrel of the gun sufficiently on his head with the other to leave no doubt that he was a trigger pull away from death.

While his hands embraced the bed with his body bent at the waist, Nadine kicked the legs of her boss, Chief Harry Lambert, apart. He stood spread eagle, his butt aimed at Nadine. "I'd give you what your wife refuses except it would sicken me worse than I already feel," she sneered at the man who had been fixing an explosive device to go off as soon as the weight of her body hit the bed.

She tapped the weapon to his head, cautioning to him to be still while she disarmed him. With his handgun secured, she stepped back and ordered him to turn around, for the first time facing him directly. She could see reflected in the beads of sweat forming on his brow, his seething and viciousness.

She had him stand next, with his hands up in the corner of the room while she took extensive pictures of the apparatus he was hooking up to kill her. When she finished, she took the camera and shoved it in her purse.

"We're going on a trip," she informed her prisoner. "If I have to blow your head off in this hotel, I will. You and your friend have really given me no choice. I'd prefer doing this in a more civilized manner, but only if you behave like a nice boy...isn't that how you like to be talked to before a woman takes off her belt to punish your fleshy ass?" Intentionally taunting to test Lambert's emotions, she cocked the trigger of her gun to remind him she was in charge and what consequence he could expect from a rash move. "I think we'll get all this settled today," she informed him.

She then had Lambert follow a string of instructions, leading them to a new rental car she had parked in the hotel lot. He drove while she sat in the back seat, her weapon aimed at him at all times.

"It was you who set it up for Chauncy to delete the file," she informed him rather than asked. "It was also you who made sure if the stolen evidence were to ever be discovered, he would be blamed. That's not nice—Chauncy's my closest friend."

"You're wrong," Lambert countered.

Nadine ignored his denial. "I'm going to want to know what role you played in the murders."

"What are you talking about?" Lambert pled.

"I'll squeeze you like a filthy mop head if necessary, so don't screw with me."

"I swear, I don't know anything about murders," Lambert vowed.

"None except mine?" she reminded him. "I hear Haley is backing you for Mayor. Is killing me part of the package?"

"I swear I don't know anything about—"

"Except he wanted me dead," she shouted angrily. "You may have known him since college, but are you really that stupid to believe that after this he wouldn't have you eliminated too?"

Lambert said nothing. The unpleasant reality she brought up to him had to be something he'd already deliberated on.

"I'll have to regret doing this, Chief, but as you're about to find out I'm going to be saving your life—and mine at the same time."

I was still in my office when I received the call from Nadine. I was pleasantly shocked to hear from her. I had assumed she wasn't alive. She afforded me no time to ask questions.

"Zach, I'll need your partner's help—the FBI agent."

"Kershaw?"

"Right. Get him to fly here immediately. I don't care what it costs. Tell him it's urgent. Can you do it?"

"I'll call you back in ten minutes," I told her.

I was on the phone immediately with Kershaw. He had become the consummate restaurant entrepreneur but the agent in him was alive. It was seven-thirty that evening when he arrived in El Paso. I picked him up at the airport. At nine fifty-five, we arrived at Kuruk—it was going to be a late night. Nadine informed me that she wanted to meet at the restaurant. She insisted that nobody be there but Kershaw and myself.

Being a Monday evening, we were thankfully closed—thankfully because Nadine had arrived before Kershaw and me. She had Lambert tied to a chair by his arms and legs; his shirt was soaking under the arms and on the chest…while it was freezing.

Nadine explained after we arrived why she wanted Kershaw there. He would be a witness. He would also be able to help her structure the material she wanted to get from Lambert before moving on to Haley. While she had been convinced that Lambert had a hand in the D. C. murders, after a couple hours of "discussion" she reversed gear. Lambert wasn't part of the scheme. Monroe and Haley handled that alone. Any complicity by Lambert was incidental; he couldn't have known the simple acts he carried out for Haley were related to murder.

Lambert had no idea why Haley wanted Nadine dead but he also knew better than to ask. What was most important to Nadine was that Lambert had attempted to kill her by exploding her car, and had arrived a second time with the aim of finishing the job. Still, he was following the direct orders of Haley.

Nadine had Lambert sign a detailed statement, including Haley's position regarding Lambert's political ambitions. Simultaneously, he also certified a tape recording of the confession of attempted murder by Lambert, along with admission of Haley's knowing involvement.

New Mexico didn't know what was coming its way that evening. A single call was placed minutes before midnight. Four hours later, the Albuquerque airport hosted an unannounced visit by our nation's President Haley. He was met by a helicopter and flown to Kuruk.

I'll dispense with every ugly detail of Nadine's meeting with Haley. Understandably, she had grown to despise the man worse than the thought of a hot pepper enema. Still, she was generous enough to give him a choice.

He could refuse to cooperate, in which case she would put Lambert on trial for his crime and force him to bring Haley down in the process for orchestrating the attempted murder of Nadine—she also promised to use the tapes to implicate him directly in several murders.

Or, as the second option, he could sign a full acknowledgement of what he had done with respect to Dr. Lawrence Monroe and his own indirect participation in the murder of over a dozen people, plus his intended murder of Nadine. Either way, the novel would be published in the name of author, Zacchaeus Miller.

If he opted for the second path, then he could go about his business as President, unimpeded by her. As for Lambert, he was given different conditions. He was to agree to resign his position as Chief effective immediately. He was also to agree not to run for public office for the remainder of his life. "You can work as a bank clerk for all I care," were her words. She also stipulated that if she or anyone precious to her were ever to be threatened or harmed by either man, then the admissions would be sent immediately to the press.

It was an easy decision for both men. They were meek. Nadine had reduced both from undaunted power brokers to weeping boys.

On the way out, Nadine couldn't repress an urge to taunt Haley. "You killed a man I loved. I can't imagine a human more evil than you."

*****

After they left, I had to ask Nadine a question that baffled me.

"Why did you let Haley off?"

"I thought a lot about it, believe me. If I had Haley prosecuted, I would have harmed our nation at a time it might be doubly damaging."

Patriot rambled quietly in my mind. Nadine pledged allegiance to the flag with one hand over her heart and the other ready to draw a sword—she wasn't joking. I still looked at her dubiously, my doubt compelling her to elaborate on her position.

"He's an evil man but people believe in him. The whole damn system in the end is based on faith, from the bottom up. I won't participate in putting millions of people through that because of one asshole."

Nadine woke Preston out of his sleep. Her words were sweet to his ear.

"Well, when can you get here? I can't wait forever to get engaged, if somebody will ask me. I might even consider a baby sometime in the future."

Preston flapped his mighty wings and was in Mescalero in no time. We had a little engagement party. Preeti carried our second child in a sac so tightly wound around her waist it looked as if it might burst through at any moment—I carried Sousche in my arms. Josea was just beginning to show signs of her pregnancy—Nadine had a yoga stomach as flat as a sidewalk.

After the formal announcement, Preston and Nadine would live temporarily in the love cottage behind Kuruk.

Preeti delivered the next day, a seven pound six ounce boy. We had already picked the name, Abraham.

I had one other worry on my mind, what Nadine had discovered about Reuben's prior life of fame. She had strong beliefs about most everything. I couldn't be sure where a matter of this sort might fall.

"Nadine, what about the business of Reuben?" I whispered. At the moment, there was nobody who could have heard me.

"What business?" She smiled. "Don't know what you're talking about."

That was the answer I wanted. From then on, she treated Reuben like Reuben. Whatever secret the man had tucked in his pocket, didn't exist to Nadine Street.

I sat thinking what a miracle it is that we had all survived and that in spite of the potential for tragedy, love was being nurtured and babies being born.

As of my writing these final words, I'm exhausted. I've been on duty feeding my son in the middle of the night. The responsibilities of being a dad will go on, but as far as this tale, it has reached…

THE END

OTHER NOVELS COMPLETED AND UPCOMING BY

Dennis A Nehamen

Mistaken Enemy
Insatiable Hate
Mescalero Blood
Misty's Place
Musicball
DOGMAi
The Making of A Madman
Juliette
The Greatest American Outlaw
Inside Trance
Crushing Dreams

ABOUT THE AUTHOR

Dennis A Nehamen, Ph.D. is a forensic and clinical psychologist who has authored novels, screenplays and musicals, including the award-winning musical *Wrapped*. He lives in Los Angeles with his wife and has two adult children.

www.ingramcontent.com/pod-product-compliance
Lightning Source LLC
Chambersburg PA
CBHW030540260626
47157CB00006B/2129